Dedicated, again, to Greg Cutler

Also by Debbie Drechsler:
Daddy's Girl

The story presented here was originally published in issues one through five of Debbie Drechsler's comic book series *Nowhere*.

First Softcover Edition: June 2003
ISBN 1-896597-65-3
Printed in Canada.
10 9 8 7 6 5 4 3 2 1

Drawn & Quarterly
P.O. Box 48056
Montreal, Quebec
Canada H2V 4S8
www.drawnandquarterly.com

Publisher: Chris Oliveros
Publicity: Elizabeth Walker

National Library of Canada
Cataloguing in Publication
Drechsler, Debbie, 1953-
  The Summer of Love / Debbie
Drechsler.
ISBN 1-896597-37-8 (bound).
ISBN 1-896597-65-3 (pbk.)
  I. Title.
PN6727.D74S85 2003
741.5'973
C2003-900721-9

Distributed in the USA and abroad by
Chronicle Books
85 Second Street
San Francisco, CA 94105
800.722.6657

Distributed in Canada by
Raincoast Books
9050 Shaughnessy Street
Vancouver, B.C. V6P 6E5
800.663.5714

The Summer of LOVE

Debbie Drechsler

Drawn & Quarterly
Montreal

ACKNOWLEDGEMENTS

Special thanks to Chris Oliveros, Richard Sala, John
Kuramoto, Paula Drechsler, and Greg Cutler. Also to
National Public Radio and the dogs (Buster and Teela) and
cats (Henry and Lucy) who keep me company while I work.

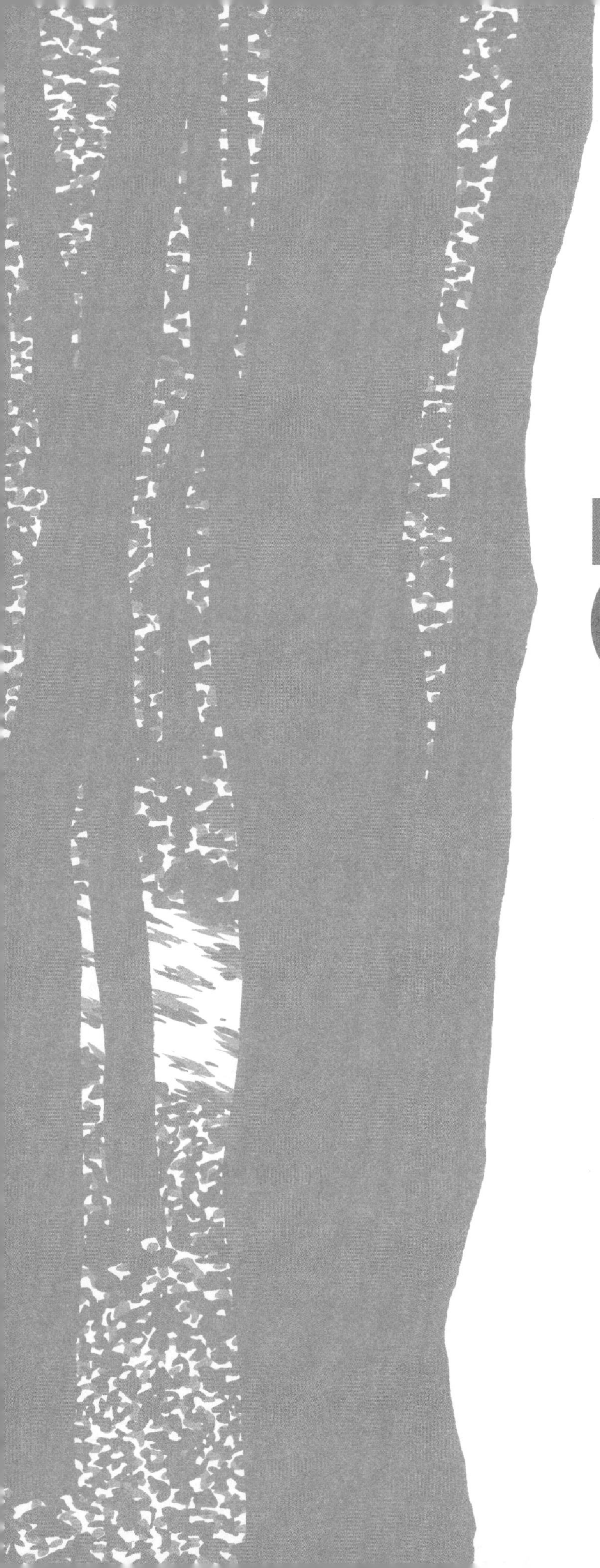

PART ONE

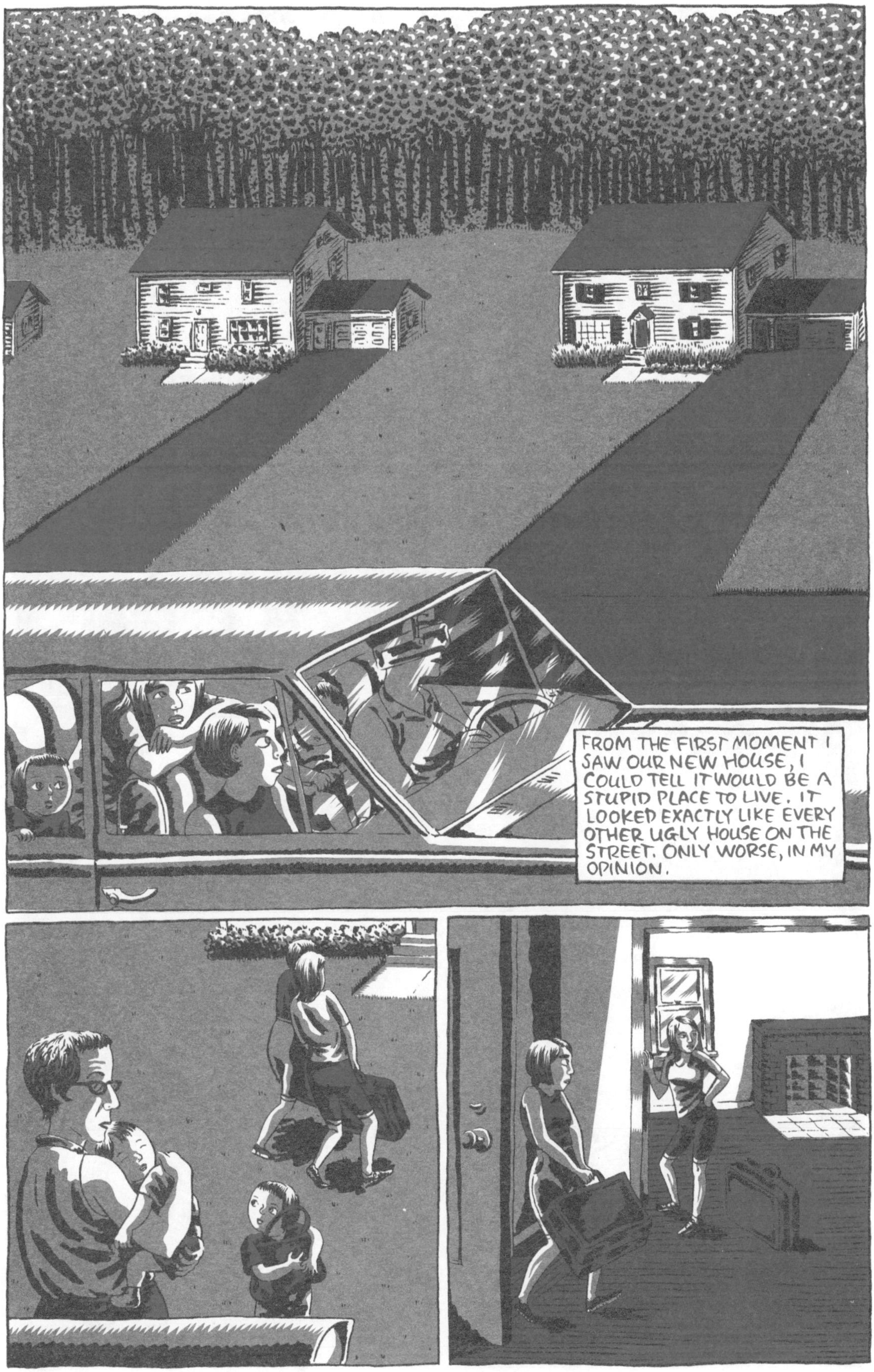
FROM THE FIRST MOMENT I SAW OUR NEW HOUSE, I COULD TELL IT WOULD BE A STUPID PLACE TO LIVE. IT LOOKED EXACTLY LIKE EVERY OTHER UGLY HOUSE ON THE STREET. ONLY WORSE, IN MY OPINION.

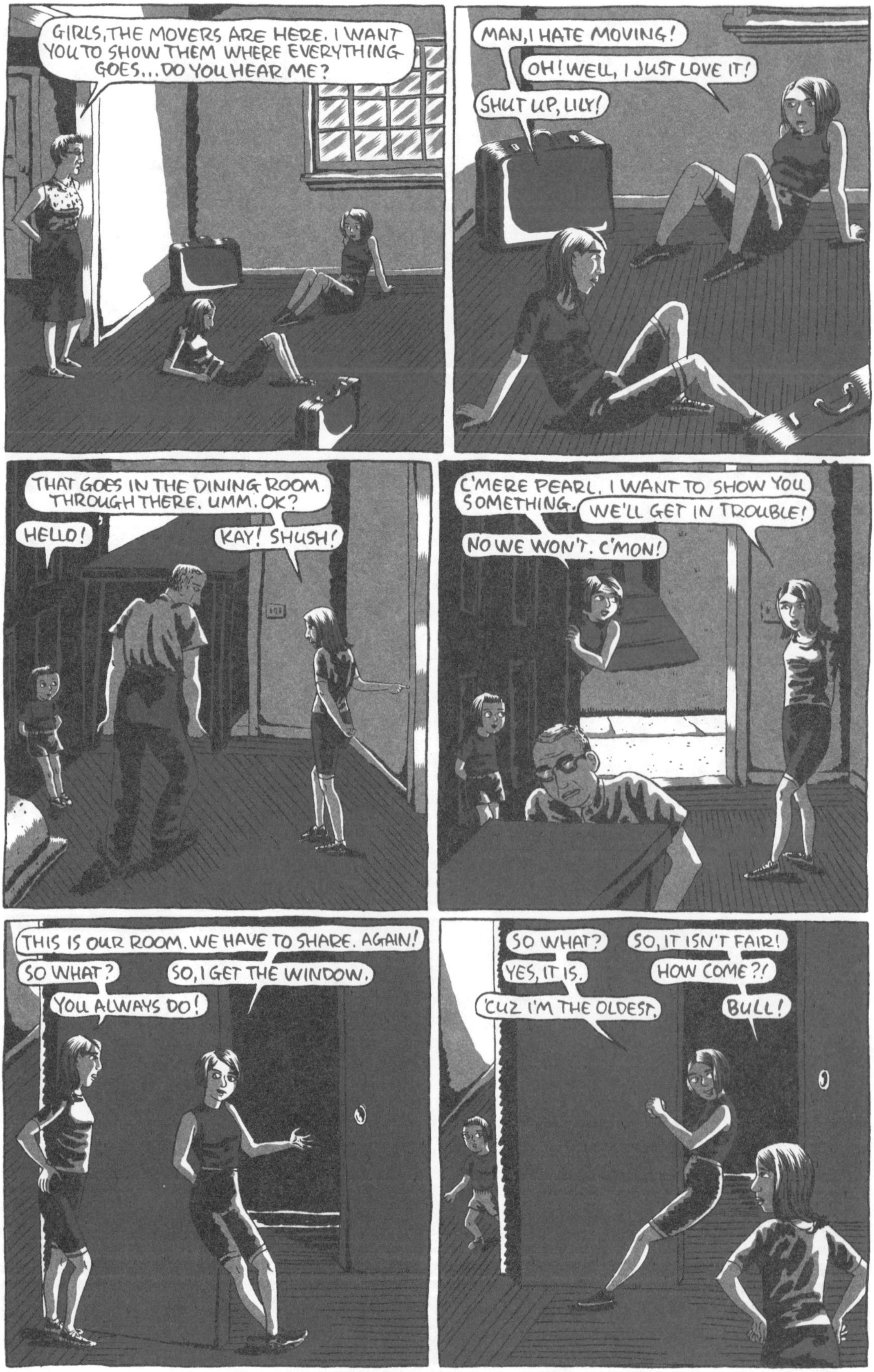
GIRLS, THE MOVERS ARE HERE. I WANT YOU TO SHOW THEM WHERE EVERYTHING GOES... DO YOU HEAR ME?
MAN, I HATE MOVING!
OH! WELL, I JUST LOVE IT!
SHUT UP, LILY!
THAT GOES IN THE DINING ROOM. THROUGH THERE. UMM. OK?
HELLO!
KAY! SHUSH!
C'MERE PEARL. I WANT TO SHOW YOU SOMETHING.
WE'LL GET IN TROUBLE!
NO WE WON'T. C'MON!
THIS IS OUR ROOM. WE HAVE TO SHARE. AGAIN!
SO WHAT?
SO, I GET THE WINDOW.
YOU ALWAYS DO!
SO WHAT?
SO, IT ISN'T FAIR!
YES, IT IS.
HOW COME?!
'CUZ I'M THE OLDEST.
BULL!

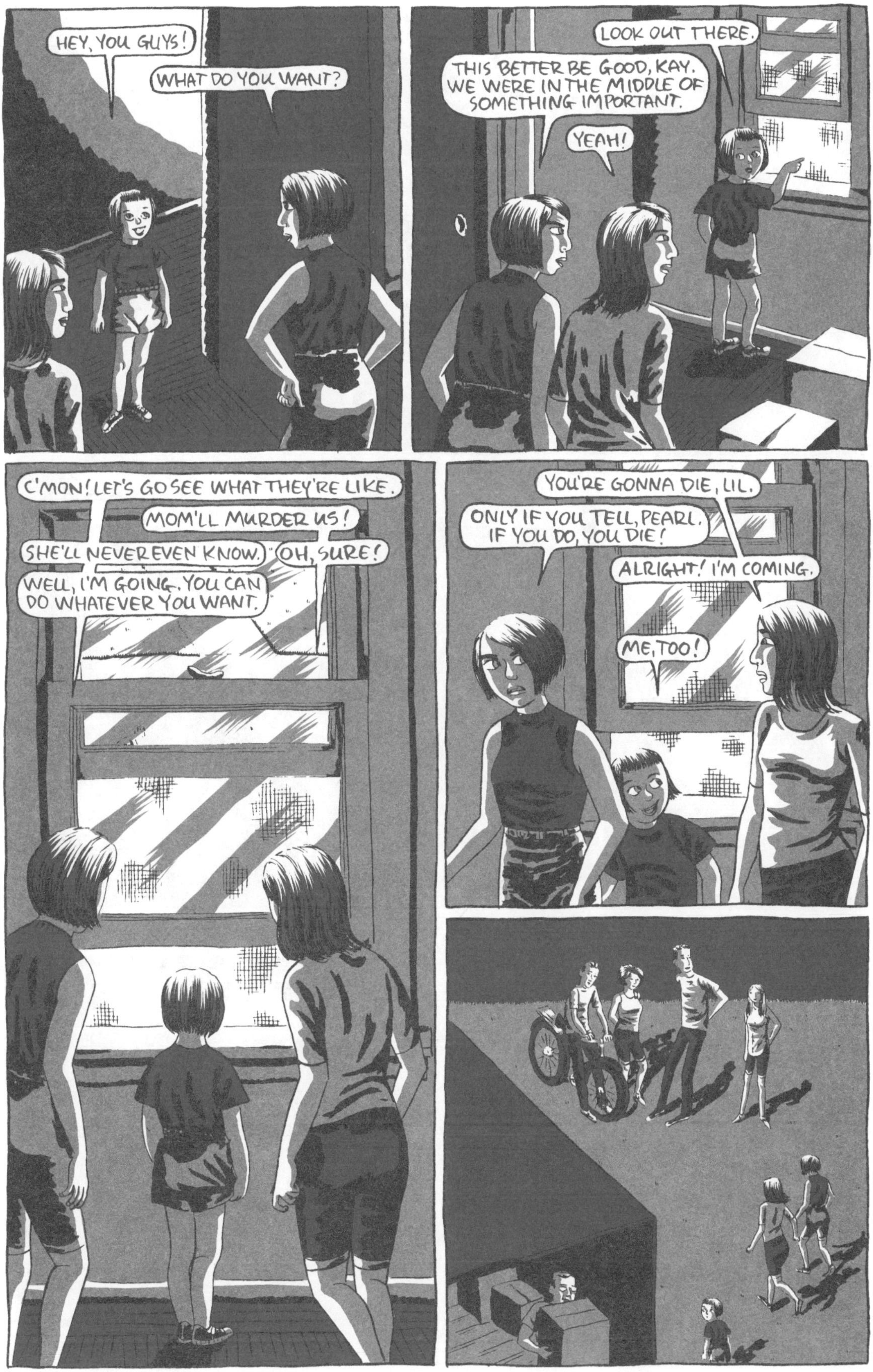
HEY, YOU GUYS!
WHAT DO YOU WANT?
LOOK OUT THERE.
THIS BETTER BE GOOD, KAY. WE WERE IN THE MIDDLE OF SOMETHING IMPORTANT.
YEAH!
C'MON! LET'S GO SEE WHAT THEY'RE LIKE.
MOM'LL MURDER US!
SHE'LL NEVER EVEN KNOW.
OH, SURE!
WELL, I'M GOING. YOU CAN DO WHATEVER YOU WANT.
YOU'RE GONNA DIE, LIL.
ONLY IF YOU TELL, PEARL. IF YOU DO, YOU DIE!
ALRIGHT! I'M COMING.
ME, TOO!

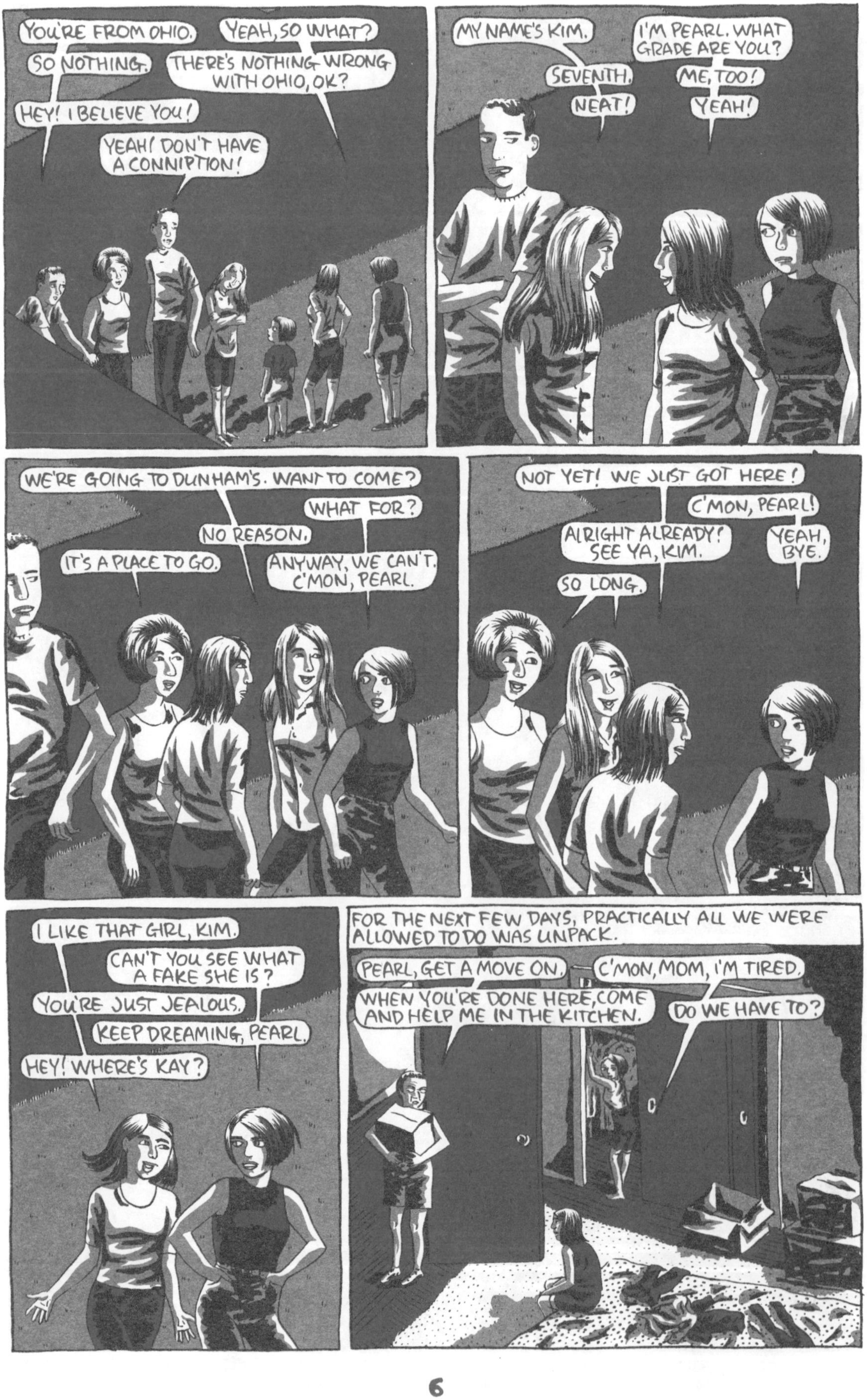
YOU'RE FROM OHIO.
YEAH, SO WHAT?
SO NOTHING.
THERE'S NOTHING WRONG WITH OHIO, OK?
HEY! I BELIEVE YOU!
YEAH! DON'T HAVE A CONNIPTION!
MY NAME'S KIM.
I'M PEARL. WHAT GRADE ARE YOU?
SEVENTH.
ME, TOO!
NEAT!
YEAH!
WE'RE GOING TO DUNHAM'S. WANT TO COME?
WHAT FOR?
NO REASON.
IT'S A PLACE TO GO.
ANYWAY, WE CAN'T. C'MON, PEARL.
NOT YET! WE JUST GOT HERE!
C'MON, PEARL!
ALRIGHT ALREADY! SEE YA, KIM.
YEAH, BYE.
SO LONG.
I LIKE THAT GIRL, KIM.
CAN'T YOU SEE WHAT A FAKE SHE IS?
YOU'RE JUST JEALOUS.
KEEP DREAMING, PEARL.
HEY! WHERE'S KAY?
FOR THE NEXT FEW DAYS, PRACTICALLY ALL WE WERE ALLOWED TO DO WAS UNPACK.
PEARL, GET A MOVE ON.
C'MON, MOM, I'M TIRED.
WHEN YOU'RE DONE HERE, COME AND HELP ME IN THE KITCHEN.
DO WE HAVE TO?

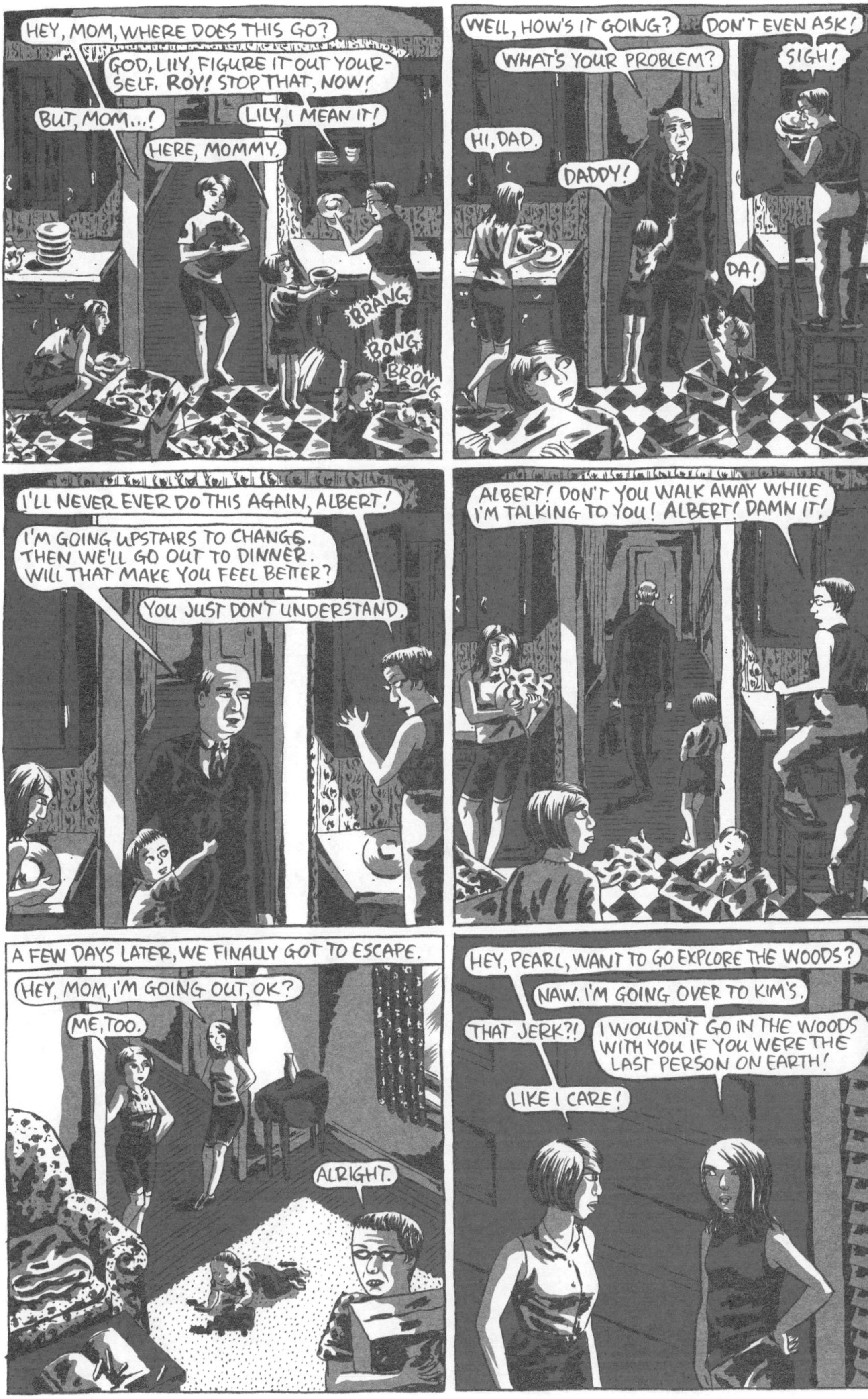
HEY, MOM, WHERE DOES THIS GO?
GOD, LILY, FIGURE IT OUT YOURSELF. ROY! STOP THAT, NOW!
BUT, MOM...!
LILY, I MEAN IT!
HERE, MOMMY.
BRANG
BONG
BRONG
WELL, HOW'S IT GOING?
DON'T EVEN ASK!
WHAT'S YOUR PROBLEM?
SIGH!
HI, DAD.
DADDY!
DA!
I'LL NEVER EVER DO THIS AGAIN, ALBERT!
I'M GOING UPSTAIRS TO CHANGE. THEN WE'LL GO OUT TO DINNER. WILL THAT MAKE YOU FEEL BETTER?
YOU JUST DON'T UNDERSTAND.
ALBERT! DON'T YOU WALK AWAY WHILE I'M TALKING TO YOU! ALBERT! DAMN IT!
A FEW DAYS LATER, WE FINALLY GOT TO ESCAPE.
HEY, MOM, I'M GOING OUT, OK?
ME, TOO.
ALRIGHT.
HEY, PEARL, WANT TO GO EXPLORE THE WOODS?
NAW. I'M GOING OVER TO KIM'S.
THAT JERK?!
I WOULDN'T GO IN THE WOODS WITH YOU IF YOU WERE THE LAST PERSON ON EARTH!
LIKE I CARE!

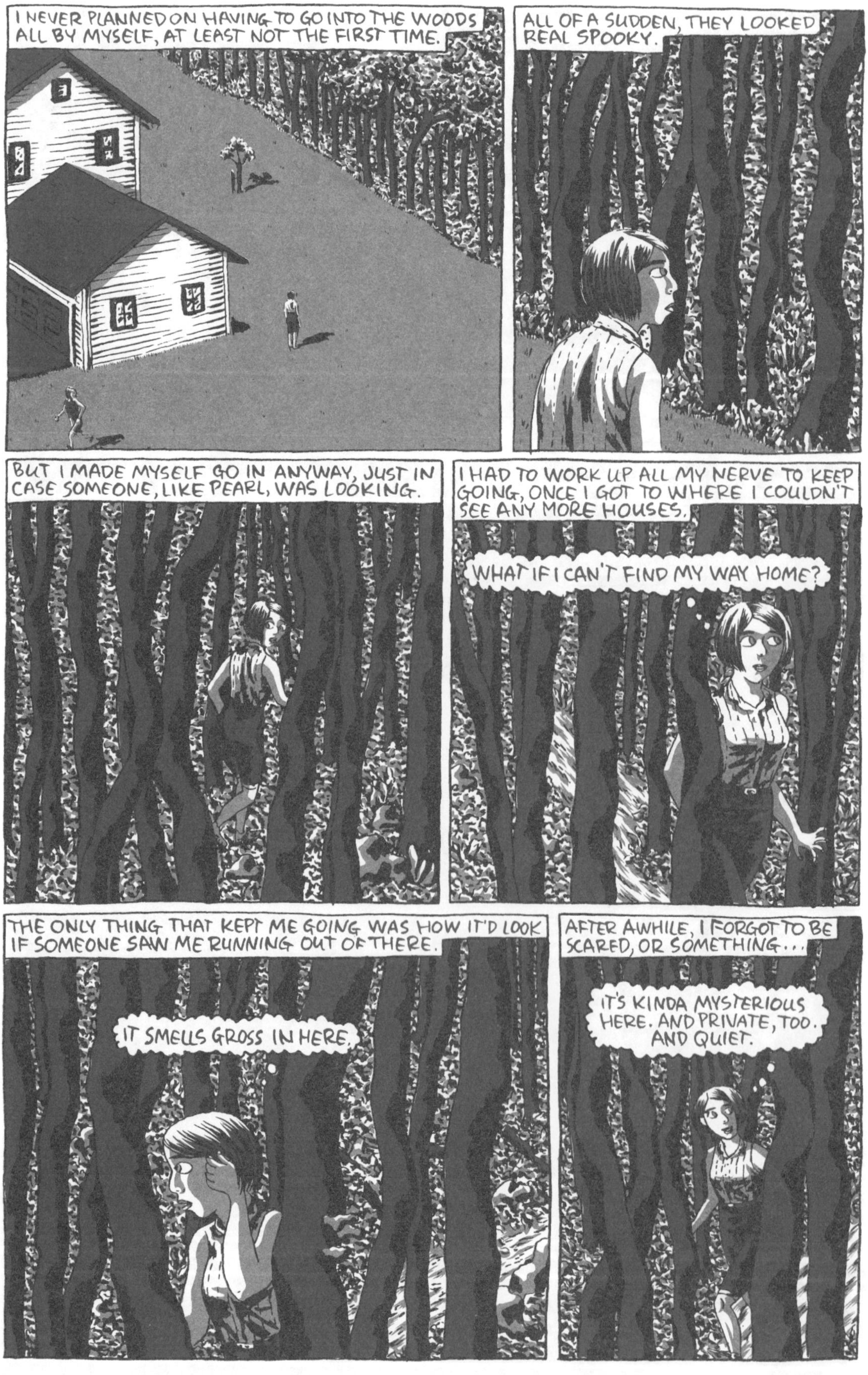
I NEVER PLANNED ON HAVING TO GO INTO THE WOODS ALL BY MYSELF, AT LEAST NOT THE FIRST TIME.
ALL OF A SUDDEN, THEY LOOKED REAL SPOOKY.
BUT I MADE MYSELF GO IN ANYWAY, JUST IN CASE SOMEONE, LIKE PEARL, WAS LOOKING.
I HAD TO WORK UP ALL MY NERVE TO KEEP GOING, ONCE I GOT TO WHERE I COULDN'T SEE ANY MORE HOUSES.
WHAT IF I CAN'T FIND MY WAY HOME?
THE ONLY THING THAT KEPT ME GOING WAS HOW IT'D LOOK IF SOMEONE SAW ME RUNNING OUT OF THERE.
IT SMELLS GROSS IN HERE.
AFTER AWHILE, I FORGOT TO BE SCARED, OR SOMETHING...
IT'S KINDA MYSTERIOUS HERE. AND PRIVATE, TOO. AND QUIET.

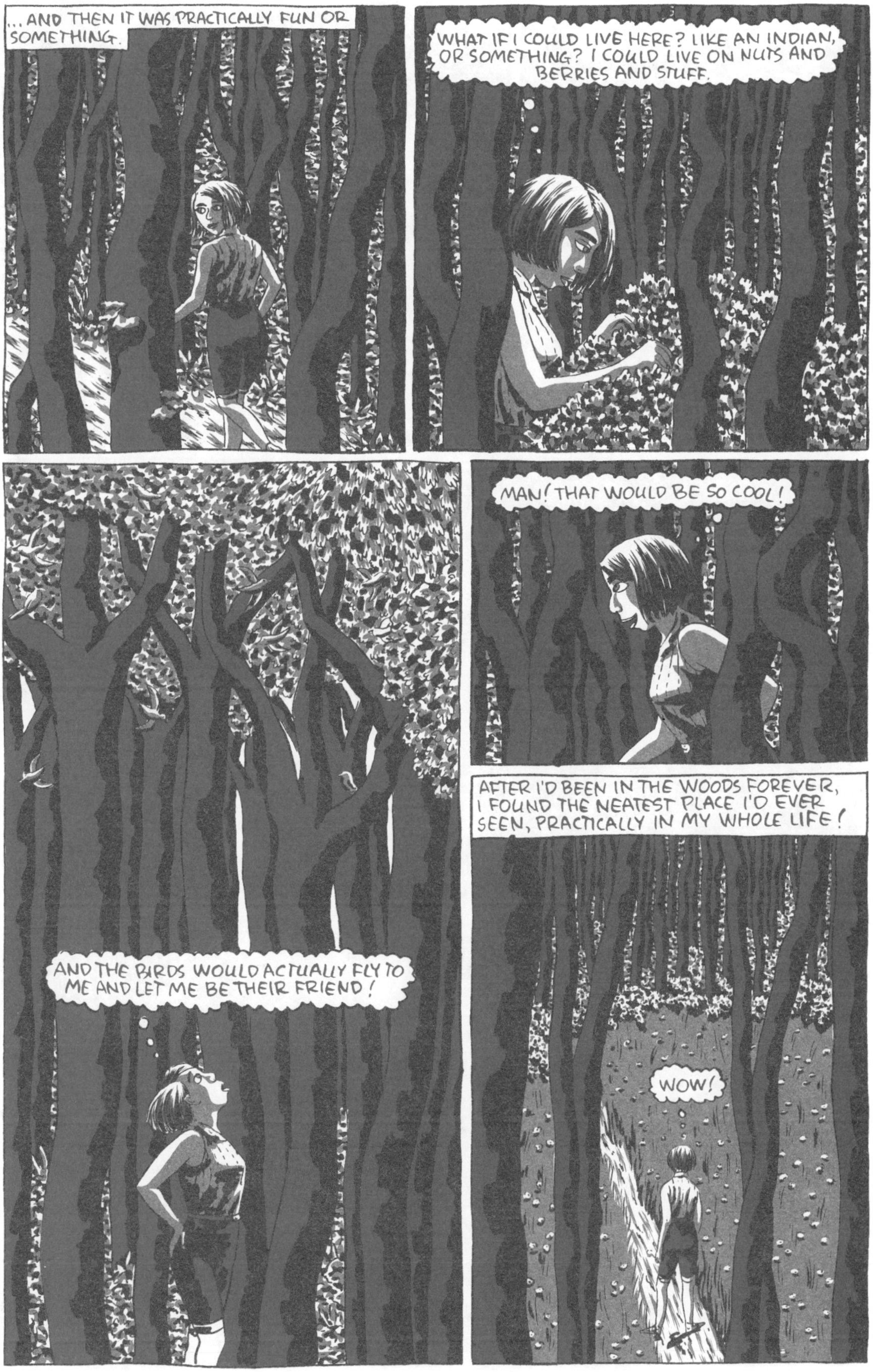
...AND THEN IT WAS PRACTICALLY FUN OR SOMETHING.
WHAT IF I COULD LIVE HERE? LIKE AN INDIAN, OR SOMETHING? I COULD LIVE ON NUTS AND BERRIES AND STUFF.
AND THE BIRDS WOULD ACTUALLY FLY TO ME AND LET ME BE THEIR FRIEND!
MAN! THAT WOULD BE SO COOL!
AFTER I'D BEEN IN THE WOODS FOREVER, I FOUND THE NEATEST PLACE I'D EVER SEEN, PRACTICALLY IN MY WHOLE LIFE!
WOW!

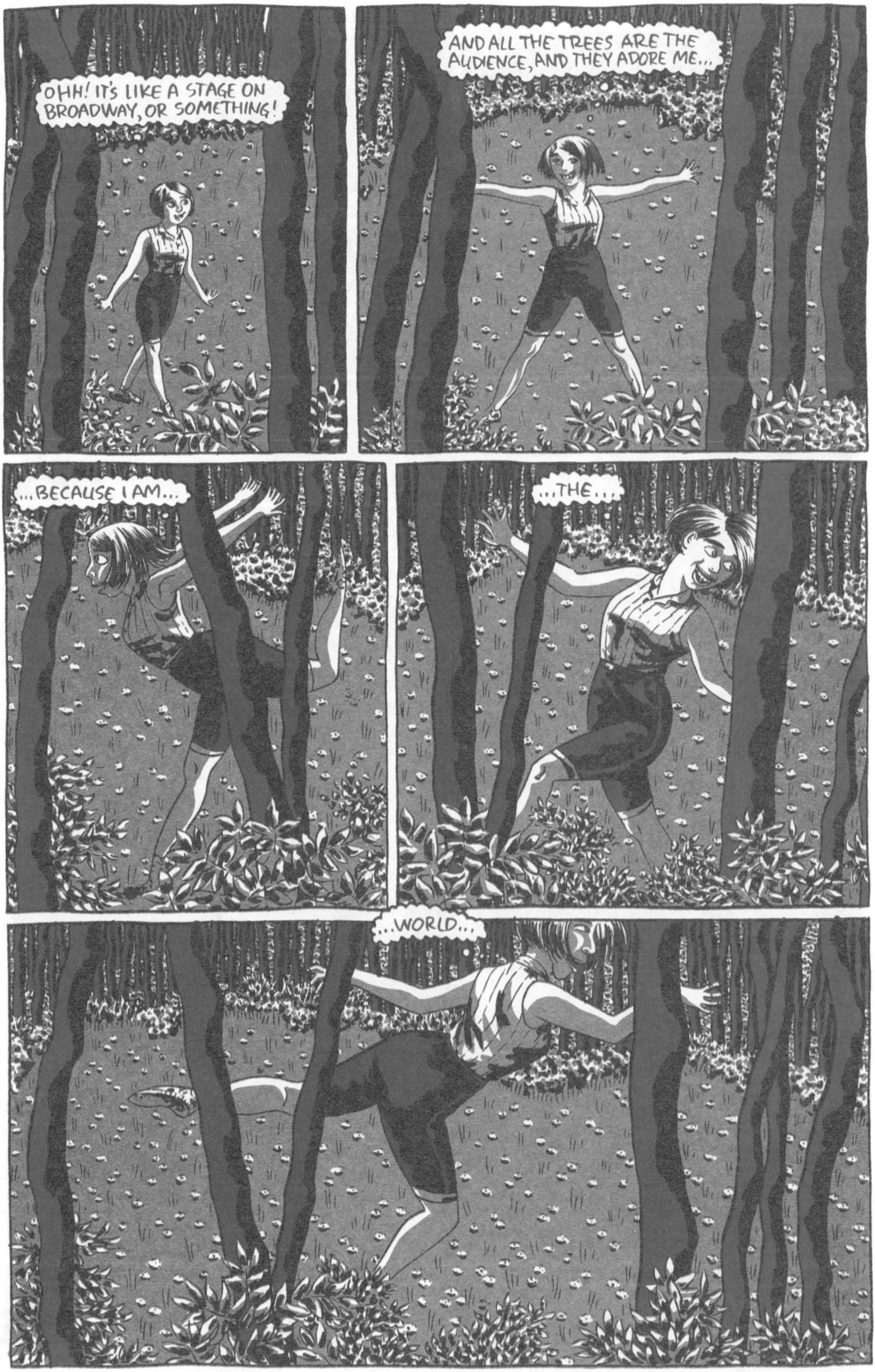
OHH! IT'S LIKE A STAGE ON BROADWAY, OR SOMETHING!
AND ALL THE TREES ARE THE AUDIENCE, AND THEY ADORE ME...
...BECAUSE I AM...
...THE...
...WORLD...

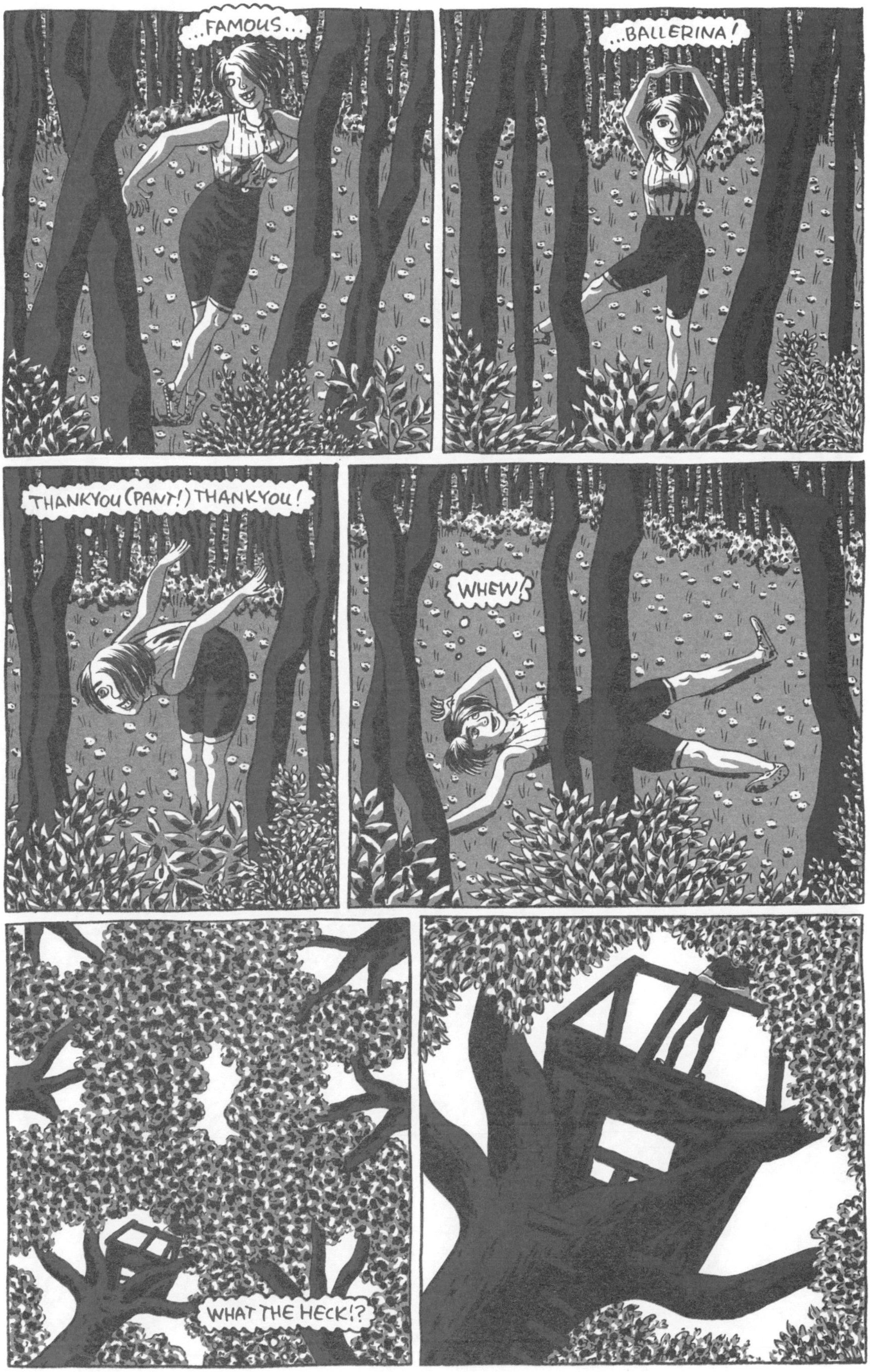
...FAMOUS...
...BALLERINA!
THANKYOU (PANT!) THANKYOU!
WHEW!
WHAT THE HECK!?

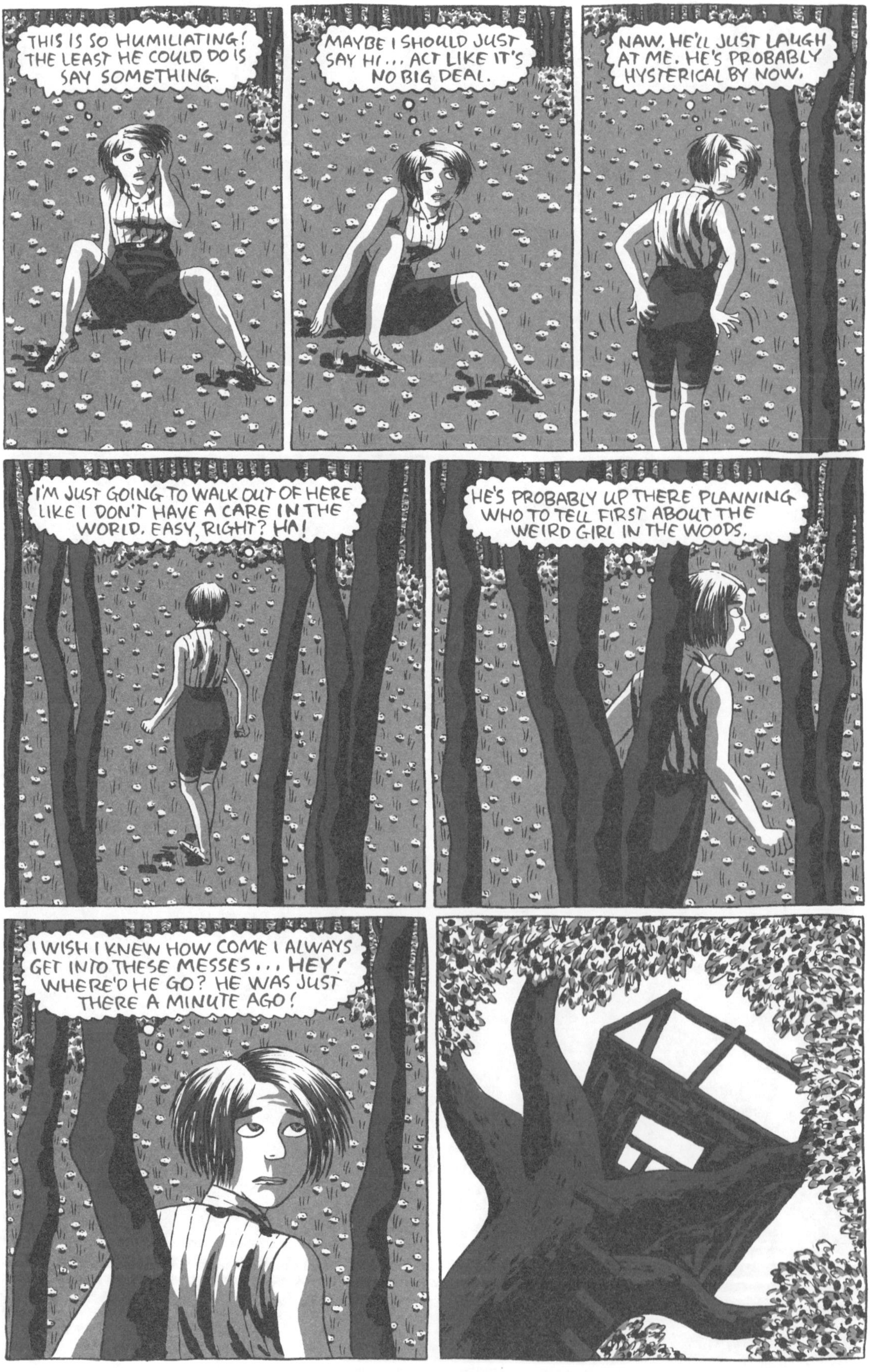
THIS IS SO HUMILIATING! THE LEAST HE COULD DO IS SAY SOMETHING.
MAYBE I SHOULD JUST SAY HI... ACT LIKE IT'S NO BIG DEAL.
NAW. HE'LL JUST LAUGH AT ME. HE'S PROBABLY HYSTERICAL BY NOW.
I'M JUST GOING TO WALK OUT OF HERE LIKE I DON'T HAVE A CARE IN THE WORLD. EASY, RIGHT? HA!
HE'S PROBABLY UP THERE PLANNING WHO TO TELL FIRST ABOUT THE WEIRD GIRL IN THE WOODS.
I WISH I KNEW HOW COME I ALWAYS GET INTO THESE MESSES... HEY! WHERE'D HE GO? HE WAS JUST THERE A MINUTE AGO!

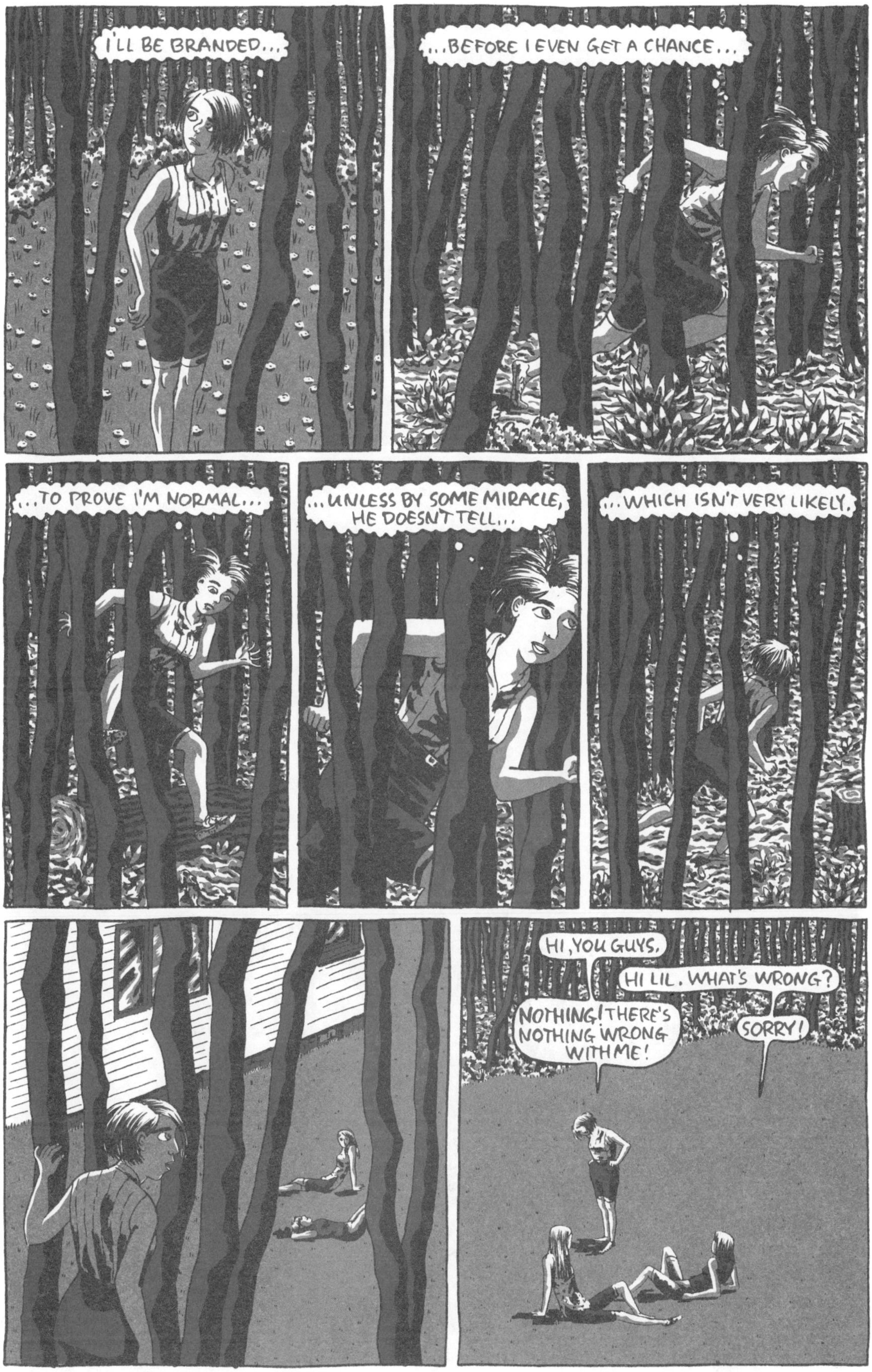
I'LL BE BRANDED...
...BEFORE I EVEN GET A CHANCE...
...TO PROVE I'M NORMAL...
...UNLESS BY SOME MIRACLE, HE DOESN'T TELL...
...WHICH ISN'T VERY LIKELY.
HI, YOU GUYS.
HI LIL. WHAT'S WRONG?
NOTHING! THERE'S NOTHING WRONG WITH ME!
SORRY!

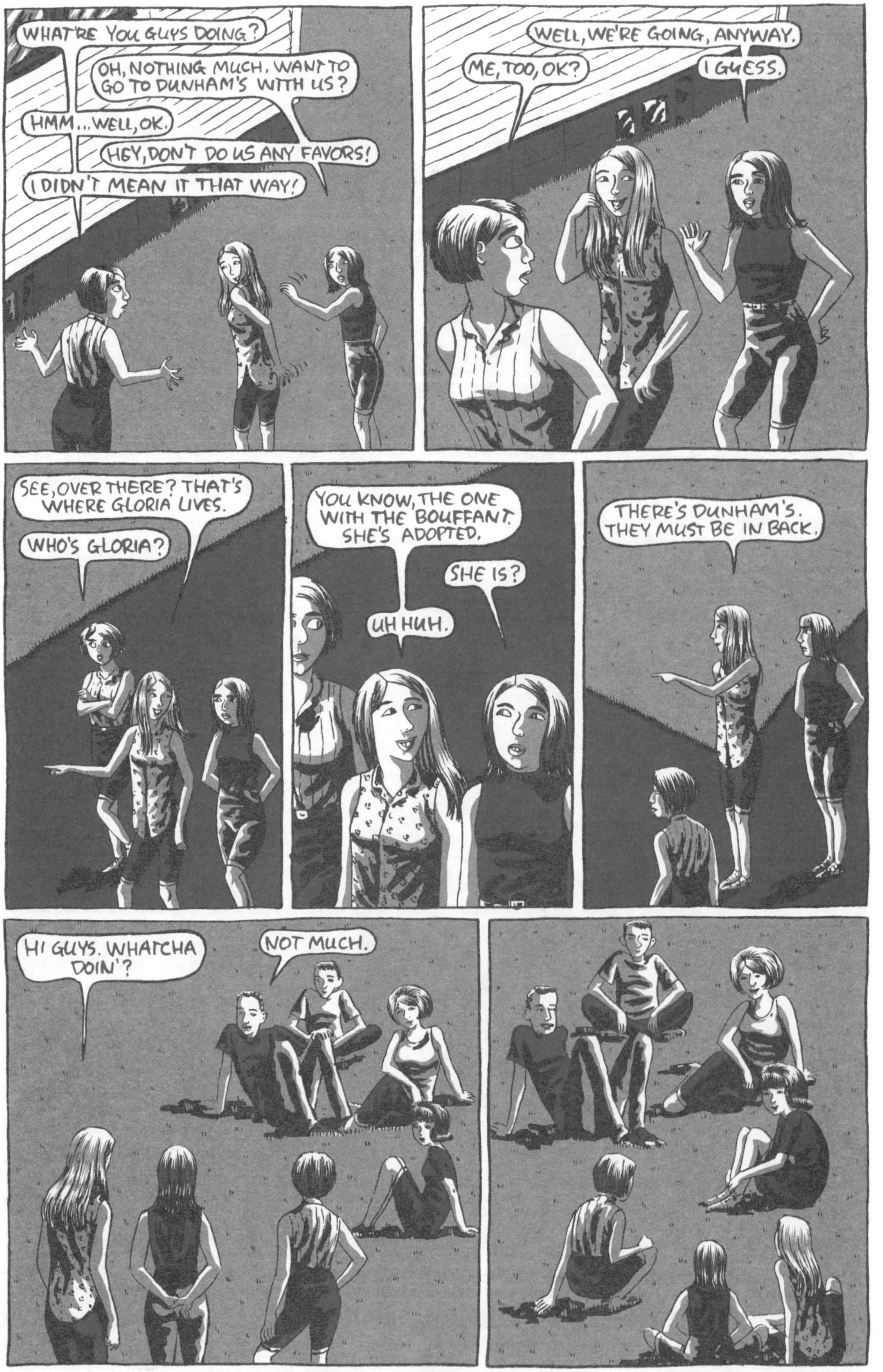
WHAT'RE YOU GUYS DOING?
OH, NOTHING MUCH. WANT TO GO TO DUNHAM'S WITH US?
HMM... WELL, OK.
HEY, DON'T DO US ANY FAVORS!
I DIDN'T MEAN IT THAT WAY!
WELL, WE'RE GOING, ANYWAY.
ME, TOO, OK?
I GUESS.
SEE, OVER THERE? THAT'S WHERE GLORIA LIVES.
WHO'S GLORIA?
YOU KNOW, THE ONE WITH THE BOUFFANT. SHE'S ADOPTED.
SHE IS?
UH HUH.
THERE'S DUNHAM'S. THEY MUST BE IN BACK.
HI GUYS. WHATCHA DOIN'?
NOT MUCH.

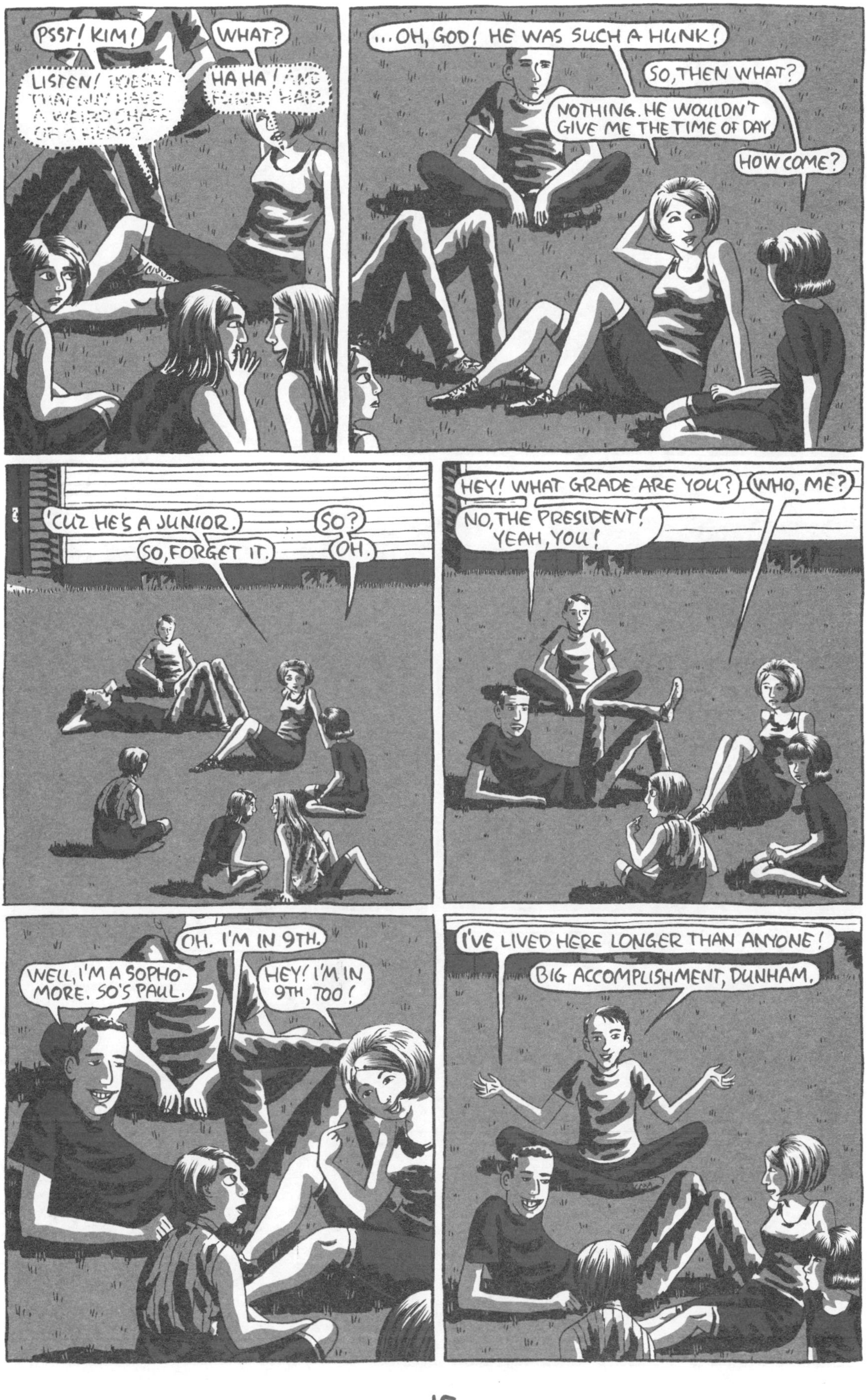
PSST! KIM!
WHAT?
LISTEN! DOESN'T THAT GUY HAVE A WEIRD SHAPE OF A HEAD?
HA HA! AND FUNNY HAIR.
...OH, GOD! HE WAS SUCH A HUNK!
SO, THEN WHAT?
NOTHING. HE WOULDN'T GIVE ME THE TIME OF DAY.
HOW COME?
'CUZ HE'S A JUNIOR.
SO?
SO, FORGET IT.
OH.
HEY! WHAT GRADE ARE YOU?
WHO, ME?
NO, THE PRESIDENT! YEAH, YOU!
OH. I'M IN 9TH.
WELL, I'M A SOPHO-MORE. SO'S PAUL.
HEY! I'M IN 9TH, TOO!
I'VE LIVED HERE LONGER THAN ANYONE!
BIG ACCOMPLISHMENT, DUNHAM.

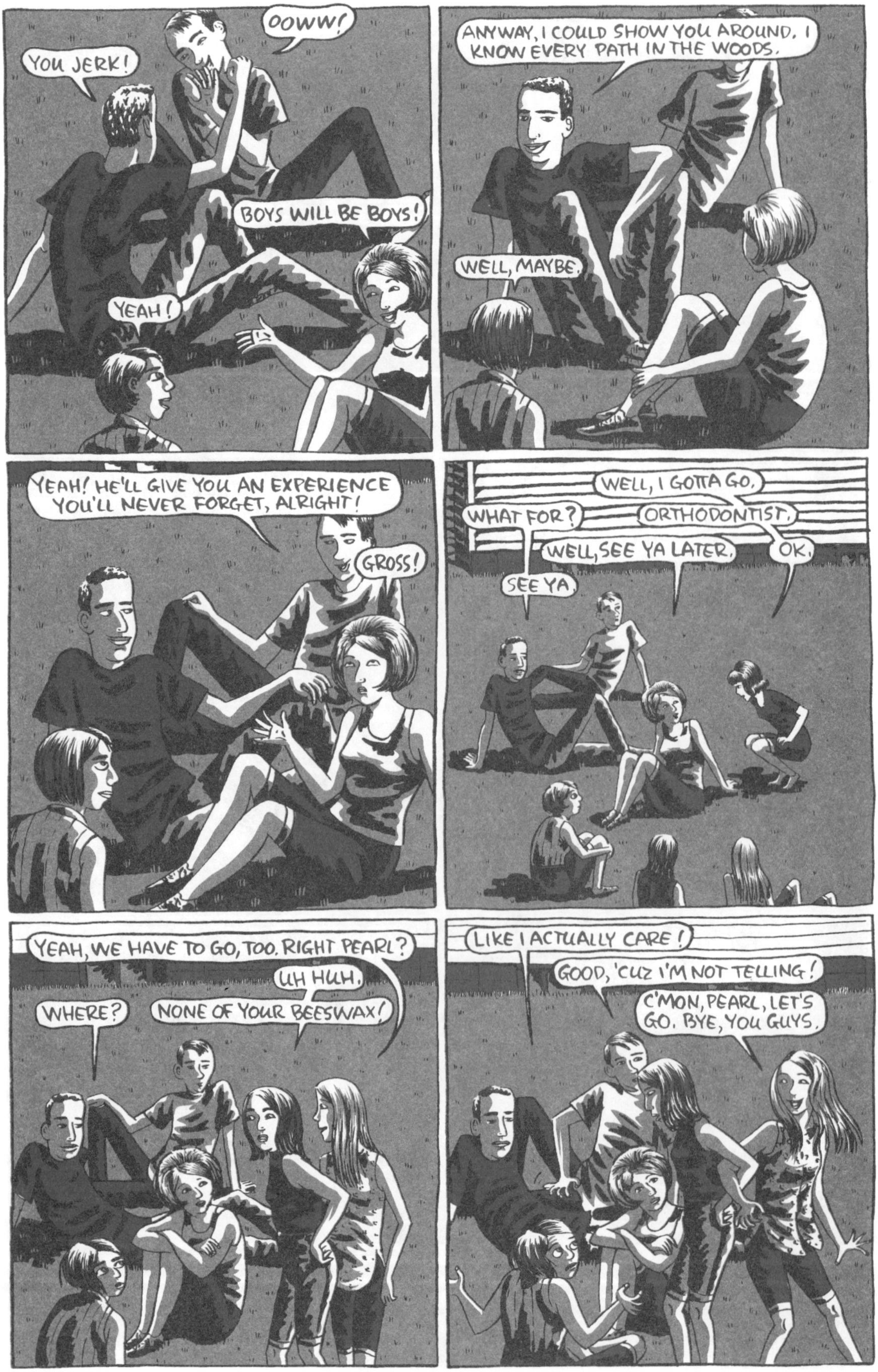
OOWW!
YOU JERK!
BOYS WILL BE BOYS!
YEAH!
ANYWAY, I COULD SHOW YOU AROUND. I KNOW EVERY PATH IN THE WOODS.
WELL, MAYBE.
YEAH! HE'LL GIVE YOU AN EXPERIENCE YOU'LL NEVER FORGET, ALRIGHT!
GROSS!
WELL, I GOTTA GO.
WHAT FOR?
ORTHODONTIST.
WELL, SEE YA LATER.
OK.
SEE YA.
YEAH, WE HAVE TO GO, TOO. RIGHT PEARL?
UH HUH.
WHERE?
NONE OF YOUR BEESWAX!
LIKE I ACTUALLY CARE!
GOOD, 'CUZ I'M NOT TELLING!
C'MON, PEARL, LET'S GO. BYE, YOU GUYS.

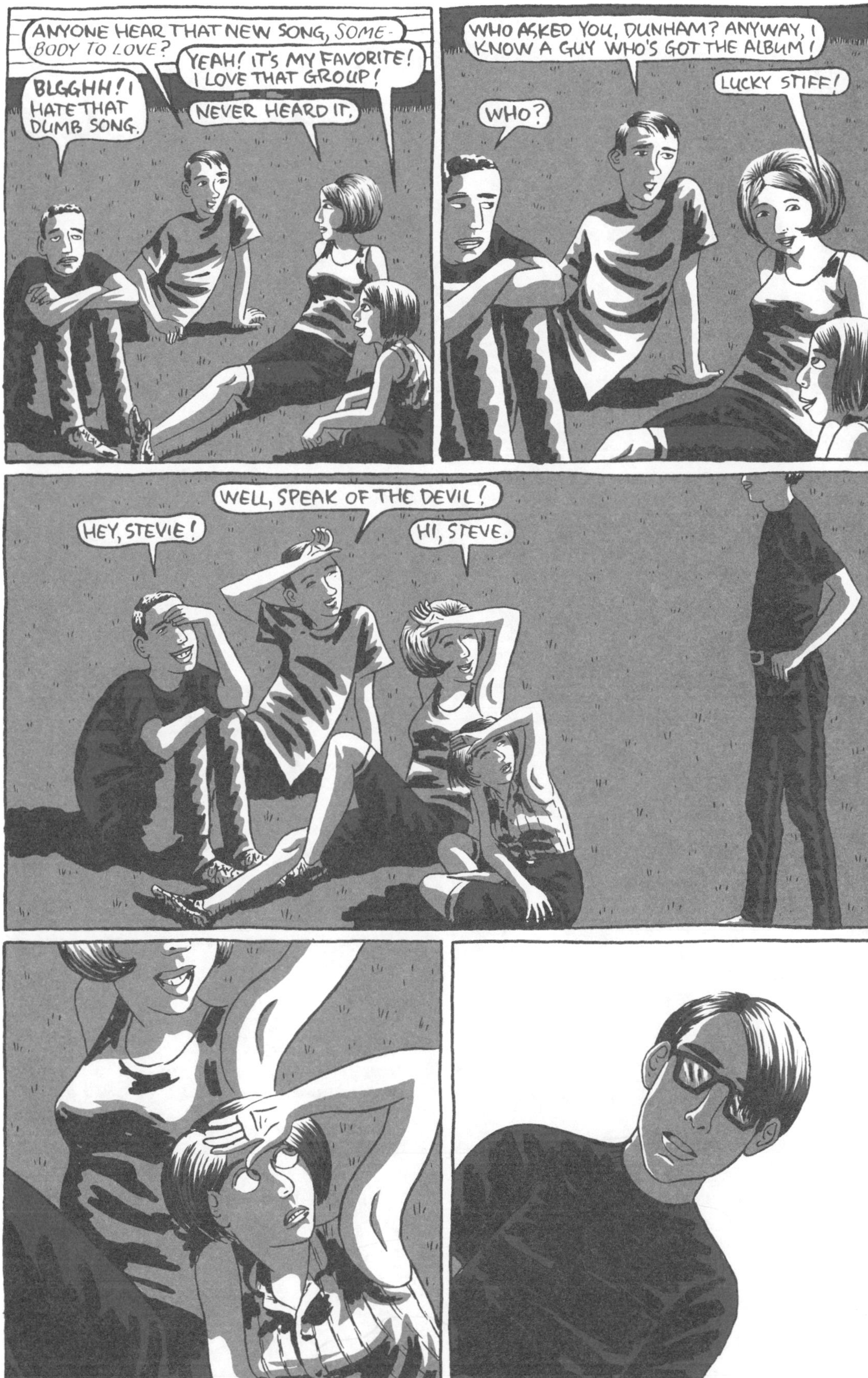
ANYONE HEAR THAT NEW SONG, SOMEBODY TO LOVE?
BLGGHH! I HATE THAT DUMB SONG.
YEAH! IT'S MY FAVORITE! I LOVE THAT GROUP!
NEVER HEARD IT.
WHO ASKED YOU, DUNHAM? ANYWAY, I KNOW A GUY WHO'S GOT THE ALBUM!
WHO?
LUCKY STIFF!
HEY, STEVIE!
WELL, SPEAK OF THE DEVIL!
HI, STEVE.

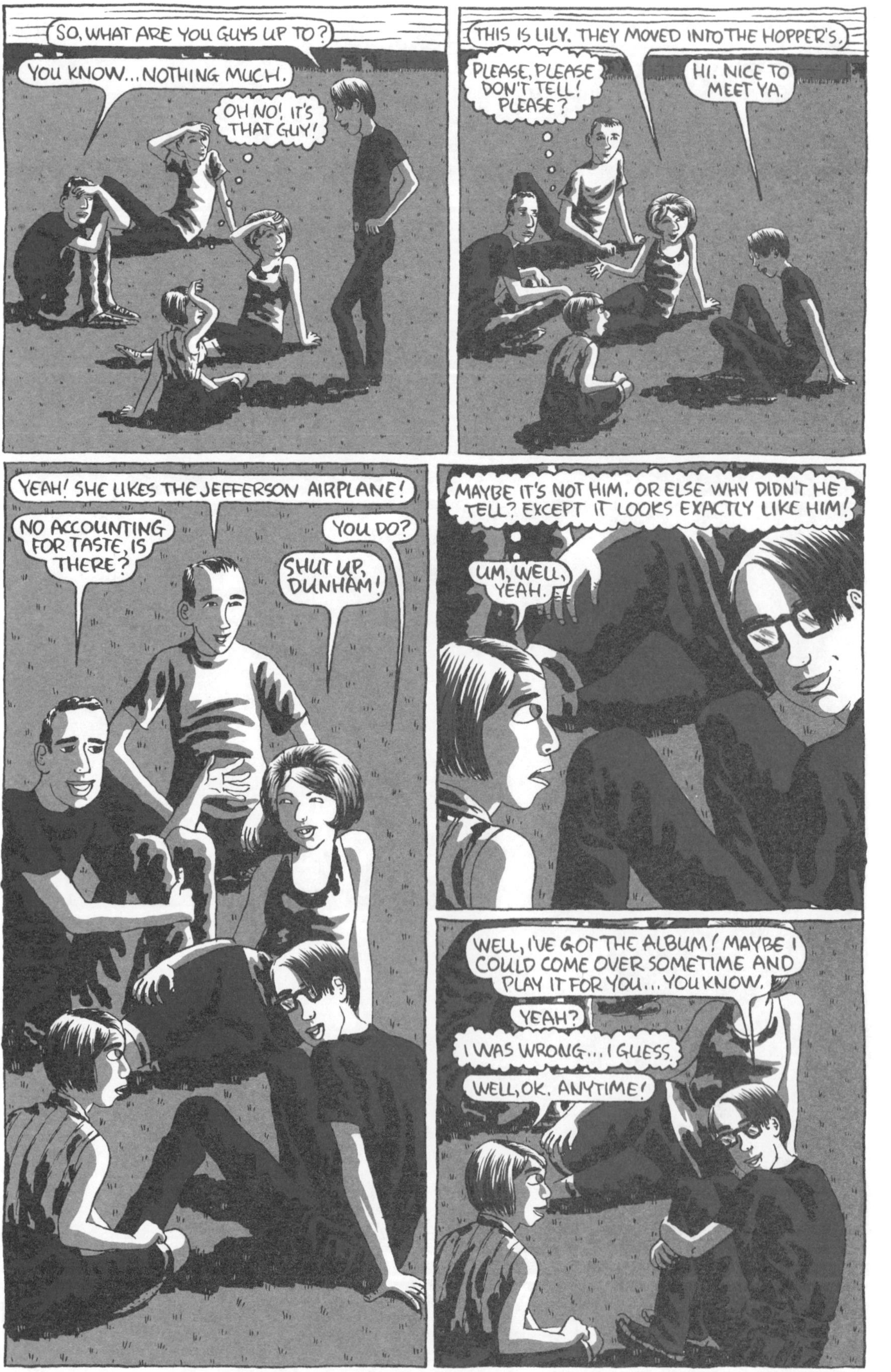
SO, WHAT ARE YOU GUYS UP TO?
YOU KNOW... NOTHING MUCH.
OH NO! IT'S THAT GUY!
THIS IS LILY. THEY MOVED INTO THE HOPPER'S.
PLEASE, PLEASE DON'T TELL! PLEASE?
HI, NICE TO MEET YA.
YEAH! SHE LIKES THE JEFFERSON AIRPLANE!
NO ACCOUNTING FOR TASTE, IS THERE?
YOU DO?
SHUT UP, DUNHAM!
MAYBE IT'S NOT HIM. OR ELSE WHY DIDN'T HE TELL? EXCEPT IT LOOKS EXACTLY LIKE HIM!
UM, WELL, YEAH.
WELL, I'VE GOT THE ALBUM! MAYBE I COULD COME OVER SOMETIME AND PLAY IT FOR YOU... YOU KNOW.
YEAH?
I WAS WRONG... I GUESS.
WELL, OK. ANYTIME!

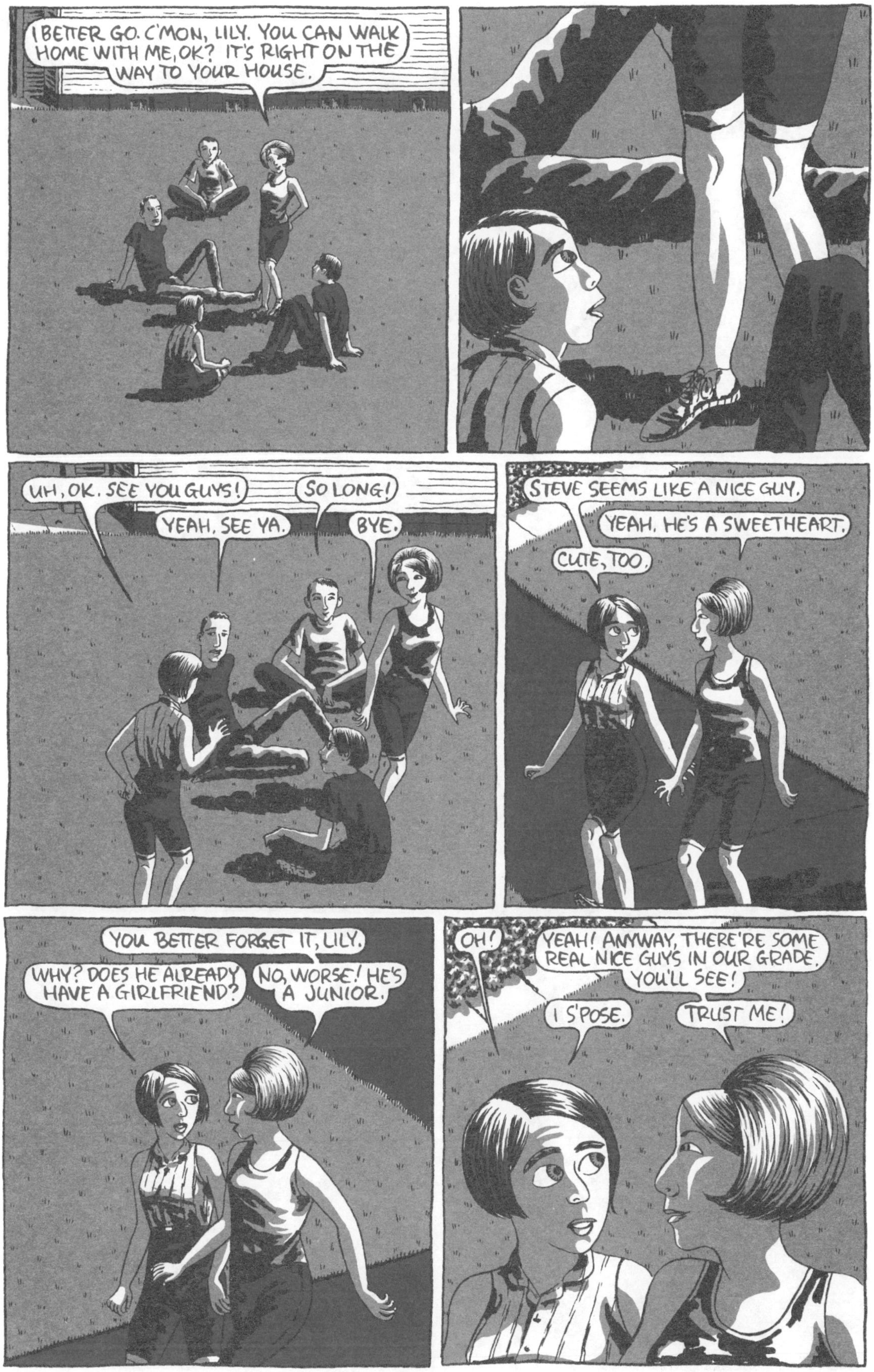
I BETTER GO. C'MON, LILY. YOU CAN WALK HOME WITH ME, OK? IT'S RIGHT ON THE WAY TO YOUR HOUSE.
UH, OK. SEE YOU GUYS!
YEAH, SEE YA.
SO LONG!
BYE.
STEVE SEEMS LIKE A NICE GUY.
YEAH. HE'S A SWEETHEART.
CUTE, TOO.
YOU BETTER FORGET IT, LILY.
WHY? DOES HE ALREADY HAVE A GIRLFRIEND?
NO, WORSE! HE'S A JUNIOR.
OH!
YEAH! ANYWAY, THERE'RE SOME REAL NICE GUYS IN OUR GRADE. YOU'LL SEE!
I S'POSE.
TRUST ME!

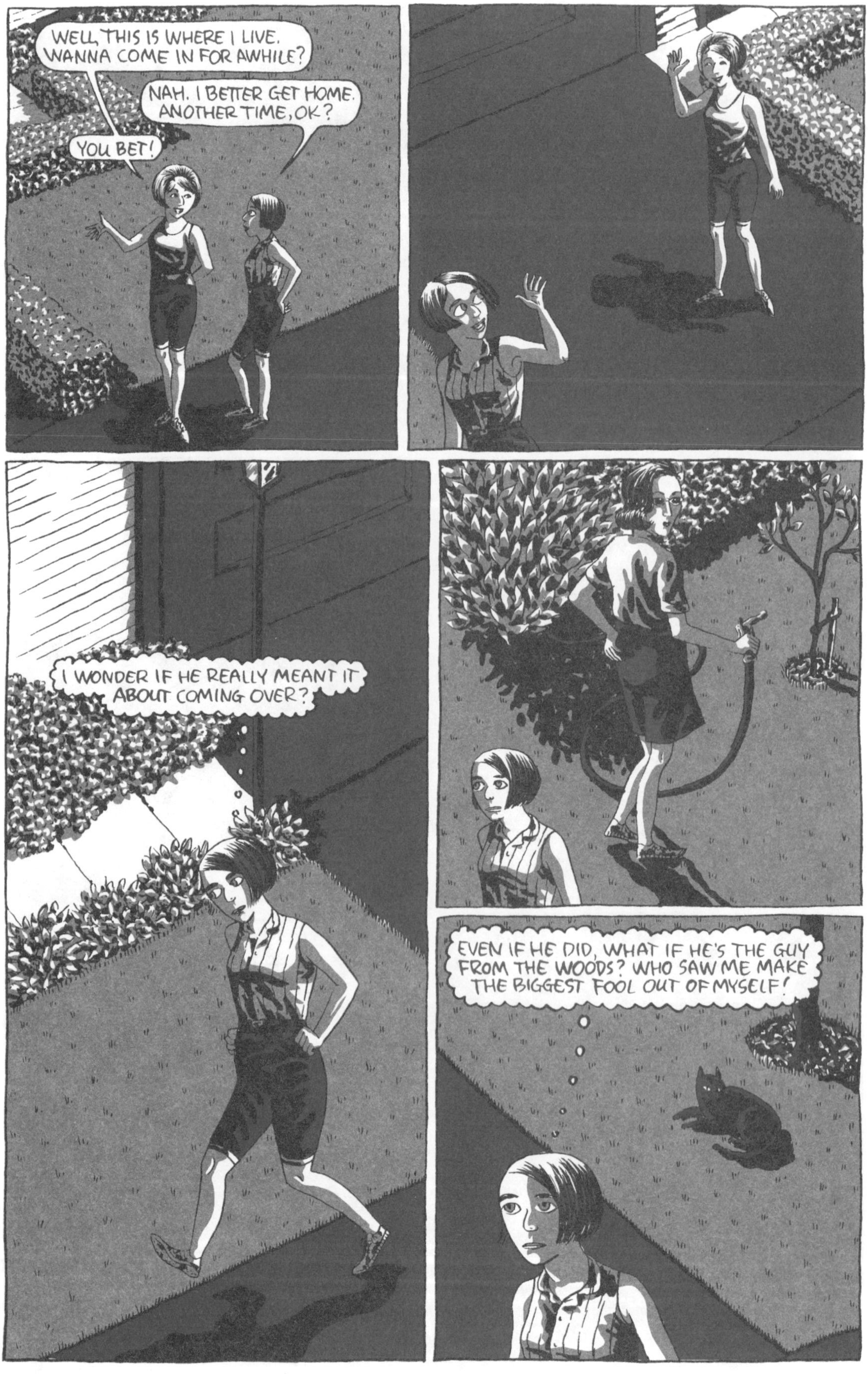
WELL, THIS IS WHERE I LIVE. WANNA COME IN FOR AWHILE?
NAH. I BETTER GET HOME. ANOTHER TIME, OK?
YOU BET!
I WONDER IF HE REALLY MEANT IT ABOUT COMING OVER?
EVEN IF HE DID, WHAT IF HE'S THE GUY FROM THE WOODS? WHO SAW ME MAKE THE BIGGEST FOOL OUT OF MYSELF!

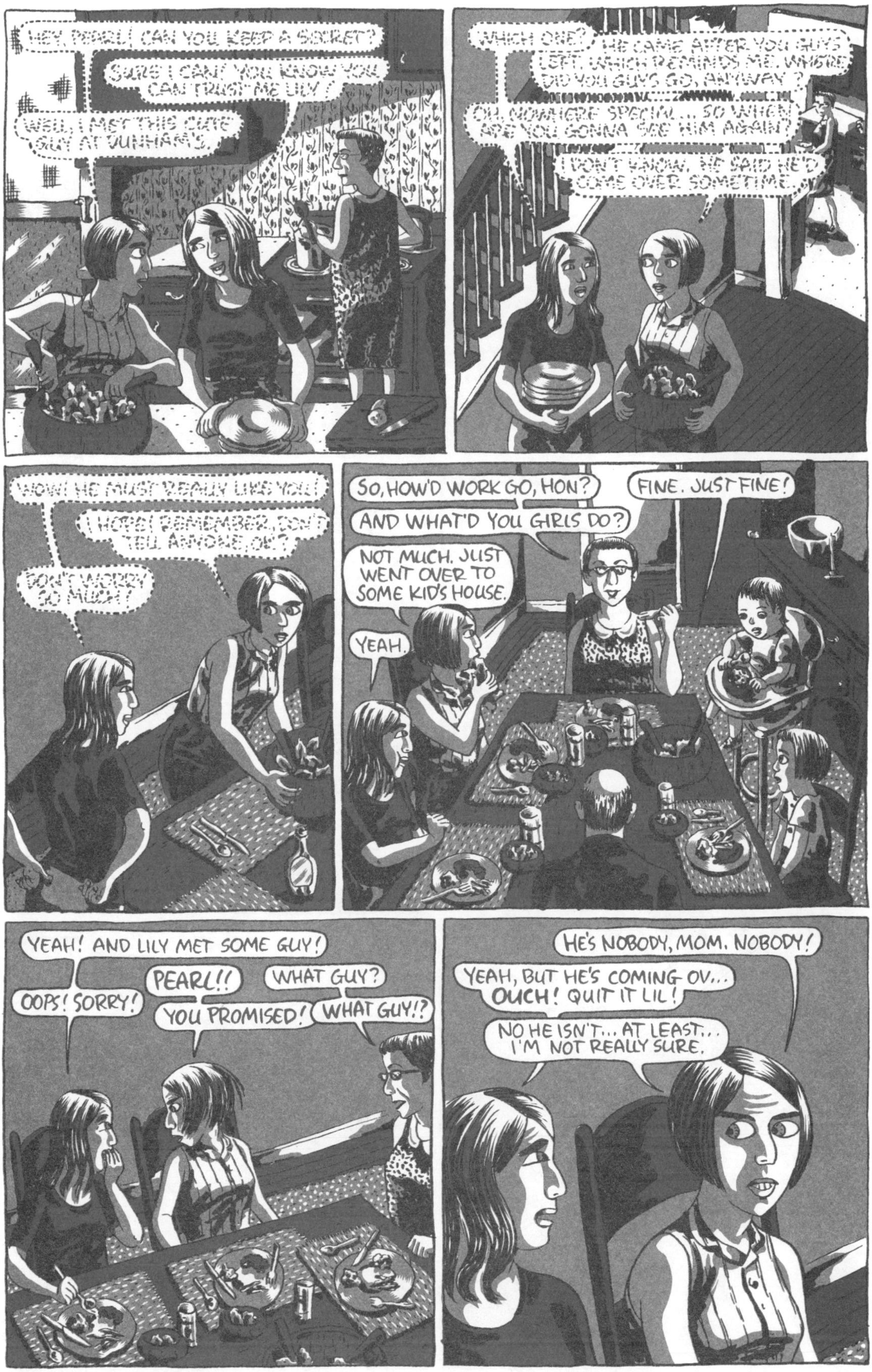
HEY, PEARL! CAN YOU KEEP A SECRET?
SURE I CAN! YOU KNOW YOU CAN TRUST ME LILY!
WELL, I MET THIS CUTE GUY AT DUNHAM'S.
WHICH ONE?
HE CAME AFTER YOU GUYS LEFT. WHICH REMINDS ME, WHERE DID YOU GUYS GO, ANYWAY?
OH, NOWHERE SPECIAL... SO WHEN ARE YOU GONNA SEE HIM AGAIN?
I DON'T KNOW. HE SAID HE'D COME OVER SOMETIME.
WOW! HE MUST REALLY LIKE YOU!
I HOPE! REMEMBER, DON'T TELL ANYONE, OK?
DON'T WORRY SO MUCH!
SO, HOW'D WORK GO, HON?
FINE. JUST FINE!
AND WHAT'D YOU GIRLS DO?
NOT MUCH. JUST WENT OVER TO SOME KID'S HOUSE.
YEAH.
YEAH! AND LILY MET SOME GUY!
OOPS! SORRY!
PEARL!!
YOU PROMISED!
WHAT GUY?
WHAT GUY!?
HE'S NOBODY, MOM. NOBODY!
YEAH, BUT HE'S COMING OV...
OUCH! QUIT IT LIL!
NO HE ISN'T... AT LEAST... I'M NOT REALLY SURE.

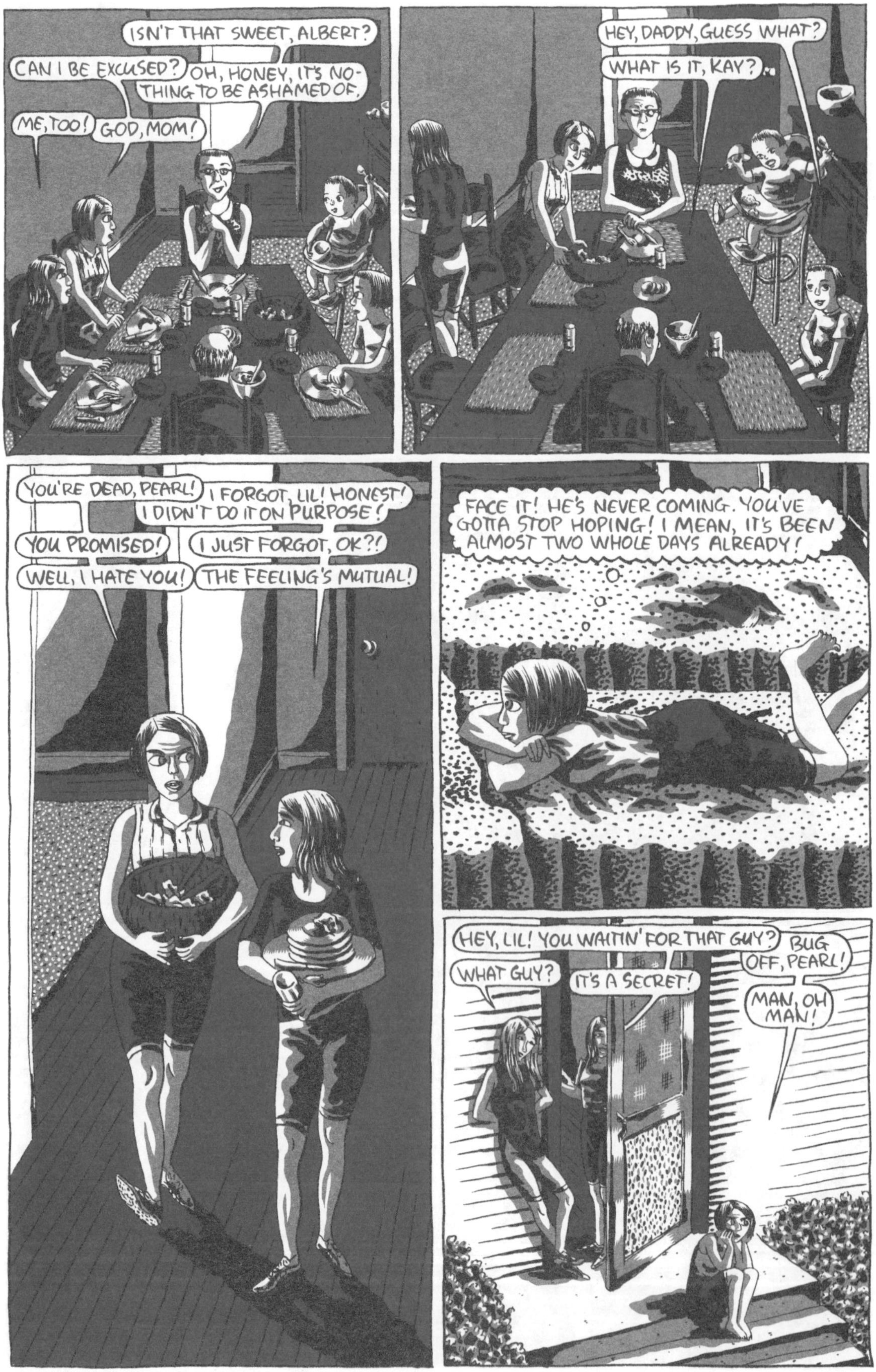

ISN'T THAT SWEET, ALBERT?
CAN I BE EXCUSED?
OH, HONEY, IT'S NOTHING TO BE ASHAMED OF.
ME, TOO!
GOD, MOM!
HEY, DADDY, GUESS WHAT?
WHAT IS IT, KAY?
YOU'RE DEAD, PEARL!
I FORGOT, LIL! HONEST! I DIDN'T DO IT ON PURPOSE!
YOU PROMISED!
I JUST FORGOT, OK?!
WELL, I HATE YOU!
THE FEELING'S MUTUAL!
FACE IT! HE'S NEVER COMING. YOU'VE GOTTA STOP HOPING! I MEAN, IT'S BEEN ALMOST TWO WHOLE DAYS ALREADY!
HEY, LIL! YOU WAITIN' FOR THAT GUY?
BUG OFF, PEARL!
WHAT GUY?
IT'S A SECRET!
MAN, OH MAN!

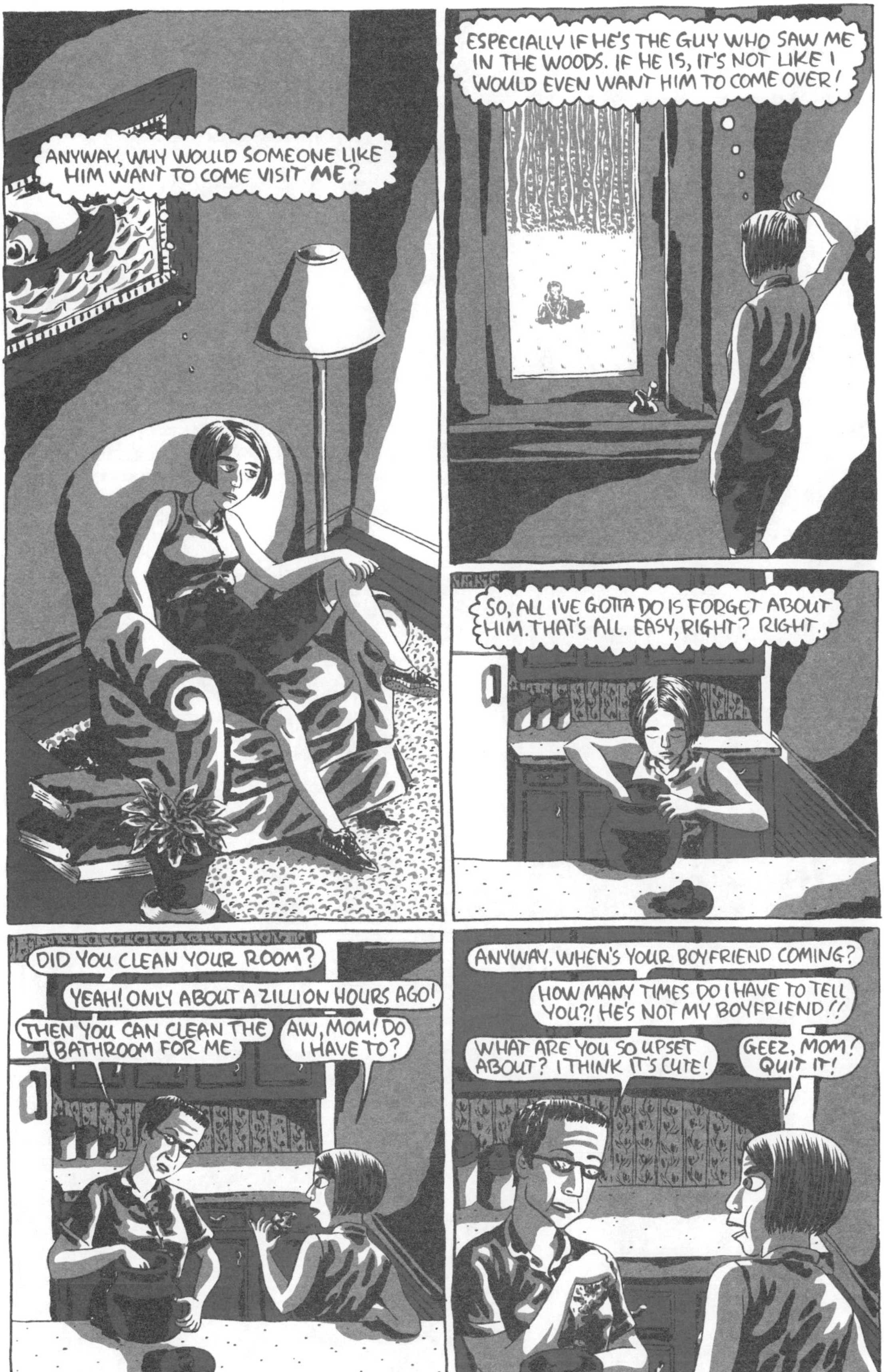
ANYWAY, WHY WOULD SOMEONE LIKE HIM WANT TO COME VISIT ME?
ESPECIALLY IF HE'S THE GUY WHO SAW ME IN THE WOODS. IF HE IS, IT'S NOT LIKE I WOULD EVEN WANT HIM TO COME OVER!
SO, ALL I'VE GOTTA DO IS FORGET ABOUT HIM. THAT'S ALL. EASY, RIGHT? RIGHT.
DID YOU CLEAN YOUR ROOM?
YEAH! ONLY ABOUT A ZILLION HOURS AGO!
THEN YOU CAN CLEAN THE BATHROOM FOR ME.
AW, MOM! DO I HAVE TO?
ANYWAY, WHEN'S YOUR BOYFRIEND COMING?
HOW MANY TIMES DO I HAVE TO TELL YOU?! HE'S NOT MY BOYFRIEND!!
WHAT ARE YOU SO UPSET ABOUT? I THINK IT'S CUTE!
GEEZ, MOM! QUIT IT!

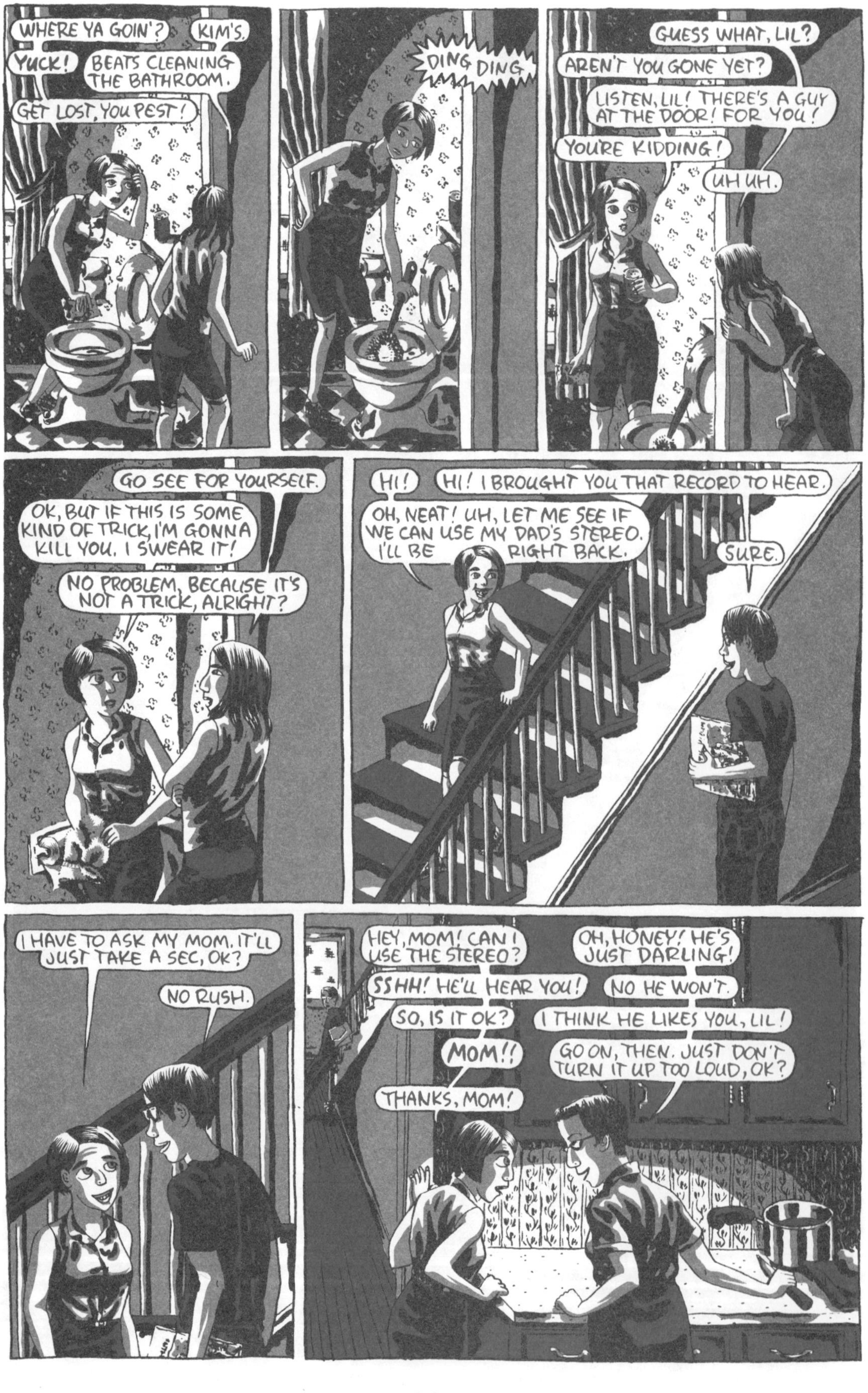
WHERE YA GOIN'?
KIM'S.
YUCK!
BEATS CLEANING THE BATHROOM.
GET LOST, YOU PEST!
DING DING
GUESS WHAT, LIL?
AREN'T YOU GONE YET?
LISTEN, LIL! THERE'S A GUY AT THE DOOR! FOR YOU!
YOU'RE KIDDING!
UH UH.
GO SEE FOR YOURSELF.
OK, BUT IF THIS IS SOME KIND OF TRICK, I'M GONNA KILL YOU. I SWEAR IT!
NO PROBLEM, BECAUSE IT'S NOT A TRICK, ALRIGHT?
HI!
HI! I BROUGHT YOU THAT RECORD TO HEAR.
OH, NEAT! UH, LET ME SEE IF WE CAN USE MY DAD'S STEREO. I'LL BE RIGHT BACK.
SURE.
I HAVE TO ASK MY MOM. IT'LL JUST TAKE A SEC, OK?
NO RUSH.
HEY, MOM! CAN I USE THE STEREO?
OH, HONEY! HE'S JUST DARLING!
SSHH! HE'LL HEAR YOU!
NO HE WON'T.
SO, IS IT OK?
I THINK HE LIKES YOU, LIL!
MOM!!
GO ON, THEN. JUST DON'T TURN IT UP TOO LOUD, OK?
THANKS, MOM!

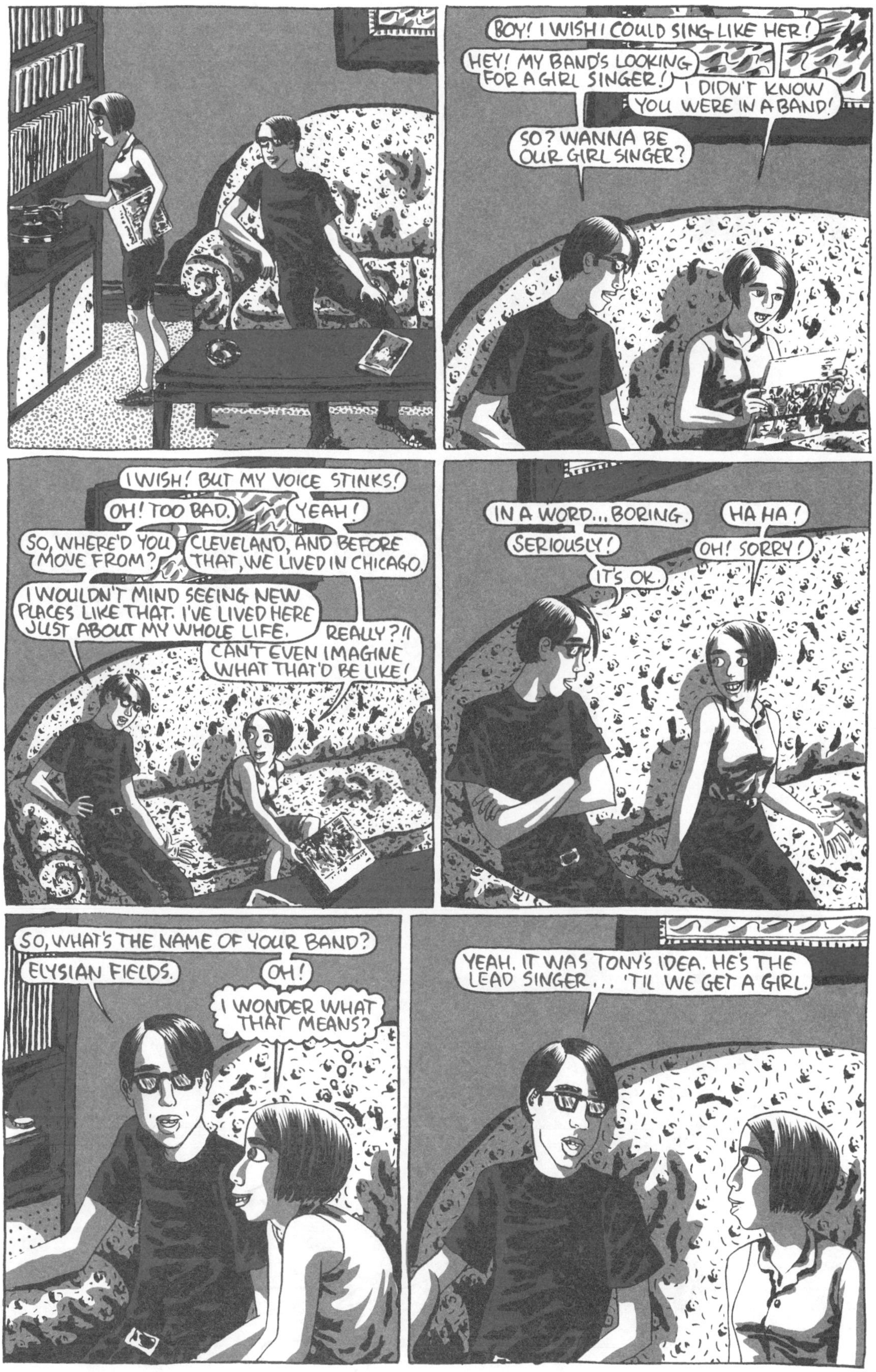
BOY! I WISH I COULD SING LIKE HER!
HEY! MY BAND'S LOOKING FOR A GIRL SINGER!
I DIDN'T KNOW YOU WERE IN A BAND!
SO? WANNA BE OUR GIRL SINGER?
I WISH! BUT MY VOICE STINKS!
OH! TOO BAD.
YEAH!
SO, WHERE'D YOU MOVE FROM?
CLEVELAND, AND BEFORE THAT, WE LIVED IN CHICAGO.
I WOULDN'T MIND SEEING NEW PLACES LIKE THAT. I'VE LIVED HERE JUST ABOUT MY WHOLE LIFE.
REALLY?!! CAN'T EVEN IMAGINE WHAT THAT'D BE LIKE!
IN A WORD... BORING.
HA HA!
SERIOUSLY!
OH! SORRY!
IT'S OK.
SO, WHAT'S THE NAME OF YOUR BAND?
ELYSIAN FIELDS.
OH!
I WONDER WHAT THAT MEANS?
YEAH. IT WAS TONY'S IDEA. HE'S THE LEAD SINGER... 'TIL WE GET A GIRL.

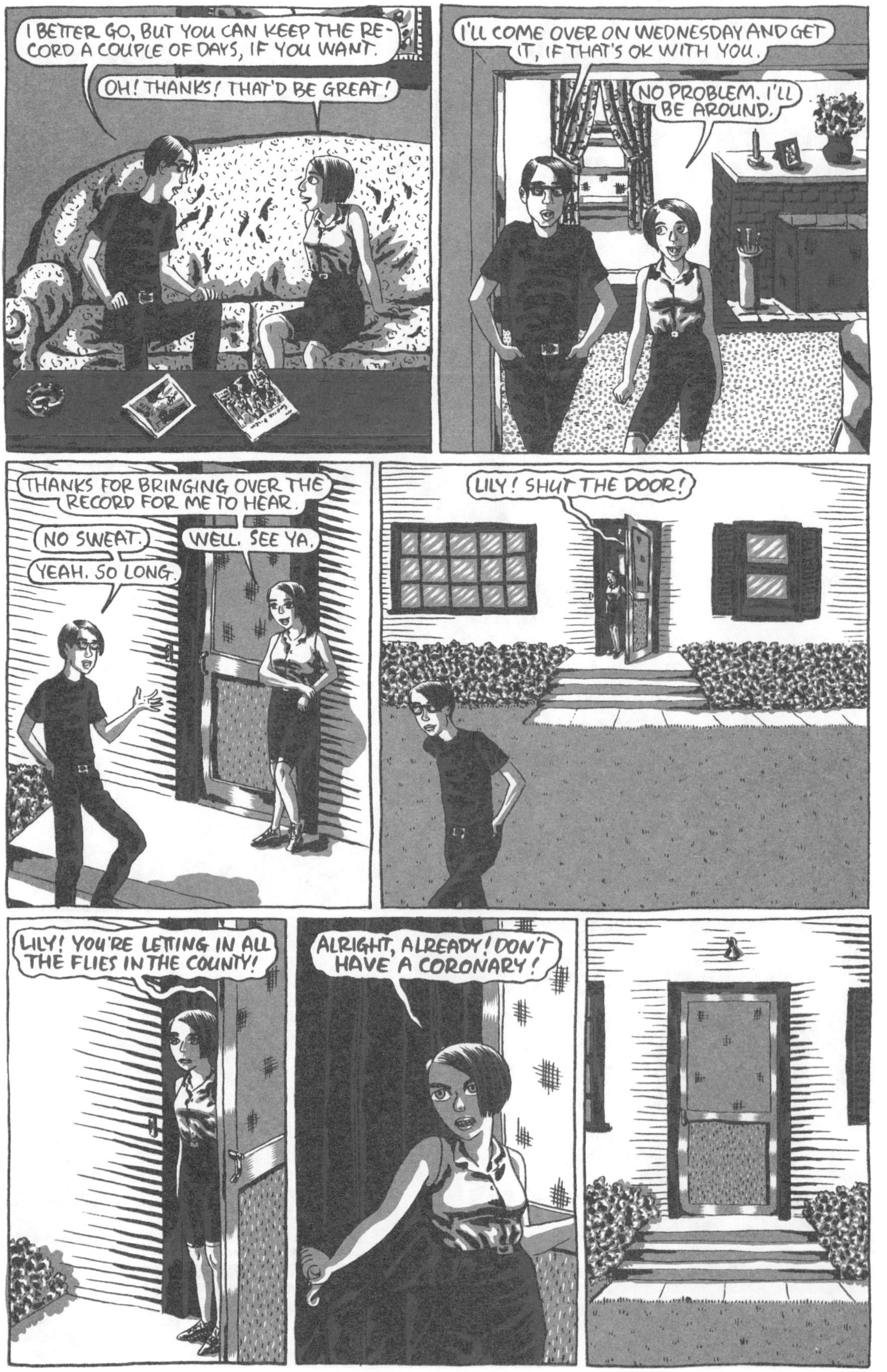
I BETTER GO, BUT YOU CAN KEEP THE RECORD A COUPLE OF DAYS, IF YOU WANT.
OH! THANKS! THAT'D BE GREAT!
I'LL COME OVER ON WEDNESDAY AND GET IT, IF THAT'S OK WITH YOU.
NO PROBLEM. I'LL BE AROUND.
THANKS FOR BRINGING OVER THE RECORD FOR ME TO HEAR.
NO SWEAT.
WELL. SEE YA.
YEAH. SO LONG.
LILY! SHUT THE DOOR!
LILY! YOU'RE LETTING IN ALL THE FLIES IN THE COUNTY!
ALRIGHT, ALREADY! DON'T HAVE A CORONARY!

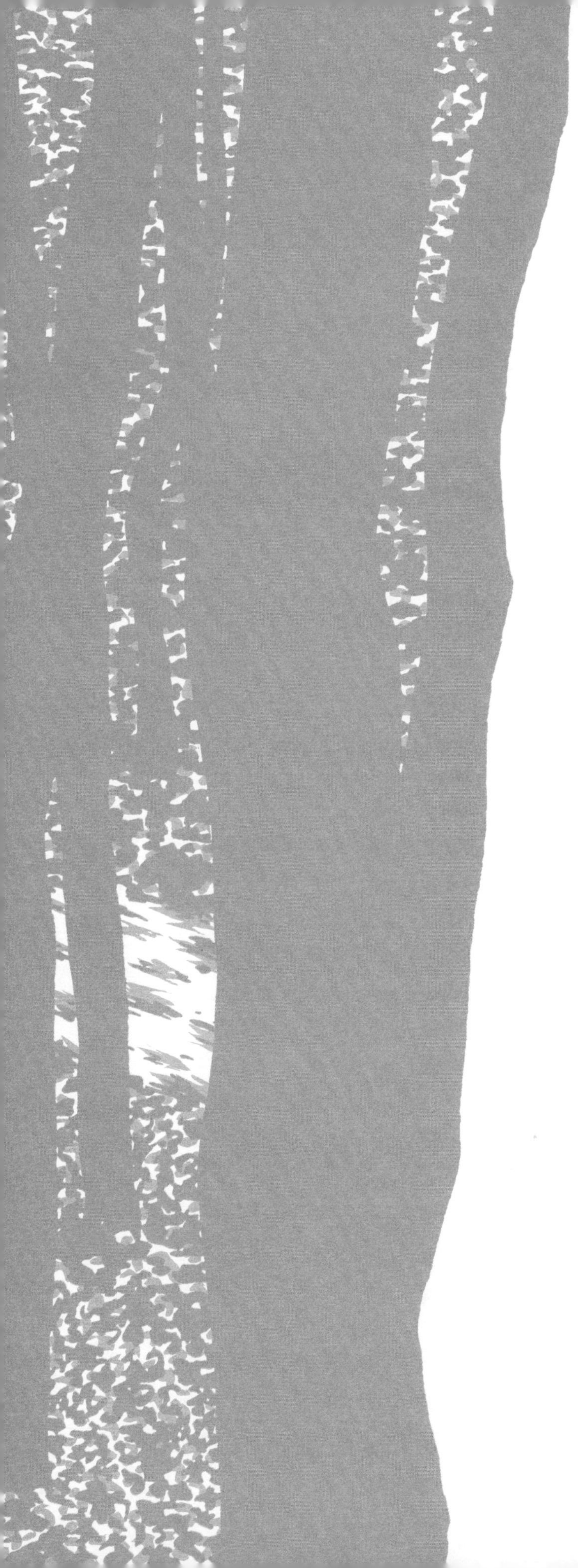

PART TWO

—

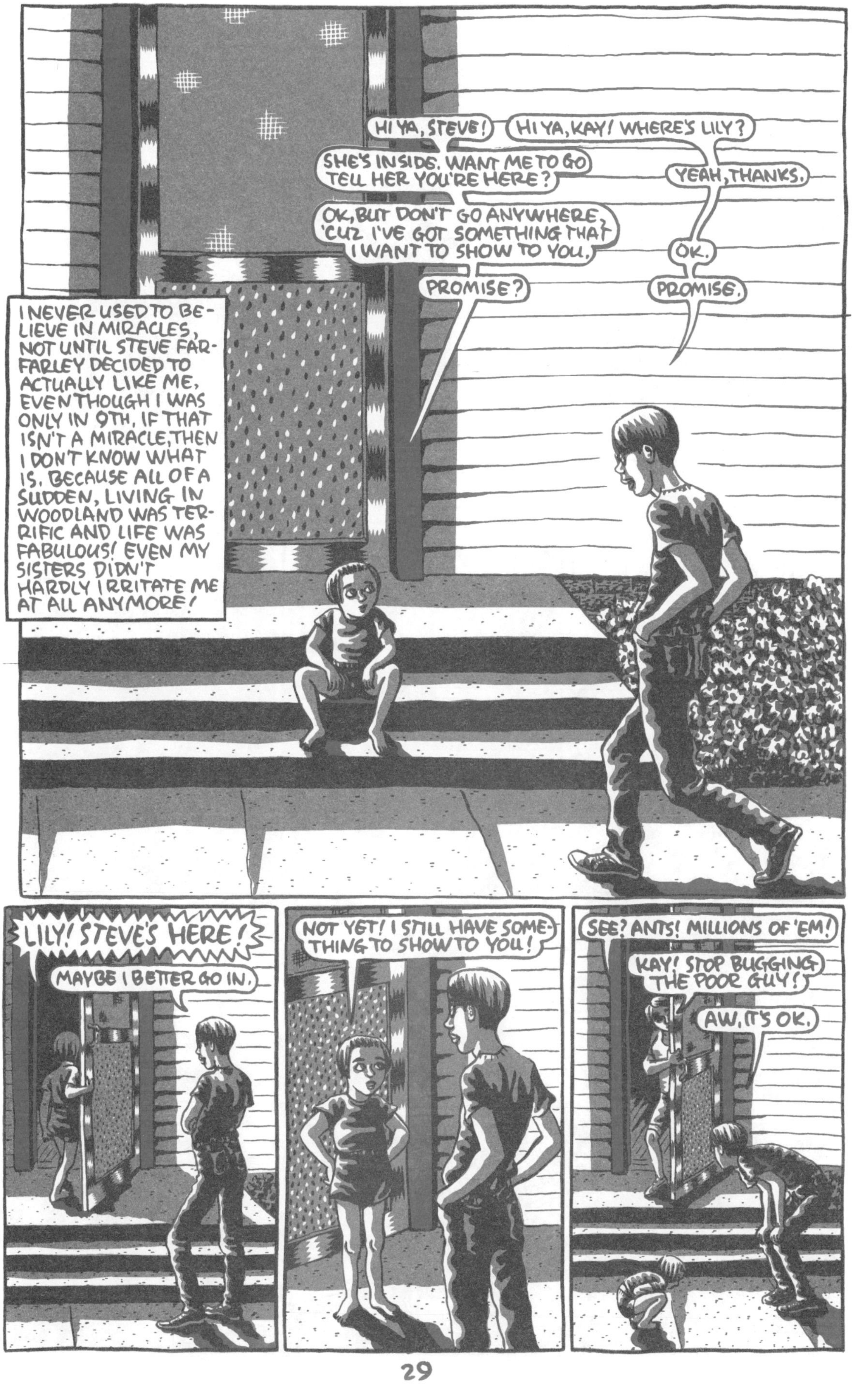
HI YA, STEVE!
HI YA, KAY! WHERE'S LILY?
SHE'S INSIDE. WANT ME TO GO TELL HER YOU'RE HERE?
YEAH, THANKS.
OK, BUT DON'T GO ANYWHERE, 'CUZ I'VE GOT SOMETHING THAT I WANT TO SHOW TO YOU.
OK.
PROMISE?
PROMISE.
I NEVER USED TO BELIEVE IN MIRACLES, NOT UNTIL STEVE FARFARLEY DECIDED TO ACTUALLY LIKE ME, EVEN THOUGH I WAS ONLY IN 9TH. IF THAT ISN'T A MIRACLE, THEN I DON'T KNOW WHAT IS. BECAUSE ALL OF A SUDDEN, LIVING IN WOODLAND WAS TERRIFIC AND LIFE WAS FABULOUS! EVEN MY SISTERS DIDN'T HARDLY IRRITATE ME AT ALL ANYMORE!
LILY! STEVE'S HERE!
MAYBE I BETTER GO IN.
NOT YET! I STILL HAVE SOMETHING TO SHOW TO YOU!
SEE? ANTS! MILLIONS OF 'EM!
KAY! STOP BUGGING THE POOR GUY!
AW, IT'S OK.

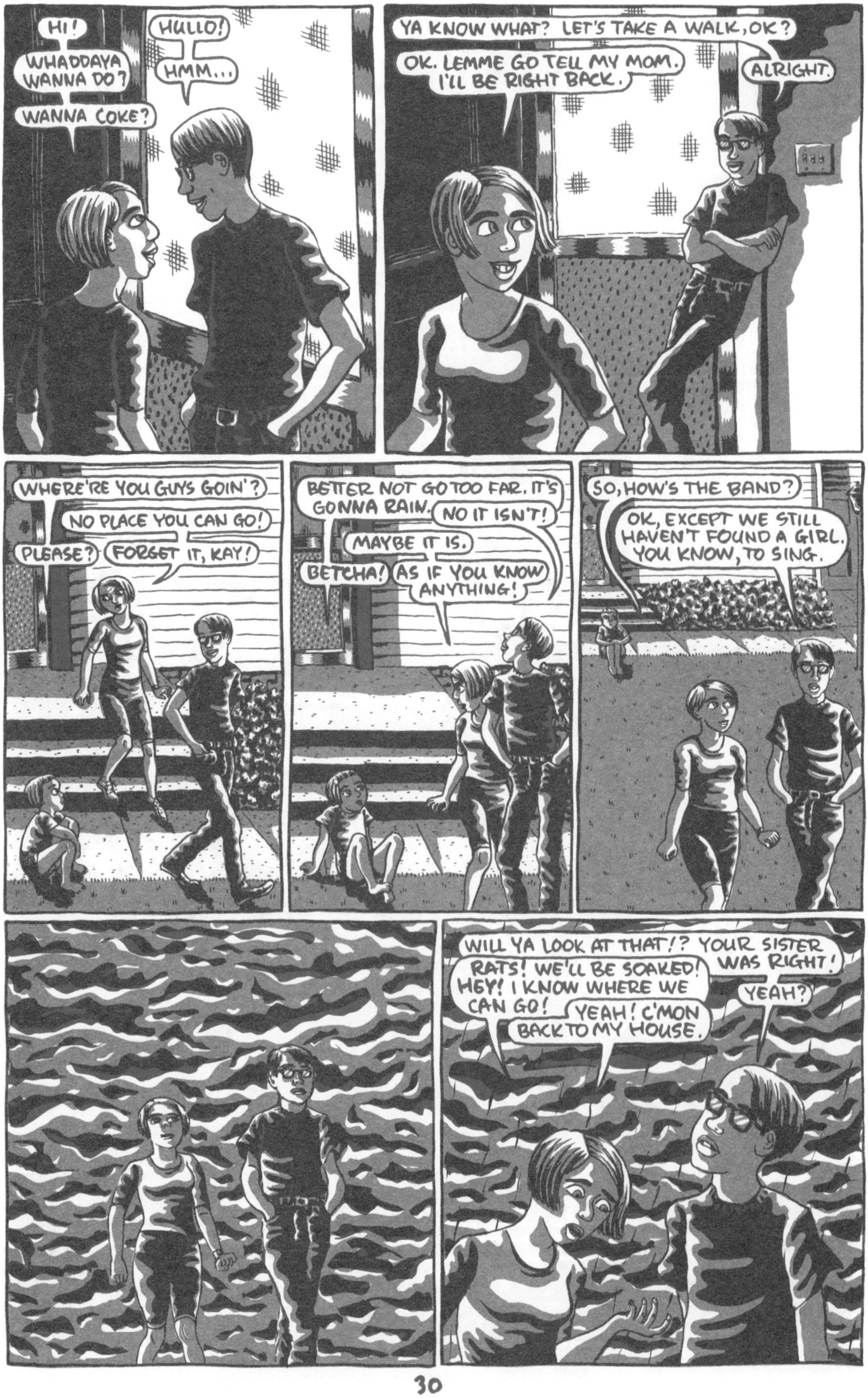
HI!
WHADDAYA WANNA DO?
WANNA COKE?
HULLO!
HMM...
YA KNOW WHAT? LET'S TAKE A WALK, OK?
OK. LEMME GO TELL MY MOM. I'LL BE RIGHT BACK.
ALRIGHT.
WHERE'RE YOU GUYS GOIN'?
NO PLACE YOU CAN GO!
PLEASE?
FORGET IT, KAY!
BETTER NOT GO TOO FAR. IT'S GONNA RAIN.
NO IT ISN'T!
MAYBE IT IS.
BETCHA!
AS IF YOU KNOW ANYTHING!
SO, HOW'S THE BAND?
OK, EXCEPT WE STILL HAVEN'T FOUND A GIRL. YOU KNOW, TO SING.
WILL YA LOOK AT THAT!? YOUR SISTER WAS RIGHT!
RATS! WE'LL BE SOAKED!
HEY! I KNOW WHERE WE CAN GO!
YEAH?
YEAH! C'MON BACK TO MY HOUSE.

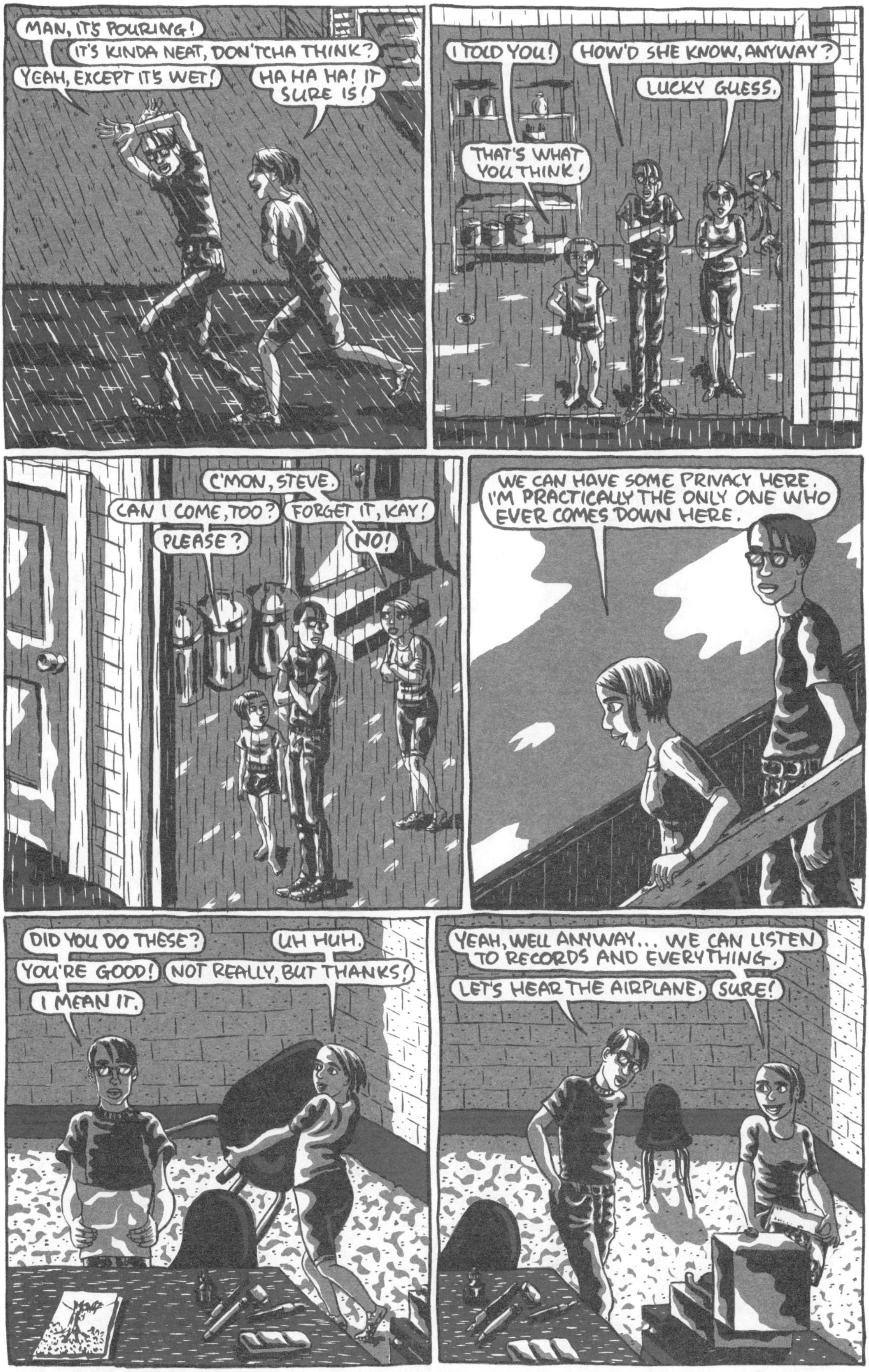
MAN, IT'S POURING!
IT'S KINDA NEAT, DON'TCHA THINK?
YEAH, EXCEPT IT'S WET!
HA HA HA! IT SURE IS!
I TOLD YOU!
THAT'S WHAT YOU THINK!
HOW'D SHE KNOW, ANYWAY?
LUCKY GUESS.
C'MON, STEVE.
CAN I COME, TOO?
FORGET IT, KAY!
PLEASE?
NO!
WE CAN HAVE SOME PRIVACY HERE. I'M PRACTICALLY THE ONLY ONE WHO EVER COMES DOWN HERE.
DID YOU DO THESE?
UH HUH.
YOU'RE GOOD!
NOT REALLY, BUT THANKS!
I MEAN IT.
YEAH, WELL ANYWAY... WE CAN LISTEN TO RECORDS AND EVERYTHING.
LET'S HEAR THE AIRPLANE.
SURE!

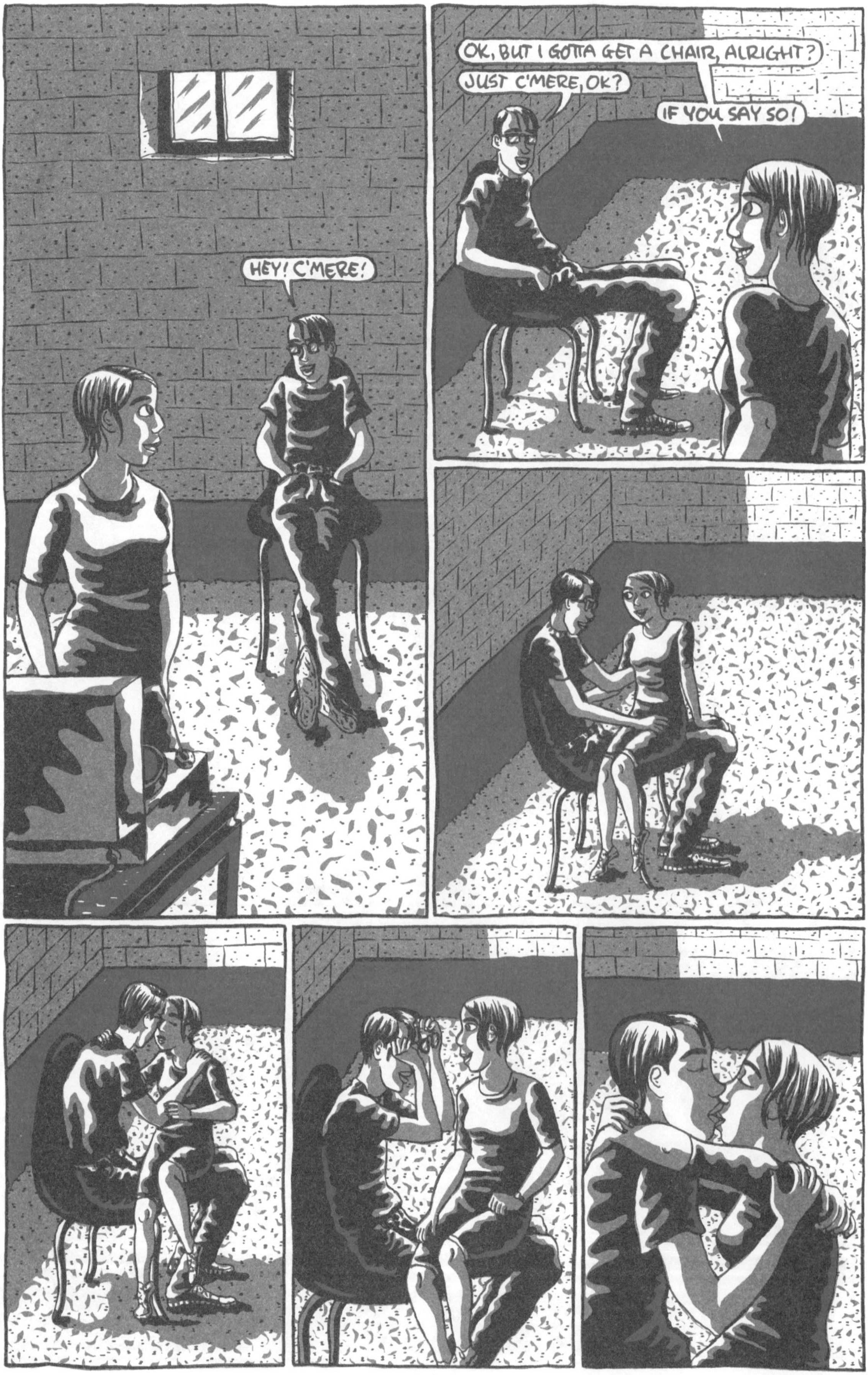
HEY! C'MERE!
OK, BUT I GOTTA GET A CHAIR, ALRIGHT?
JUST C'MERE, OK?
IF YOU SAY SO!

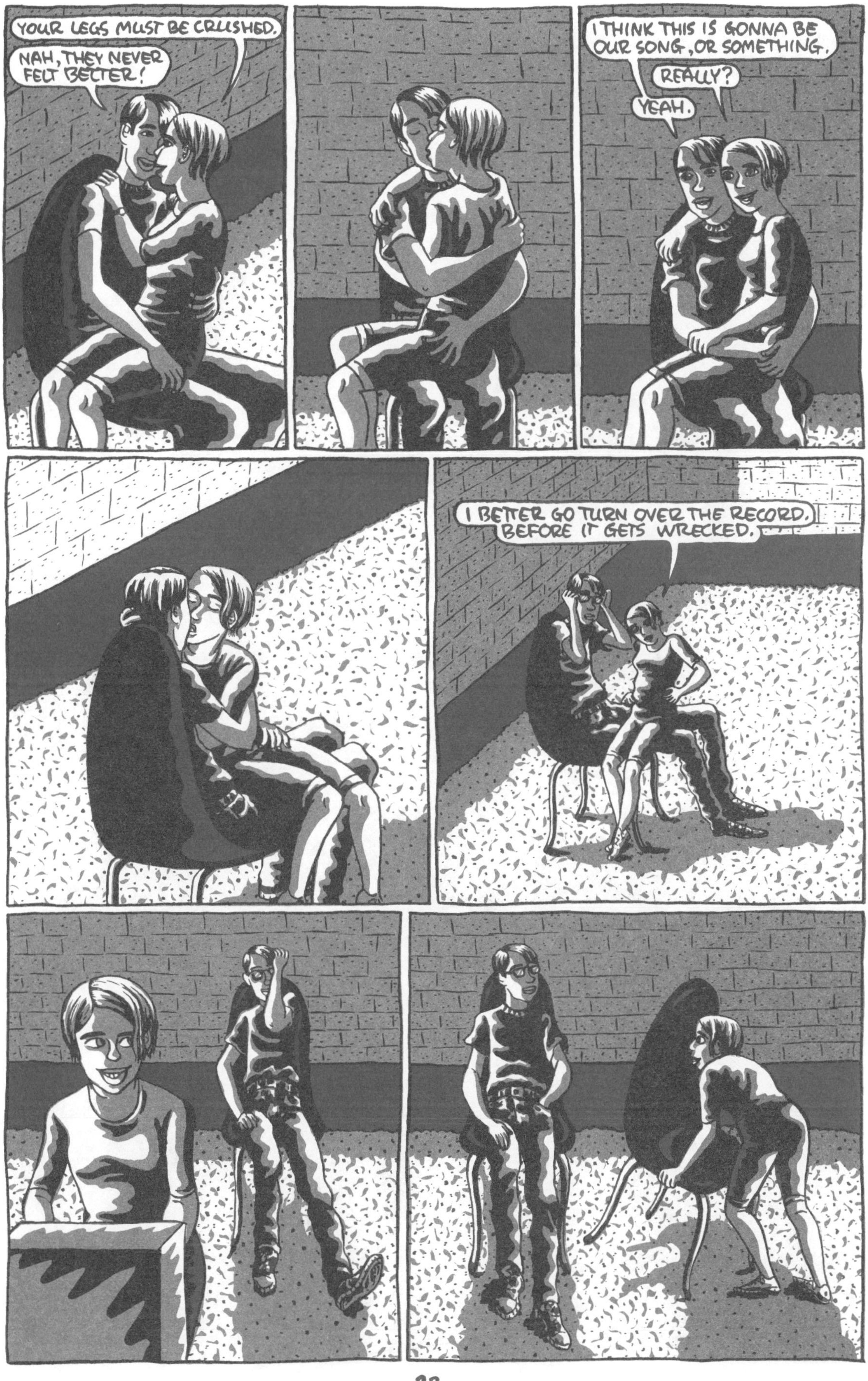
YOUR LEGS MUST BE CRUSHED.
NAH, THEY NEVER FELT BETTER!
I THINK THIS IS GONNA BE OUR SONG, OR SOMETHING.
REALLY?
YEAH.
I BETTER GO TURN OVER THE RECORD, BEFORE IT GETS WRECKED.

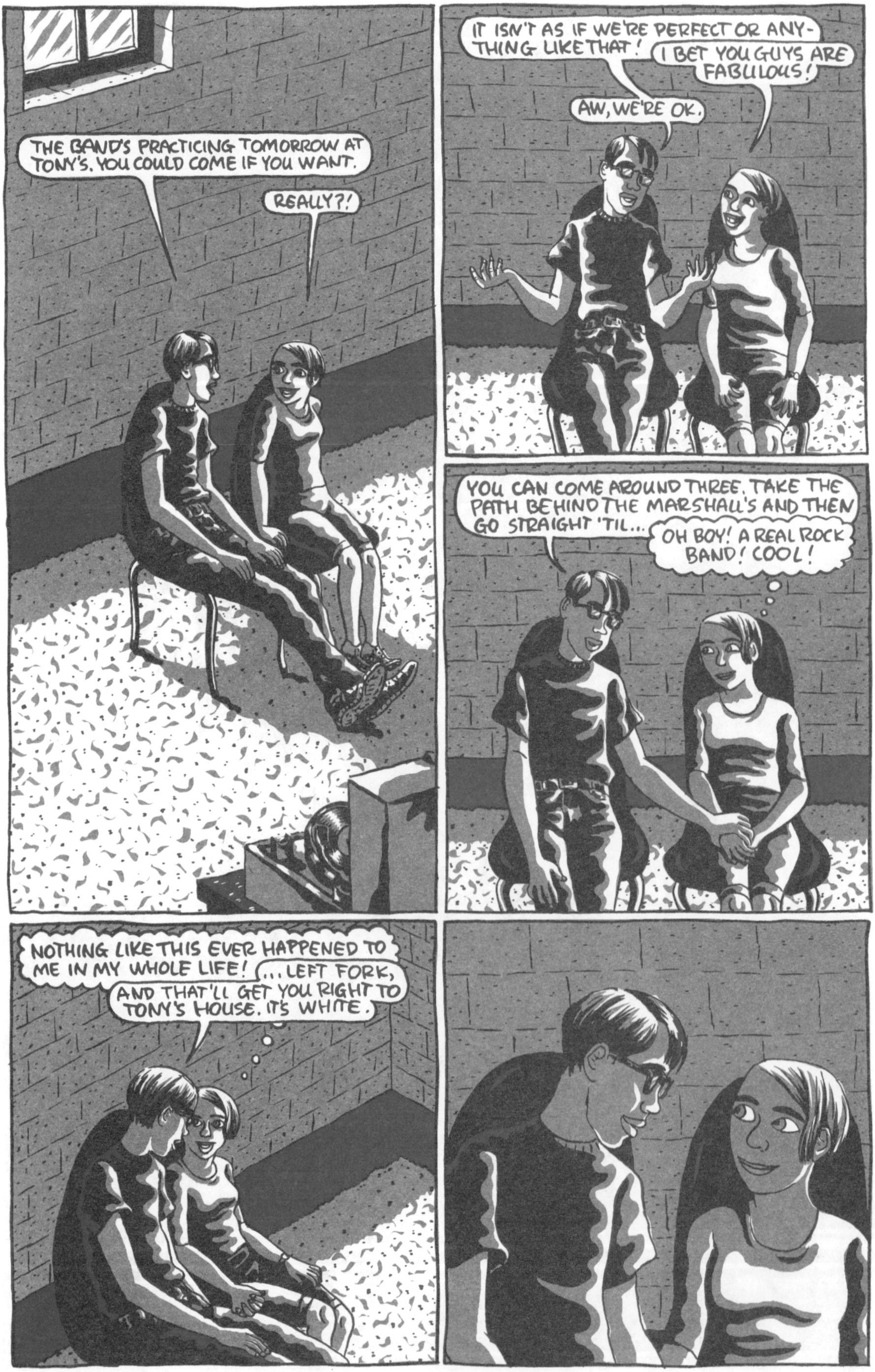
THE BAND'S PRACTICING TOMORROW AT TONY'S. YOU COULD COME IF YOU WANT.
REALLY?!
IT ISN'T AS IF WE'RE PERFECT OR ANY-THING LIKE THAT!
I BET YOU GUYS ARE FABULOUS!
AW, WE'RE OK.
YOU CAN COME AROUND THREE. TAKE THE PATH BEHIND THE MARSHALL'S AND THEN GO STRAIGHT 'TIL...
OH BOY! A REAL ROCK BAND! COOL!
NOTHING LIKE THIS EVER HAPPENED TO ME IN MY WHOLE LIFE!
...LEFT FORK, AND THAT'LL GET YOU RIGHT TO TONY'S HOUSE. IT'S WHITE.

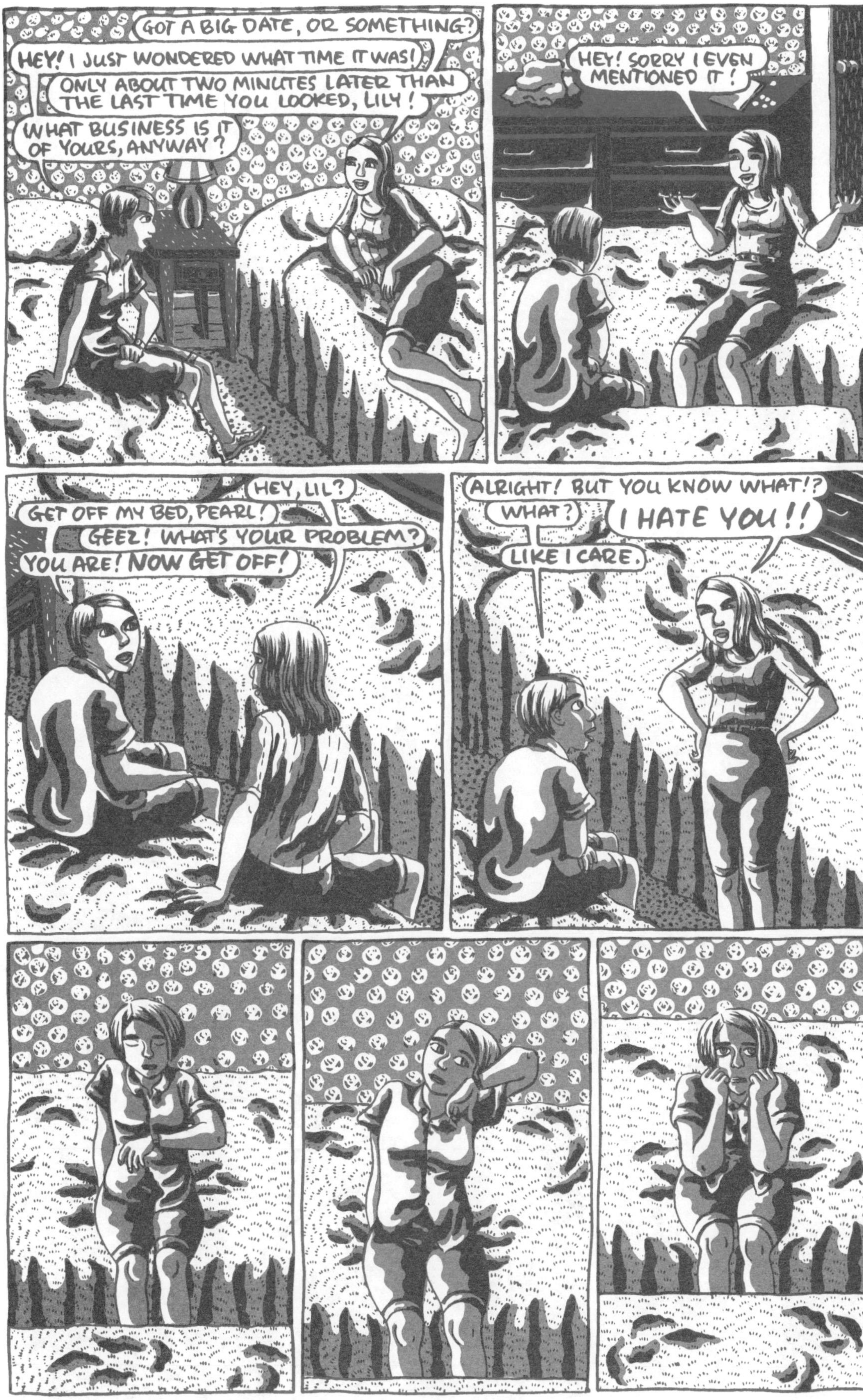
GOT A BIG DATE, OR SOMETHING?
HEY! I JUST WONDERED WHAT TIME IT WAS!
ONLY ABOUT TWO MINUTES LATER THAN THE LAST TIME YOU LOOKED, LILY!
WHAT BUSINESS IS IT OF YOURS, ANYWAY?
HEY! SORRY I EVEN MENTIONED IT!
HEY, LIL?
GET OFF MY BED, PEARL!
GEEZ! WHAT'S YOUR PROBLEM?
YOU ARE! NOW GET OFF!
ALRIGHT! BUT YOU KNOW WHAT!?
WHAT?
I HATE YOU!!
LIKE I CARE.

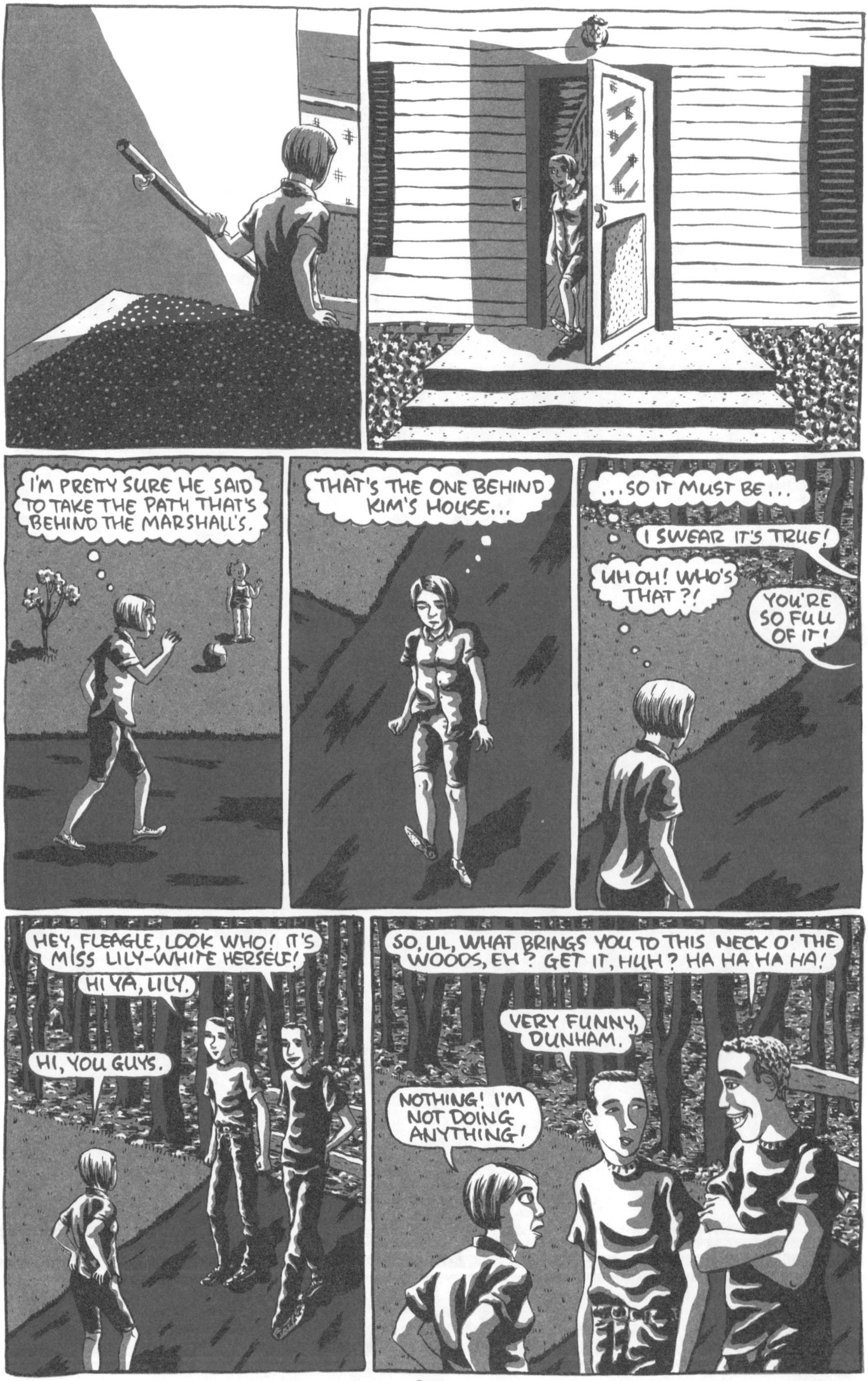
I'M PRETTY SURE HE SAID TO TAKE THE PATH THAT'S BEHIND THE MARSHALL'S.
THAT'S THE ONE BEHIND KIM'S HOUSE...
...SO IT MUST BE...
I SWEAR IT'S TRUE!
UH OH! WHO'S THAT?!
YOU'RE SO FULL OF IT!
HEY, FLEAGLE, LOOK WHO! IT'S MISS LILY-WHITE HERSELF!
HI YA, LILY.
HI, YOU GUYS.
SO, LIL, WHAT BRINGS YOU TO THIS NECK O' THE WOODS, EH? GET IT, HUH? HA HA HA HA!
VERY FUNNY, DUNHAM.
NOTHING! I'M NOT DOING ANYTHING!

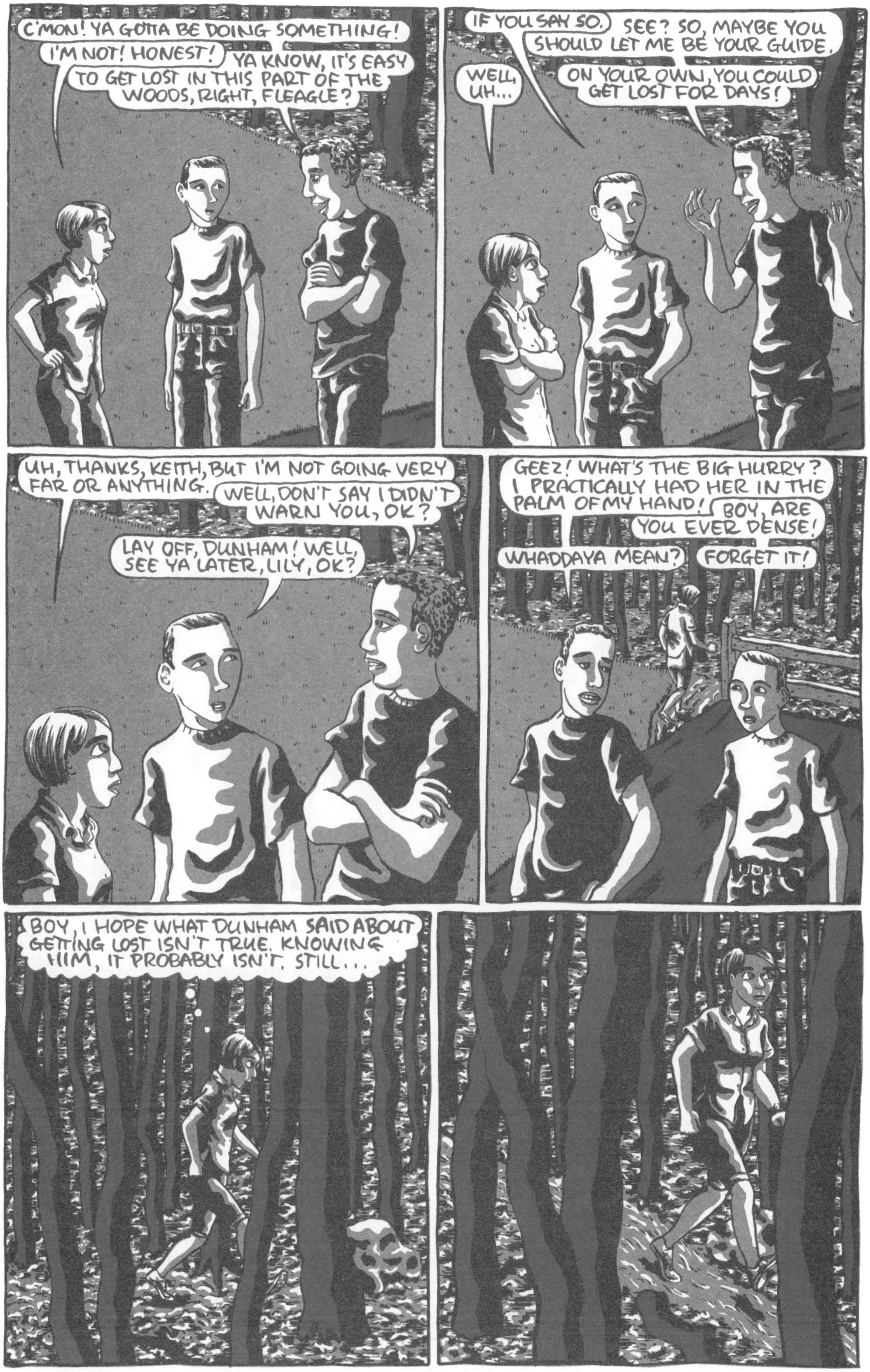
C'MON! YA GOTTA BE DOING SOMETHING!
I'M NOT! HONEST!
YA KNOW, IT'S EASY TO GET LOST IN THIS PART OF THE WOODS, RIGHT, FLEAGLE?
IF YOU SAY SO.
SEE? SO, MAYBE YOU SHOULD LET ME BE YOUR GUIDE.
WELL, UH...
ON YOUR OWN, YOU COULD GET LOST FOR DAYS!
UH, THANKS, KEITH, BUT I'M NOT GOING VERY FAR OR ANYTHING.
WELL, DON'T SAY I DIDN'T WARN YOU, OK?
LAY OFF, DUNHAM! WELL, SEE YA LATER, LILY, OK?
GEEZ! WHAT'S THE BIG HURRY? I PRACTICALLY HAD HER IN THE PALM OF MY HAND!
BOY, ARE YOU EVER DENSE!
WHADDAYA MEAN?
FORGET IT!
BOY, I HOPE WHAT DUNHAM SAID ABOUT GETTING LOST ISN'T TRUE. KNOWING HIM, IT PROBABLY ISN'T. STILL...

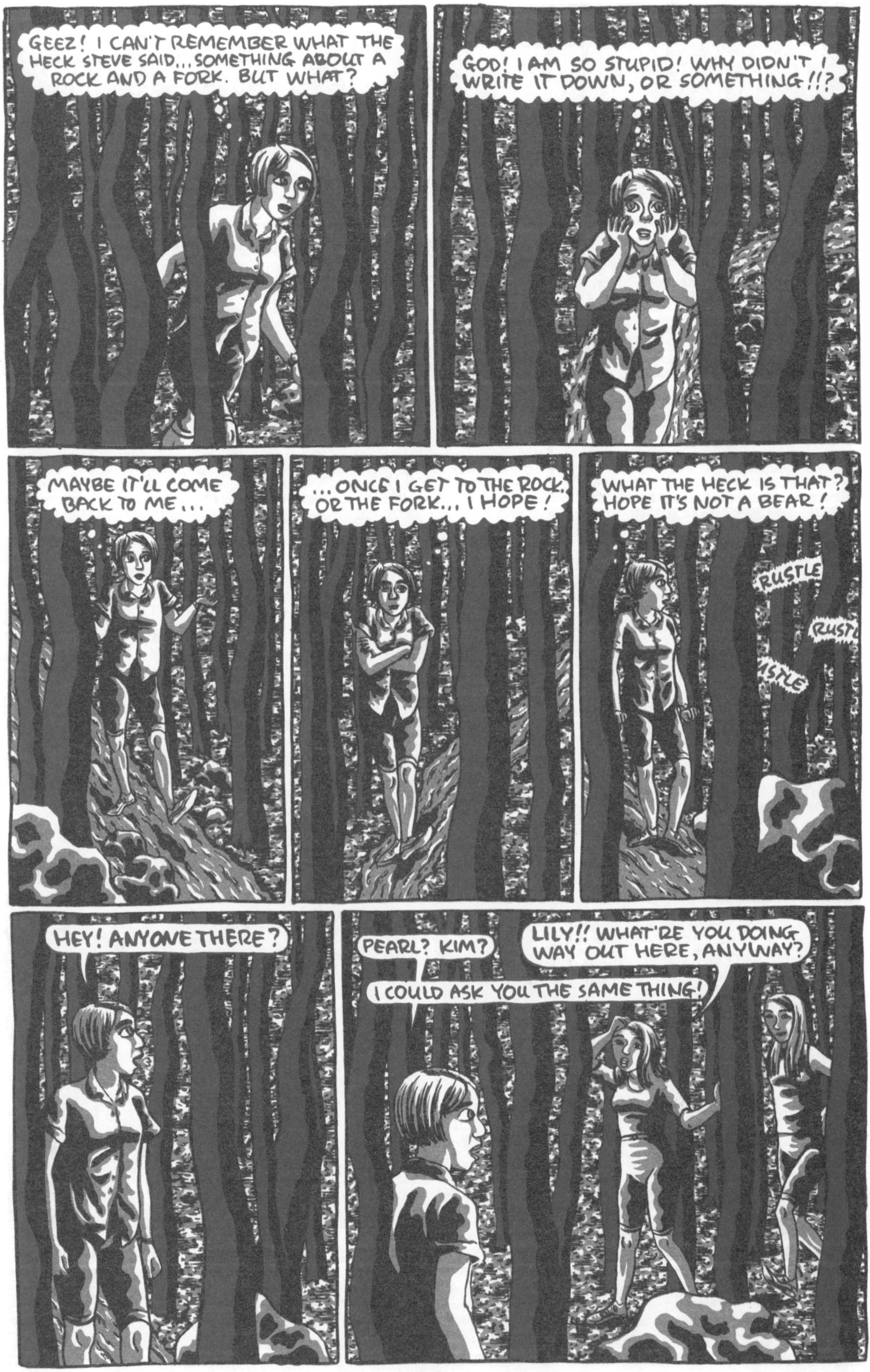
GEEZ! I CAN'T REMEMBER WHAT THE HECK STEVE SAID... SOMETHING ABOUT A ROCK AND A FORK. BUT WHAT?
GOD! I AM SO STUPID! WHY DIDN'T I WRITE IT DOWN, OR SOMETHING!!?
MAYBE IT'LL COME BACK TO ME...
...ONCE I GET TO THE ROCK. OR THE FORK... I HOPE!
WHAT THE HECK IS THAT? HOPE IT'S NOT A BEAR!
RUSTLE
HEY! ANYONE THERE?
PEARL? KIM?
LILY!! WHAT'RE YOU DOING WAY OUT HERE, ANYWAY?
I COULD ASK YOU THE SAME THING!

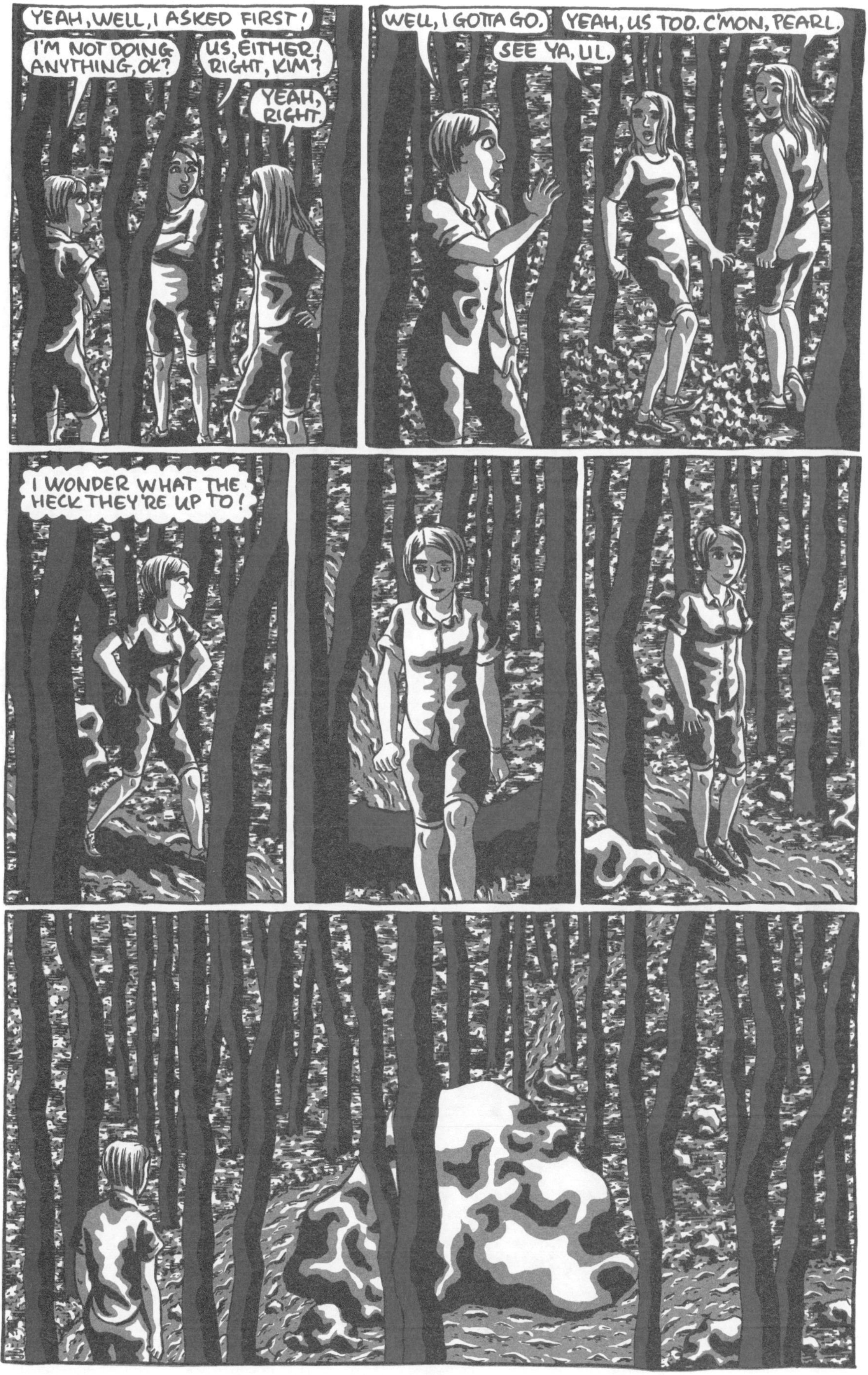
YEAH, WELL, I ASKED FIRST!
I'M NOT DOING ANYTHING, OK?
US, EITHER! RIGHT, KIM?
YEAH, RIGHT.
WELL, I GOTTA GO.
SEE YA, UL.
YEAH, US TOO. C'MON, PEARL.
I WONDER WHAT THE HECK THEY'RE UP TO!

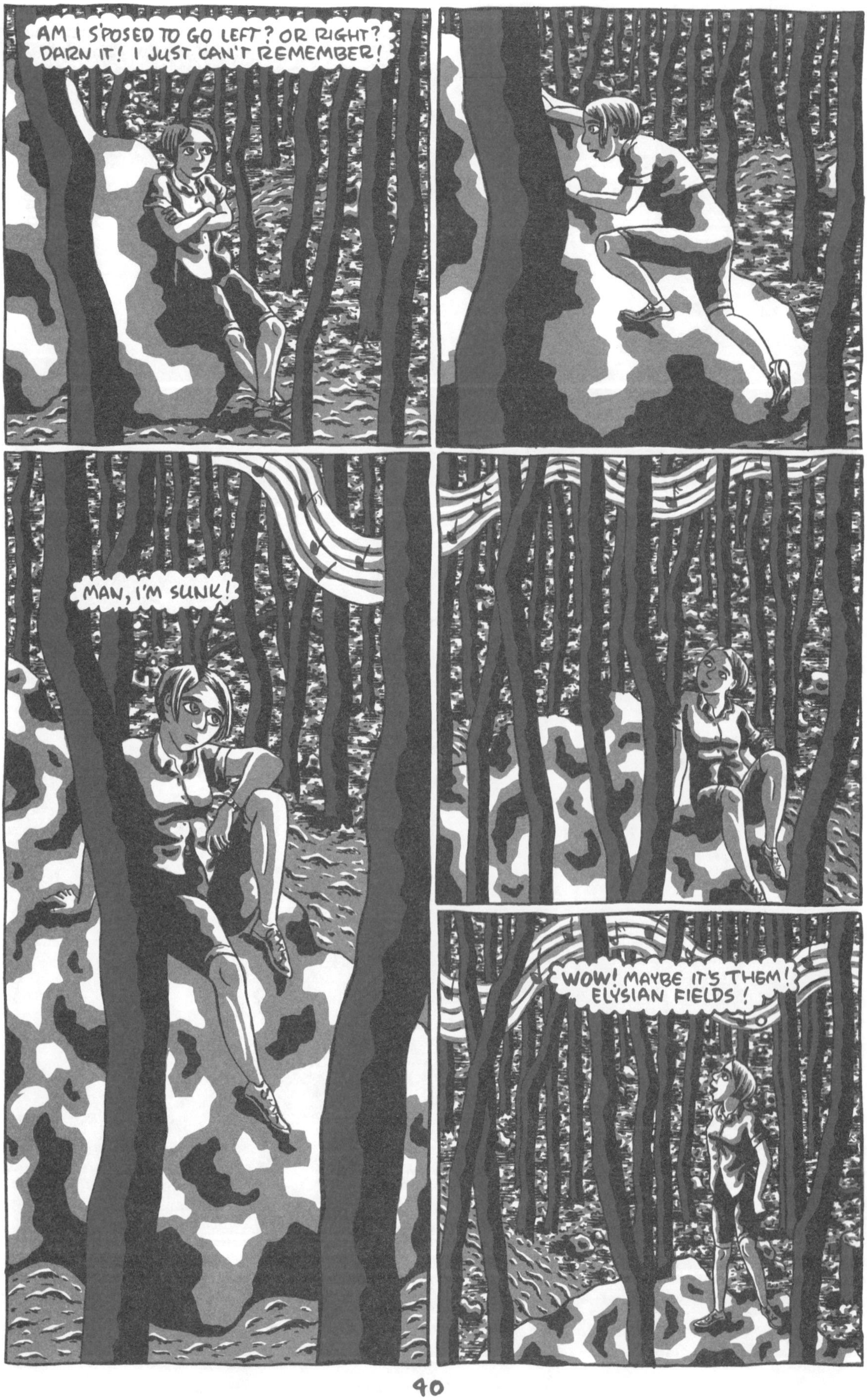
AM I S'POSED TO GO LEFT? OR RIGHT? DARN IT! I JUST CAN'T REMEMBER!
MAN, I'M SUNK!
WOW! MAYBE IT'S THEM! ELYSIAN FIELDS!

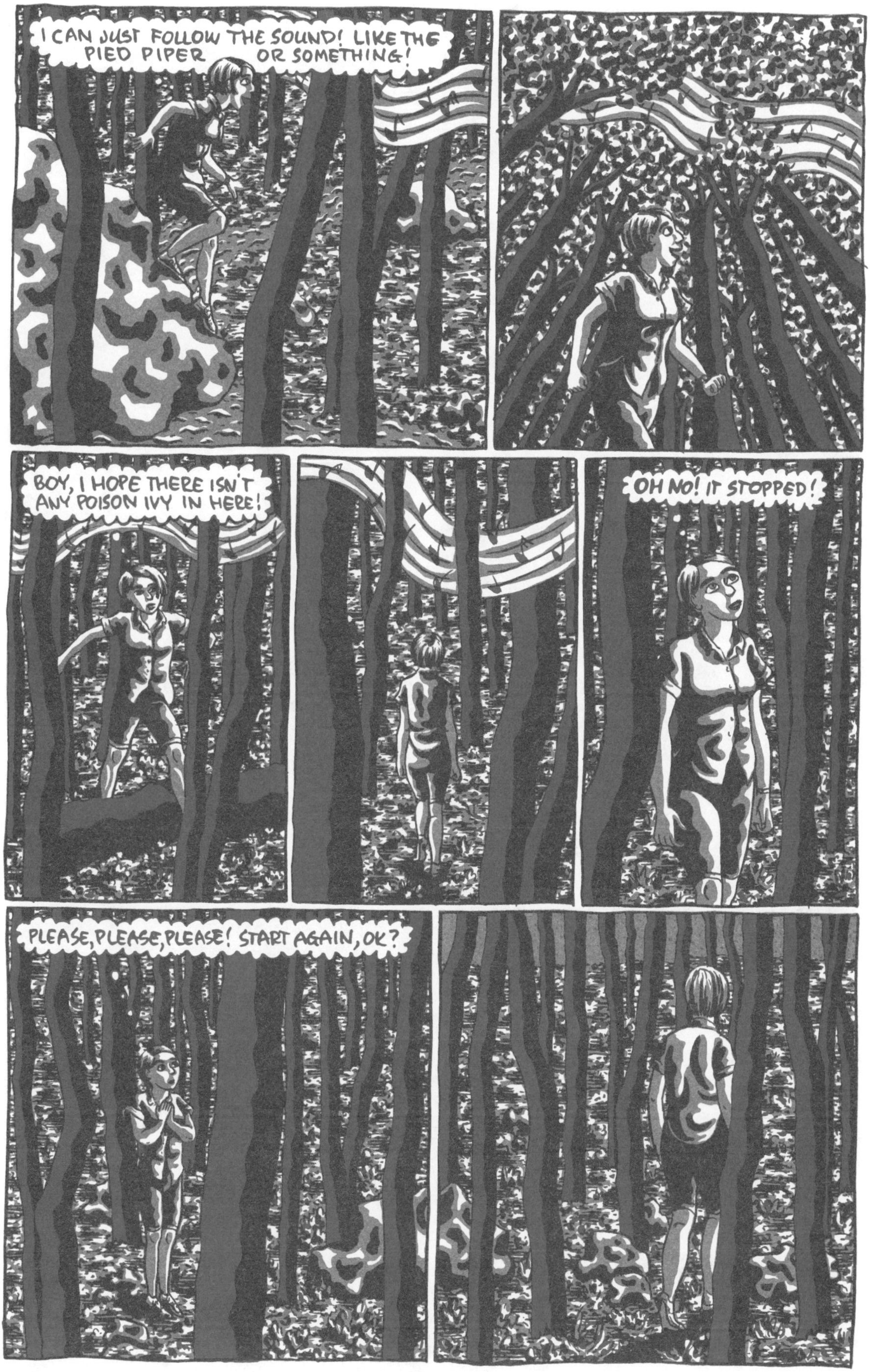
I CAN JUST FOLLOW THE SOUND! LIKE THE PIED PIPER OR SOMETHING!
BOY, I HOPE THERE ISN'T ANY POISON IVY IN HERE!
OH NO! IT STOPPED!
PLEASE, PLEASE, PLEASE! START AGAIN, OK?

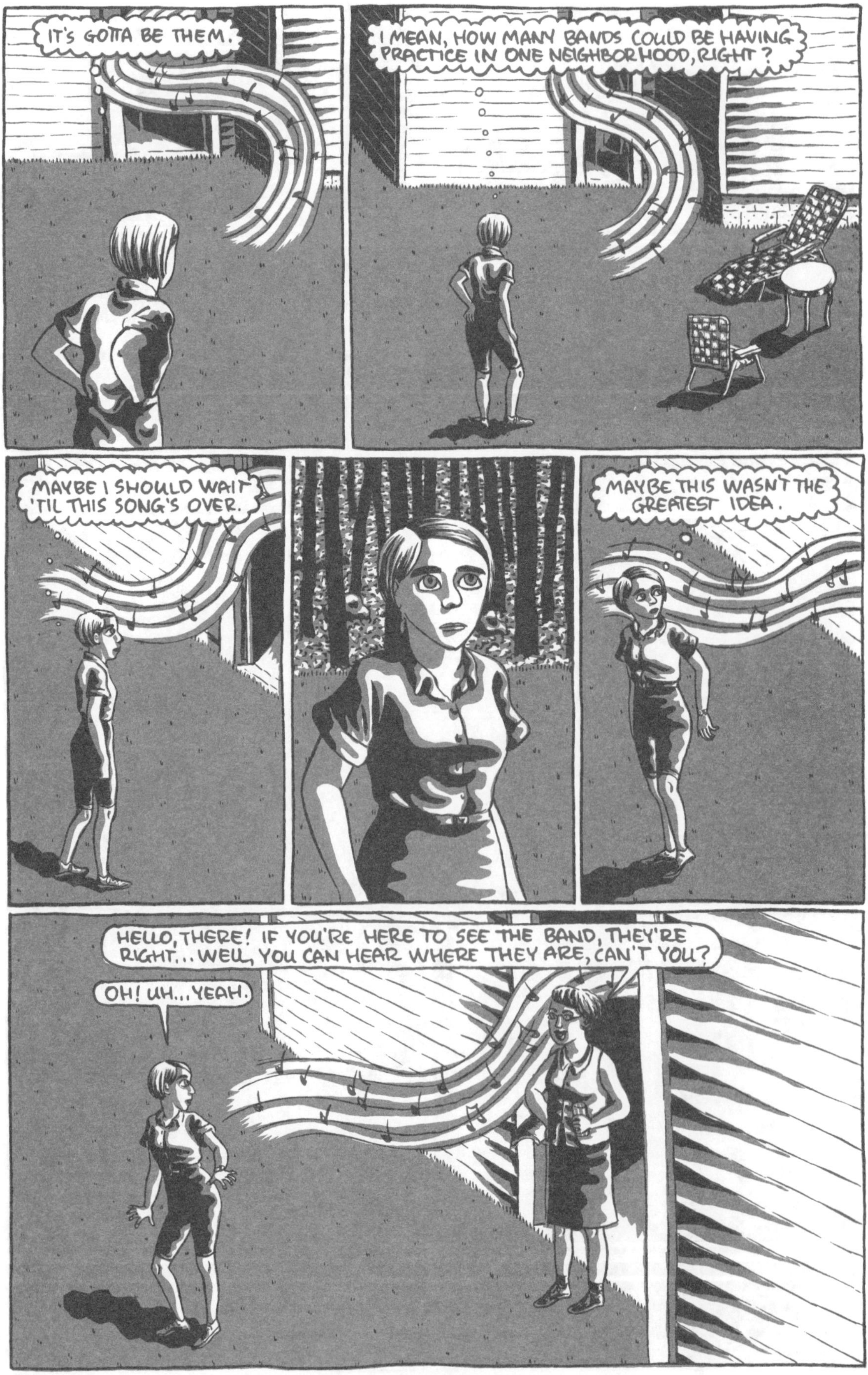
IT'S GOTTA BE THEM.
I MEAN, HOW MANY BANDS COULD BE HAVING PRACTICE IN ONE NEIGHBORHOOD, RIGHT?
MAYBE I SHOULD WAIT 'TIL THIS SONG'S OVER.
MAYBE THIS WASN'T THE GREATEST IDEA.
HELLO, THERE! IF YOU'RE HERE TO SEE THE BAND, THEY'RE RIGHT... WELL, YOU CAN HEAR WHERE THEY ARE, CAN'T YOU?
OH! UH... YEAH.

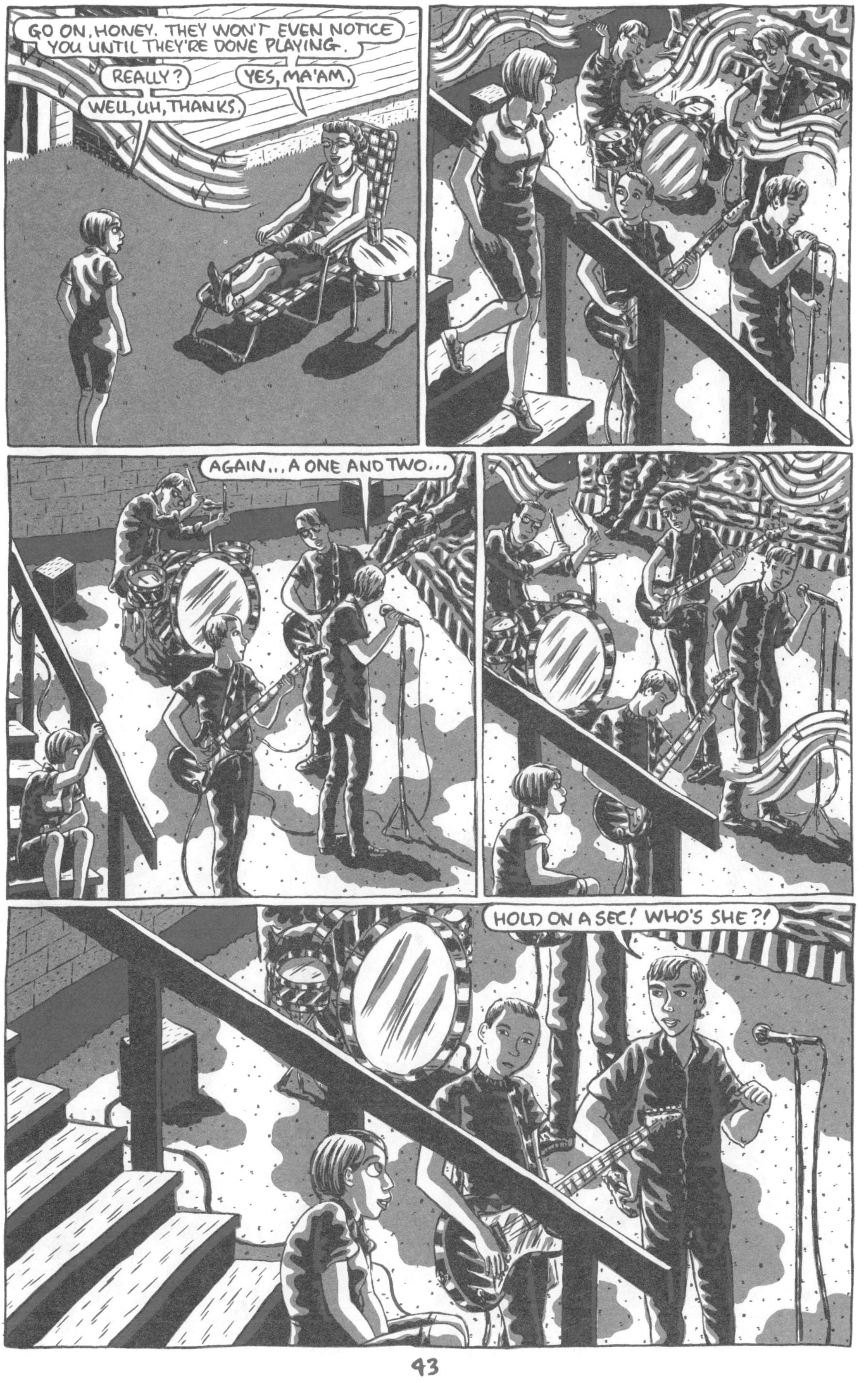
GO ON, HONEY. THEY WON'T EVEN NOTICE YOU UNTIL THEY'RE DONE PLAYING.
REALLY?
YES, MA'AM.
WELL, UH, THANKS.
AGAIN... A ONE AND TWO...
HOLD ON A SEC! WHO'S SHE?!

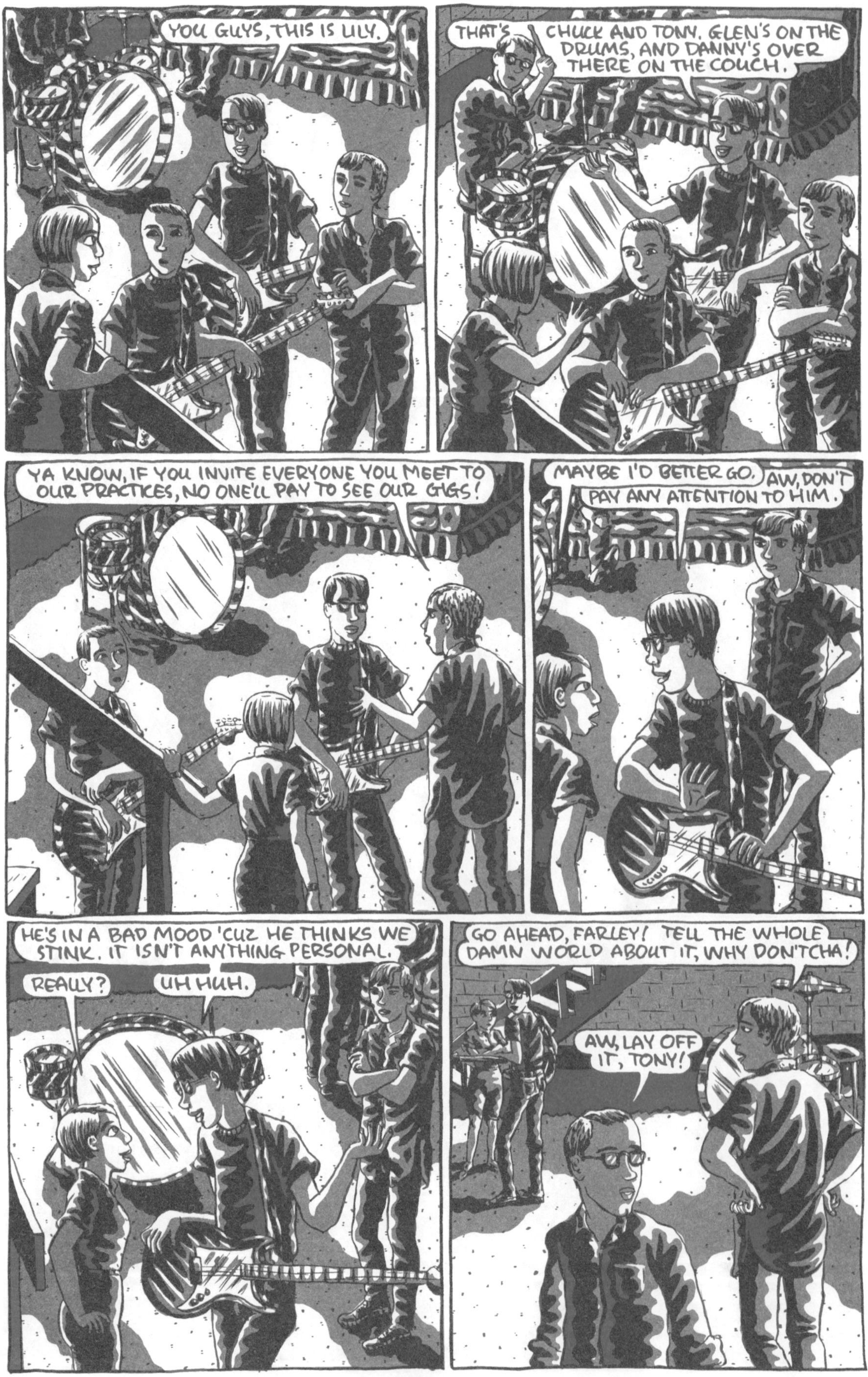
YOU GUYS, THIS IS LILY.
THAT'S CHUCK AND TONY. GLEN'S ON THE DRUMS, AND DANNY'S OVER THERE ON THE COUCH.
YA KNOW, IF YOU INVITE EVERYONE YOU MEET TO OUR PRACTICES, NO ONE'LL PAY TO SEE OUR GIGS!
MAYBE I'D BETTER GO.
AW, DON'T PAY ANY ATTENTION TO HIM.
HE'S IN A BAD MOOD 'CUZ HE THINKS WE STINK. IT ISN'T ANYTHING PERSONAL.
REALLY?
UH HUH.
GO AHEAD, FARLEY! TELL THE WHOLE DAMN WORLD ABOUT IT, WHY DON'TCHA!
AW, LAY OFF IT, TONY!

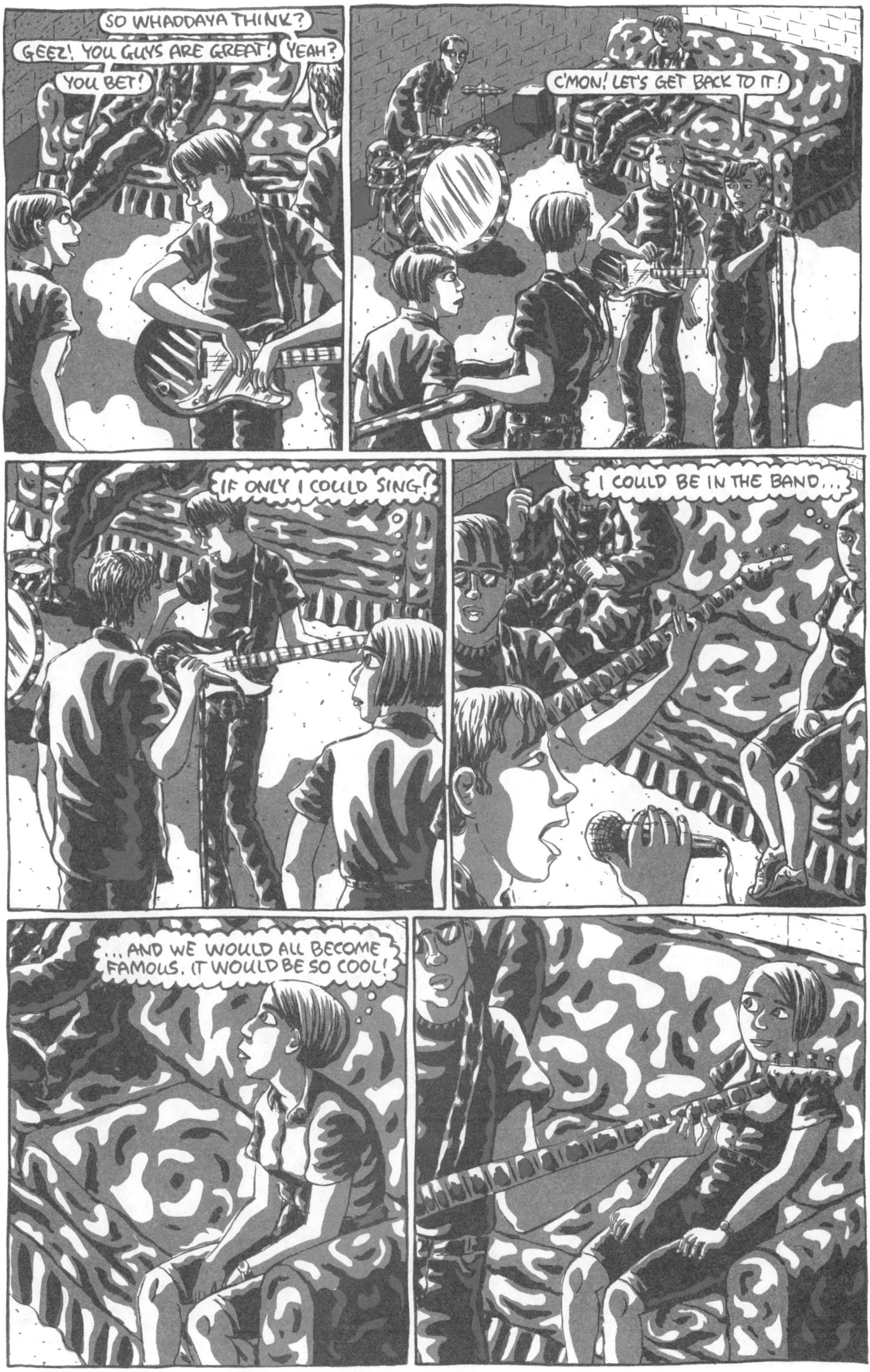
SO WHADDAYA THINK?
GEEZ! YOU GUYS ARE GREAT!
YEAH?
YOU BET!
C'MON! LET'S GET BACK TO IT!
IF ONLY I COULD SING!
I COULD BE IN THE BAND...
...AND WE WOULD ALL BECOME FAMOUS. IT WOULD BE SO COOL!

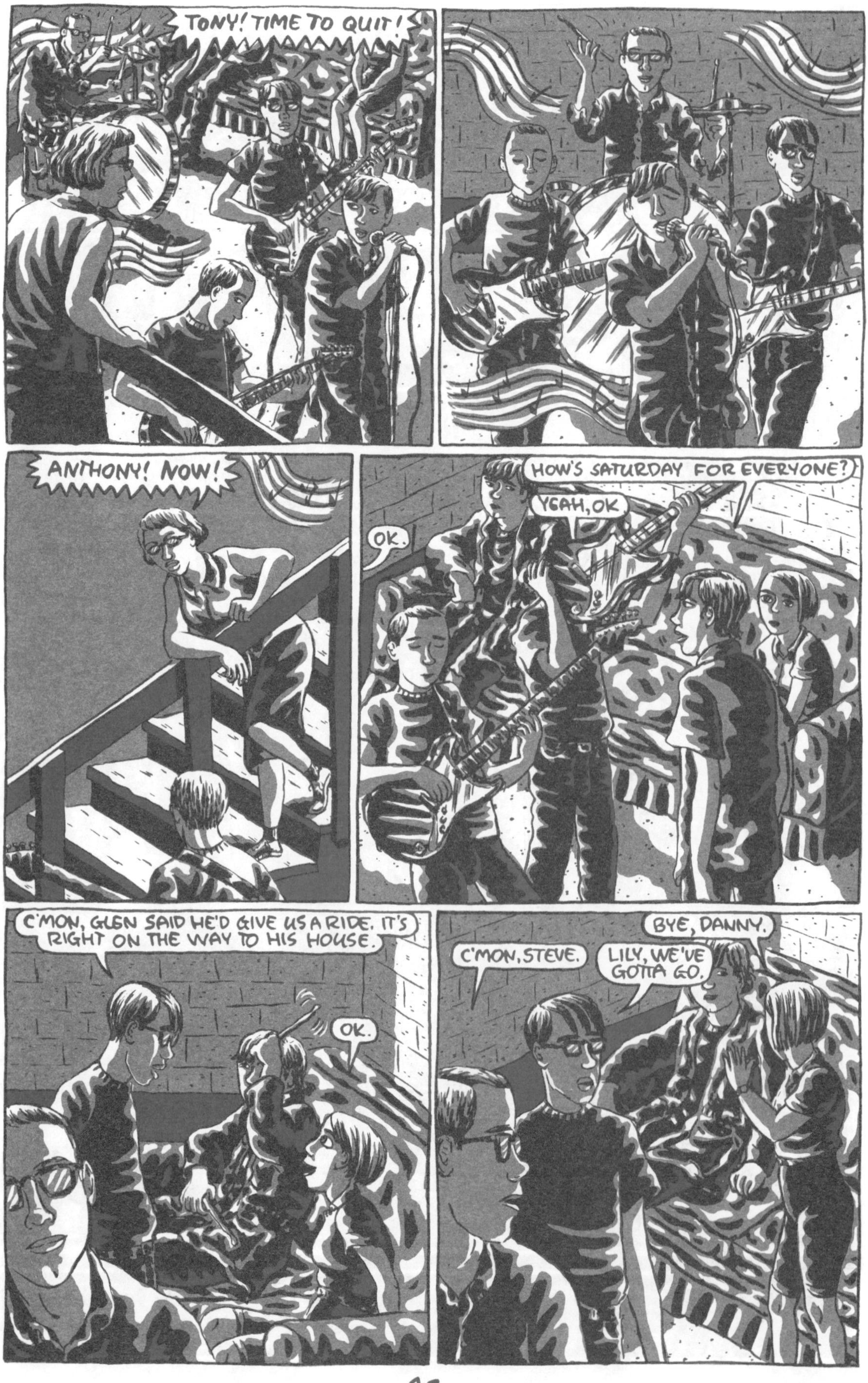
TONY! TIME TO QUIT!
ANTHONY! NOW!
HOW'S SATURDAY FOR EVERYONE?
YEAH, OK
OK.
C'MON, GLEN SAID HE'D GIVE US A RIDE. IT'S RIGHT ON THE WAY TO HIS HOUSE.
OK.
BYE, DANNY.
C'MON, STEVE.
LILY, WE'VE GOTTA GO.

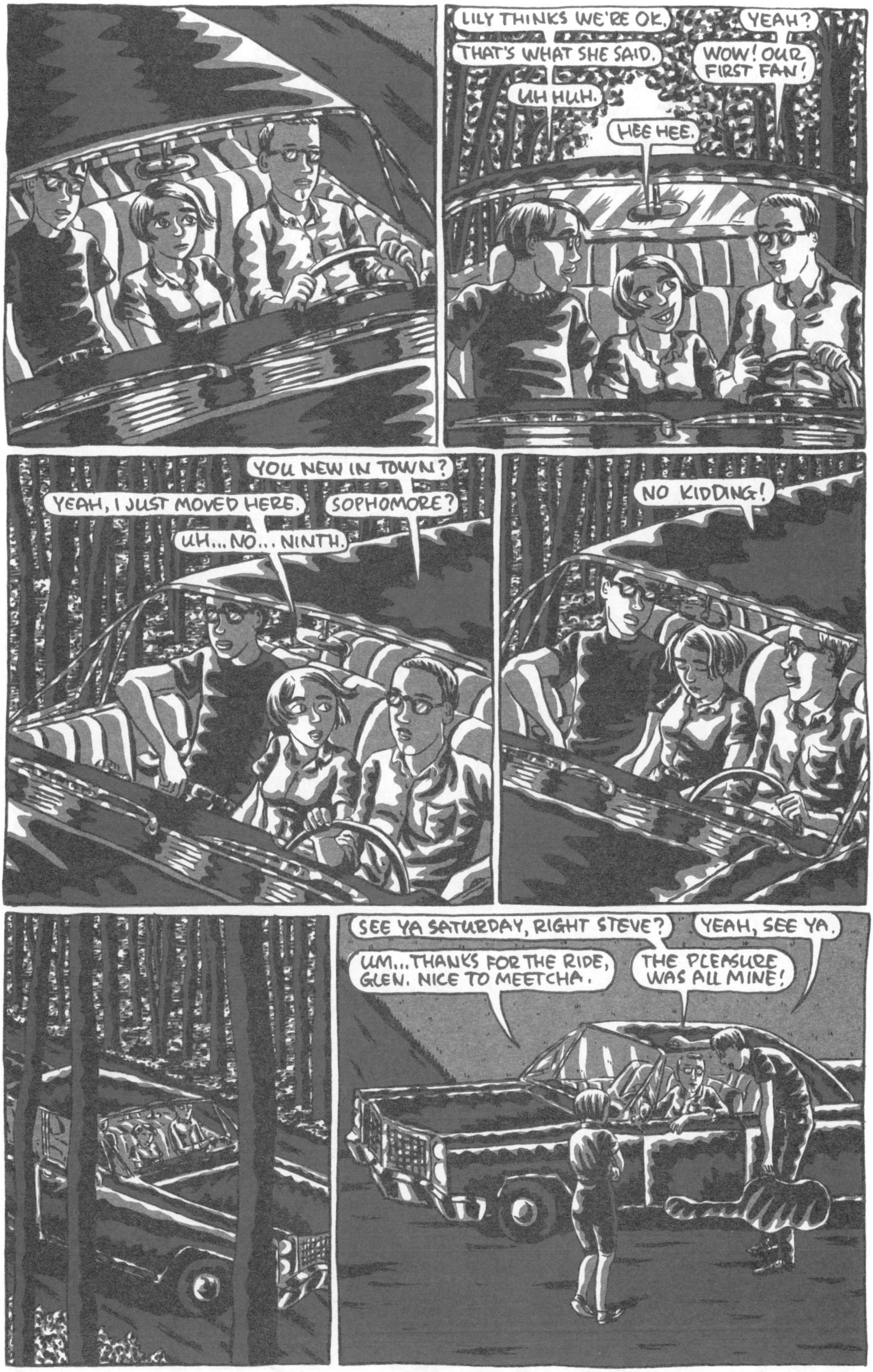
LILY THINKS WE'RE OK.
YEAH?
THAT'S WHAT SHE SAID.
WOW! OUR FIRST FAN!
UH HUH.
HEE HEE.
YOU NEW IN TOWN?
YEAH, I JUST MOVED HERE.
SOPHOMORE?
UH... NO... NINTH.
NO KIDDING!
SEE YA SATURDAY, RIGHT STEVE?
YEAH, SEE YA.
UM... THANKS FOR THE RIDE, GLEN. NICE TO MEETCHA.
THE PLEASURE WAS ALL MINE!

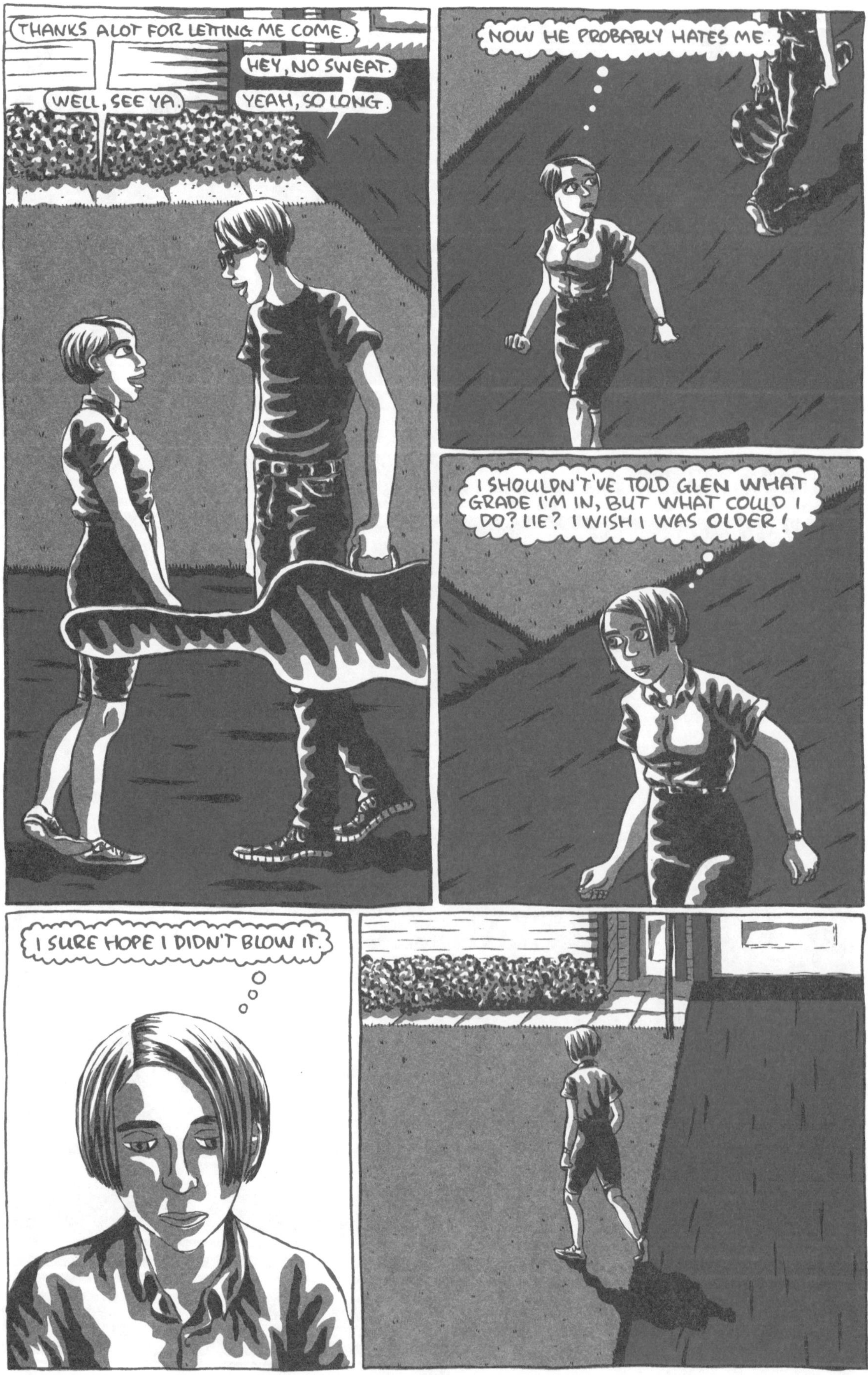
THANKS ALOT FOR LETTING ME COME.
HEY, NO SWEAT.
WELL, SEE YA.
YEAH, SO LONG.
NOW HE PROBABLY HATES ME.
I SHOULDN'T'VE TOLD GLEN WHAT GRADE I'M IN, BUT WHAT COULD I DO? LIE? I WISH I WAS OLDER!
I SURE HOPE I DIDN'T BLOW IT.

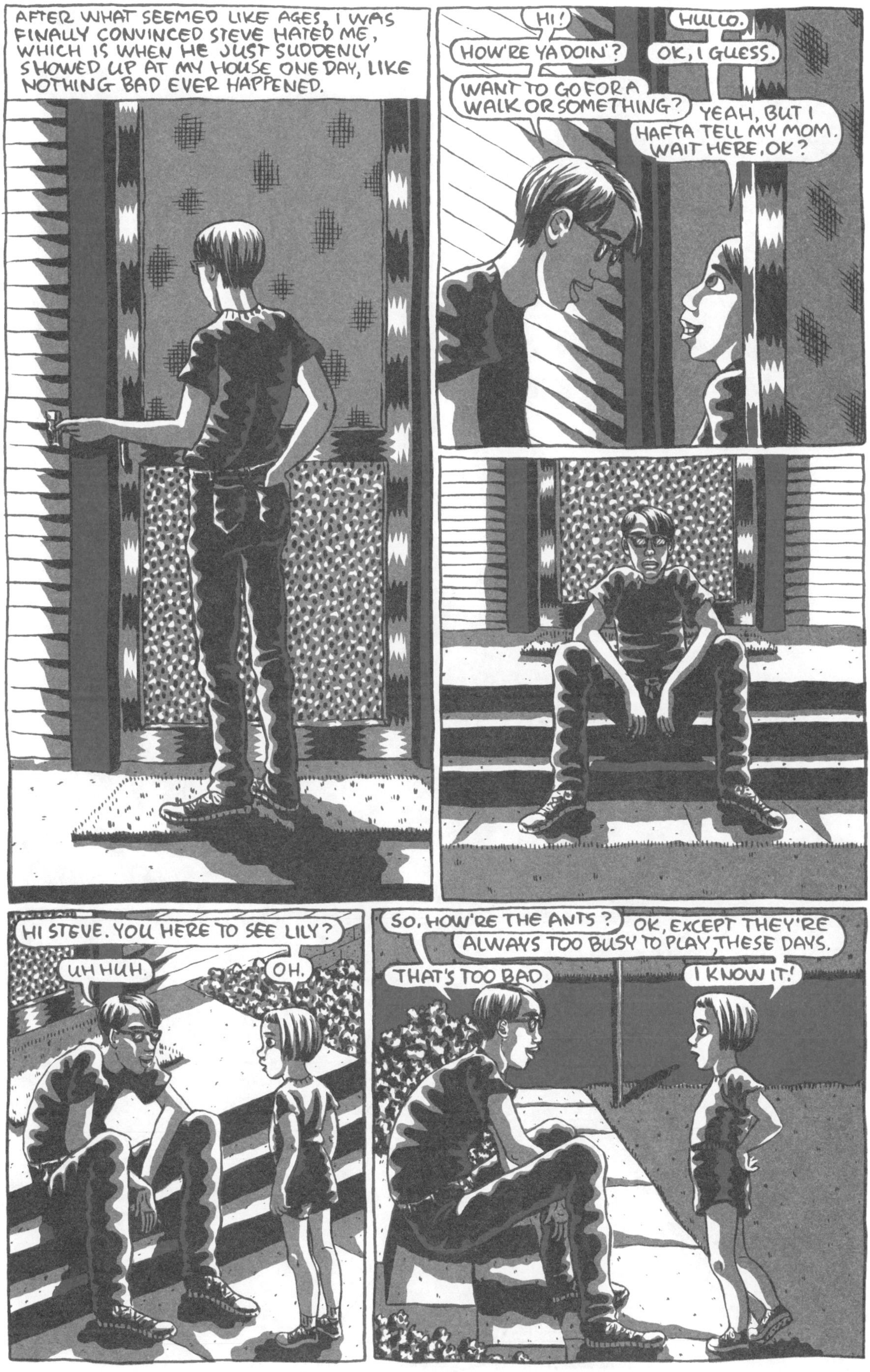

AFTER WHAT SEEMED LIKE AGES, I WAS FINALLY CONVINCED STEVE HATED ME, WHICH IS WHEN HE JUST SUDDENLY SHOWED UP AT MY HOUSE ONE DAY, LIKE NOTHING BAD EVER HAPPENED.
HI!
HULLO.
HOW'RE YA DOIN'?
OK, I GUESS.
WANT TO GO FOR A WALK OR SOMETHING?
YEAH, BUT I HAFTA TELL MY MOM. WAIT HERE, OK?
HI STEVE. YOU HERE TO SEE LILY?
UH HUH.
OH.
SO, HOW'RE THE ANTS?
OK, EXCEPT THEY'RE ALWAYS TOO BUSY TO PLAY, THESE DAYS.
THAT'S TOO BAD.
I KNOW IT!

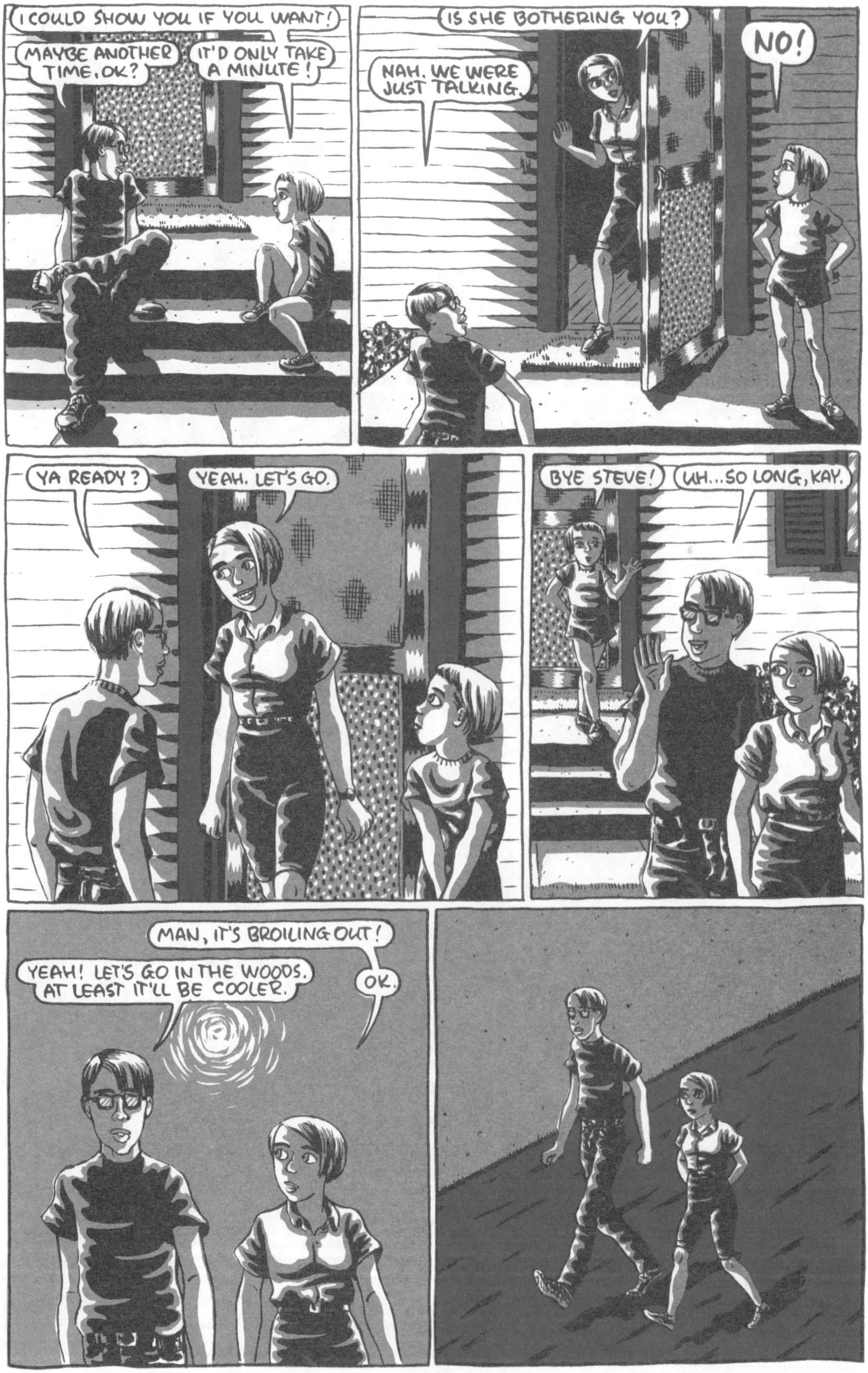

I COULD SHOW YOU IF YOU WANT!
MAYBE ANOTHER TIME, OK?
IT'D ONLY TAKE A MINUTE!
IS SHE BOTHERING YOU?
NAH. WE WERE JUST TALKING.
NO!
YA READY?
YEAH. LET'S GO.
BYE STEVE!
UH...SO LONG, KAY.
MAN, IT'S BROILING OUT!
YEAH! LET'S GO IN THE WOODS. AT LEAST IT'LL BE COOLER.
OK.

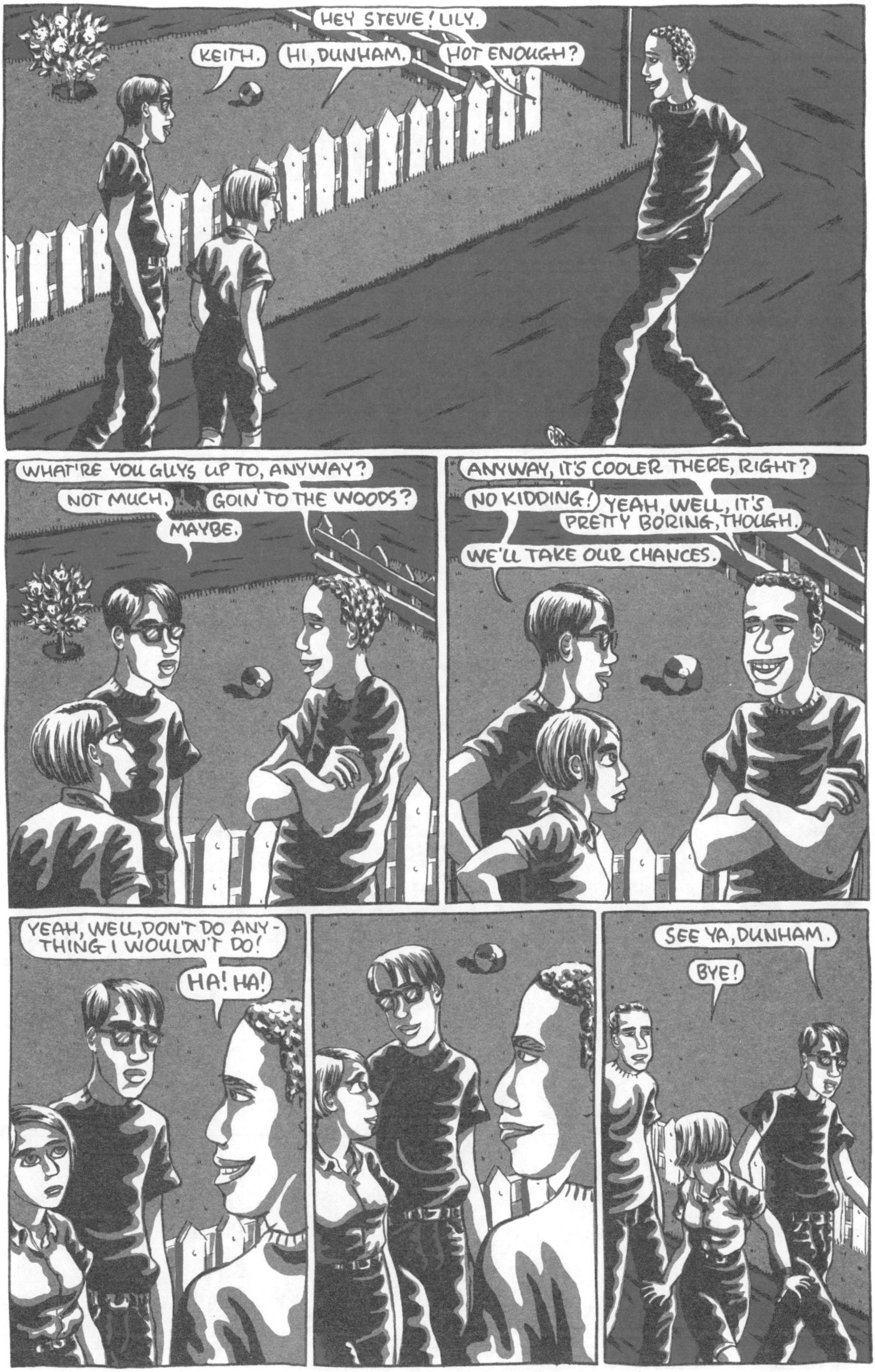
HEY STEVIE! LILY.
KEITH.
HI, DUNHAM.
HOT ENOUGH?
WHAT'RE YOU GUYS UP TO, ANYWAY?
NOT MUCH.
GOIN TO THE WOODS?
MAYBE.
ANYWAY, IT'S COOLER THERE, RIGHT?
NO KIDDING!
YEAH, WELL, IT'S PRETTY BORING, THOUGH.
WE'LL TAKE OUR CHANCES.
YEAH, WELL, DON'T DO ANY-THING I WOULDN'T DO!
HA! HA!
SEE YA, DUNHAM.
BYE!

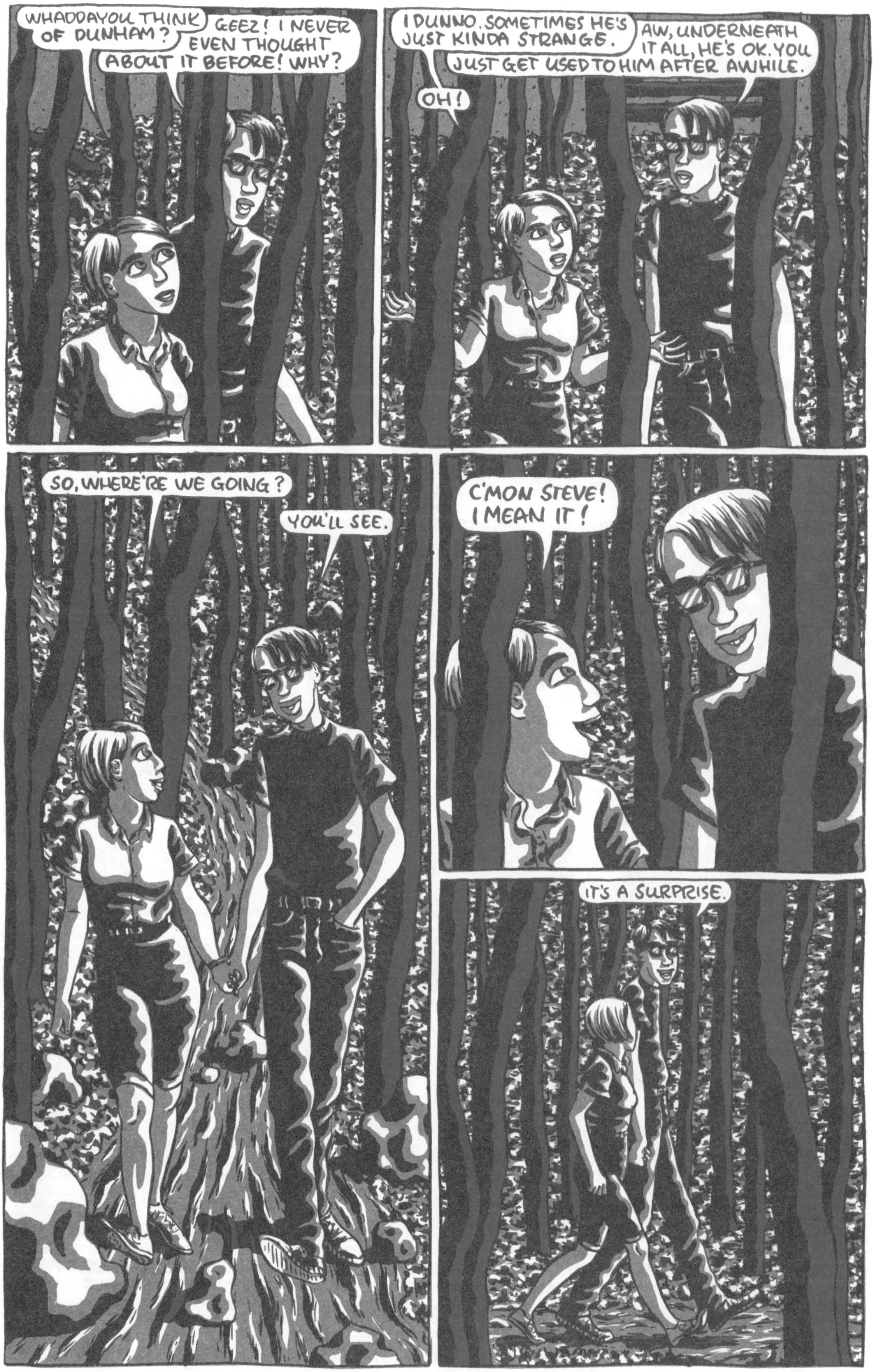
WHADDAYOU THINK OF DUNHAM?
GEEZ! I NEVER EVEN THOUGHT ABOUT IT BEFORE! WHY?
I DUNNO. SOMETIMES HE'S JUST KINDA STRANGE.
AW, UNDERNEATH IT ALL, HE'S OK. YOU JUST GET USED TO HIM AFTER AWHILE.
OH!
SO, WHERE'RE WE GOING?
YOU'LL SEE.
C'MON STEVE! I MEAN IT!
IT'S A SURPRISE.

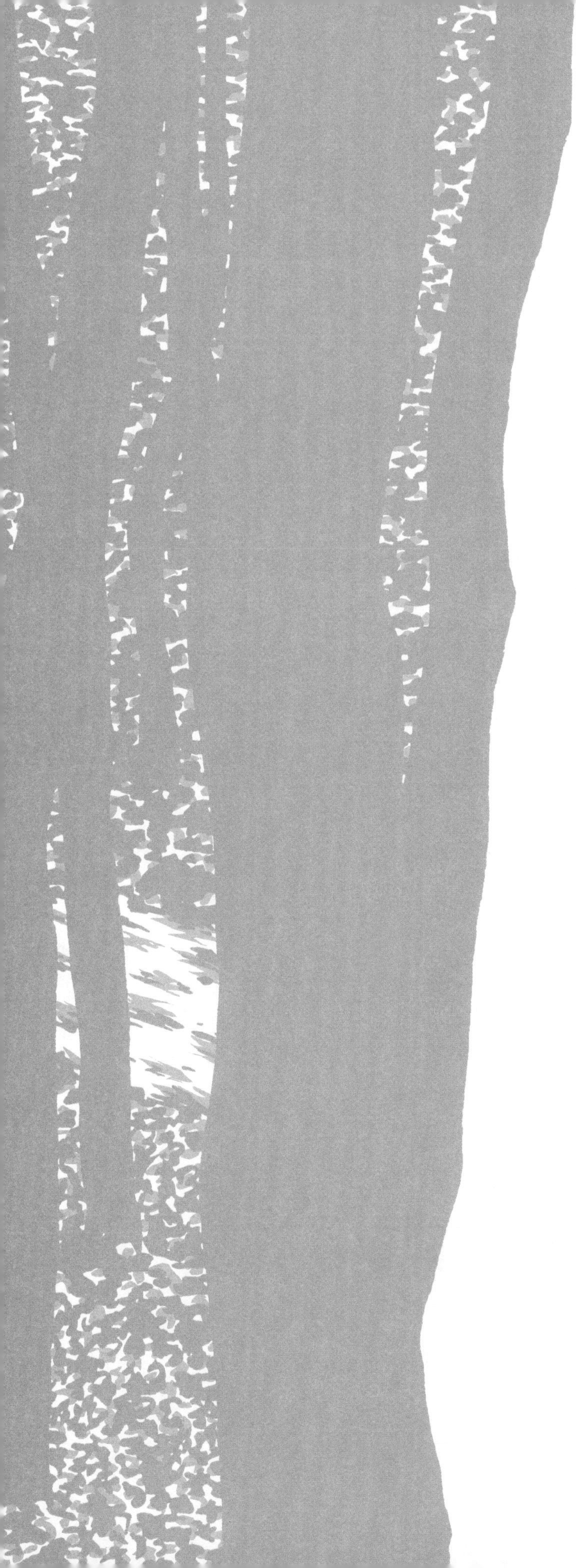

PART
THREE

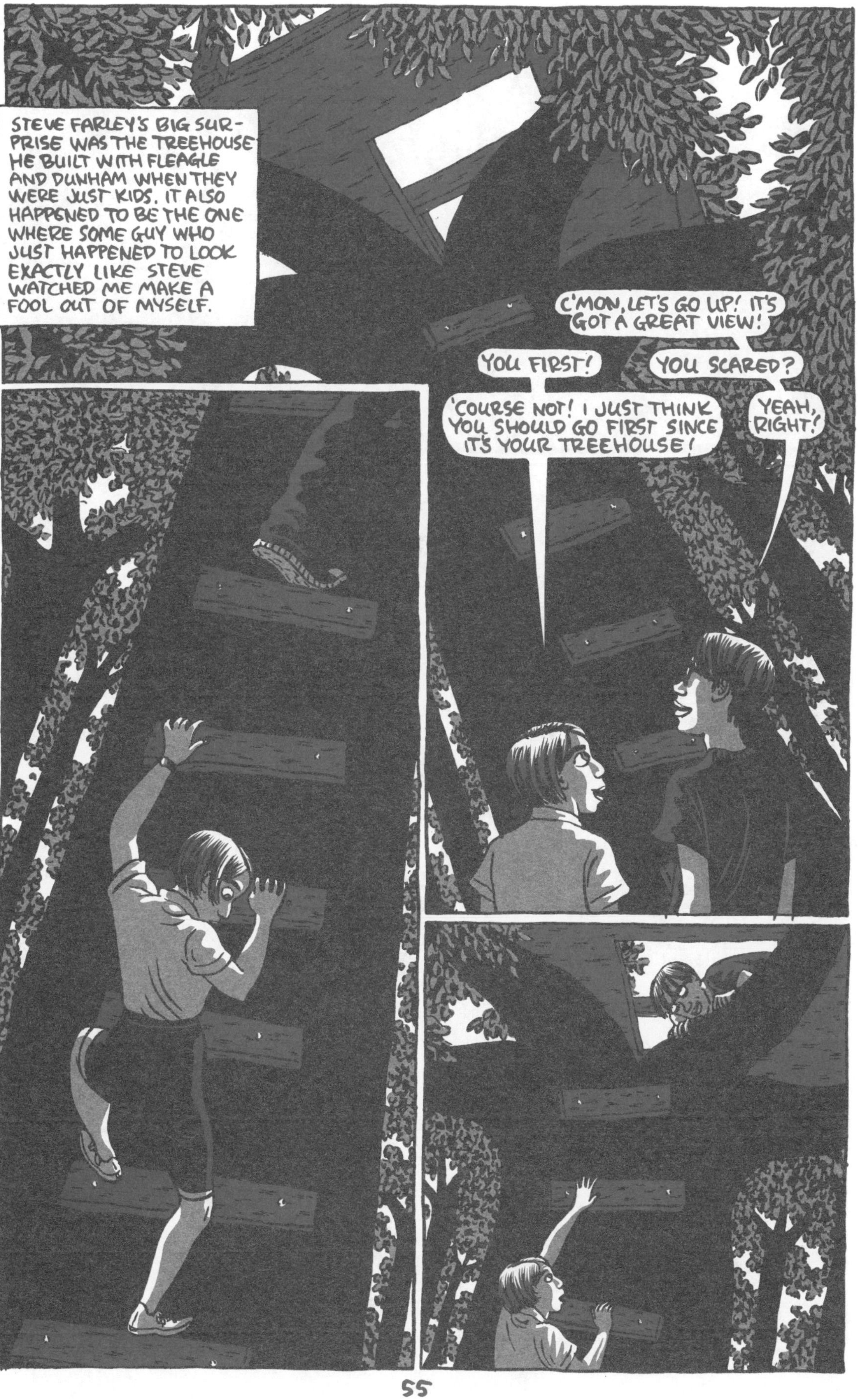
STEVE FARLEY'S BIG SURPRISE WAS THE TREEHOUSE HE BUILT WITH FLEAGLE AND DUNHAM WHEN THEY WERE JUST KIDS. IT ALSO HAPPENED TO BE THE ONE WHERE SOME GUY WHO JUST HAPPENED TO LOOK EXACTLY LIKE STEVE WATCHED ME MAKE A FOOL OUT OF MYSELF.
C'MON, LET'S GO UP! IT'S GOT A GREAT VIEW!
YOU FIRST!
YOU SCARED?
'COURSE NOT! I JUST THINK YOU SHOULD GO FIRST SINCE IT'S YOUR TREEHOUSE!
YEAH, RIGHT!

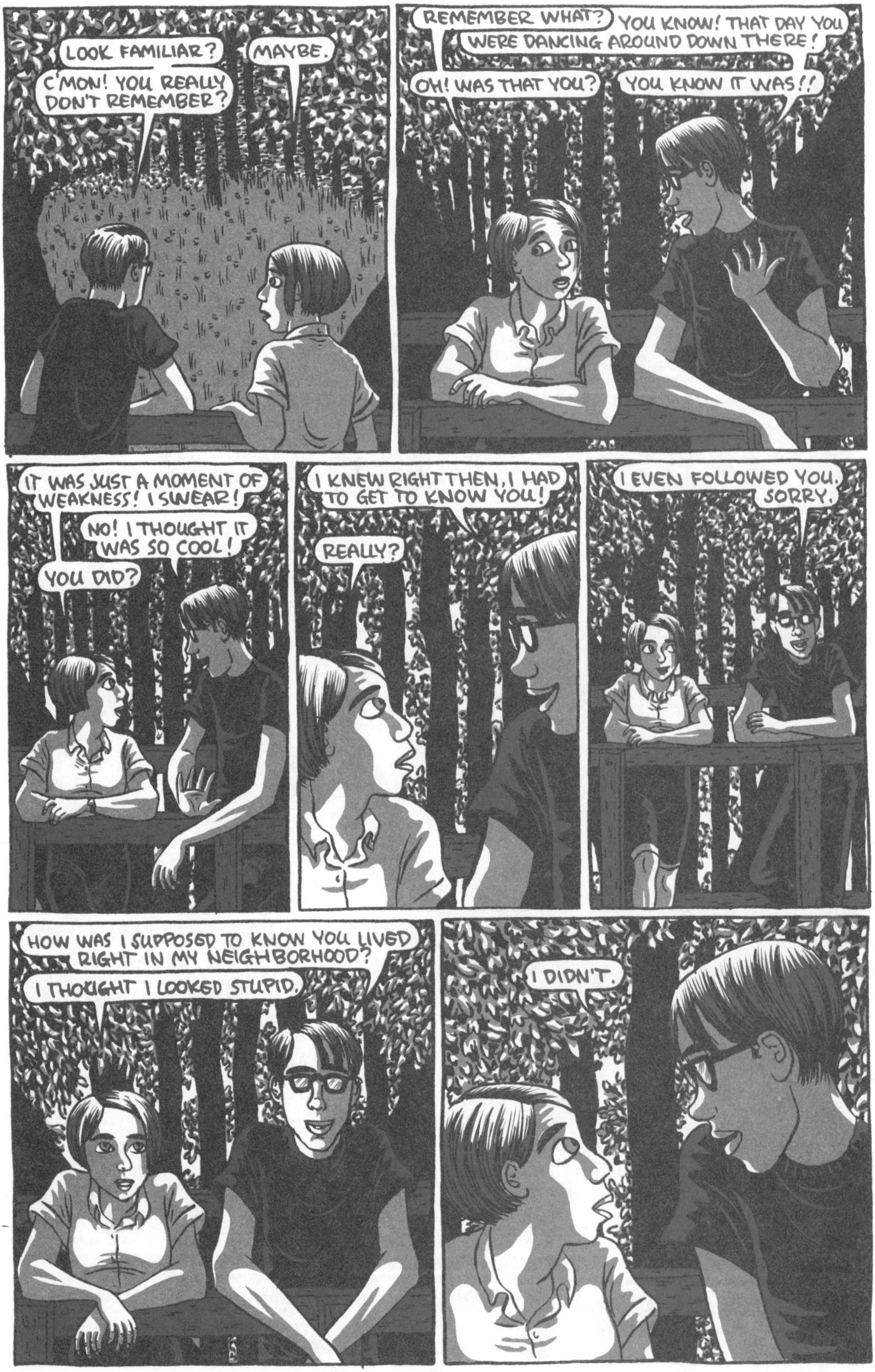
LOOK FAMILIAR?
MAYBE.
C'MON! YOU REALLY DON'T REMEMBER?
REMEMBER WHAT?
YOU KNOW! THAT DAY YOU WERE DANCING AROUND DOWN THERE!
OH! WAS THAT YOU?
YOU KNOW IT WAS!!
IT WAS JUST A MOMENT OF WEAKNESS! I SWEAR!
NO! I THOUGHT IT WAS SO COOL!
YOU DID?
I KNEW RIGHT THEN, I HAD TO GET TO KNOW YOU!
REALLY?
I EVEN FOLLOWED YOU. SORRY.
HOW WAS I SUPPOSED TO KNOW YOU LIVED RIGHT IN MY NEIGHBORHOOD?
I THOUGHT I LOOKED STUPID.
I DIDN'T.

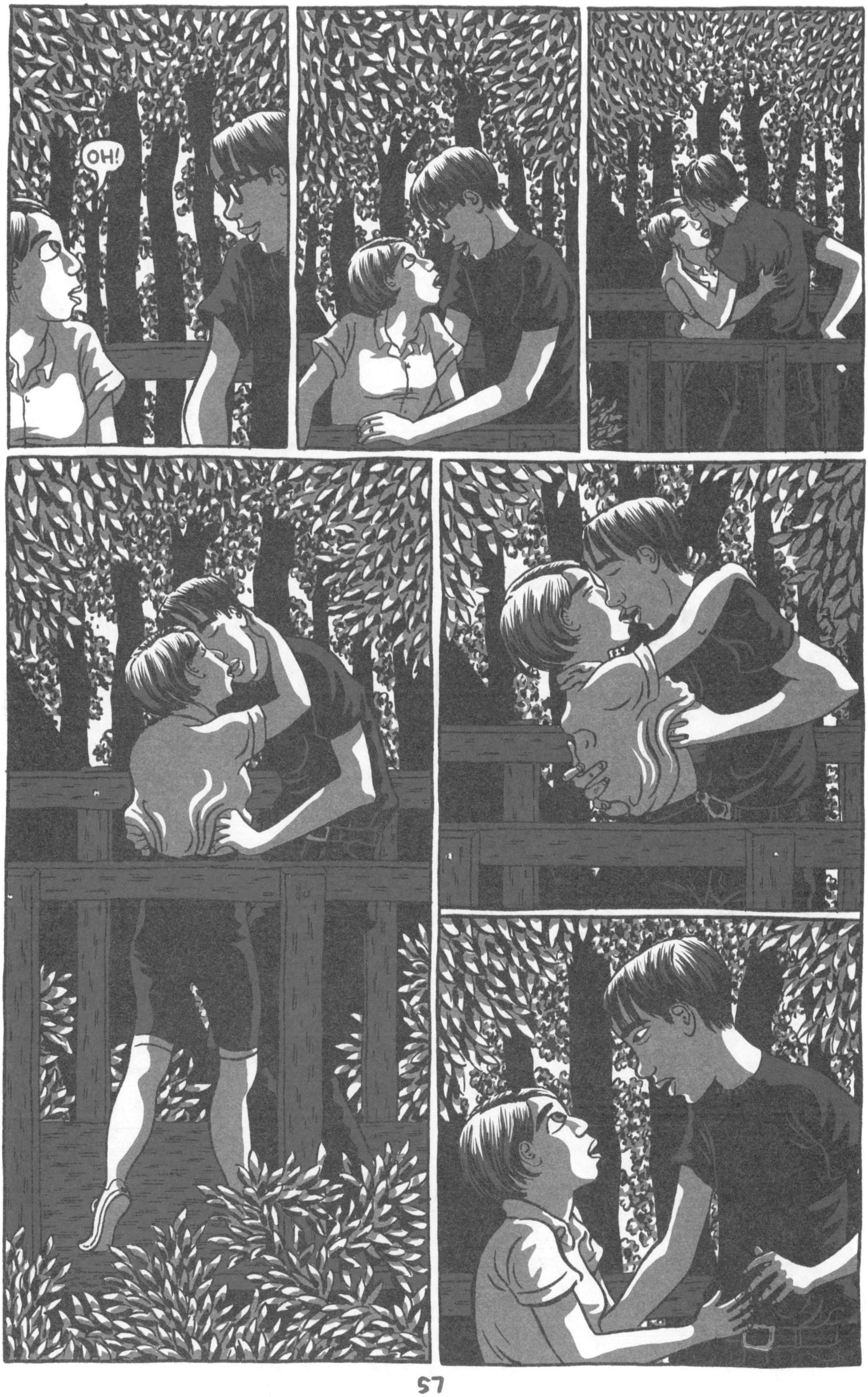
OH!

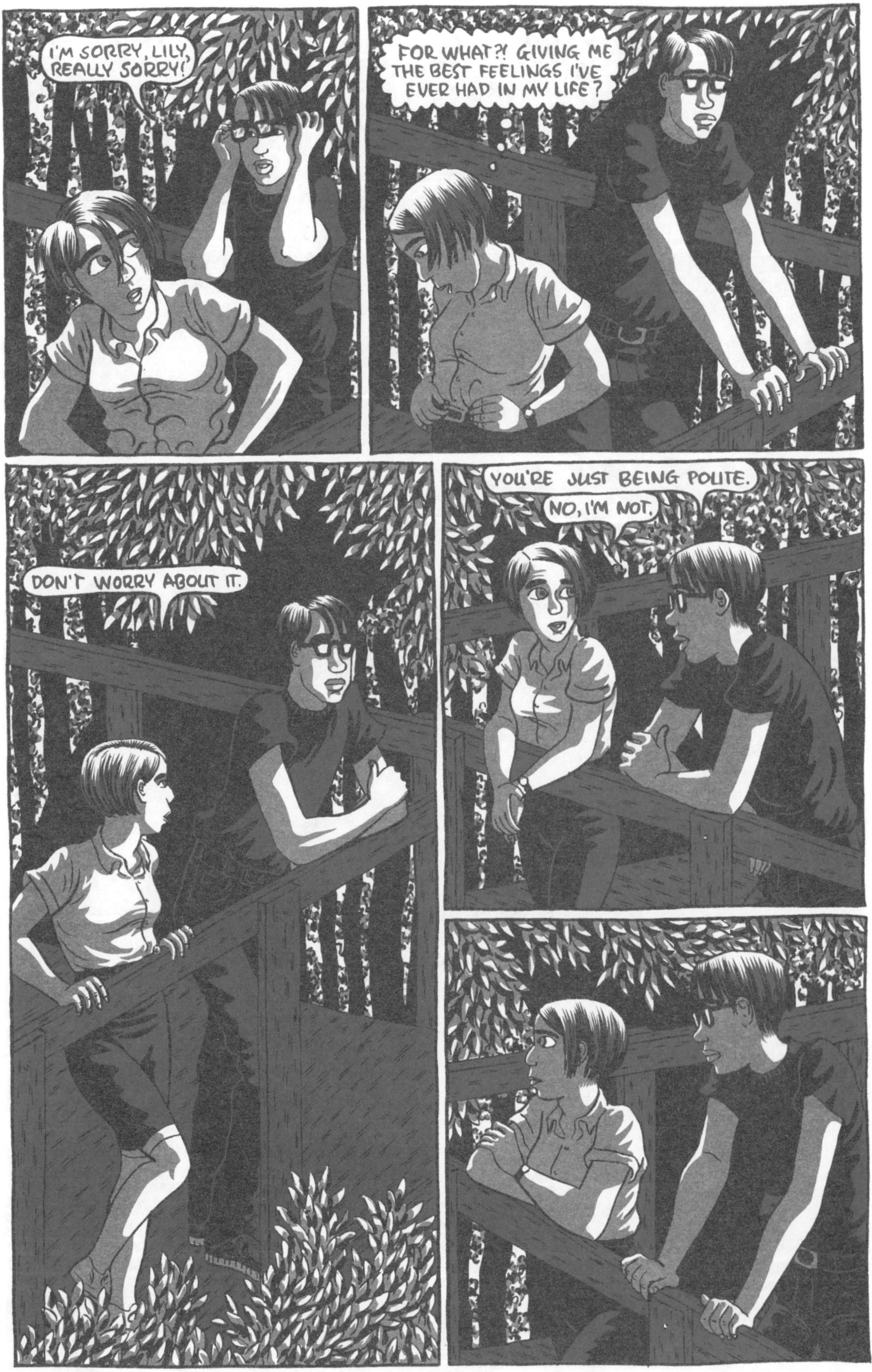
I'M SORRY, LILY, REALLY SORRY!
FOR WHAT?! GIVING ME THE BEST FEELINGS I'VE EVER HAD IN MY LIFE?
DON'T WORRY ABOUT IT.
YOU'RE JUST BEING POLITE.
NO, I'M NOT.

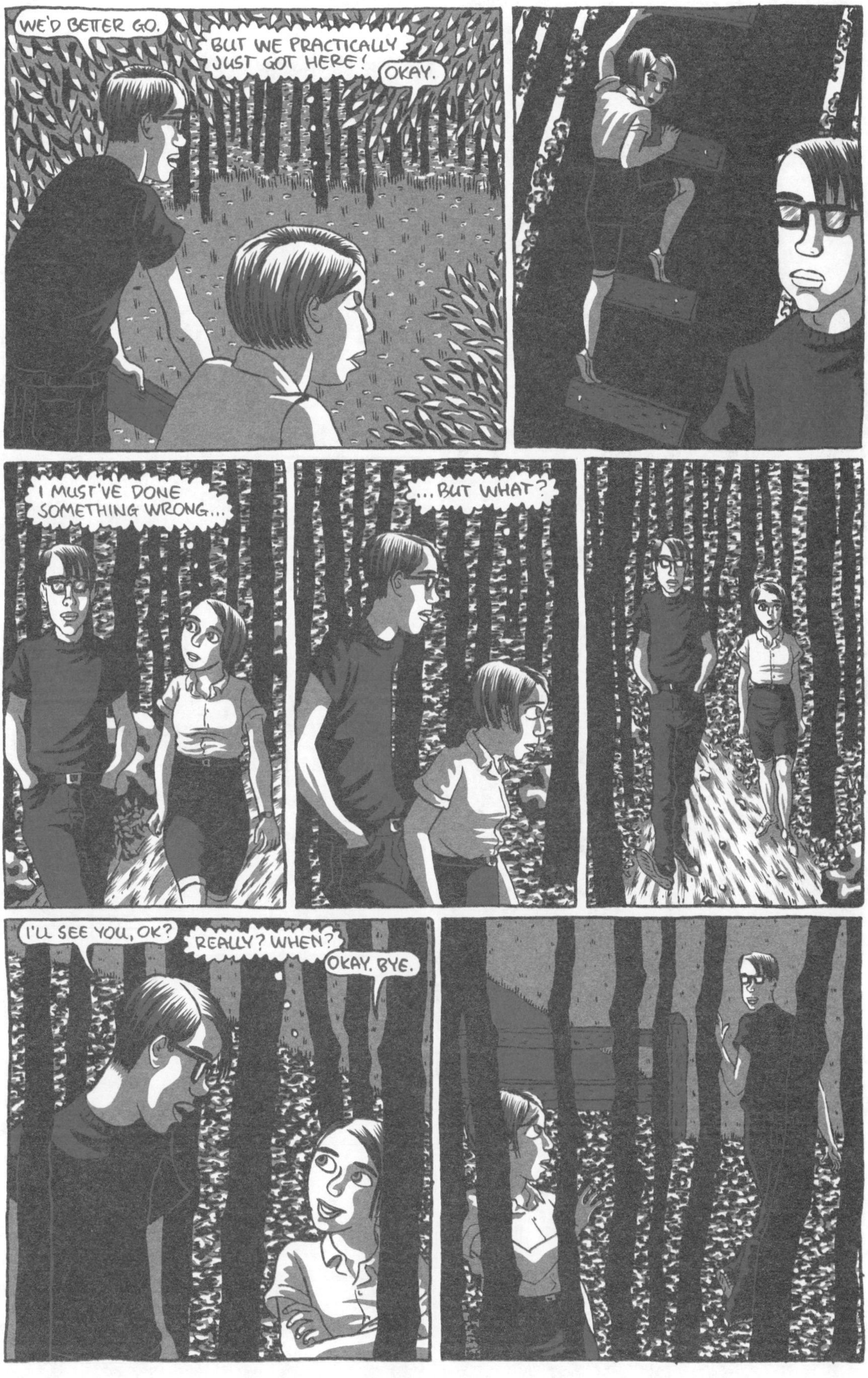
WE'D BETTER GO.
BUT WE PRACTICALLY JUST GOT HERE!
OKAY.
I MUST'VE DONE SOMETHING WRONG...
...BUT WHAT?
I'LL SEE YOU, OK?
REALLY? WHEN?
OKAY. BYE.

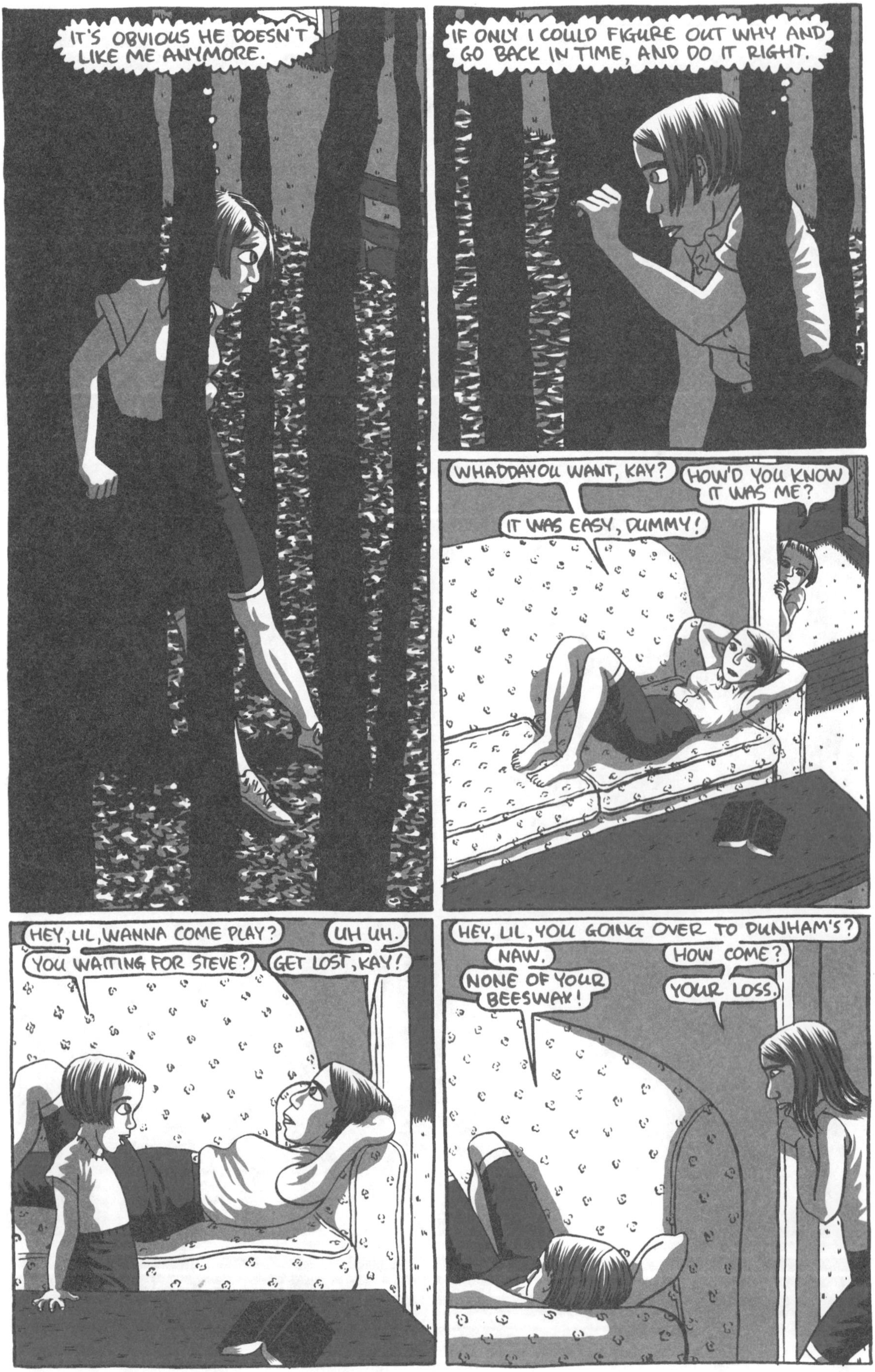
IT'S OBVIOUS HE DOESN'T LIKE ME ANYMORE.
IF ONLY I COULD FIGURE OUT WHY AND GO BACK IN TIME, AND DO IT RIGHT.
WHADDAYOU WANT, KAY?
HOW'D YOU KNOW IT WAS ME?
IT WAS EASY, DUMMY!
HEY, LIL, WANNA COME PLAY?
UH UH.
YOU WAITING FOR STEVE?
GET LOST, KAY!
HEY, LIL, YOU GOING OVER TO DUNHAM'S?
NAW.
HOW COME?
NONE OF YOUR BEESWAX!
YOUR LOSS.

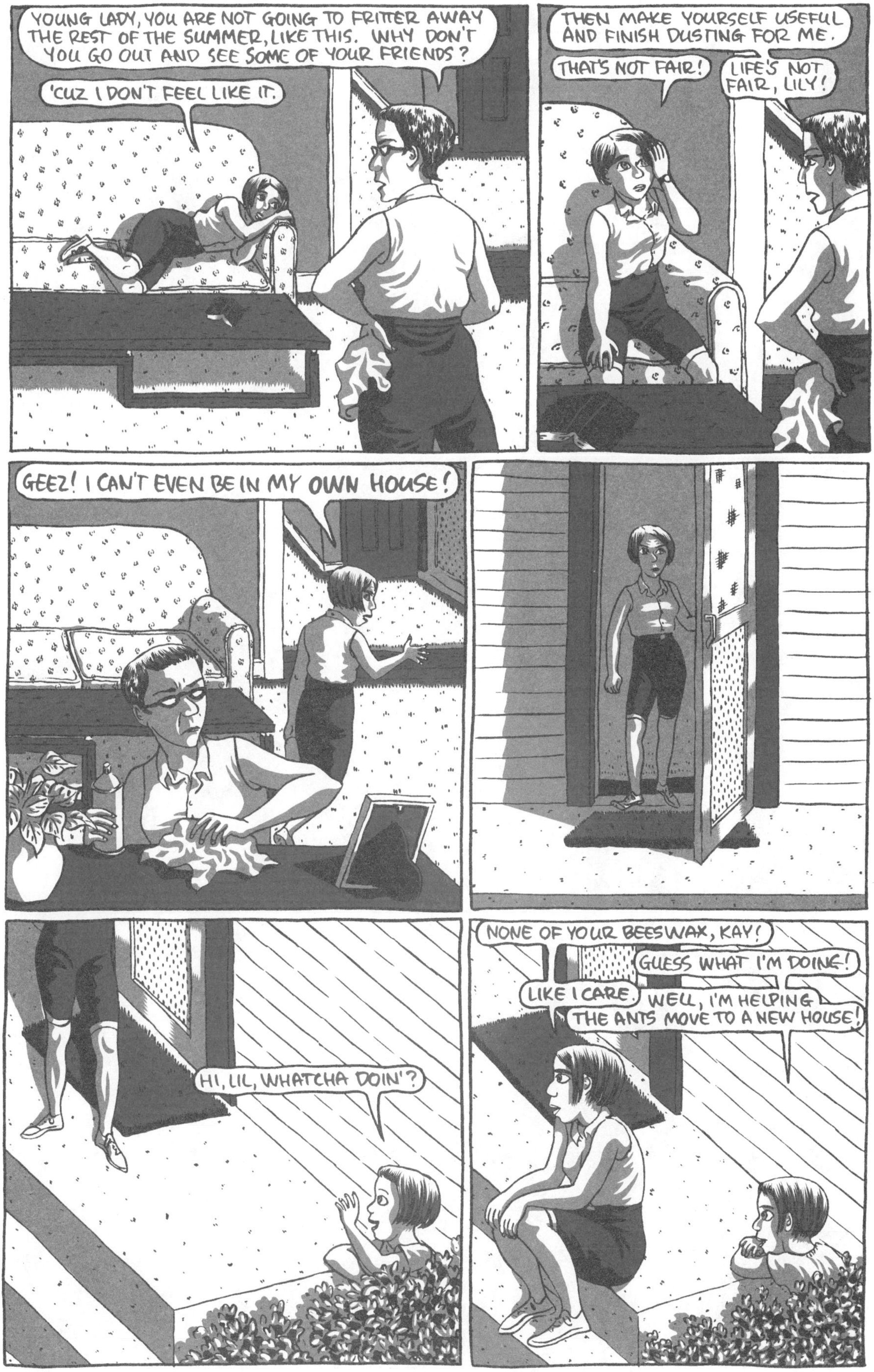
YOUNG LADY, YOU ARE NOT GOING TO FRITTER AWAY THE REST OF THE SUMMER, LIKE THIS. WHY DON'T YOU GO OUT AND SEE SOME OF YOUR FRIENDS?
'CUZ I DON'T FEEL LIKE IT.
THEN MAKE YOURSELF USEFUL AND FINISH DUSTING FOR ME.
THAT'S NOT FAIR!
LIFE'S NOT FAIR, LILY!
GEEZ! I CAN'T EVEN BE IN MY OWN HOUSE!
HI, LIL, WHATCHA DOIN'?
NONE OF YOUR BEESWAX, KAY!
GUESS WHAT I'M DOING!
LIKE I CARE.
WELL, I'M HELPING THE ANTS MOVE TO A NEW HOUSE!

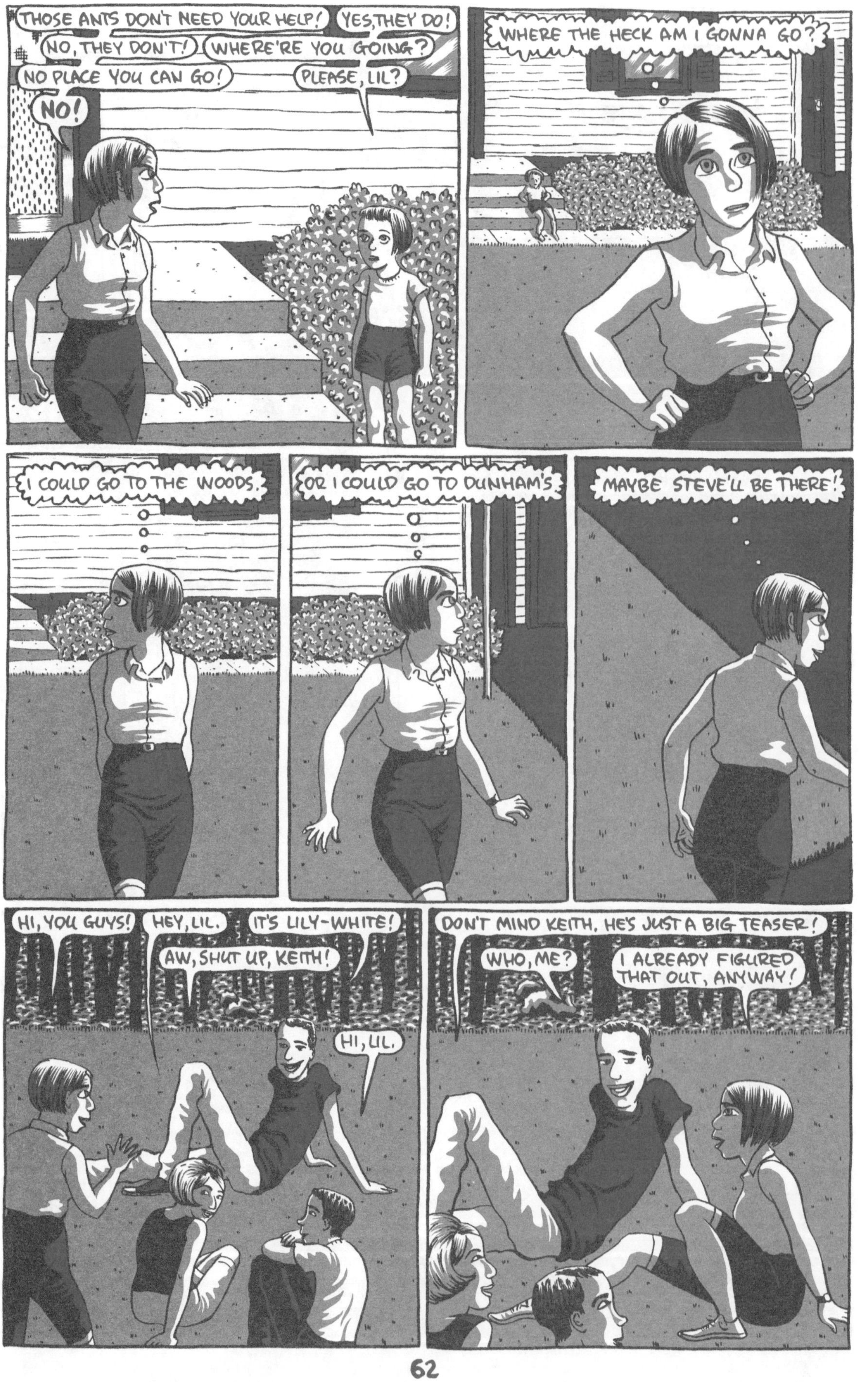
THOSE ANTS DON'T NEED YOUR HELP!
YES, THEY DO!
NO, THEY DON'T!
WHERE'RE YOU GOING?
NO PLACE YOU CAN GO!
PLEASE, LIL?
NO!
WHERE THE HECK AM I GONNA GO?
I COULD GO TO THE WOODS.
OR I COULD GO TO DUNHAM'S.
MAYBE STEVE'LL BE THERE!
HI, YOU GUYS!
HEY, LIL.
IT'S LILY-WHITE!
AW, SHUT UP, KEITH!
HI, LIL.
DON'T MIND KEITH. HE'S JUST A BIG TEASER!
WHO, ME?
I ALREADY FIGURED THAT OUT, ANYWAY!

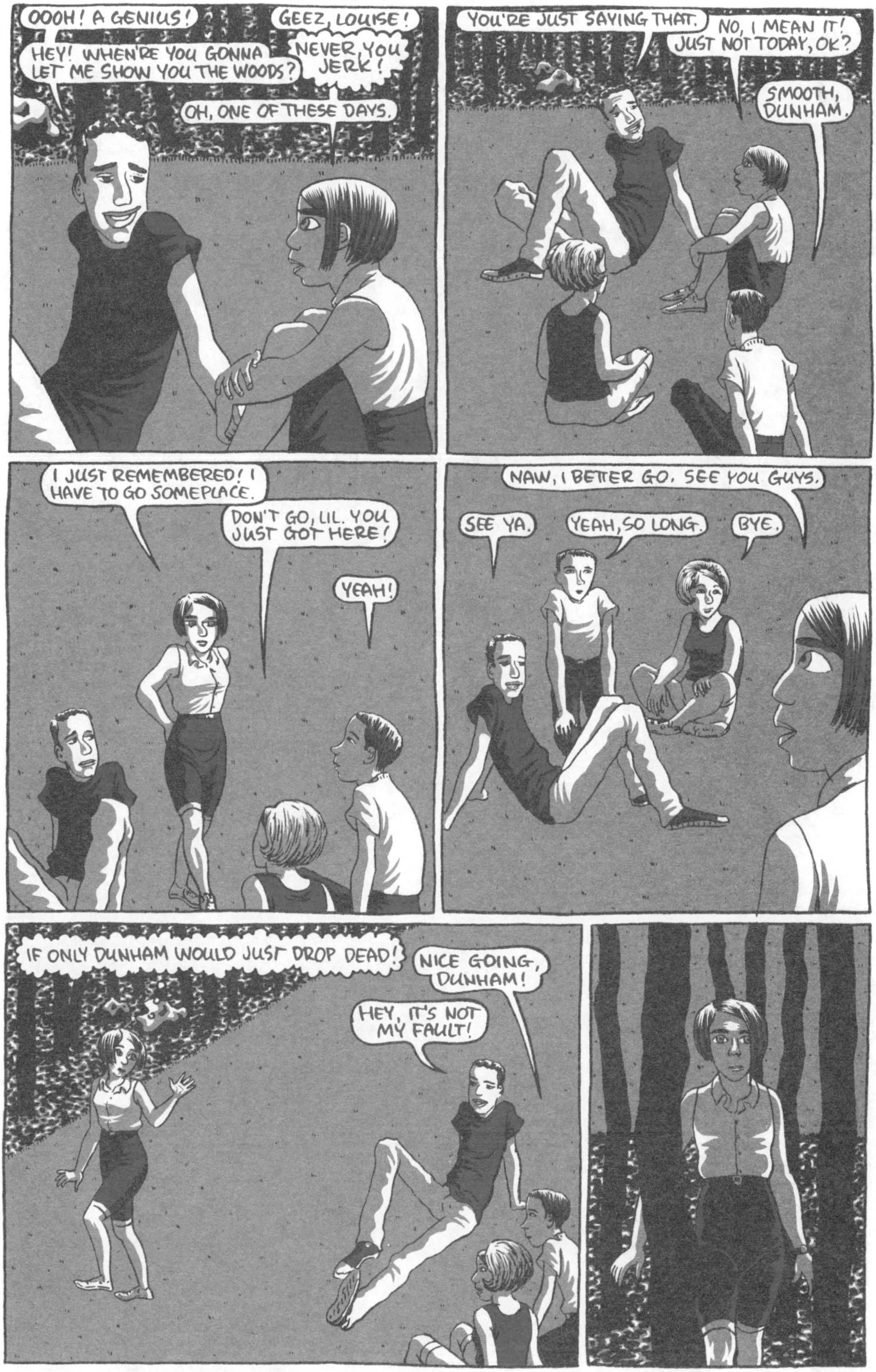
OOOH! A GENIUS!
GEEZ, LOUISE!
HEY! WHEN'RE YOU GONNA LET ME SHOW YOU THE WOODS?
NEVER, YOU JERK!
OH, ONE OF THESE DAYS.
YOU'RE JUST SAYING THAT.
NO, I MEAN IT! JUST NOT TODAY, OK?
SMOOTH, DUNHAM.
I JUST REMEMBERED! I HAVE TO GO SOMEPLACE.
DON'T GO, LIL. YOU JUST GOT HERE!
YEAH!
NAW, I BETTER GO. SEE YOU GUYS.
SEE YA.
YEAH, SO LONG.
BYE.
IF ONLY DUNHAM WOULD JUST DROP DEAD!
NICE GOING, DUNHAM!
HEY, IT'S NOT MY FAULT!

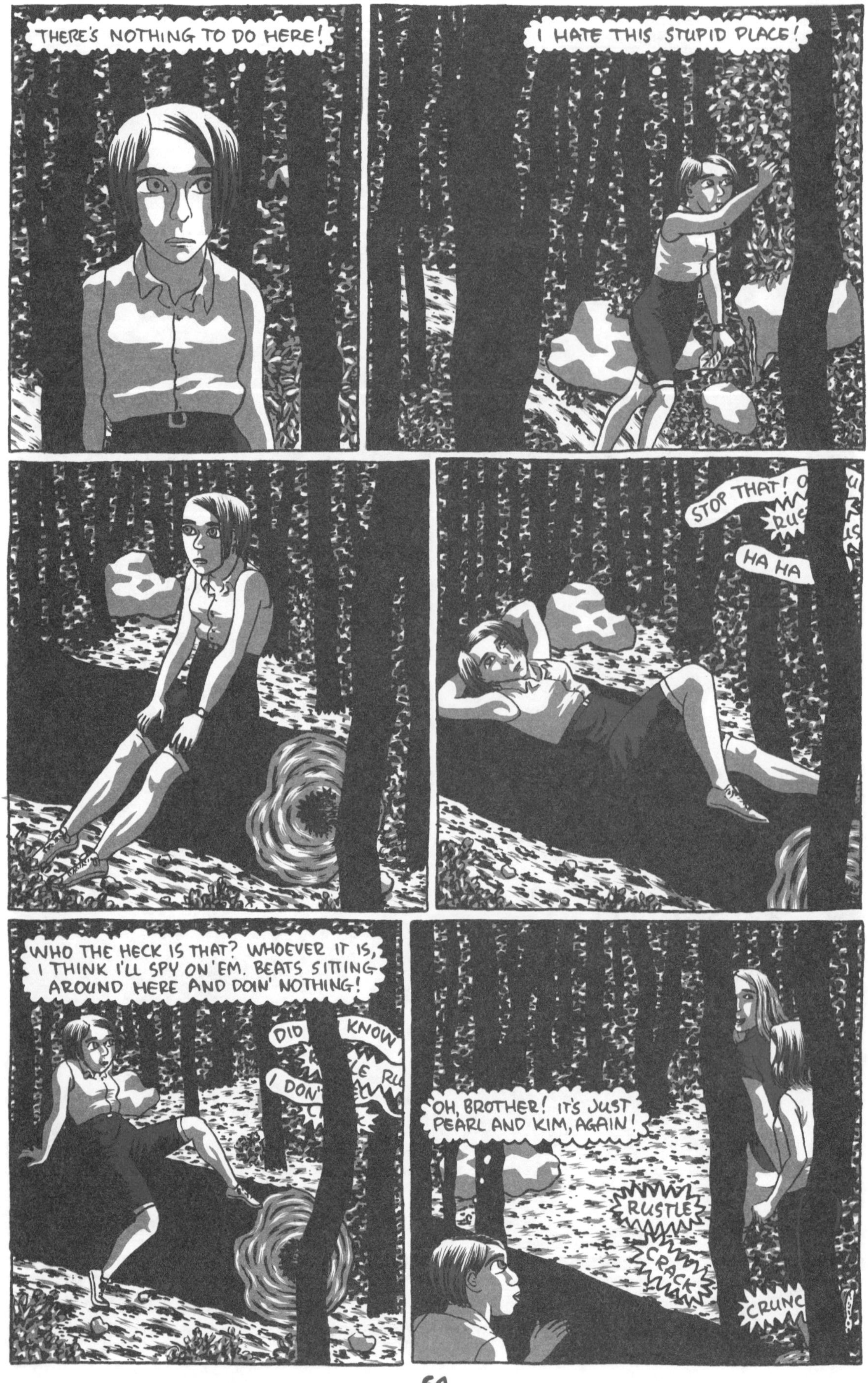
THERE'S NOTHING TO DO HERE!
I HATE THIS STUPID PLACE!
STOP THAT!
HA HA
WHO THE HECK IS THAT? WHOEVER IT IS, I THINK I'LL SPY ON 'EM. BEATS SITTING AROUND HERE AND DOIN' NOTHING!
DID
KNOW
OH, BROTHER! IT'S JUST PEARL AND KIM, AGAIN!
RUSTLE
CRACK

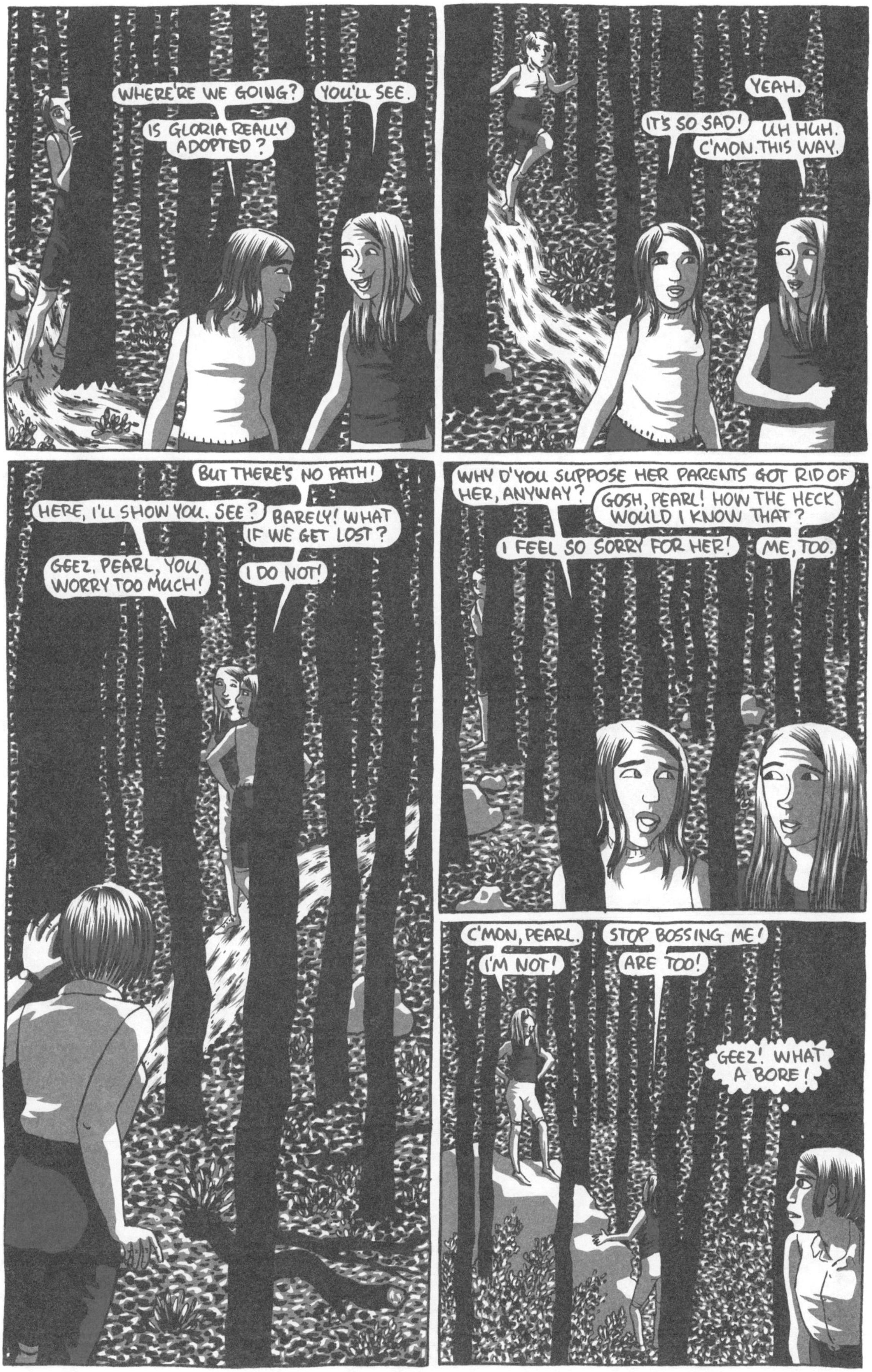
WHERE'RE WE GOING?
IS GLORIA REALLY ADOPTED?
YOU'LL SEE.
IT'S SO SAD!
YEAH.
UH HUH. C'MON. THIS WAY.
BUT THERE'S NO PATH!
HERE, I'LL SHOW YOU. SEE?
BARELY! WHAT IF WE GET LOST?
GEEZ, PEARL, YOU WORRY TOO MUCH!
I DO NOT!
WHY D'YOU SUPPOSE HER PARENTS GOT RID OF HER, ANYWAY?
GOSH, PEARL! HOW THE HECK WOULD I KNOW THAT?
I FEEL SO SORRY FOR HER!
ME, TOO.
C'MON, PEARL.
I'M NOT!
STOP BOSSING ME!
ARE TOO!
GEEZ! WHAT A BORE!

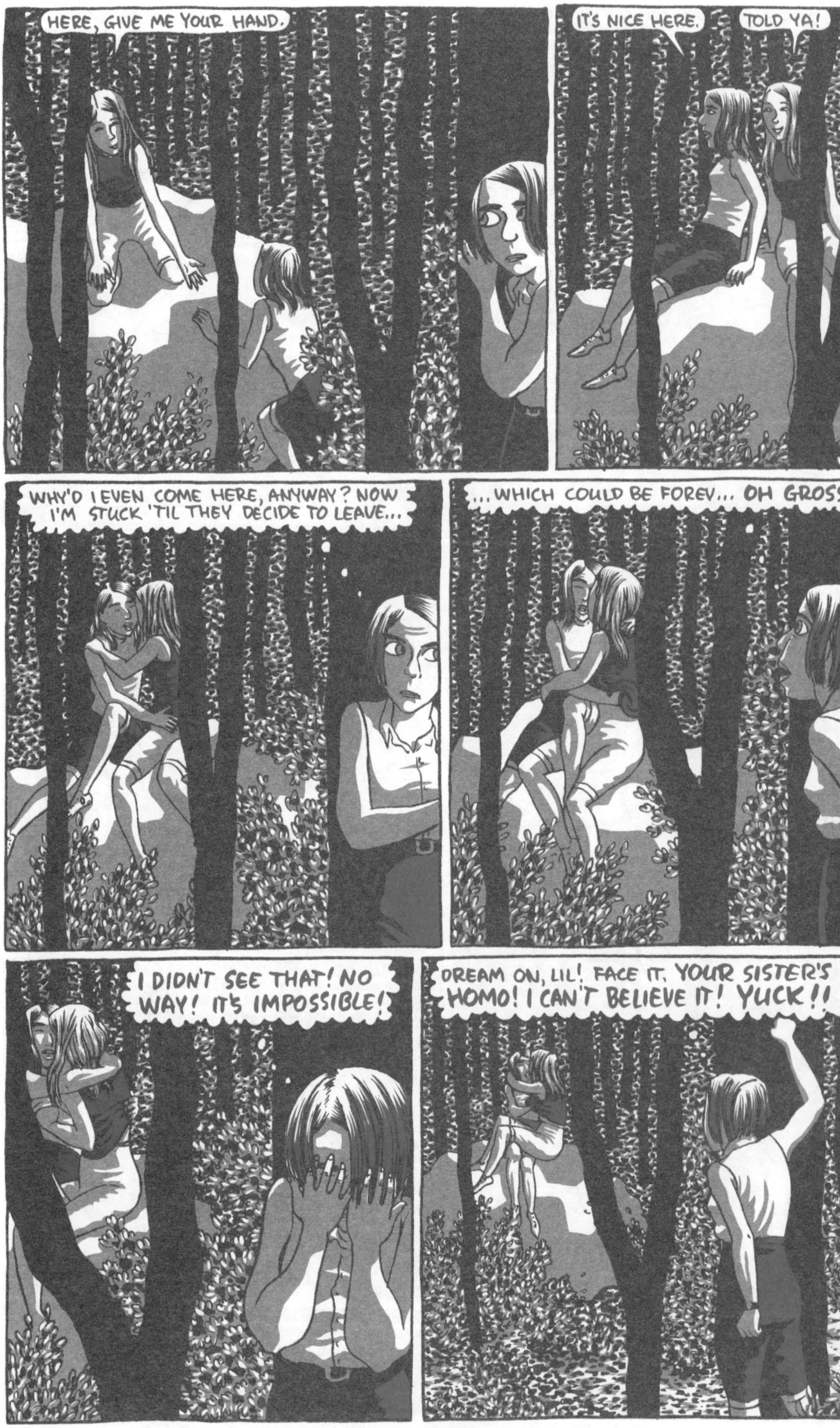
HERE, GIVE ME YOUR HAND.
IT'S NICE HERE.
TOLD YA!
WHY'D I EVEN COME HERE, ANYWAY? NOW I'M STUCK 'TIL THEY DECIDE TO LEAVE...
...WHICH COULD BE FOREV... OH GROSS!
I DIDN'T SEE THAT! NO WAY! IT'S IMPOSSIBLE!
DREAM ON, LIL! FACE IT, YOUR SISTER'S A HOMO! I CAN'T BELIEVE IT! YUCK!!

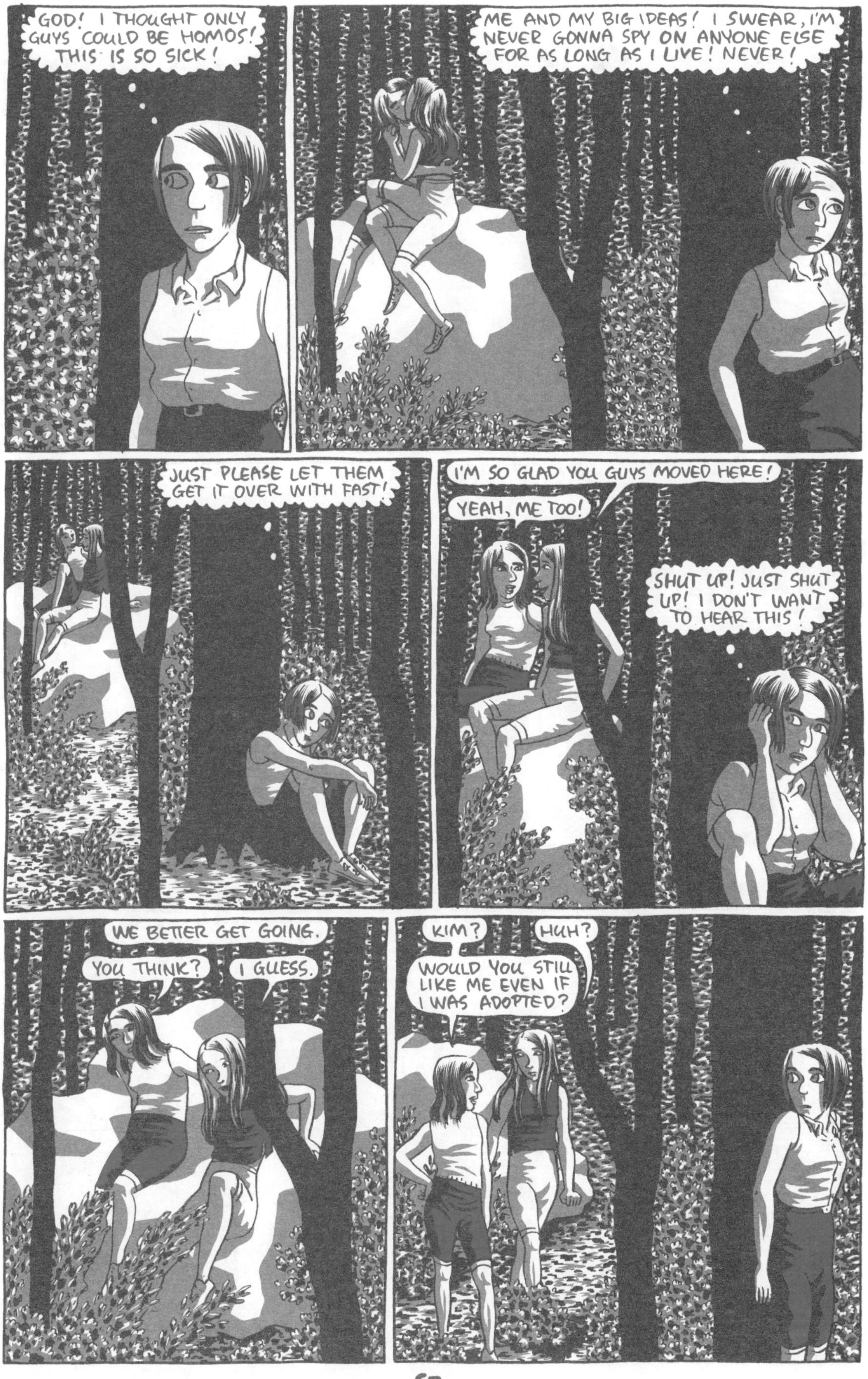
GOD! I THOUGHT ONLY GUYS COULD BE HOMOS! THIS IS SO SICK!
ME AND MY BIG IDEAS! I SWEAR, I'M NEVER GONNA SPY ON ANYONE ELSE FOR AS LONG AS I LIVE! NEVER!
JUST PLEASE LET THEM GET IT OVER WITH FAST!
I'M SO GLAD YOU GUYS MOVED HERE!
YEAH, ME TOO!
SHUT UP! JUST SHUT UP! I DON'T WANT TO HEAR THIS!
WE BETTER GET GOING.
YOU THINK?
I GUESS.
KIM?
HUH?
WOULD YOU STILL LIKE ME EVEN IF I WAS ADOPTED?

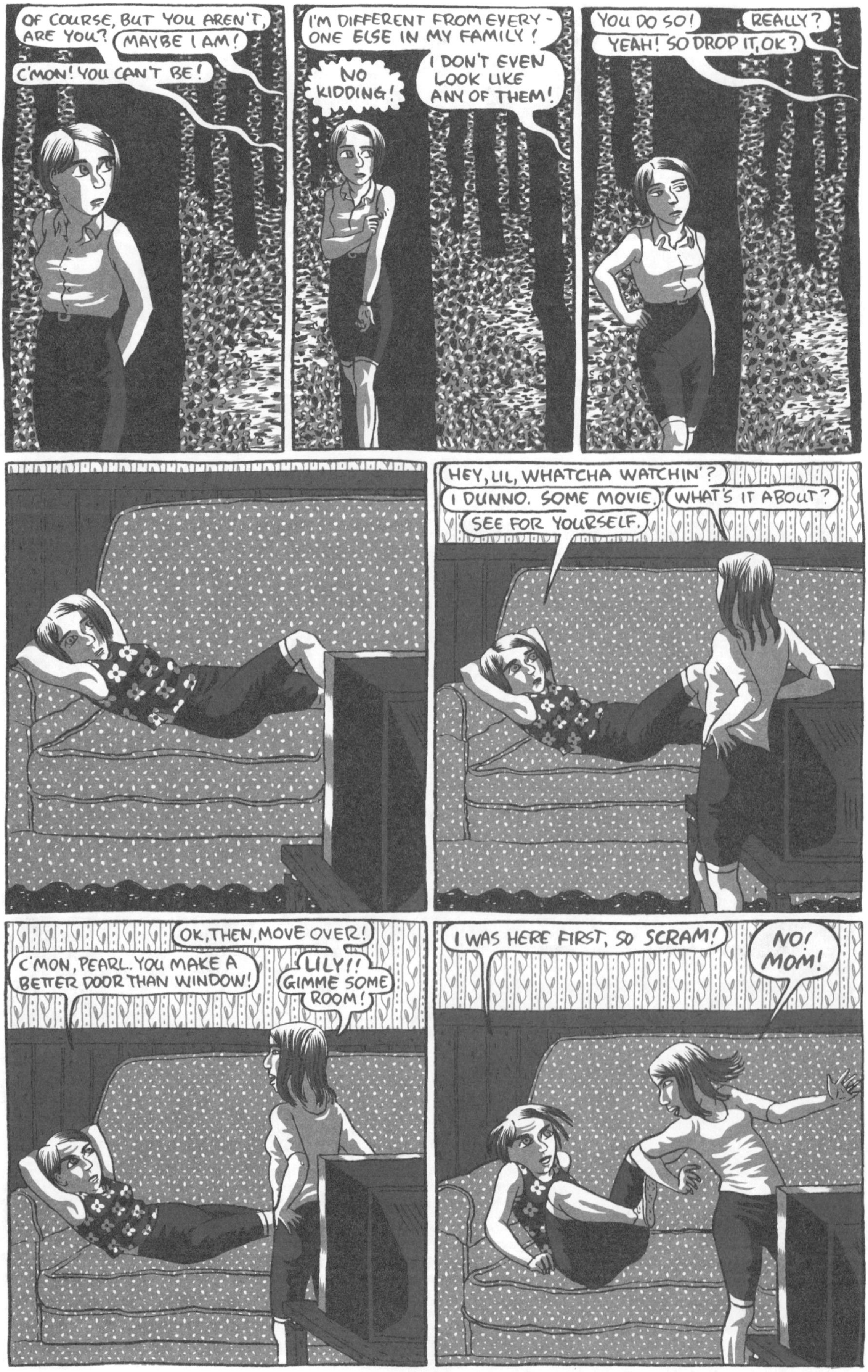
OF COURSE, BUT YOU AREN'T, ARE YOU?
MAYBE I AM!
C'MON! YOU CAN'T BE!
I'M DIFFERENT FROM EVERY-ONE ELSE IN MY FAMILY!
NO KIDDING!
I DON'T EVEN LOOK LIKE ANY OF THEM!
YOU DO SO!
REALLY?
YEAH! SO DROP IT, OK?
HEY, LIL, WHATCHA WATCHIN'?
I DUNNO. SOME MOVIE.
WHAT'S IT ABOUT?
SEE FOR YOURSELF.
OK, THEN, MOVE OVER!
C'MON, PEARL. YOU MAKE A BETTER DOOR THAN WINDOW!
LILY!! GIMME SOME ROOM!
I WAS HERE FIRST, SO SCRAM!
NO! MOM!

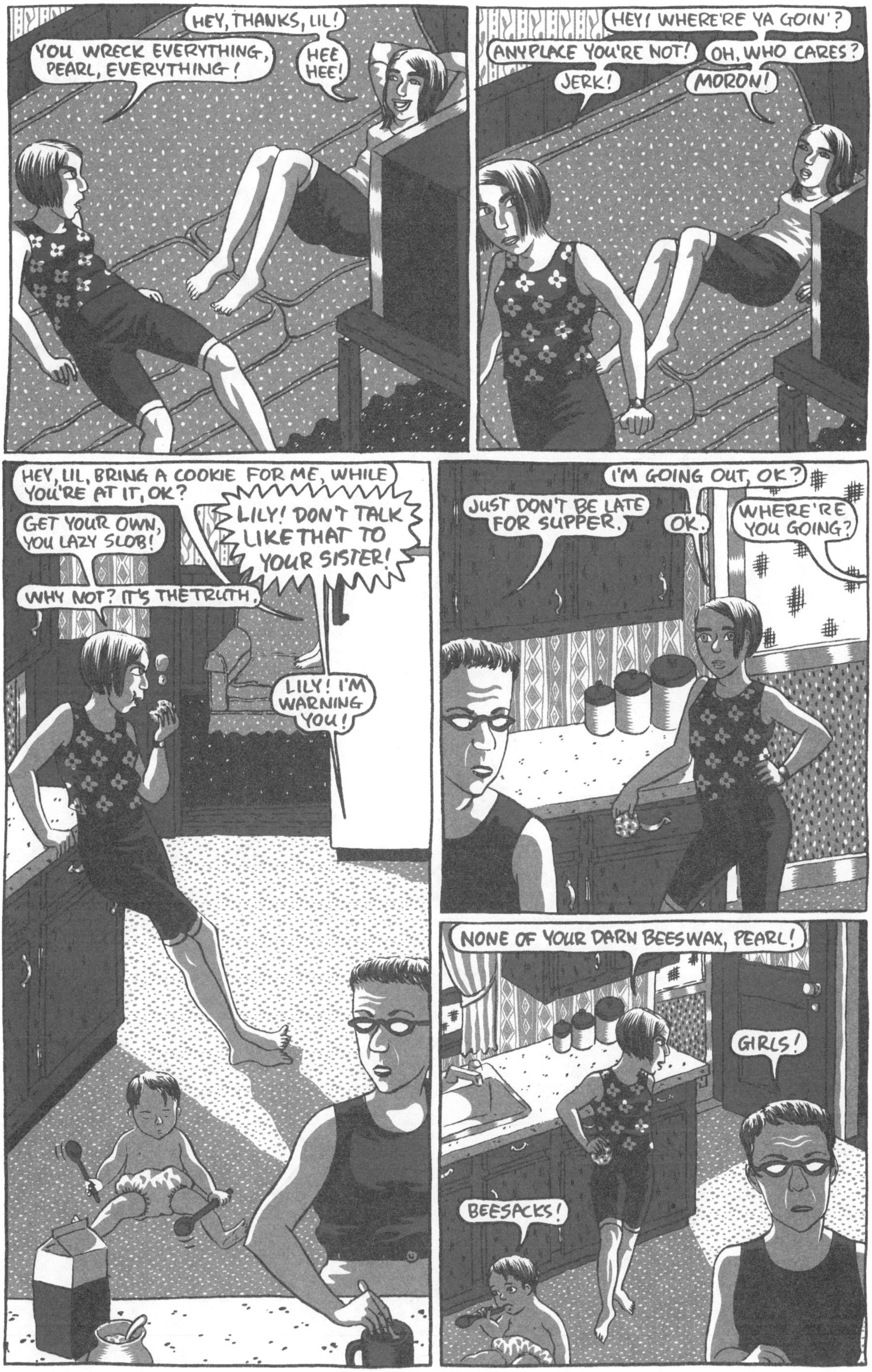
YOU WRECK EVERYTHING, PEARL, EVERYTHING!
HEY, THANKS, LIL!
HEE HEE!
HEY! WHERE'RE YA GOIN'?
ANYPLACE YOU'RE NOT!
OH, WHO CARES?
JERK!
MORON!
HEY, LIL, BRING A COOKIE FOR ME, WHILE YOU'RE AT IT, OK?
GET YOUR OWN, YOU LAZY SLOB!
LILY! DON'T TALK LIKE THAT TO YOUR SISTER!
WHY NOT? IT'S THE TRUTH.
LILY! I'M WARNING YOU!
I'M GOING OUT, OK?
JUST DON'T BE LATE FOR SUPPER.
OK.
WHERE'RE YOU GOING?
NONE OF YOUR DARN BEESWAX, PEARL!
GIRLS!
BEESACKS!

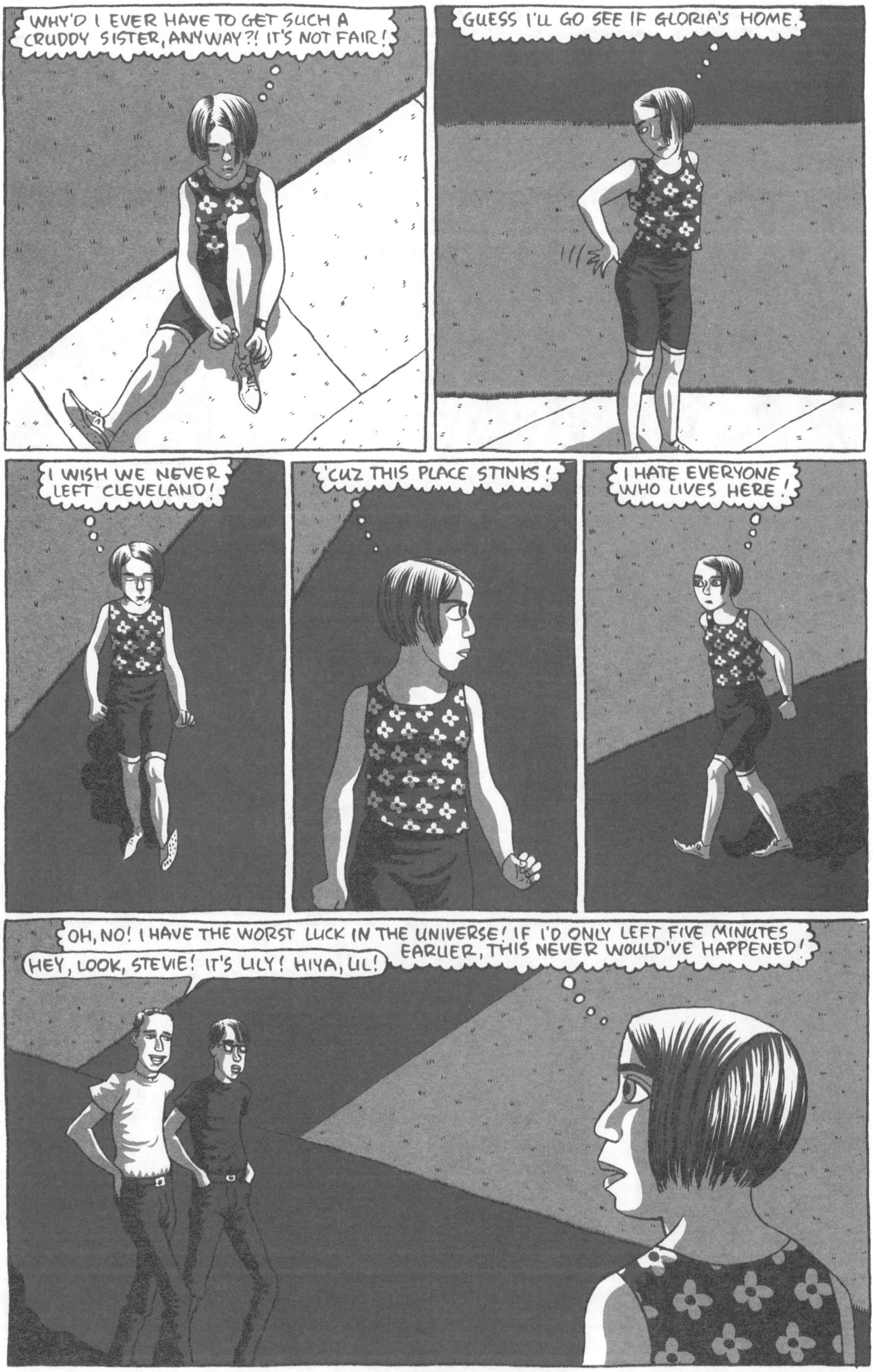
WHY'D I EVER HAVE TO GET SUCH A CRUDDY SISTER, ANYWAY?! IT'S NOT FAIR!
GUESS I'LL GO SEE IF GLORIA'S HOME.
I WISH WE NEVER LEFT CLEVELAND!
'CUZ THIS PLACE STINKS!
I HATE EVERYONE WHO LIVES HERE!
OH, NO! I HAVE THE WORST LUCK IN THE UNIVERSE! IF I'D ONLY LEFT FIVE MINUTES EARLIER, THIS NEVER WOULD'VE HAPPENED!
HEY, LOOK, STEVIE! IT'S LILY! HIYA, LIL!

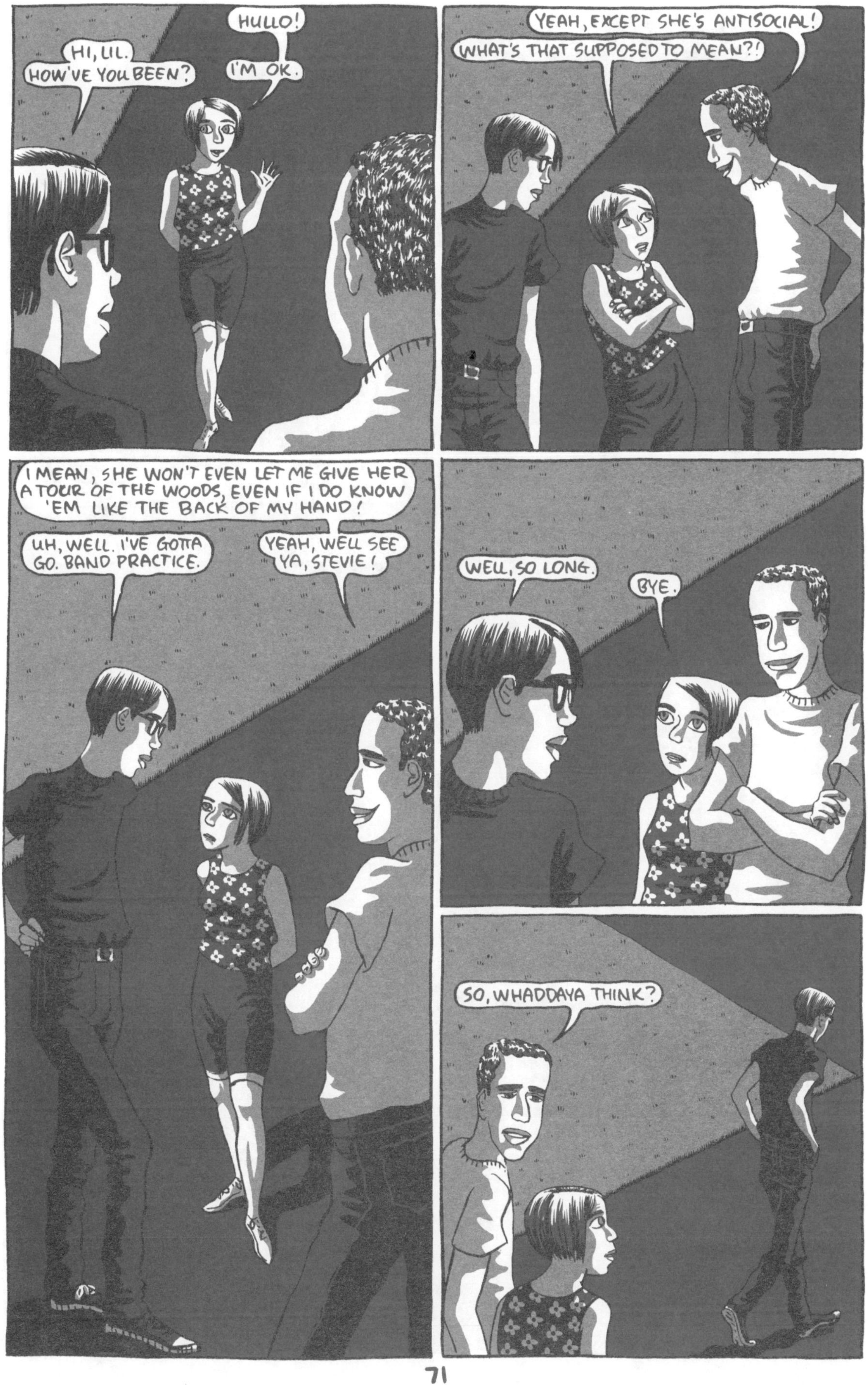
HI, LIL. HOW'VE YOU BEEN?
HULLO!
I'M OK.
YEAH, EXCEPT SHE'S ANTISOCIAL!
WHAT'S THAT SUPPOSED TO MEAN?!
I MEAN, SHE WON'T EVEN LET ME GIVE HER A TOUR OF THE WOODS, EVEN IF I DO KNOW 'EM LIKE THE BACK OF MY HAND!
UH, WELL. I'VE GOTTA GO. BAND PRACTICE.
YEAH, WELL SEE YA, STEVIE!
WELL, SO LONG.
BYE.
SO, WHADDAYA THINK?

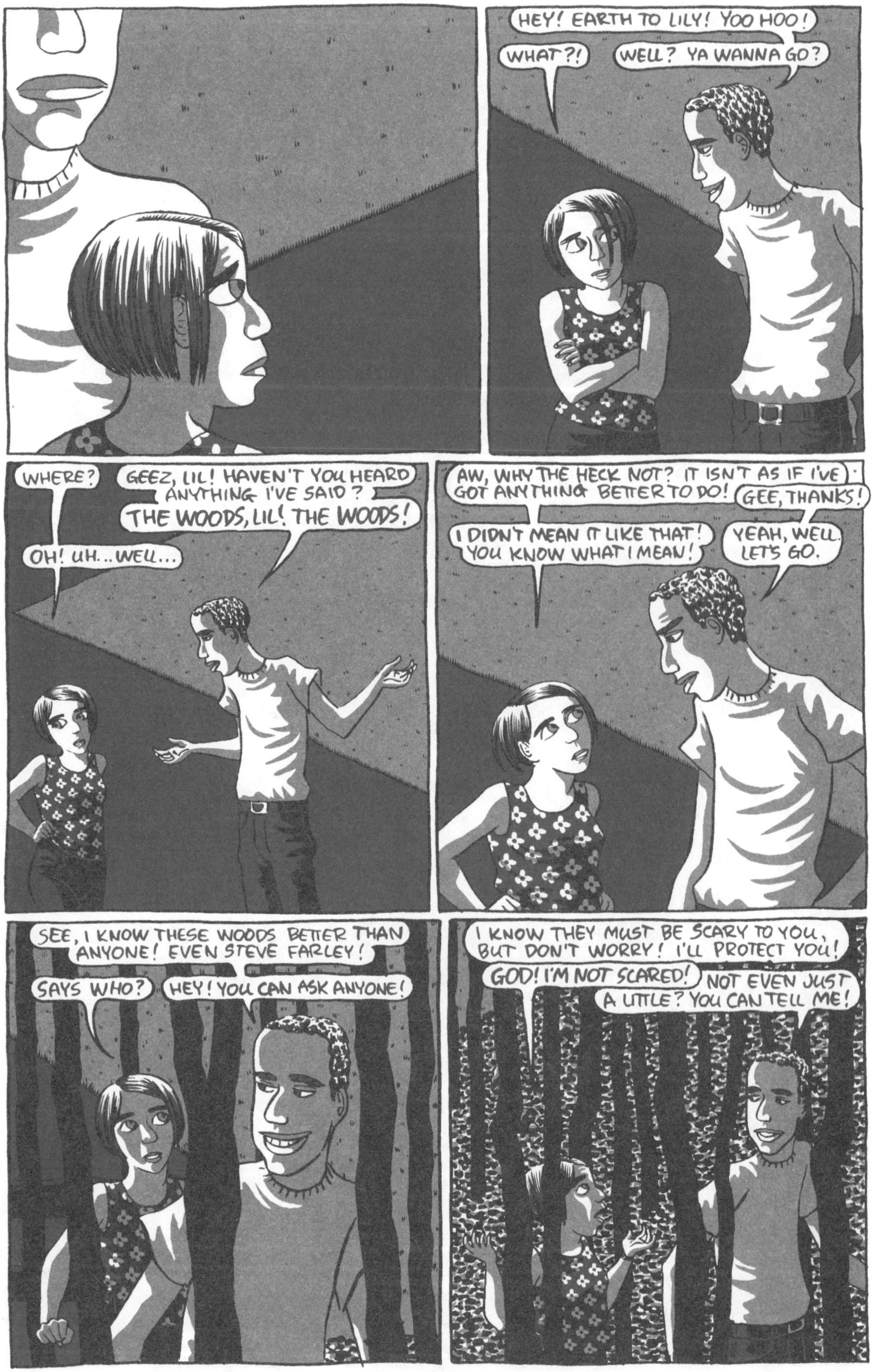
HEY! EARTH TO LILY! YOO HOO!
WHAT?!
WELL? YA WANNA GO?
WHERE?
GEEZ, LIL! HAVEN'T YOU HEARD ANYTHING I'VE SAID?
THE WOODS, LIL! THE WOODS!
OH! UH... WELL...
AW, WHY THE HECK NOT? IT ISN'T AS IF I'VE GOT ANYTHING BETTER TO DO!
GEE, THANKS!
I DIDN'T MEAN IT LIKE THAT! YOU KNOW WHAT I MEAN!
YEAH, WELL. LET'S GO.
SEE, I KNOW THESE WOODS BETTER THAN ANYONE! EVEN STEVE FARLEY!
SAYS WHO?
HEY! YOU CAN ASK ANYONE!
I KNOW THEY MUST BE SCARY TO YOU, BUT DON'T WORRY! I'LL PROTECT YOU!
GOD! I'M NOT SCARED!
NOT EVEN JUST A LITTLE? YOU CAN TELL ME!

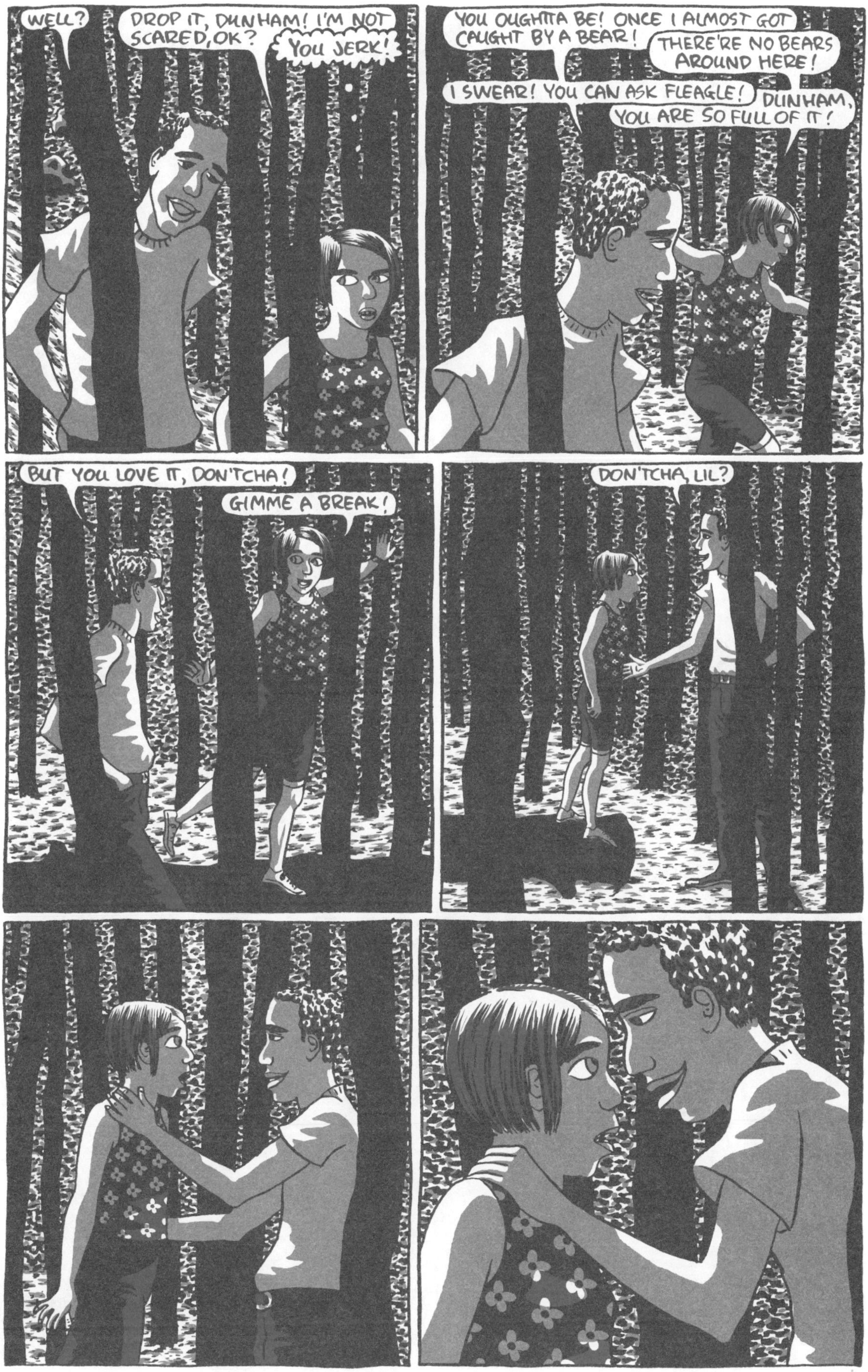
WELL?
DROP IT, DUNHAM! I'M NOT SCARED, OK?
YOU JERK!
YOU OUGHTTA BE! ONCE I ALMOST GOT CAUGHT BY A BEAR!
THERE'RE NO BEARS AROUND HERE!
I SWEAR! YOU CAN ASK FLEAGLE!
DUNHAM, YOU ARE SO FULL OF IT!
BUT YOU LOVE IT, DON'TCHA!
GIMME A BREAK!
DON'TCHA, LIL?

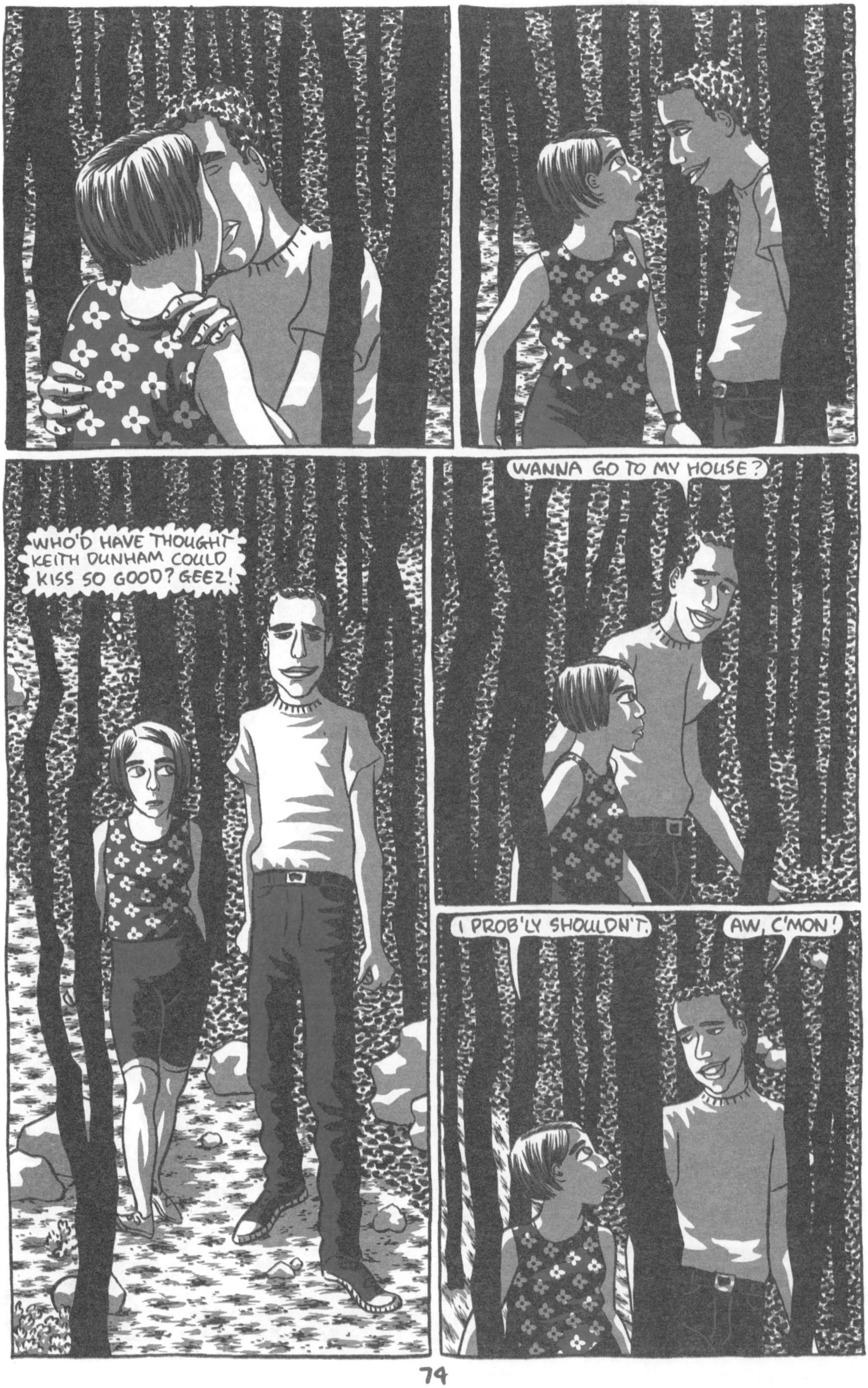
WHO'D HAVE THOUGHT KEITH DUNHAM COULD KISS SO GOOD? GEEZ!
WANNA GO TO MY HOUSE?
I PROB'LY SHOULDN'T.
AW, C'MON!

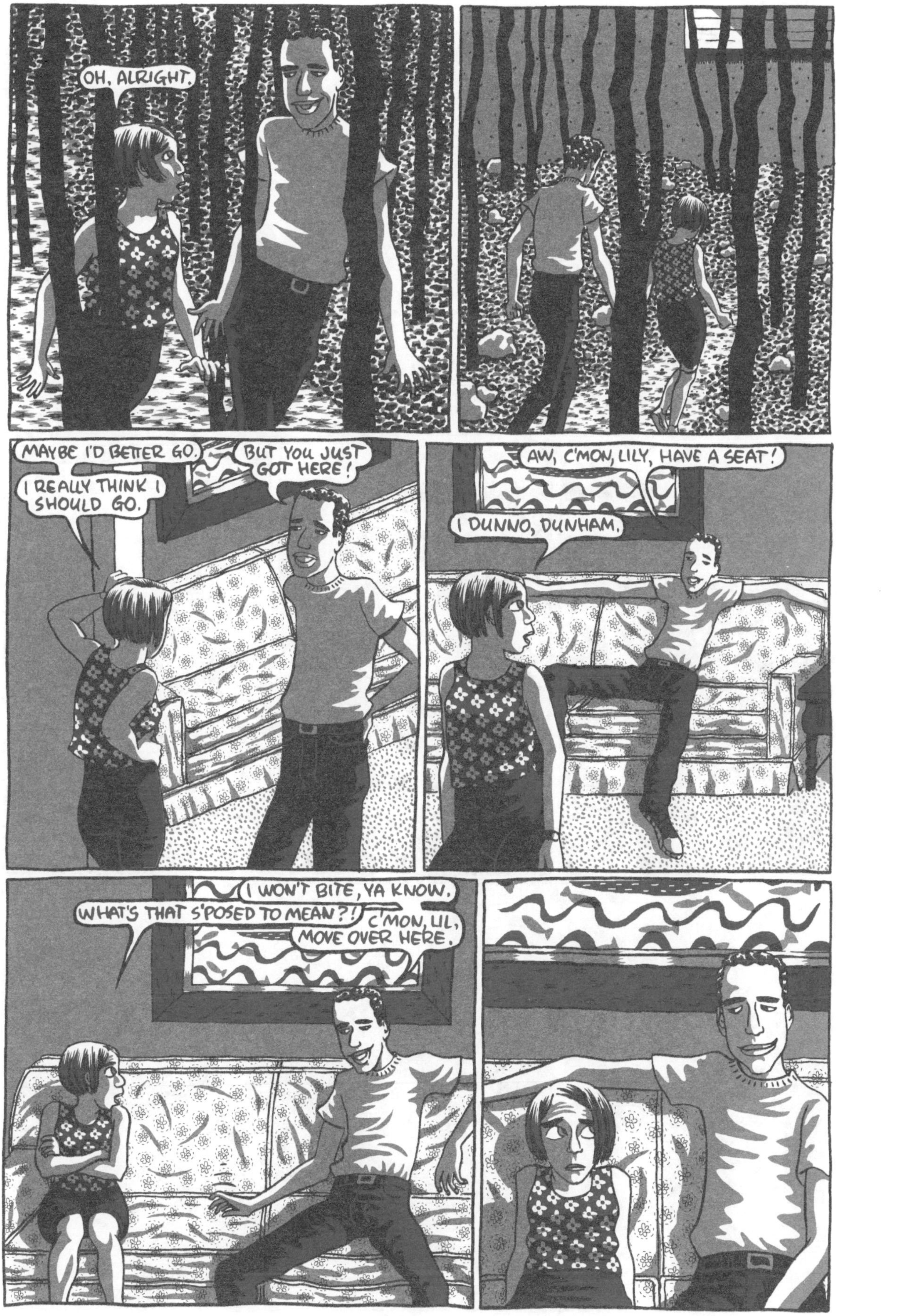
OH, ALRIGHT.
MAYBE I'D BETTER GO.
BUT YOU JUST GOT HERE!
I REALLY THINK I SHOULD GO.
AW, C'MON, LILY, HAVE A SEAT!
I DUNNO, DUNHAM.
I WON'T BITE, YA KNOW.
WHAT'S THAT S'POSED TO MEAN?!
C'MON, LIL, MOVE OVER HERE.

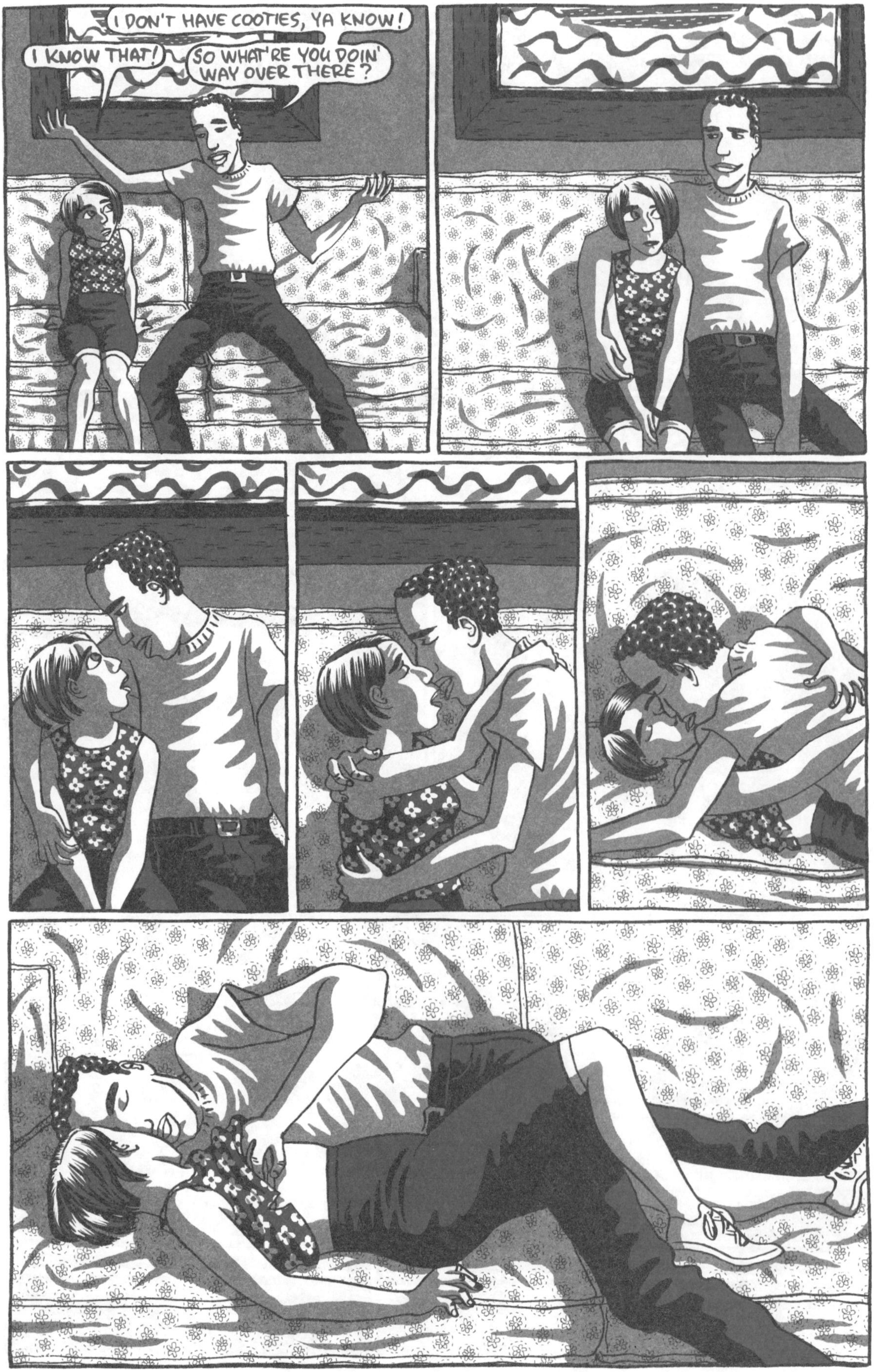
I DON'T HAVE COOTIES, YA KNOW!
I KNOW THAT!
SO WHAT'RE YOU DOIN' WAY OVER THERE?

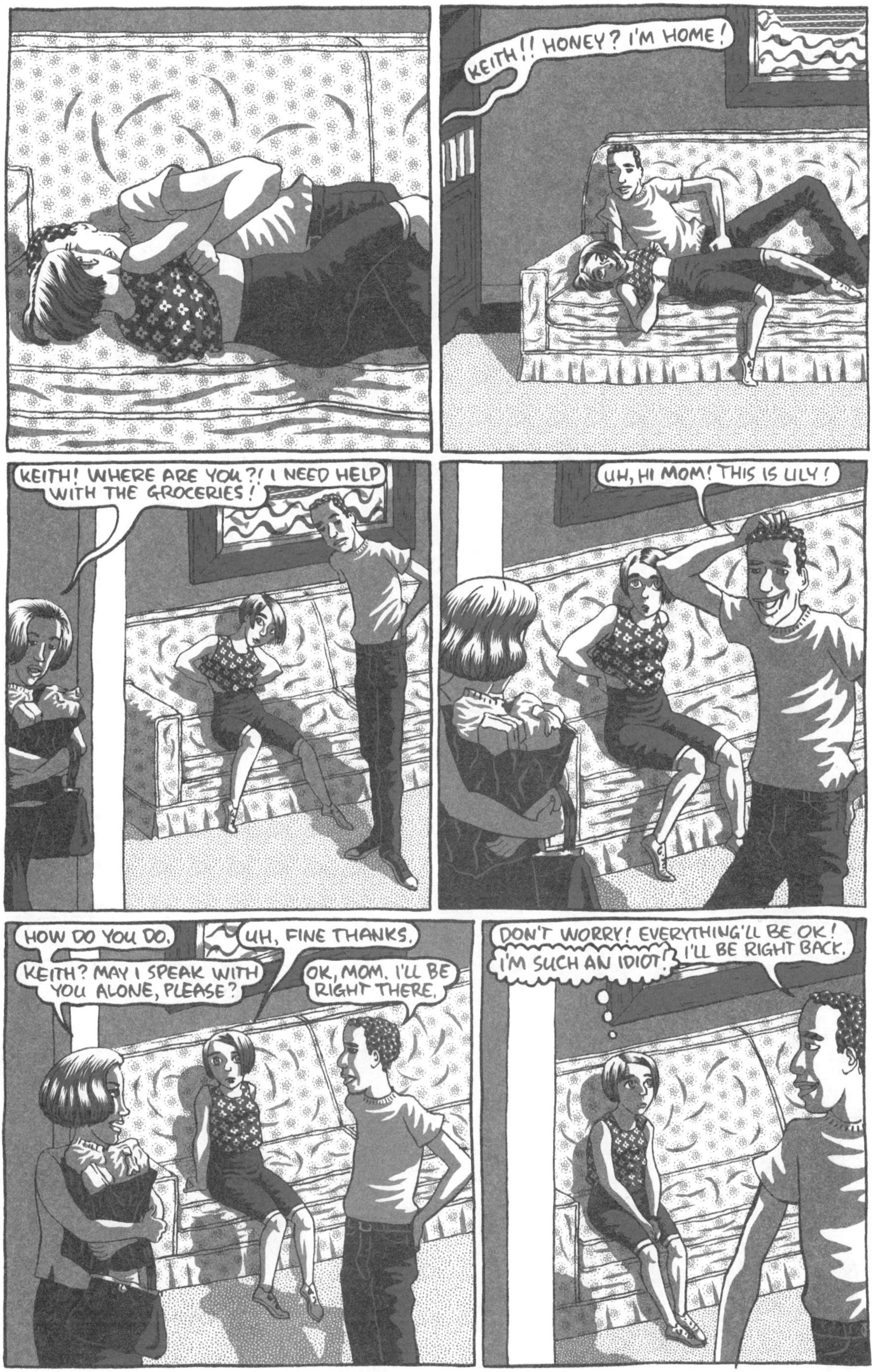
KEITH!! HONEY? I'M HOME!
KEITH! WHERE ARE YOU?! I NEED HELP WITH THE GROCERIES!
UH, HI MOM! THIS IS LILY!
HOW DO YOU DO.
UH, FINE THANKS.
KEITH? MAY I SPEAK WITH YOU ALONE, PLEASE?
OK, MOM. I'LL BE RIGHT THERE.
DON'T WORRY! EVERYTHING'LL BE OK! I'LL BE RIGHT BACK.
I'M SUCH AN IDIOT!

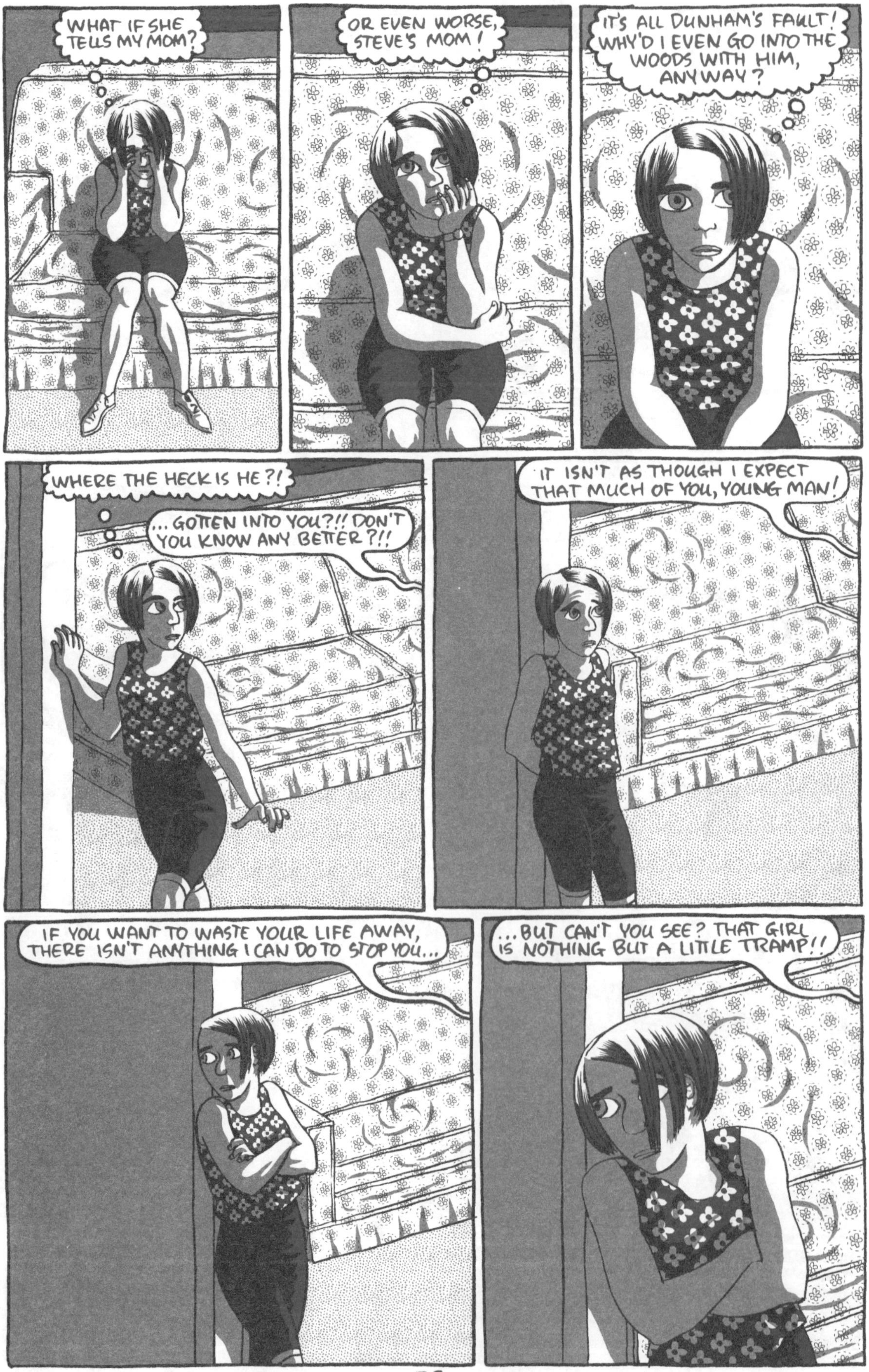
WHAT IF SHE TELLS MY MOM?
OR EVEN WORSE, STEVE'S MOM!
IT'S ALL DUNHAM'S FAULT! WHY'D I EVEN GO INTO THE WOODS WITH HIM, ANYWAY?
WHERE THE HECK IS HE?!
...GOTTEN INTO YOU?!! DON'T YOU KNOW ANY BETTER?!!
IT ISN'T AS THOUGH I EXPECT THAT MUCH OF YOU, YOUNG MAN!
IF YOU WANT TO WASTE YOUR LIFE AWAY, THERE ISN'T ANYTHING I CAN DO TO STOP YOU...
...BUT CAN'T YOU SEE? THAT GIRL IS NOTHING BUT A LITTLE TRAMP!!

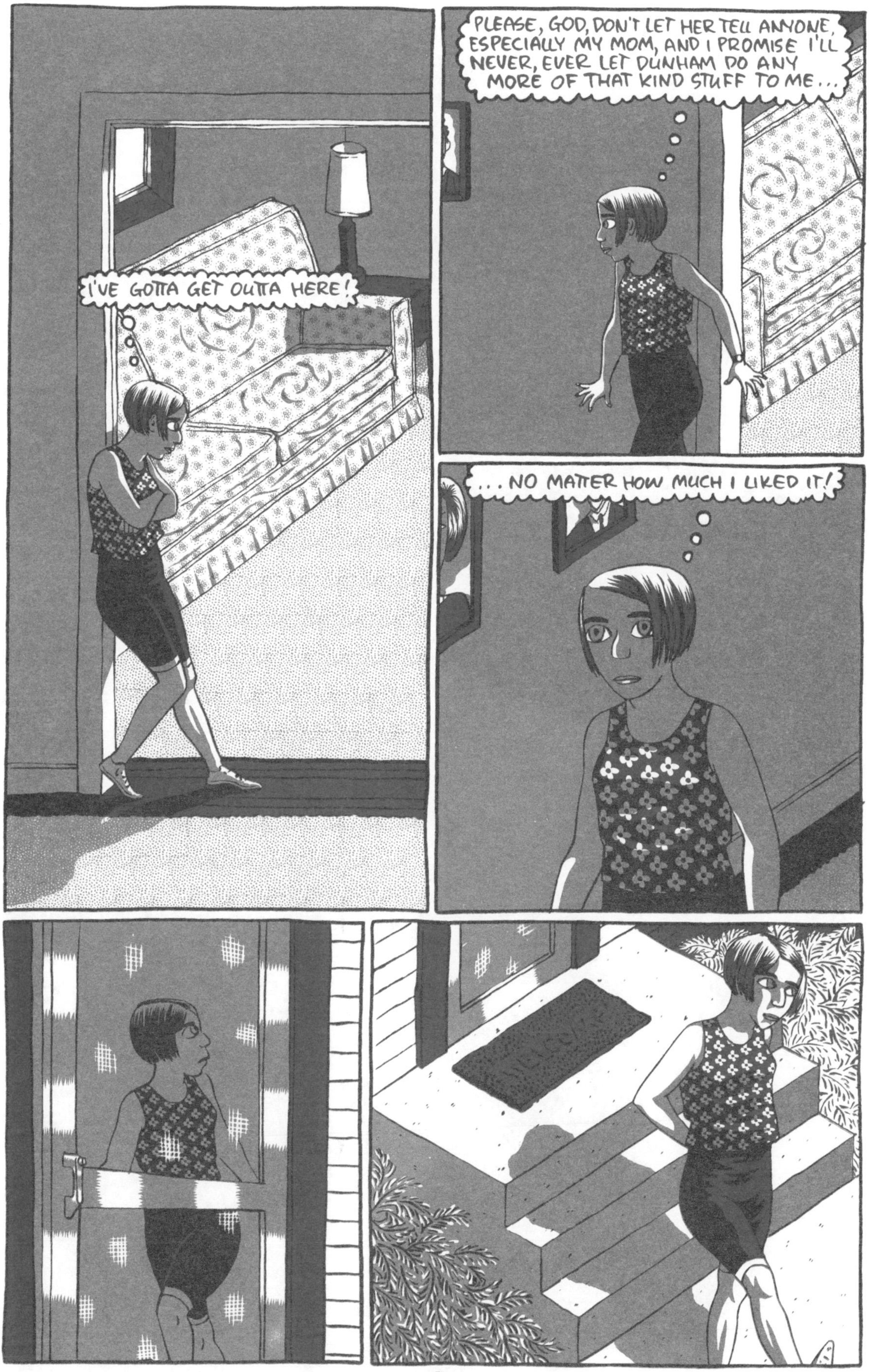
I'VE GOTTA GET OUTTA HERE!
PLEASE, GOD, DON'T LET HER TELL ANYONE, ESPECIALLY MY MOM, AND I PROMISE I'LL NEVER, EVER LET DUNHAM DO ANY MORE OF THAT KIND STUFF TO ME...
...NO MATTER HOW MUCH I LIKED IT!

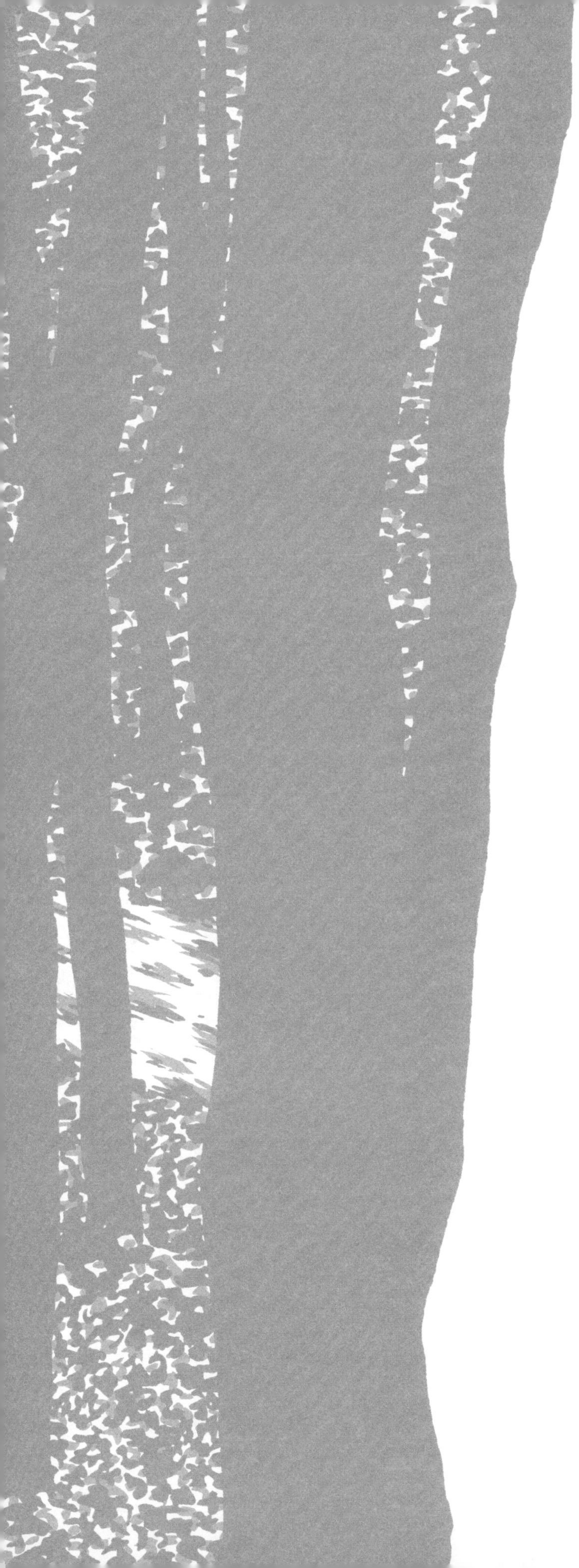

PART FOUR

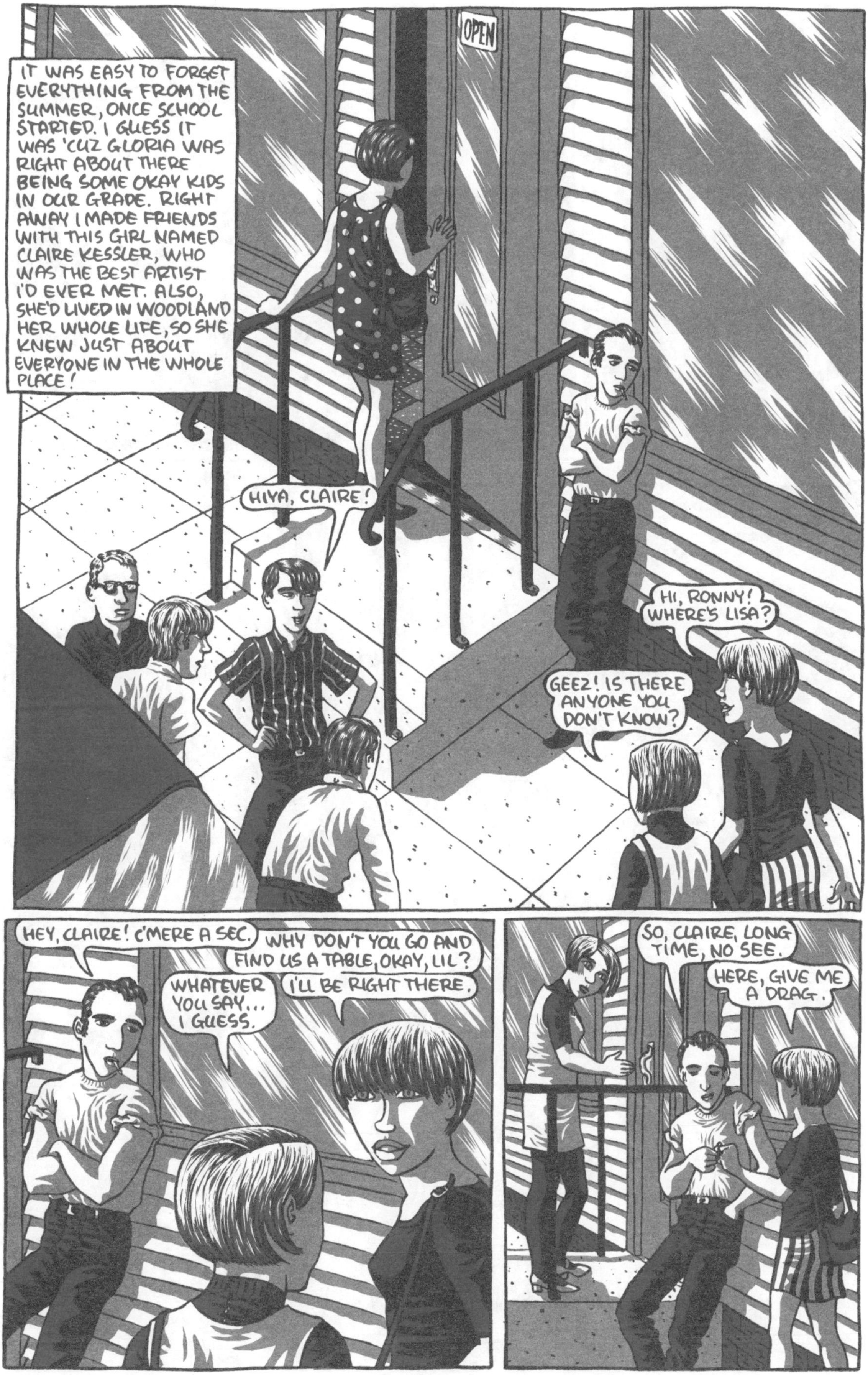
OPEN
IT WAS EASY TO FORGET EVERYTHING FROM THE SUMMER, ONCE SCHOOL STARTED. I GUESS IT WAS 'CUZ GLORIA WAS RIGHT ABOUT THERE BEING SOME OKAY KIDS IN OUR GRADE. RIGHT AWAY I MADE FRIENDS WITH THIS GIRL NAMED CLAIRE KESSLER, WHO WAS THE BEST ARTIST I'D EVER MET. ALSO, SHE'D LIVED IN WOODLAND HER WHOLE LIFE, SO SHE KNEW JUST ABOUT EVERYONE IN THE WHOLE PLACE!
HIYA, CLAIRE!
HI, RONNY! WHERE'S LISA?
GEEZ! IS THERE ANYONE YOU DON'T KNOW?
HEY, CLAIRE! C'MERE A SEC.
WHY DON'T YOU GO AND FIND US A TABLE, OKAY, LIL?
I'LL BE RIGHT THERE.
WHATEVER YOU SAY... I GUESS.
SO, CLAIRE, LONG TIME, NO SEE.
HERE, GIVE ME A DRAG.

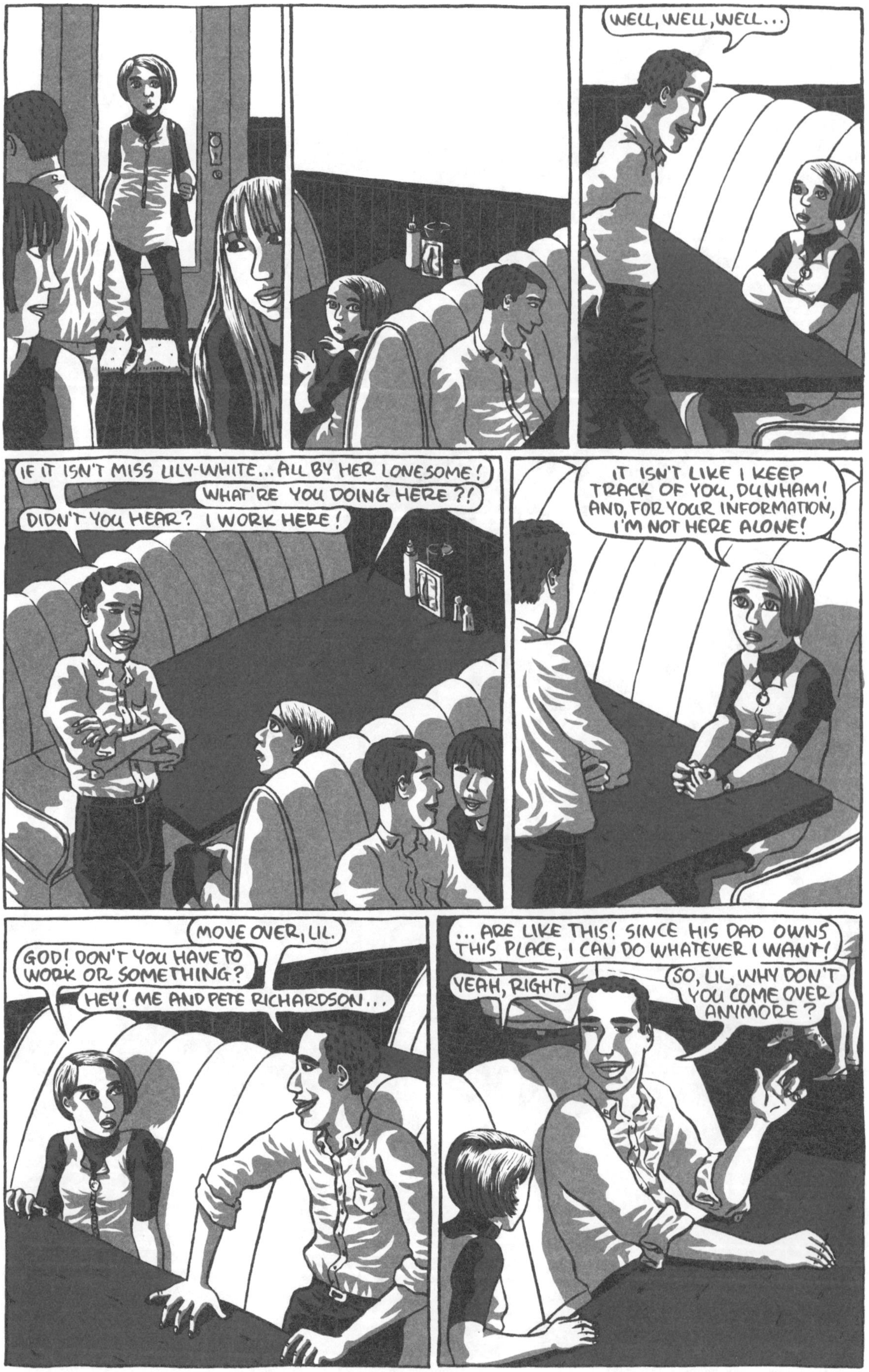
WELL, WELL, WELL...
IF IT ISN'T MISS LILY-WHITE... ALL BY HER LONESOME!
WHAT'RE YOU DOING HERE?!
DIDN'T YOU HEAR? I WORK HERE!
IT ISN'T LIKE I KEEP TRACK OF YOU, DUNHAM! AND, FOR YOUR INFORMATION, I'M NOT HERE ALONE!
MOVE OVER, LIL.
GOD! DON'T YOU HAVE TO WORK OR SOMETHING?
HEY! ME AND PETE RICHARDSON...
... ARE LIKE THIS! SINCE HIS DAD OWNS THIS PLACE, I CAN DO WHATEVER I WANT!
YEAH, RIGHT.
SO, LIL, WHY DON'T YOU COME OVER ANYMORE?

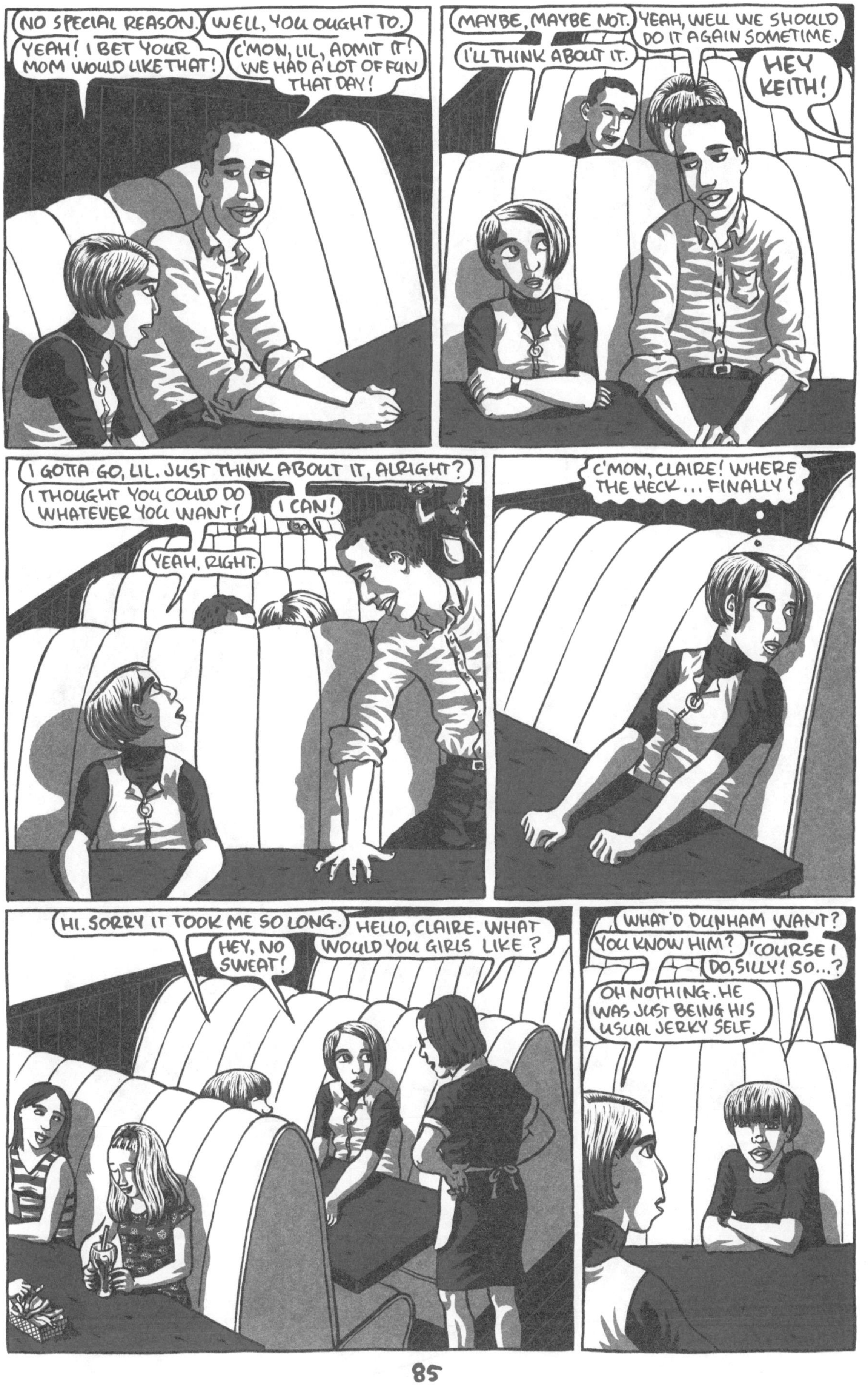
NO SPECIAL REASON.
WELL, YOU OUGHT TO.
YEAH! I BET YOUR MOM WOULD LIKE THAT!
C'MON, LIL, ADMIT IT! WE HAD A LOT OF FUN THAT DAY!
MAYBE, MAYBE NOT.
YEAH, WELL WE SHOULD DO IT AGAIN SOMETIME.
I'LL THINK ABOUT IT.
HEY KEITH!
I GOTTA GO, LIL. JUST THINK ABOUT IT, ALRIGHT?
I THOUGHT YOU COULD DO WHATEVER YOU WANT!
I CAN!
YEAH, RIGHT.
C'MON, CLAIRE! WHERE THE HECK... FINALLY!
HI. SORRY IT TOOK ME SO LONG.
HEY, NO SWEAT!
HELLO, CLAIRE. WHAT WOULD YOU GIRLS LIKE?
WHAT'D DUNHAM WANT?
YOU KNOW HIM?
'COURSE I DO, SILLY! SO...?
OH NOTHING. HE WAS JUST BEING HIS USUAL JERKY SELF.

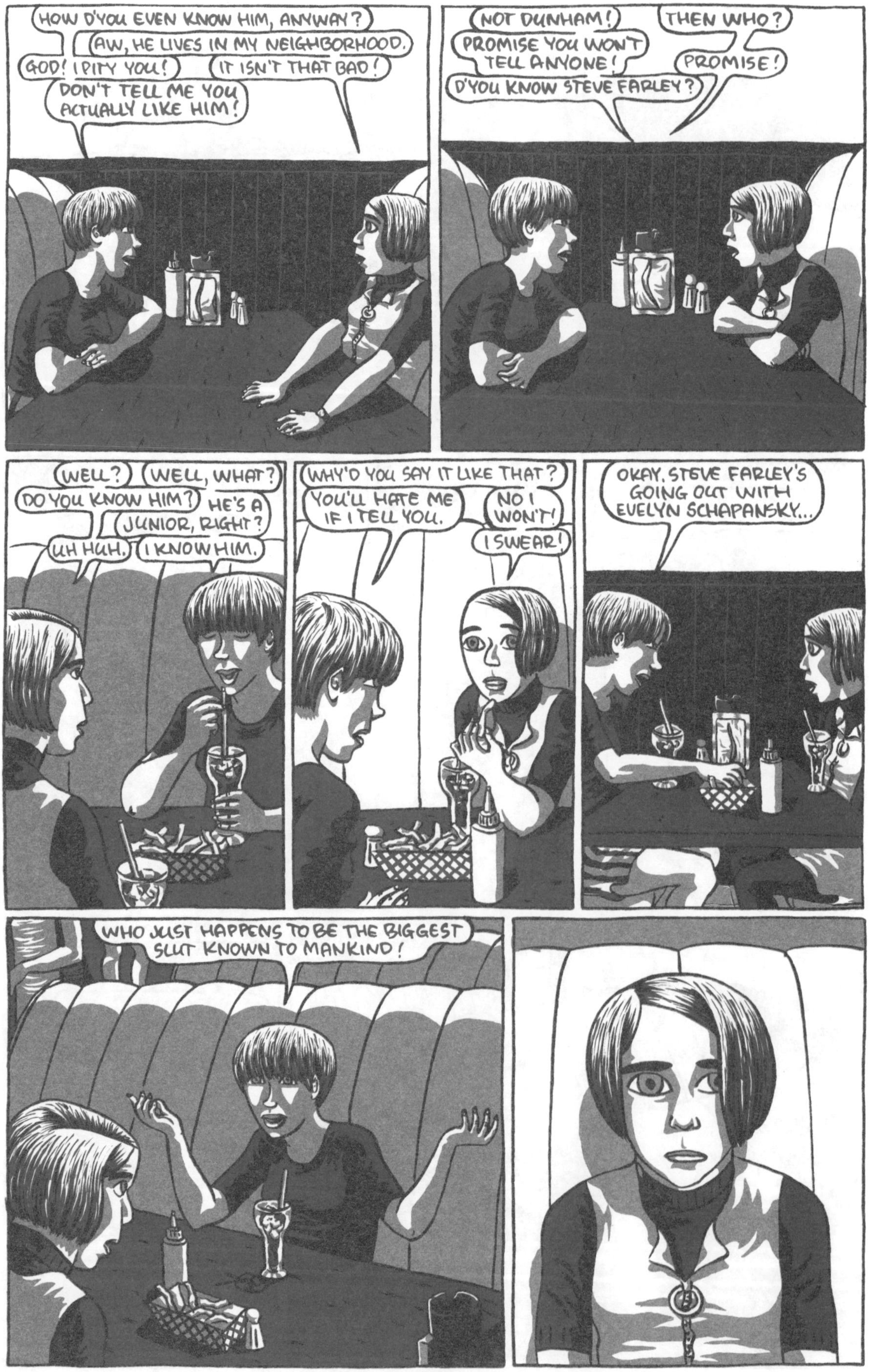
HOW D'YOU EVEN KNOW HIM, ANYWAY?
AW, HE LIVES IN MY NEIGHBORHOOD.
GOD! I PITY YOU!
IT ISN'T THAT BAD!
DON'T TELL ME YOU ACTUALLY LIKE HIM!
NOT DUNHAM!
THEN WHO?
PROMISE YOU WON'T TELL ANYONE!
PROMISE!
D'YOU KNOW STEVE FARLEY?
WELL?
WELL, WHAT?
DO YOU KNOW HIM?
HE'S A JUNIOR, RIGHT?
UH HUH.
I KNOW HIM.
WHY'D YOU SAY IT LIKE THAT?
YOU'LL HATE ME IF I TELL YOU.
NO I WON'T!
I SWEAR!
OKAY. STEVE FARLEY'S GOING OUT WITH EVELYN SCHAPANSKY...
WHO JUST HAPPENS TO BE THE BIGGEST SLUT KNOWN TO MANKIND!

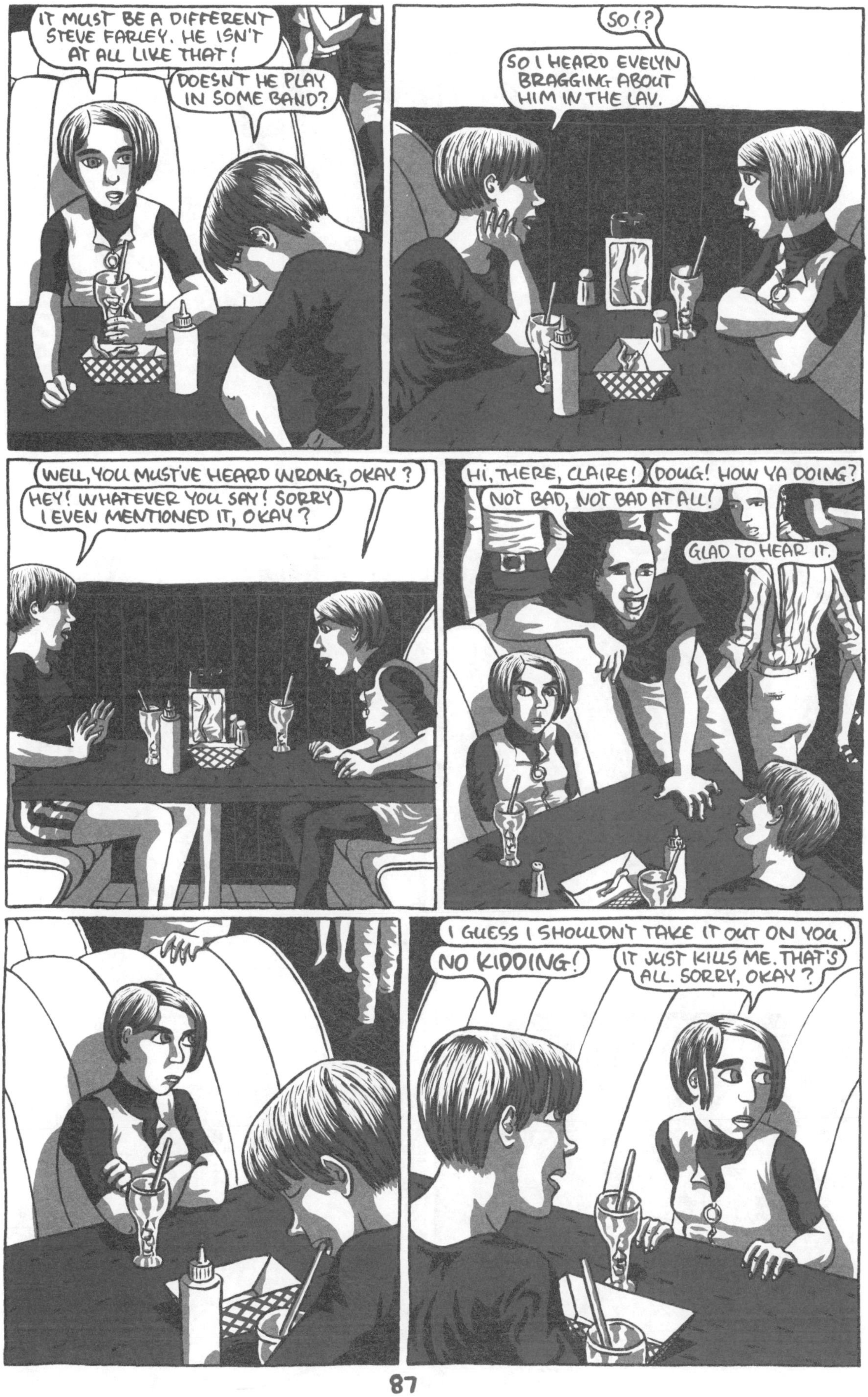
IT MUST BE A DIFFERENT STEVE FARLEY. HE ISN'T AT ALL LIKE THAT!
DOESN'T HE PLAY IN SOME BAND?
SO!?
SO I HEARD EVELYN BRAGGING ABOUT HIM IN THE LAV.
WELL, YOU MUST'VE HEARD WRONG, OKAY?
HEY! WHATEVER YOU SAY! SORRY I EVEN MENTIONED IT, OKAY?
HI, THERE, CLAIRE!
DOUG! HOW YA DOING?
NOT BAD, NOT BAD AT ALL!
GLAD TO HEAR IT.
I GUESS I SHOULDN'T TAKE IT OUT ON YOU.
NO KIDDING!
IT JUST KILLS ME. THAT'S ALL. SORRY, OKAY?

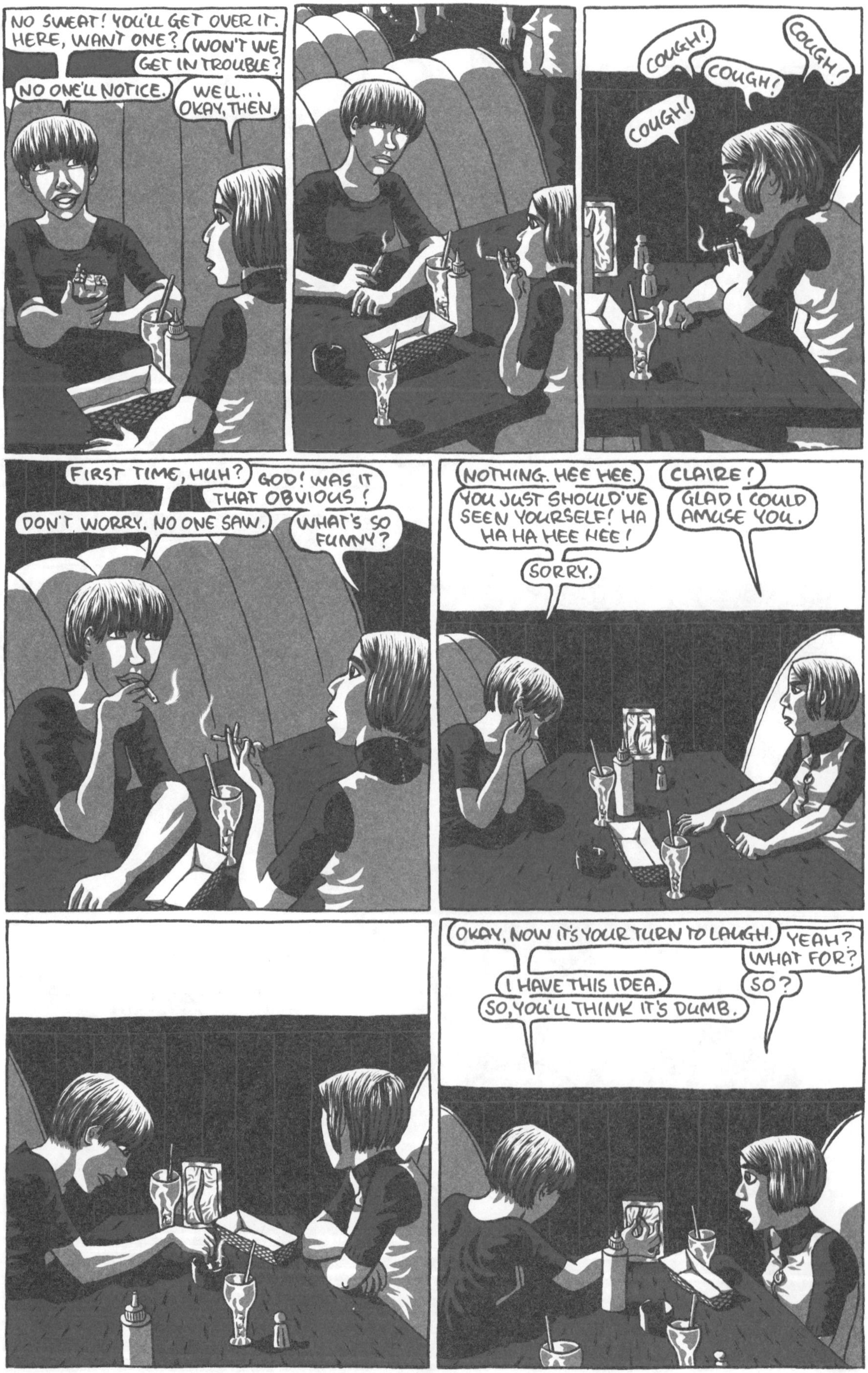
NO SWEAT! YOU'LL GET OVER IT. HERE, WANT ONE?
WON'T WE GET IN TROUBLE?
NO ONE'LL NOTICE.
WELL... OKAY, THEN.
COUGH!
COUGH!
COUGH!
COUGH!
FIRST TIME, HUH?
GOD! WAS IT THAT OBVIOUS!
DON'T WORRY. NO ONE SAW.
WHAT'S SO FUNNY?
NOTHING. HEE HEE.
YOU JUST SHOULD'VE SEEN YOURSELF! HA HA HA HEE HEE!
CLAIRE!
GLAD I COULD AMUSE YOU.
SORRY.
OKAY, NOW IT'S YOUR TURN TO LAUGH.
YEAH? WHAT FOR?
I HAVE THIS IDEA.
SO?
SO, YOU'LL THINK IT'S DUMB.

TRY ME! OKAY. I THINK WE SHOULD JOIN ART CLUB.

THAT IS A LAUGH! YOU'RE JOKING, RIGHT?

NOT REALLY.

OH. SO WHAT'S SO GREAT ABOUT ART CLUB?

NOTHING! I JUST THINK IT MIGHT BE FUN. BESIDES, THEY COULD USE SOME BETTER ARTISTS.

BOY, ARE YOU EVER CONCEITED!

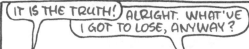

IT IS THE TRUTH! ALRIGHT. WHAT'VE I GOT TO LOSE, ANYWAY?

I HOPE WE WON'T BE SORRY. WELL, AT LEAST IF WE ARE, WE WON'T BE ALONE.

I GUESS... OH, NO!

WHAT?

THERE'S MY STUPID SISTER!

WHERE?!

OVER THERE...WEARING THE BROWN DRESS.

HIYA, LIL.

PEARL.

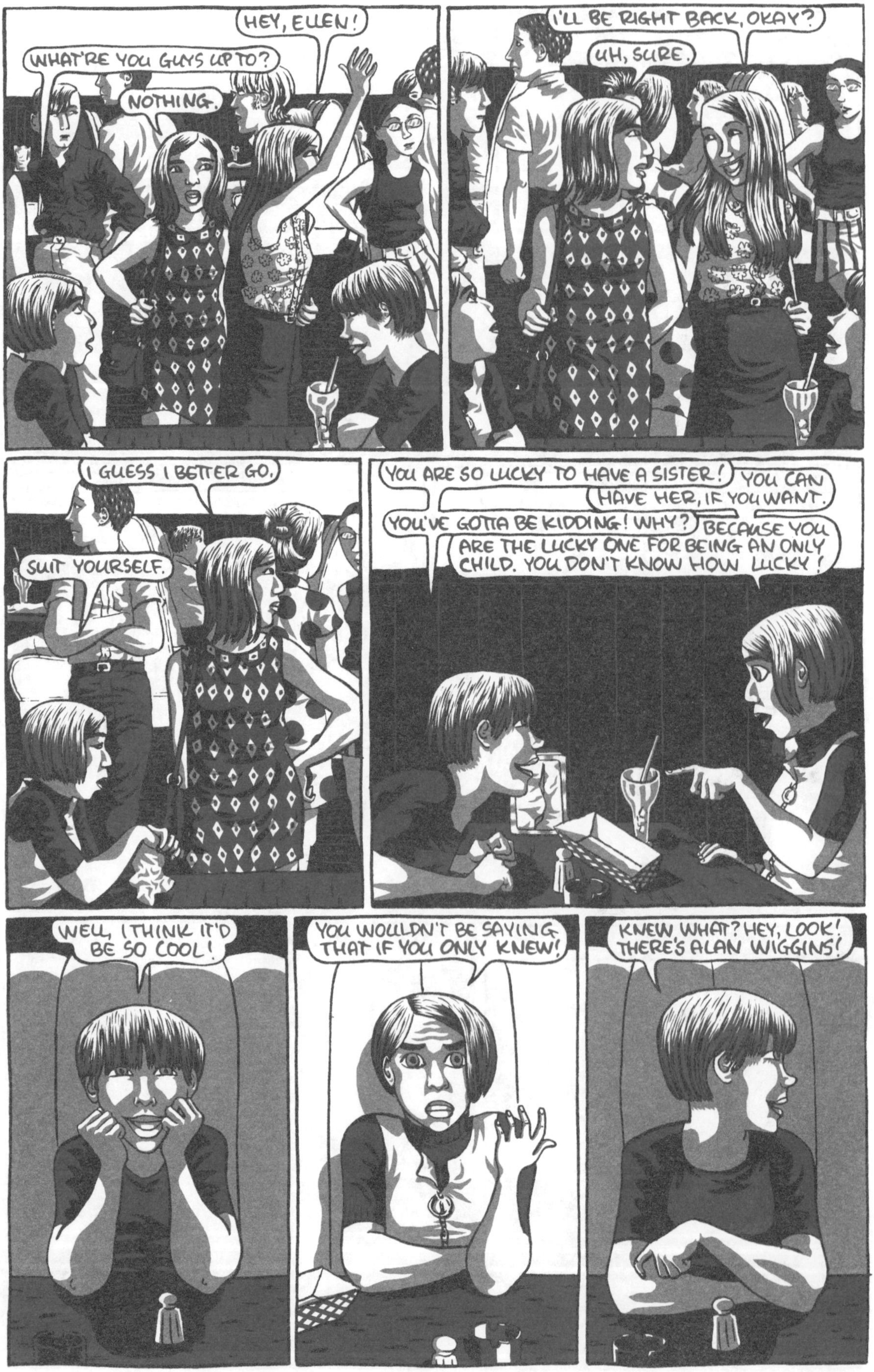
WHAT'RE YOU GUYS UP TO?
HEY, ELLEN!
NOTHING.
I'LL BE RIGHT BACK, OKAY?
UH, SURE.
I GUESS I BETTER GO.
SUIT YOURSELF.
YOU ARE SO LUCKY TO HAVE A SISTER!
YOU CAN HAVE HER, IF YOU WANT.
YOU'VE GOTTA BE KIDDING! WHY?
BECAUSE YOU ARE THE LUCKY ONE FOR BEING AN ONLY CHILD. YOU DON'T KNOW HOW LUCKY!
WELL, I THINK IT'D BE SO COOL!
YOU WOULDN'T BE SAYING THAT IF YOU ONLY KNEW!
KNEW WHAT? HEY, LOOK! THERE'S ALAN WIGGINS!

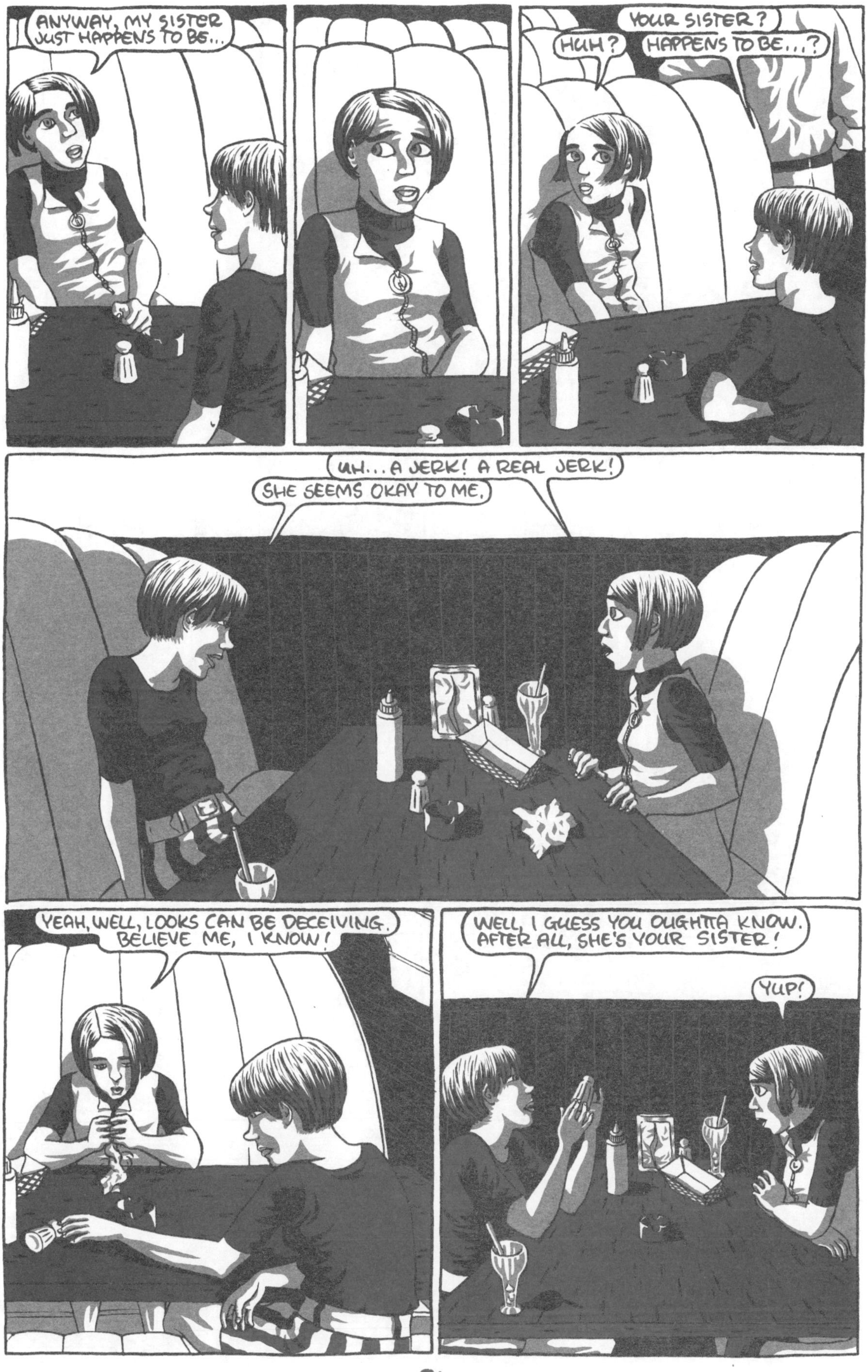
ANYWAY, MY SISTER JUST HAPPENS TO BE...
YOUR SISTER?
HUH?
HAPPENS TO BE...?
UH... A JERK! A REAL JERK!
SHE SEEMS OKAY TO ME.
YEAH, WELL, LOOKS CAN BE DECEIVING. BELIEVE ME, I KNOW!
WELL, I GUESS YOU OUGHTTA KNOW. AFTER ALL, SHE'S YOUR SISTER!
YUP!

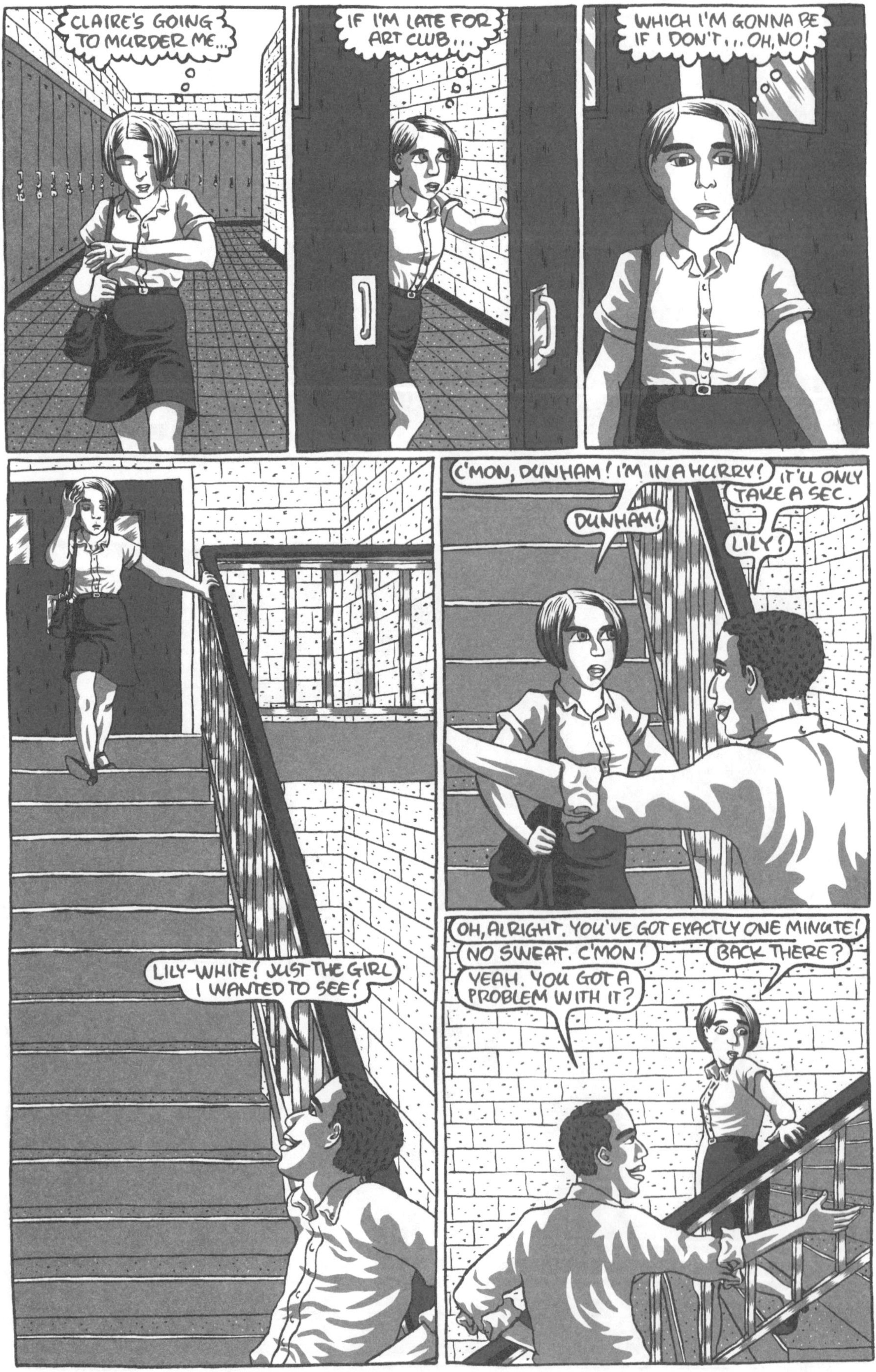
CLAIRE'S GOING TO MURDER ME...
IF I'M LATE FOR ART CLUB...
WHICH I'M GONNA BE IF I DON'T... OH, NO!
LILY-WHITE! JUST THE GIRL I WANTED TO SEE!
DUNHAM!
LILY!
C'MON, DUNHAM! I'M IN A HURRY!
IT'LL ONLY TAKE A SEC.
OH, ALRIGHT. YOU'VE GOT EXACTLY ONE MINUTE!
NO SWEAT. C'MON!
BACK THERE?
YEAH. YOU GOT A PROBLEM WITH IT?

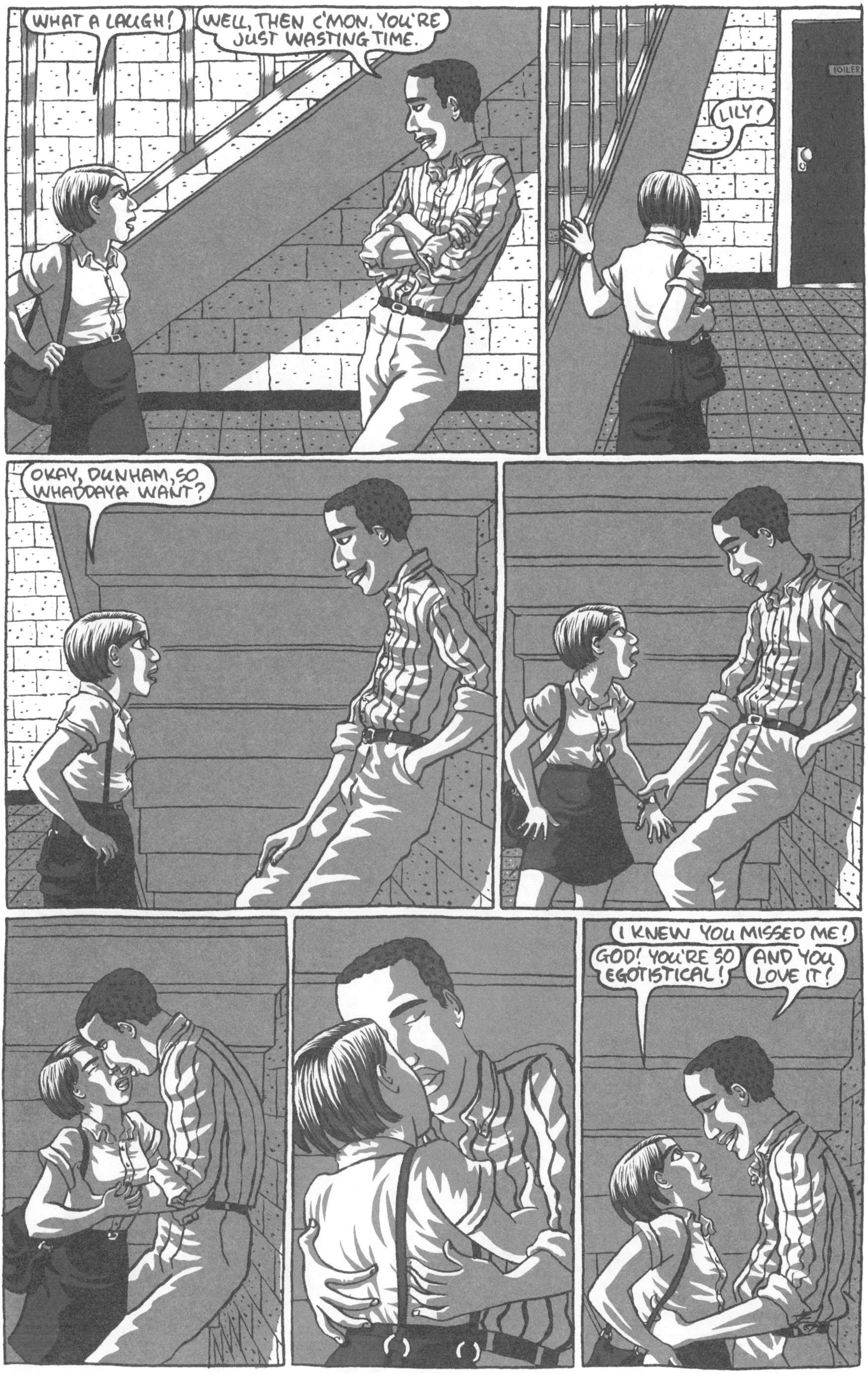
WHAT A LAUGH!
WELL, THEN C'MON. YOU'RE JUST WASTING TIME.
BOILER
LILY!
OKAY, DUNHAM, SO WHADDAYA WANT?
I KNEW YOU MISSED ME!
GOD! YOU'RE SO EGOTISTICAL!
AND YOU LOVE IT!

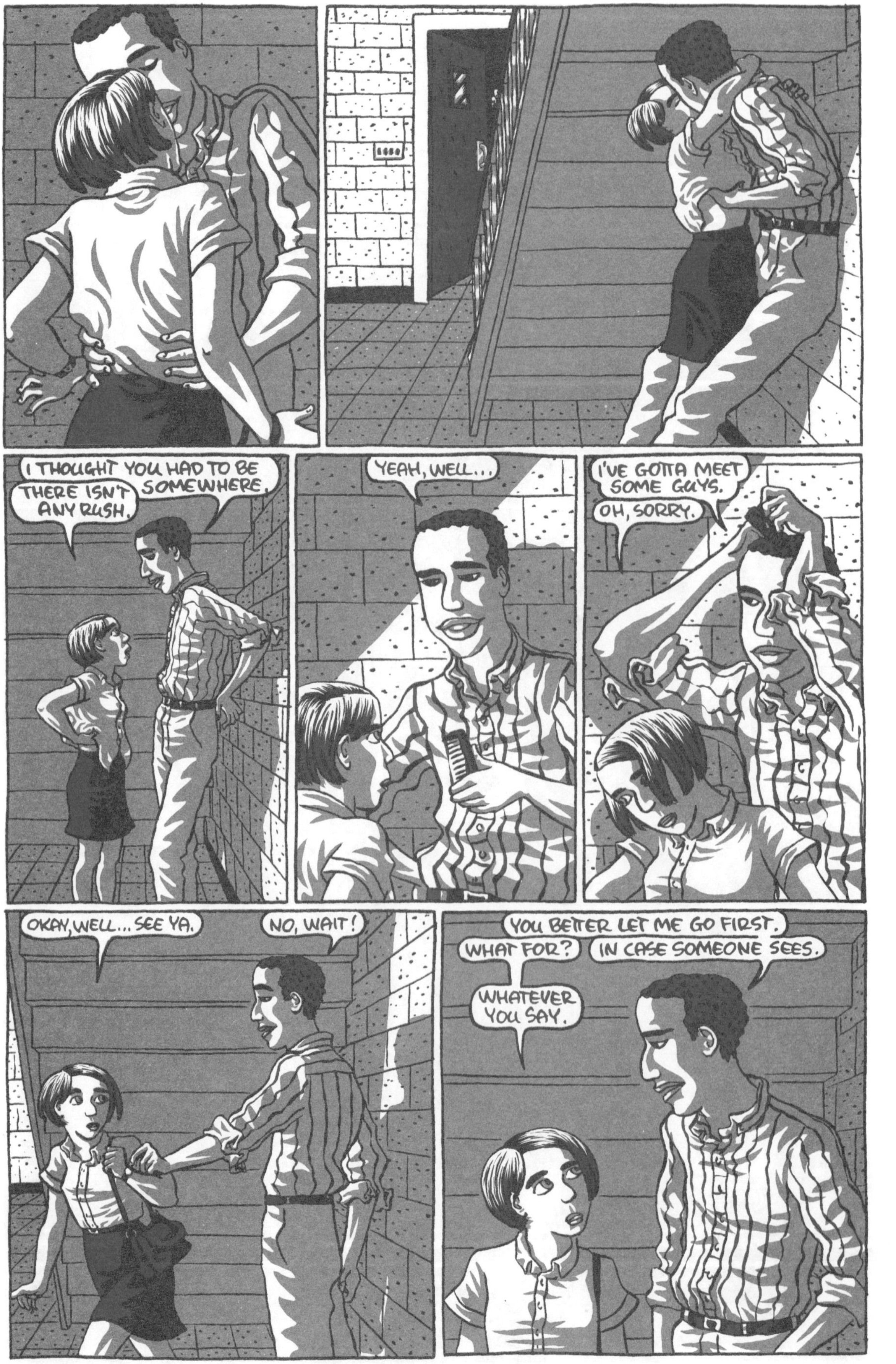
I THOUGHT YOU HAD TO BE SOMEWHERE.
THERE ISN'T ANY RUSH.
YEAH, WELL...
I'VE GOTTA MEET SOME GUYS.
OH, SORRY.
OKAY, WELL... SEE YA.
NO, WAIT!
YOU BETTER LET ME GO FIRST.
WHAT FOR?
IN CASE SOMEONE SEES.
WHATEVER YOU SAY.

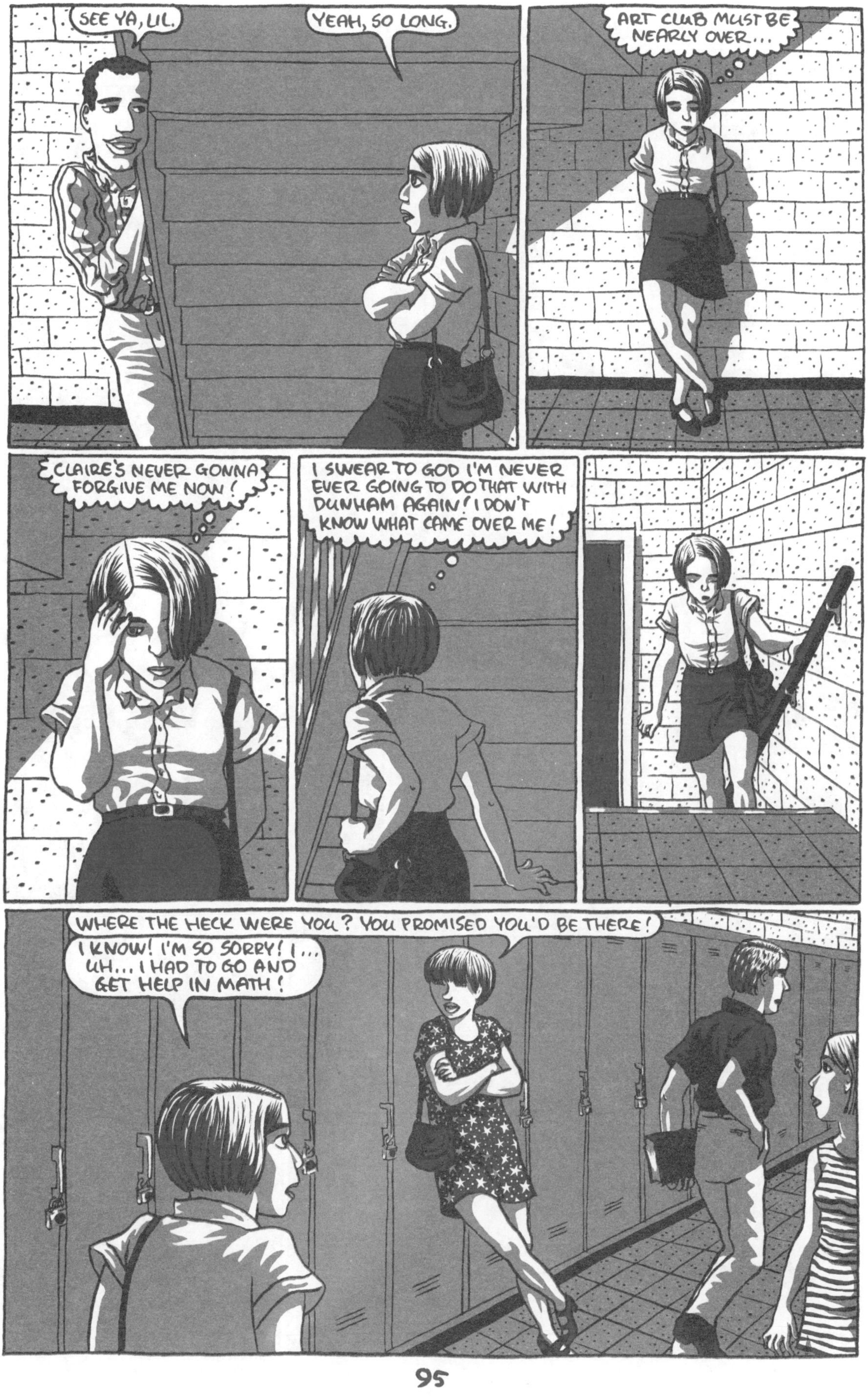
SEE YA, LIL.
YEAH, SO LONG.
ART CLUB MUST BE NEARLY OVER...
CLAIRE'S NEVER GONNA FORGIVE ME NOW!
I SWEAR TO GOD I'M NEVER EVER GOING TO DO THAT WITH DUNHAM AGAIN! I DON'T KNOW WHAT CAME OVER ME!
WHERE THE HECK WERE YOU? YOU PROMISED YOU'D BE THERE!
I KNOW! I'M SO SORRY! I... UH... I HAD TO GO AND GET HELP IN MATH!

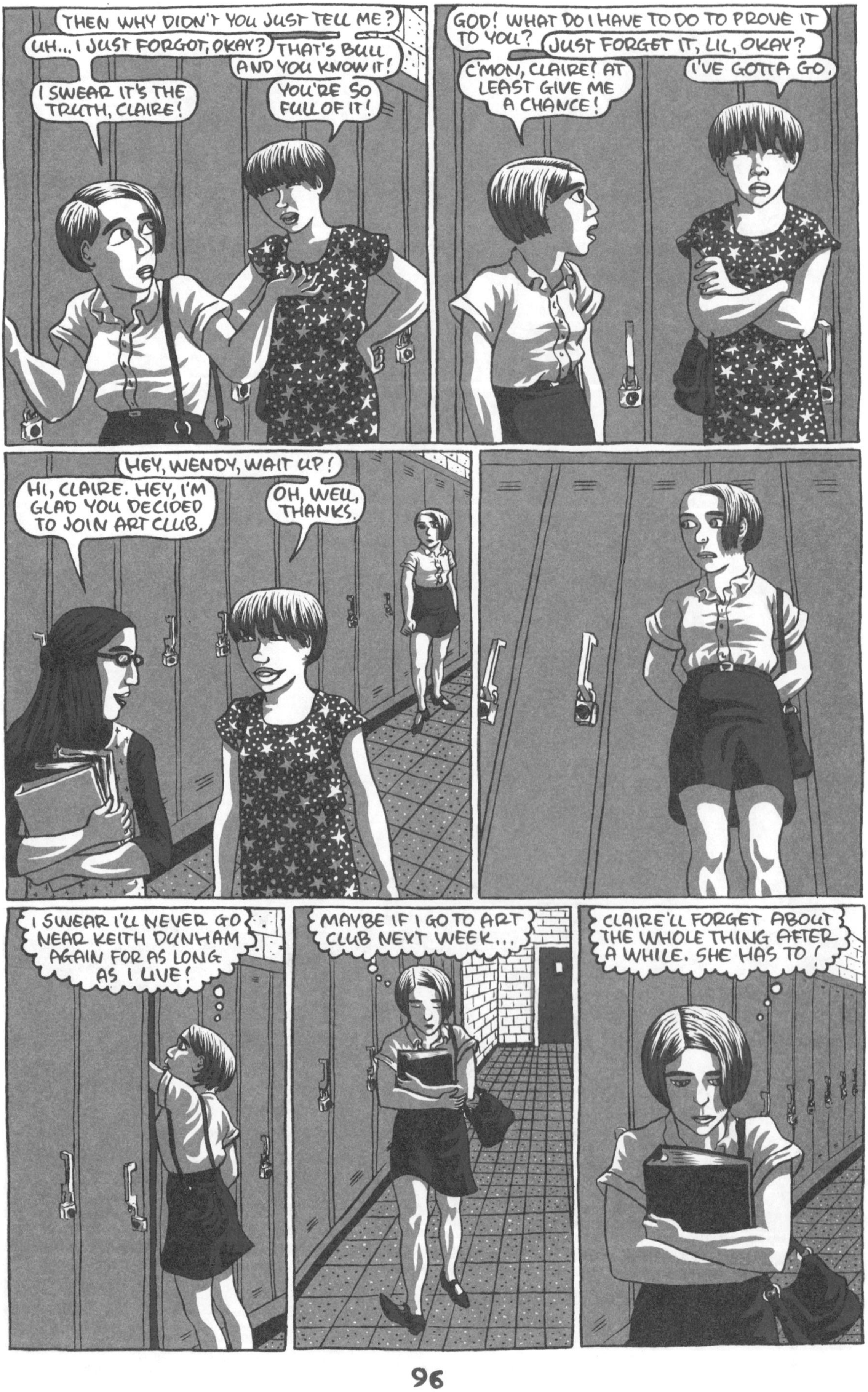
THEN WHY DIDN'T YOU JUST TELL ME?
UH... I JUST FORGOT, OKAY?
THAT'S BULL AND YOU KNOW IT!
I SWEAR IT'S THE TRUTH, CLAIRE!
YOU'RE SO FULL OF IT!
GOD! WHAT DO I HAVE TO DO TO PROVE IT TO YOU?
JUST FORGET IT, LIL, OKAY?
C'MON, CLAIRE! AT LEAST GIVE ME A CHANCE!
I'VE GOTTA GO.
HEY, WENDY, WAIT UP!
HI, CLAIRE. HEY, I'M GLAD YOU DECIDED TO JOIN ART CLUB.
OH, WELL, THANKS.
I SWEAR I'LL NEVER GO NEAR KEITH DUNHAM AGAIN FOR AS LONG AS I LIVE!
MAYBE IF I GO TO ART CLUB NEXT WEEK...
CLAIRE'LL FORGET ABOUT THE WHOLE THING AFTER A WHILE. SHE HAS TO!

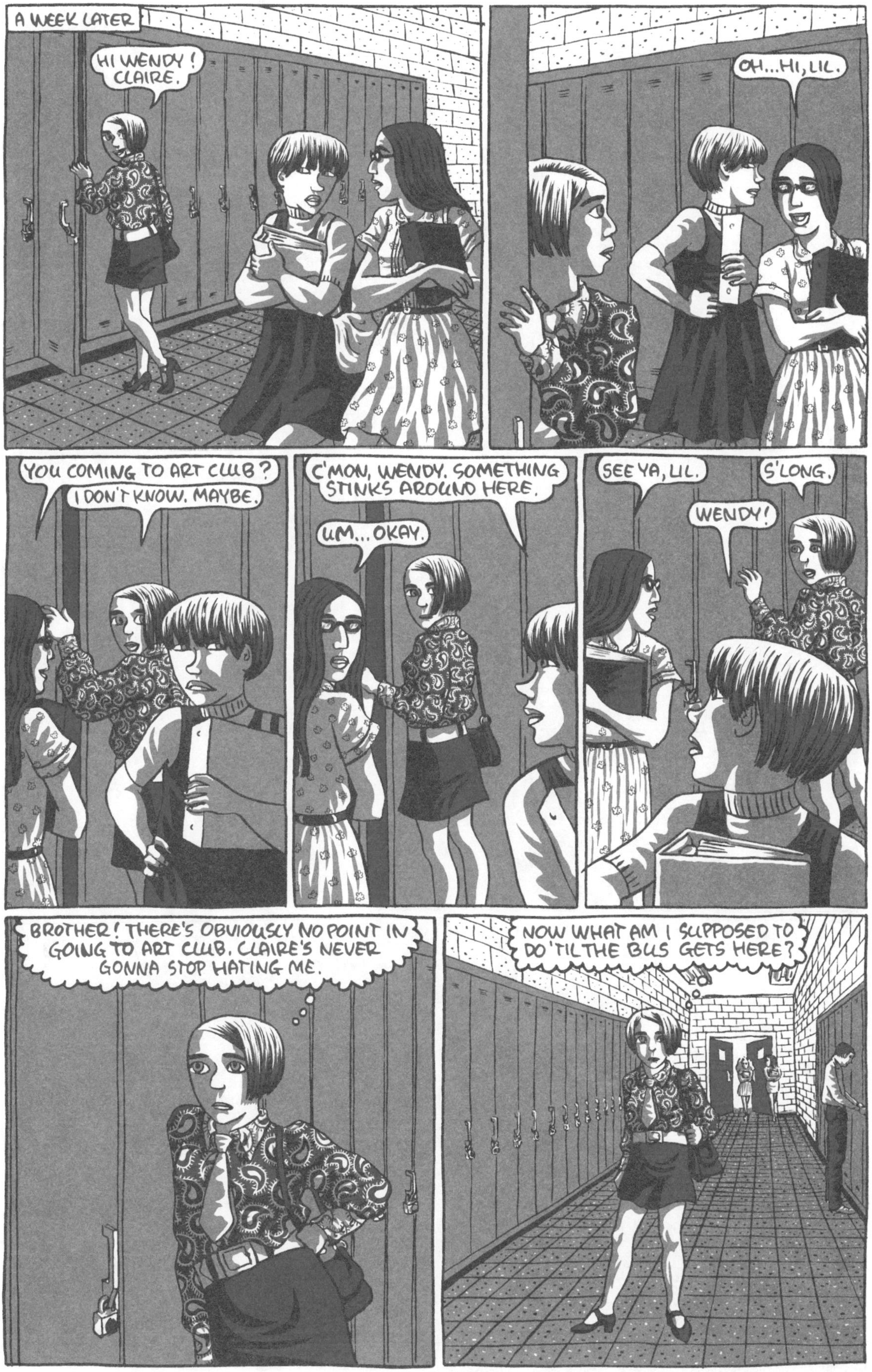
A WEEK LATER
HI WENDY! CLAIRE.
OH...HI, LIL.
YOU COMING TO ART CLUB?
I DON'T KNOW. MAYBE.
C'MON, WENDY. SOMETHING STINKS AROUND HERE.
UM...OKAY.
SEE YA, LIL.
S'LONG.
WENDY!
BROTHER! THERE'S OBVIOUSLY NO POINT IN GOING TO ART CLUB. CLAIRE'S NEVER GONNA STOP HATING ME.
NOW WHAT AM I SUPPOSED TO DO 'TIL THE BUS GETS HERE?

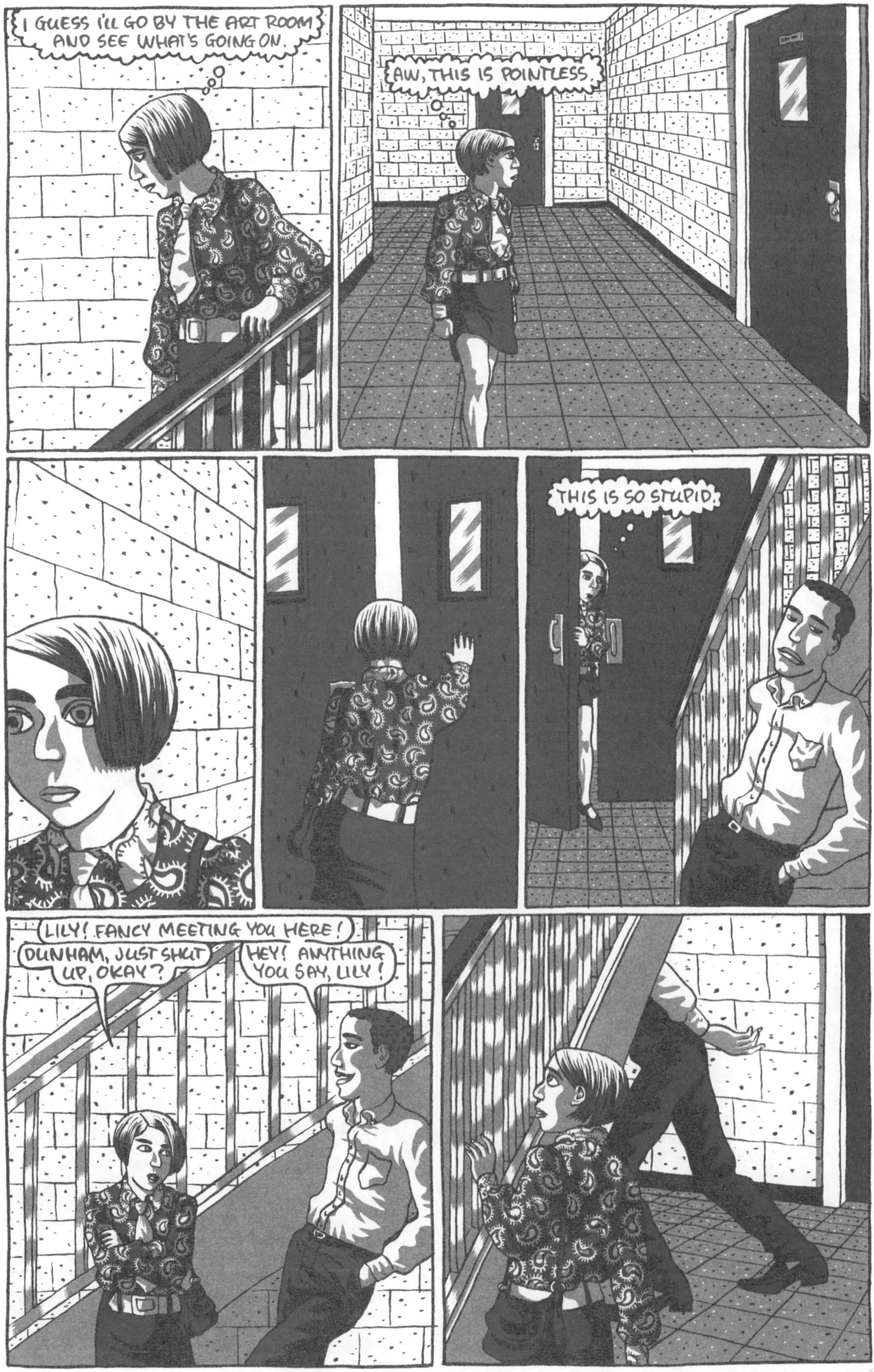
I GUESS I'LL GO BY THE ART ROOM AND SEE WHAT'S GOING ON.
AW, THIS IS POINTLESS.
THIS IS SO STUPID.
LILY! FANCY MEETING YOU HERE!
DUNHAM, JUST SHUT UP, OKAY?
HEY! ANYTHING YOU SAY, LILY!

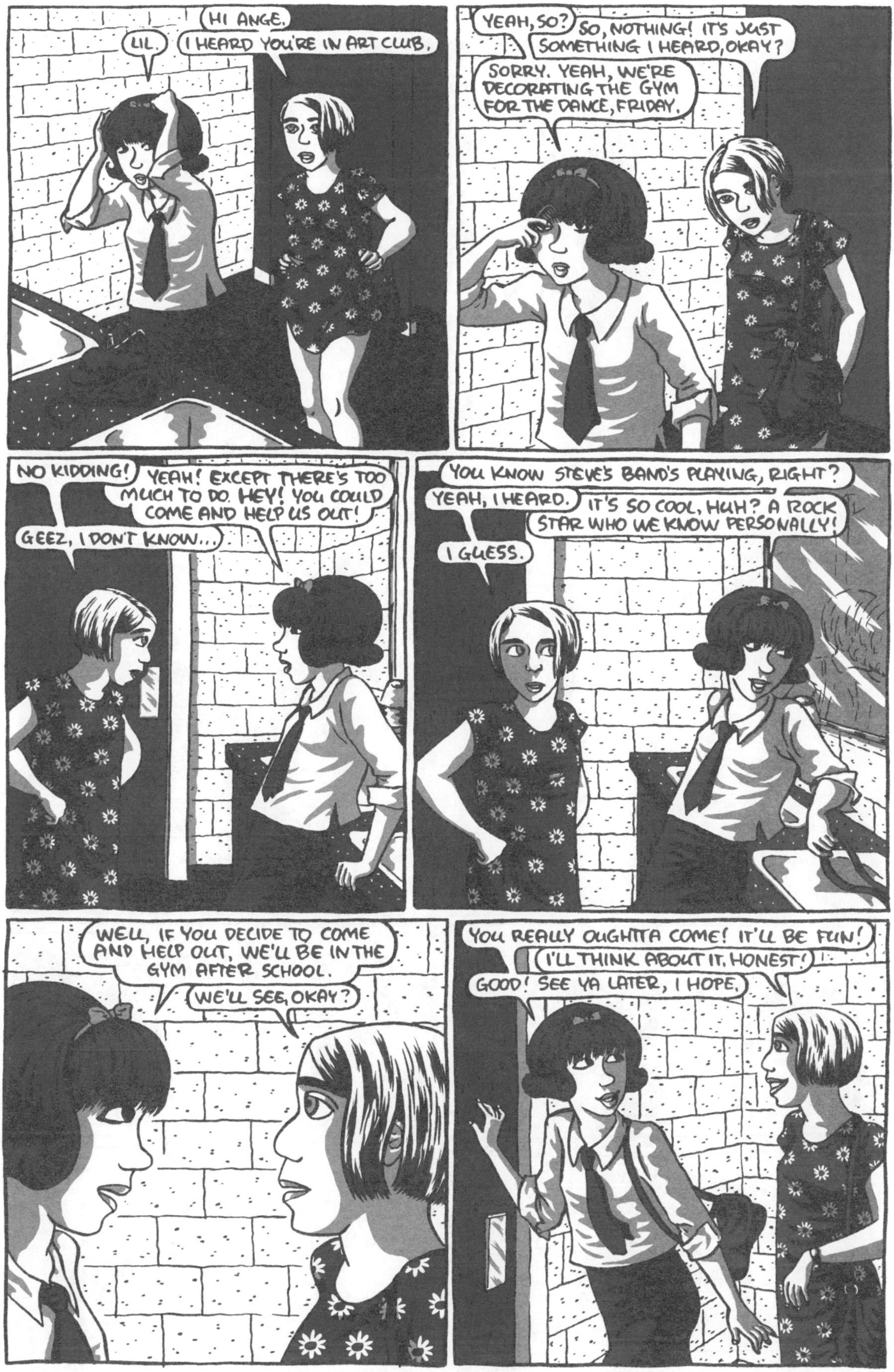
HI ANGE.
LIL.
I HEARD YOU'RE IN ART CLUB.
YEAH, SO?
SO, NOTHING! IT'S JUST SOMETHING I HEARD, OKAY?
SORRY. YEAH, WE'RE DECORATING THE GYM FOR THE DANCE, FRIDAY.
NO KIDDING!
YEAH! EXCEPT THERE'S TOO MUCH TO DO. HEY! YOU COULD COME AND HELP US OUT!
GEEZ, I DON'T KNOW...
YOU KNOW STEVE'S BAND'S PLAYING, RIGHT?
YEAH, I HEARD.
IT'S SO COOL, HUH? A ROCK STAR WHO WE KNOW PERSONALLY!
I GUESS.
WELL, IF YOU DECIDE TO COME AND HELP OUT, WE'LL BE IN THE GYM AFTER SCHOOL.
WE'LL SEE, OKAY?
YOU REALLY OUGHTTA COME! IT'LL BE FUN!
I'LL THINK ABOUT IT. HONEST!
GOOD! SEE YA LATER, I HOPE.

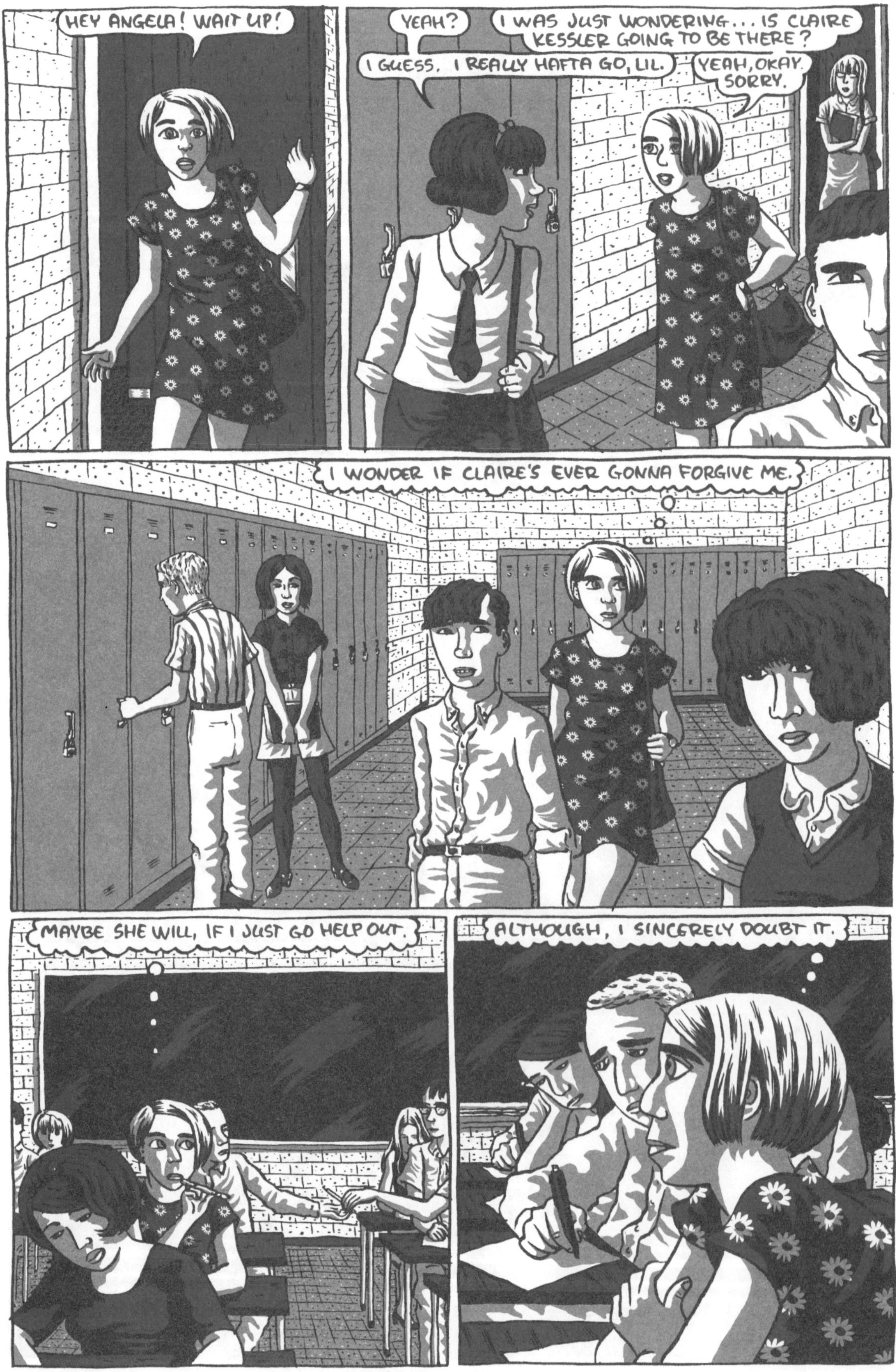
HEY ANGELA! WAIT UP!
YEAH?
I WAS JUST WONDERING... IS CLAIRE KESSLER GOING TO BE THERE?
I GUESS. I REALLY HAFTA GO, LIL.
YEAH, OKAY. SORRY.
I WONDER IF CLAIRE'S EVER GONNA FORGIVE ME.
MAYBE SHE WILL, IF I JUST GO HELP OUT.
ALTHOUGH, I SINCERELY DOUBT IT.

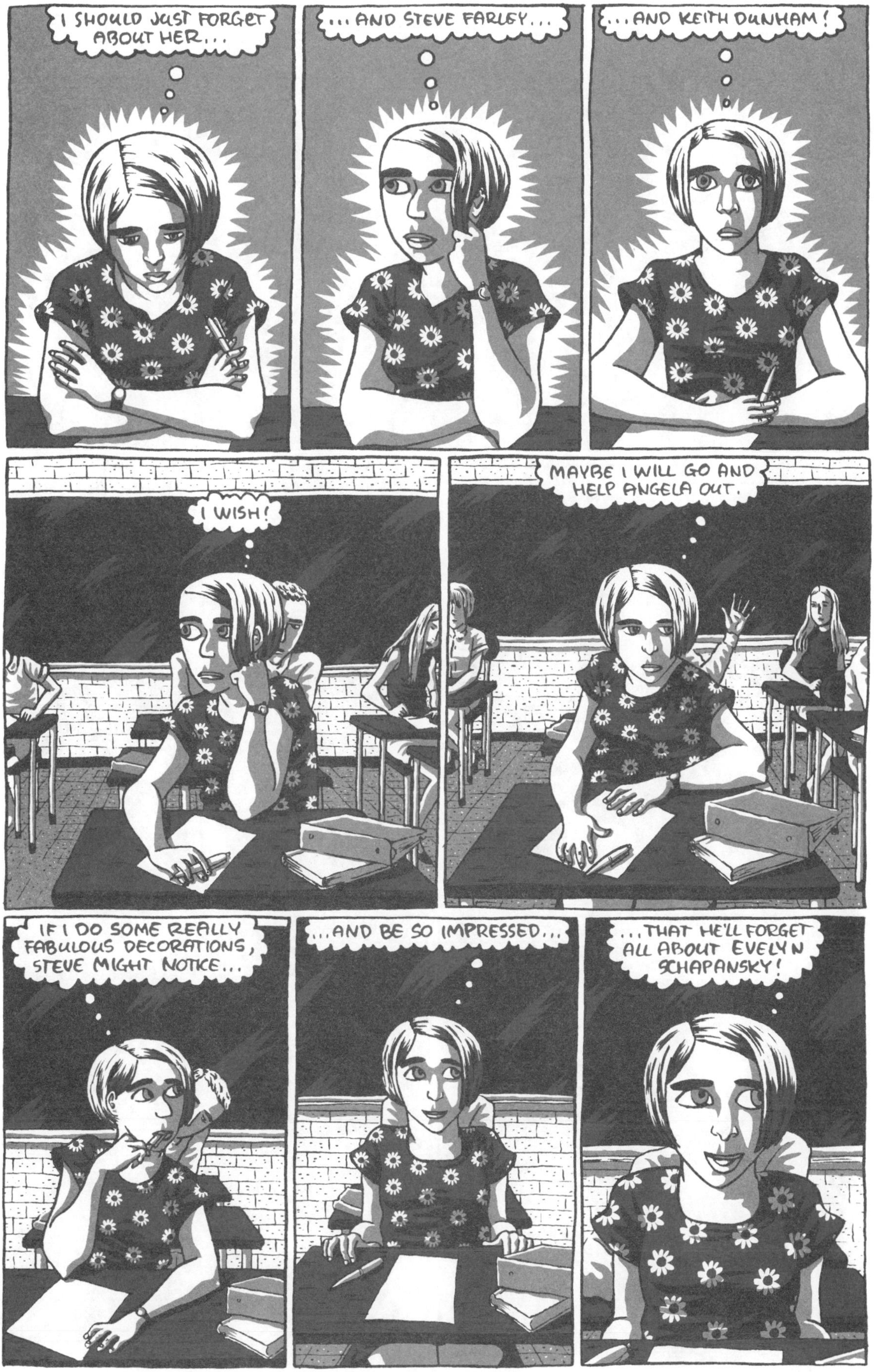
I SHOULD JUST FORGET ABOUT HER...
...AND STEVE FARLEY...
...AND KEITH DUNHAM!
I WISH!
MAYBE I WILL GO AND HELP ANGELA OUT.
IF I DO SOME REALLY FABULOUS DECORATIONS, STEVE MIGHT NOTICE...
...AND BE SO IMPRESSED...
...THAT HE'LL FORGET ALL ABOUT EVELYN SCHAPANSKY!

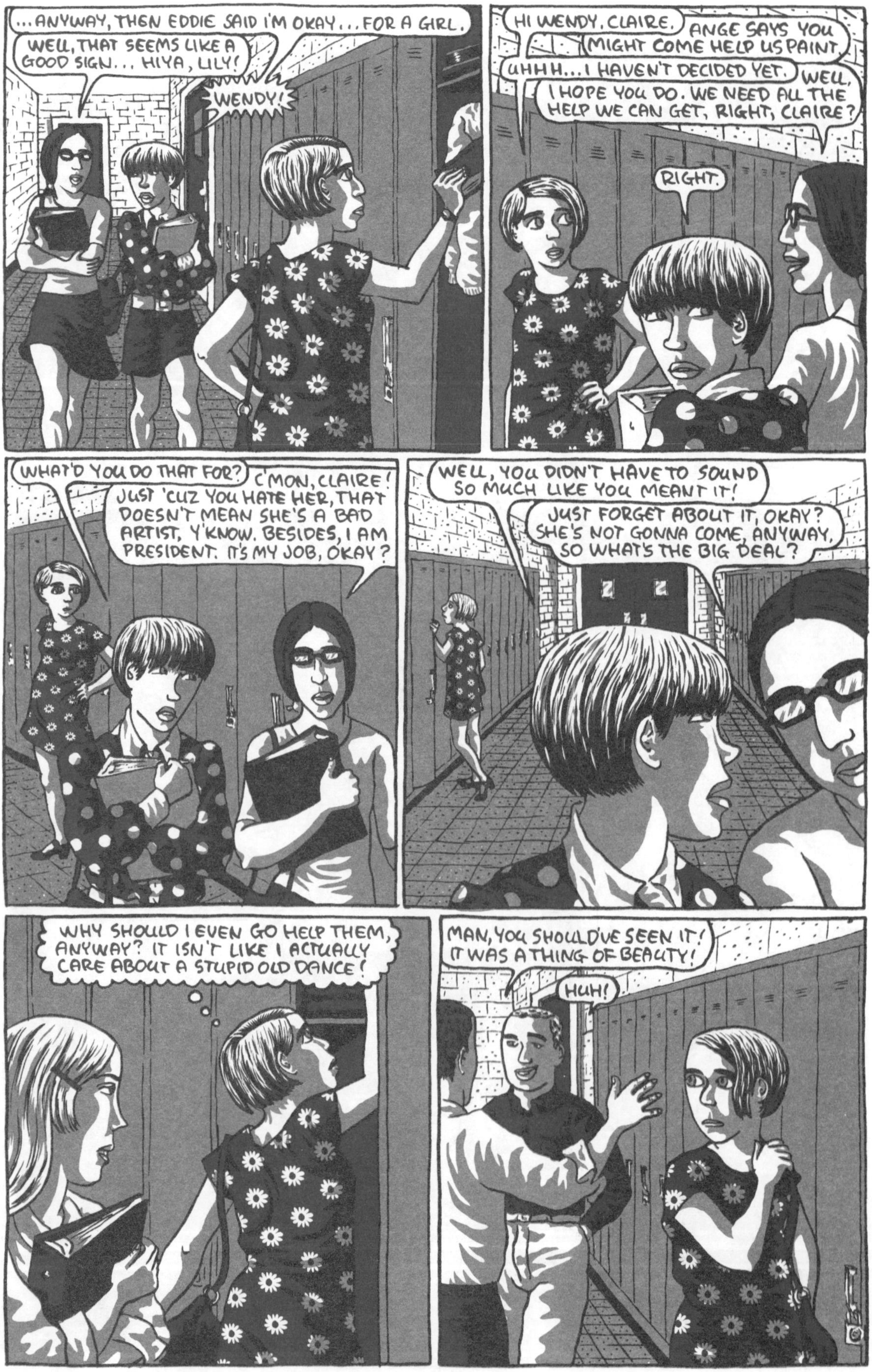

...ANYWAY, THEN EDDIE SAID I'M OKAY... FOR A GIRL.
WELL, THAT SEEMS LIKE A GOOD SIGN... HIYA, LILY!
WENDY!
HI WENDY, CLAIRE.
ANGE SAYS YOU MIGHT COME HELP US PAINT.
UHHH... I HAVEN'T DECIDED YET.
WELL, I HOPE YOU DO. WE NEED ALL THE HELP WE CAN GET, RIGHT, CLAIRE?
RIGHT.
WHAT'D YOU DO THAT FOR?
C'MON, CLAIRE! JUST 'CUZ YOU HATE HER, THAT DOESN'T MEAN SHE'S A BAD ARTIST, Y'KNOW. BESIDES, I AM PRESIDENT. IT'S MY JOB, OKAY?
WELL, YOU DIDN'T HAVE TO SOUND SO MUCH LIKE YOU MEANT IT!
JUST FORGET ABOUT IT, OKAY? SHE'S NOT GONNA COME, ANYWAY, SO WHAT'S THE BIG DEAL?
WHY SHOULD I EVEN GO HELP THEM, ANYWAY? IT ISN'T LIKE I ACTUALLY CARE ABOUT A STUPID OLD DANCE!
MAN, YOU SHOULD'VE SEEN IT! IT WAS A THING OF BEAUTY!
HUH!

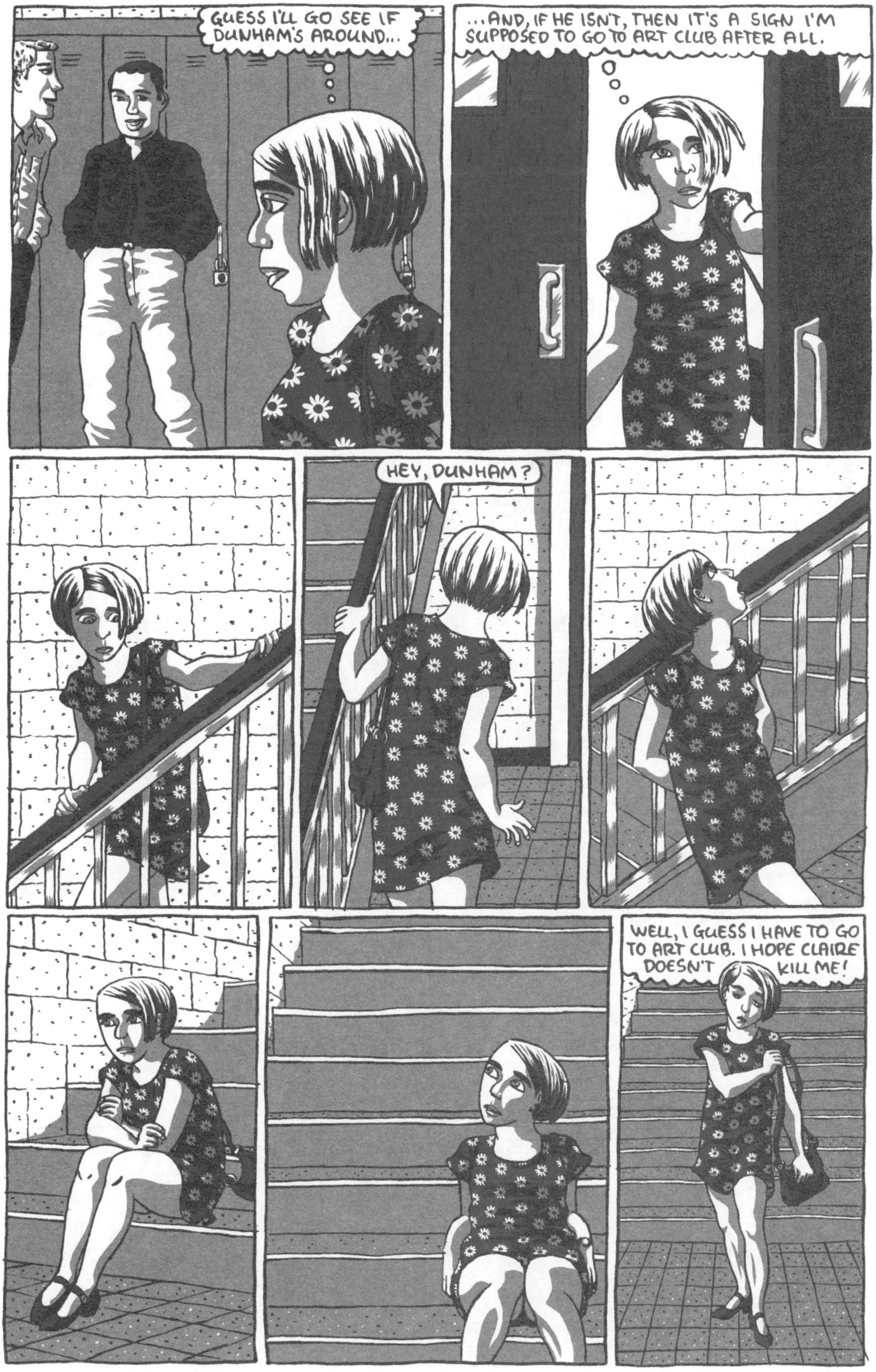
GUESS I'LL GO SEE IF DUNHAM'S AROUND...
...AND, IF HE ISN'T, THEN IT'S A SIGN I'M SUPPOSED TO GO TO ART CLUB AFTER ALL.
HEY, DUNHAM?
WELL, I GUESS I HAVE TO GO TO ART CLUB. I HOPE CLAIRE DOESN'T KILL ME!

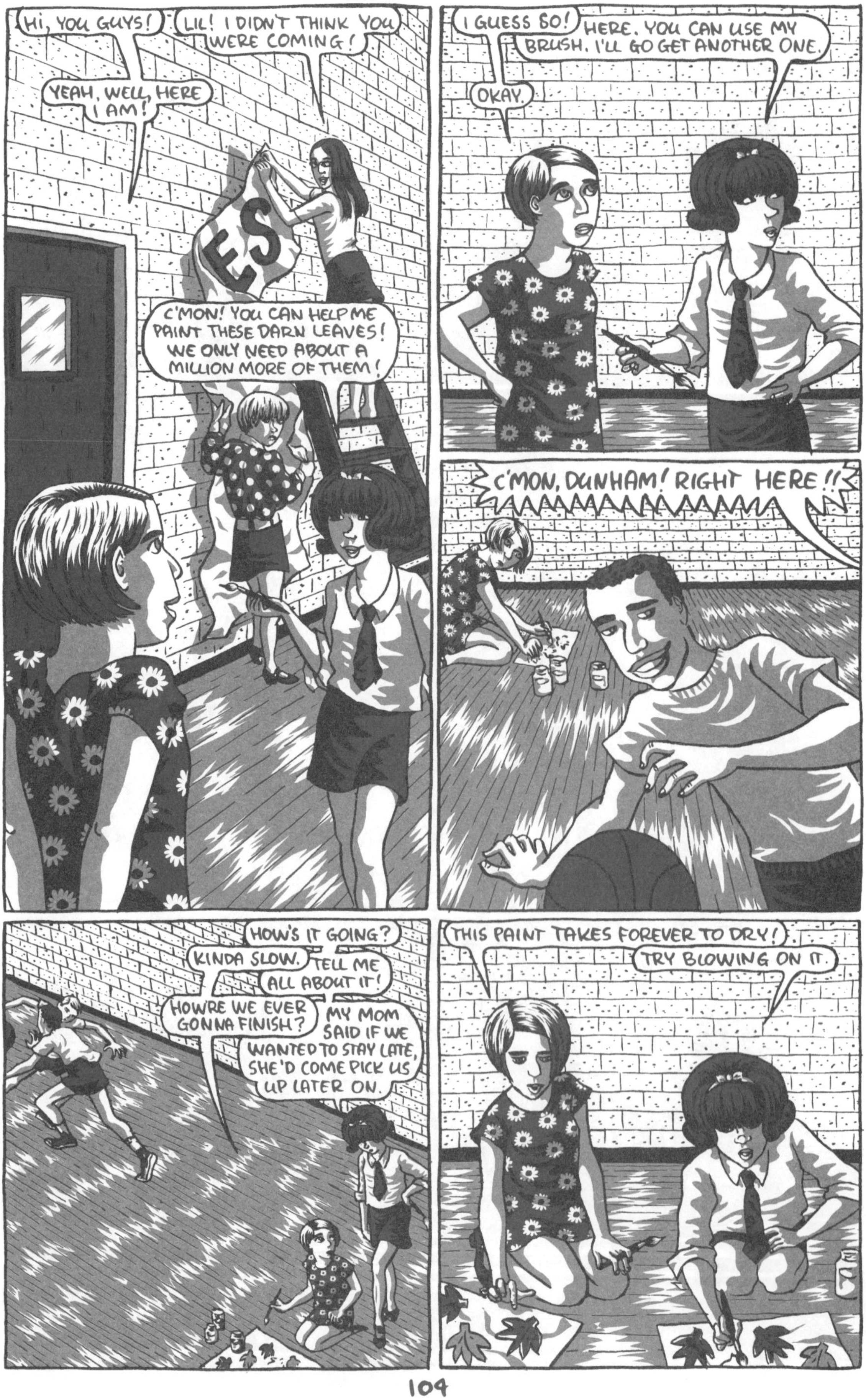
HI, YOU GUYS!
LIL! I DIDN'T THINK YOU WERE COMING!
YEAH, WELL, HERE I AM!
C'MON! YOU CAN HELP ME PAINT THESE DARN LEAVES! WE ONLY NEED ABOUT A MILLION MORE OF THEM!
I GUESS SO!
HERE. YOU CAN USE MY BRUSH. I'LL GO GET ANOTHER ONE.
OKAY.
C'MON, DUNHAM! RIGHT HERE!!
HOW'S IT GOING?
KINDA SLOW.
TELL ME ALL ABOUT IT!
HOW'RE WE EVER GONNA FINISH?
MY MOM SAID IF WE WANTED TO STAY LATE, SHE'D COME PICK US UP LATER ON.
THIS PAINT TAKES FOREVER TO DRY!
TRY BLOWING ON IT.

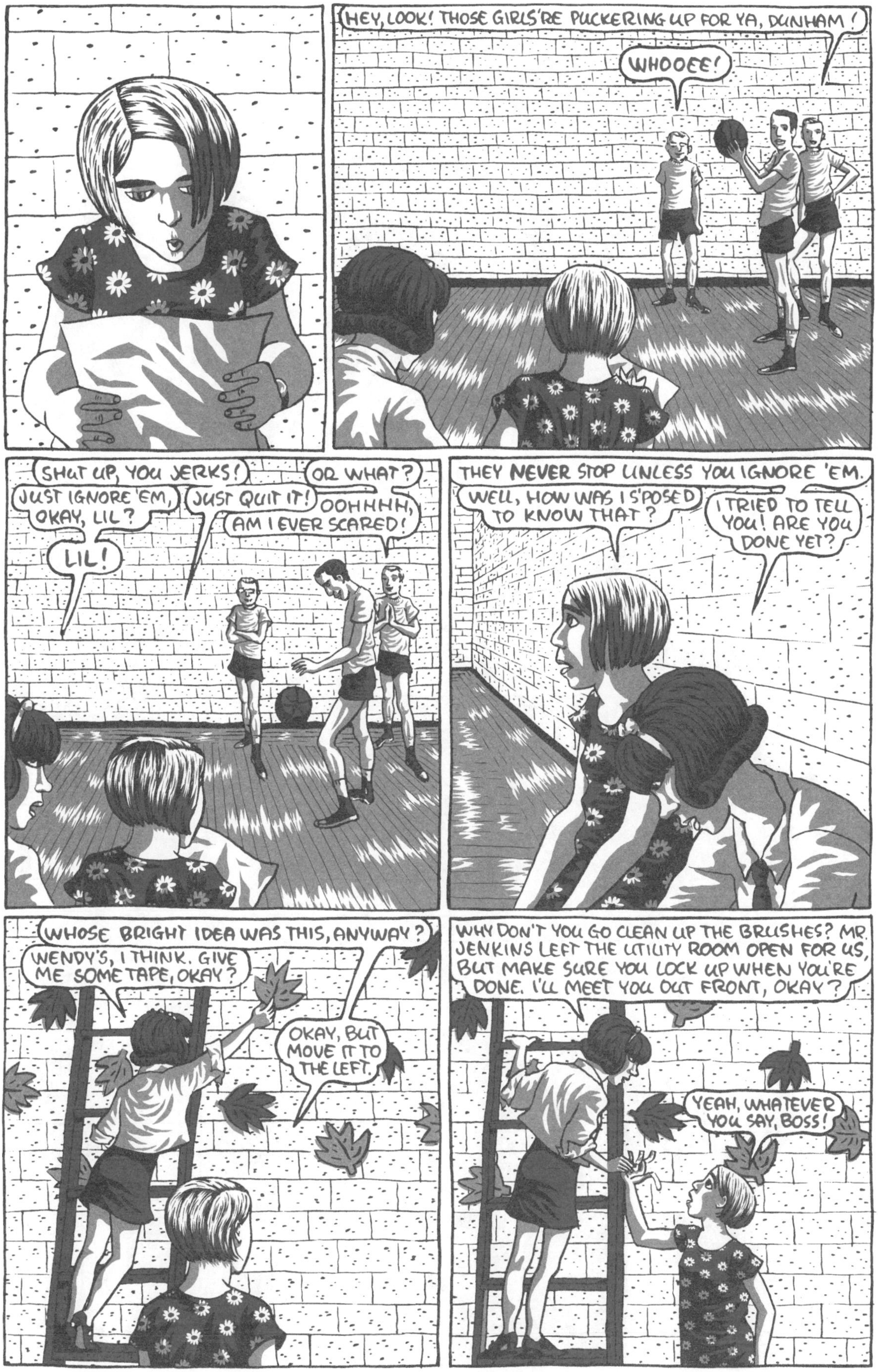
HEY, LOOK! THOSE GIRLS'RE PUCKERING UP FOR YA, DUNHAM!
WHOOEE!
SHUT UP, YOU JERKS!
OR WHAT?
JUST IGNORE 'EM, OKAY, LIL?
JUST QUIT IT!
OOHHHHH, AM I EVER SCARED!
LIL!
THEY NEVER STOP UNLESS YOU IGNORE 'EM.
WELL, HOW WAS I S'POSED TO KNOW THAT?
I TRIED TO TELL YOU! ARE YOU DONE YET?
WHOSE BRIGHT IDEA WAS THIS, ANYWAY?
WENDY'S, I THINK. GIVE ME SOME TAPE, OKAY?
OKAY, BUT MOVE IT TO THE LEFT.
WHY DON'T YOU GO CLEAN UP THE BRUSHES? MR JENKINS LEFT THE UTILITY ROOM OPEN FOR US, BUT MAKE SURE YOU LOCK UP WHEN YOU'RE DONE. I'LL MEET YOU OUT FRONT, OKAY?
YEAH, WHATEVER YOU SAY, BOSS!

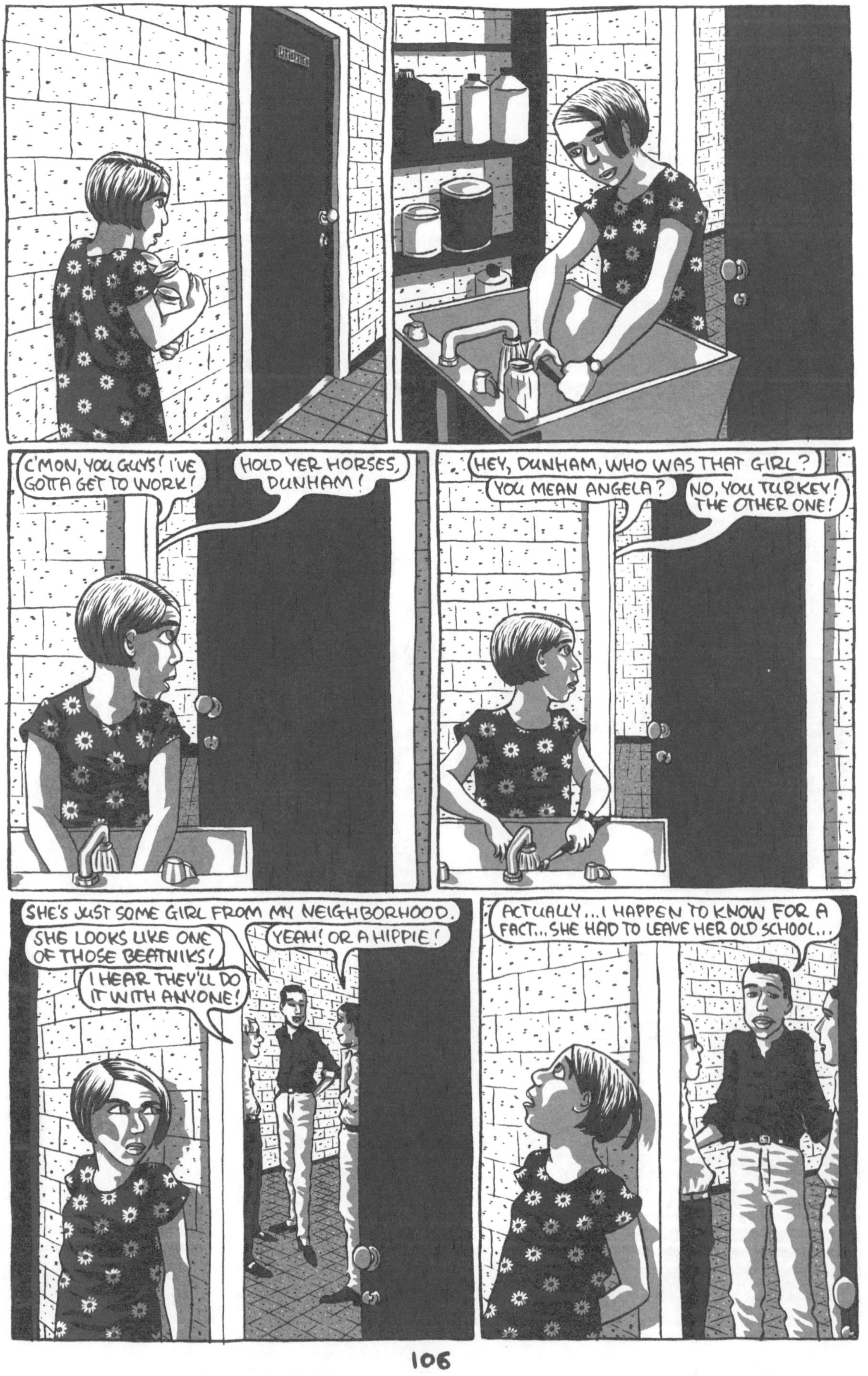
C'MON, YOU GUYS! I'VE GOTTA GET TO WORK!
HOLD YER HORSES, DUNHAM!
HEY, DUNHAM, WHO WAS THAT GIRL?
YOU MEAN ANGELA?
NO, YOU TURKEY! THE OTHER ONE!
SHE'S JUST SOME GIRL FROM MY NEIGHBORHOOD.
SHE LOOKS LIKE ONE OF THOSE BEATNIKS!
YEAH! OR A HIPPIE!
I HEAR THEY'LL DO IT WITH ANYONE!
ACTUALLY... I HAPPEN TO KNOW FOR A FACT... SHE HAD TO LEAVE HER OLD SCHOOL...

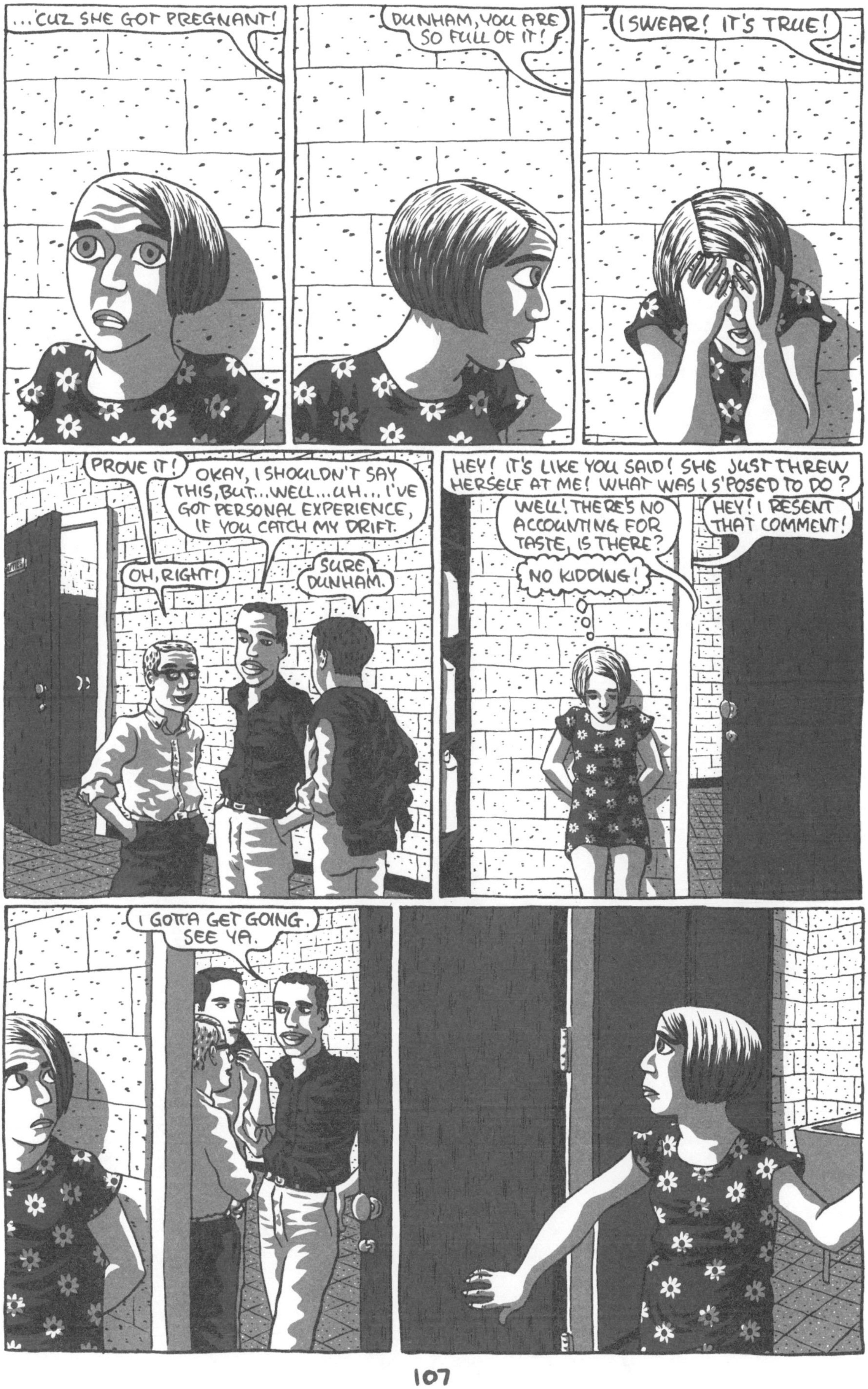
...CUZ SHE GOT PREGNANT!
DUNHAM, YOU ARE SO FULL OF IT!
I SWEAR! IT'S TRUE!
PROVE IT!
OKAY, I SHOULDN'T SAY THIS, BUT... WELL... UH... I'VE GOT PERSONAL EXPERIENCE, IF YOU CATCH MY DRIFT.
OH, RIGHT!
SURE, DUNHAM.
HEY! IT'S LIKE YOU SAID! SHE JUST THREW HERSELF AT ME! WHAT WAS I S'POSED TO DO?
WELL! THERE'S NO ACCOUNTING FOR TASTE, IS THERE?
HEY! I RESENT THAT COMMENT!
NO KIDDING!
I GOTTA GET GOING. SEE YA.

PART
FIVE

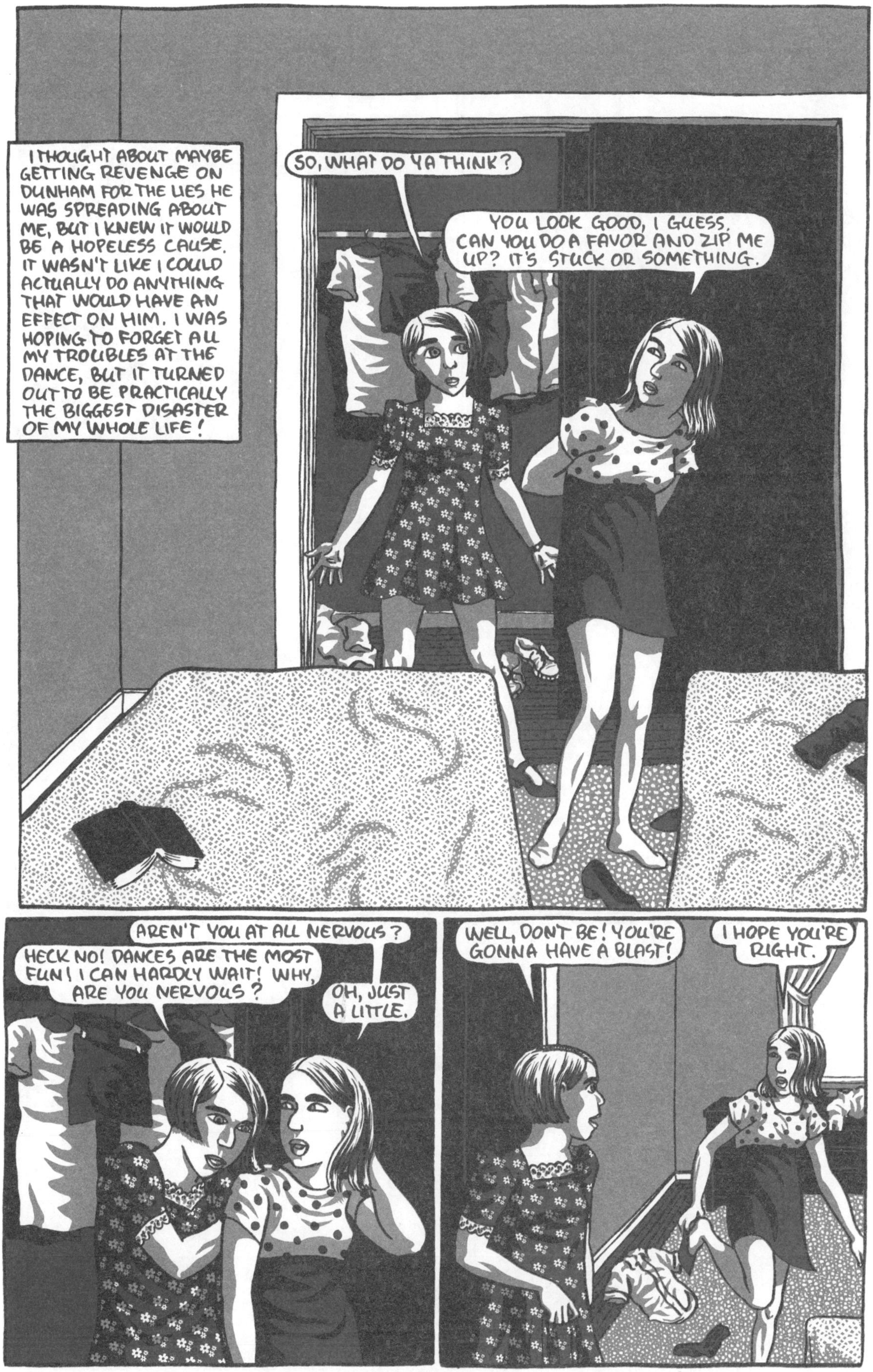
I THOUGHT ABOUT MAYBE GETTING REVENGE ON DUNHAM FOR THE LIES HE WAS SPREADING ABOUT ME, BUT I KNEW IT WOULD BE A HOPELESS CAUSE. IT WASN'T LIKE I COULD ACTUALLY DO ANYTHING THAT WOULD HAVE AN EFFECT ON HIM. I WAS HOPING TO FORGET ALL MY TROUBLES AT THE DANCE, BUT IT TURNED OUT TO BE PRACTICALLY THE BIGGEST DISASTER OF MY WHOLE LIFE!
SO, WHAT DO YA THINK?
YOU LOOK GOOD, I GUESS. CAN YOU DO A FAVOR AND ZIP ME UP? IT'S STUCK OR SOMETHING.
AREN'T YOU AT ALL NERVOUS?
HECK NO! DANCES ARE THE MOST FUN! I CAN HARDLY WAIT! WHY, ARE YOU NERVOUS?
OH, JUST A LITTLE.
WELL, DON'T BE! YOU'RE GONNA HAVE A BLAST!
I HOPE YOU'RE RIGHT.

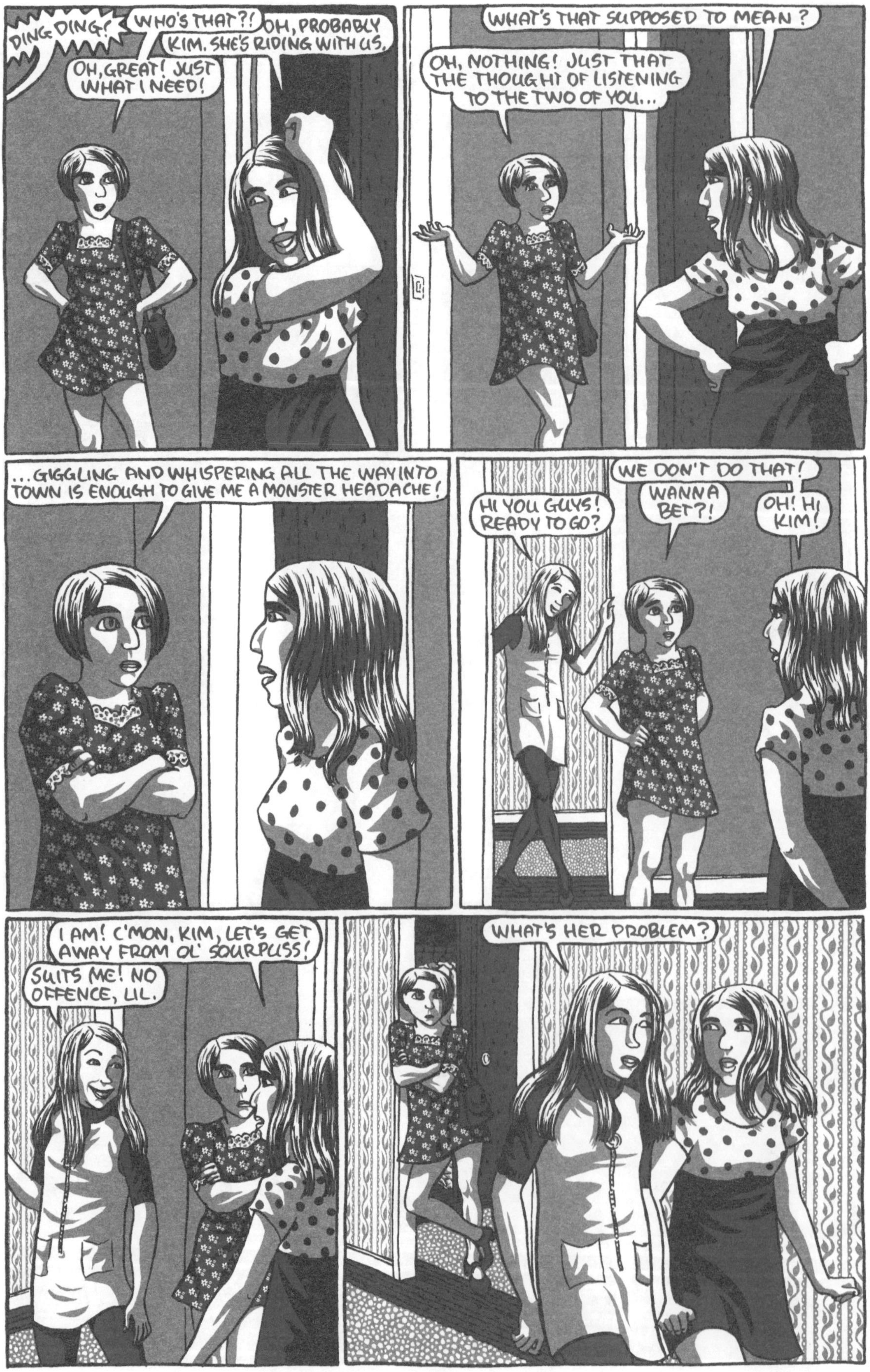
DING DING!
WHO'S THAT?!
OH, PROBABLY KIM. SHE'S RIDING WITH US.
OH, GREAT! JUST WHAT I NEED!
WHAT'S THAT SUPPOSED TO MEAN?
OH, NOTHING! JUST THAT THE THOUGHT OF LISTENING TO THE TWO OF YOU...
...GIGGLING AND WHISPERING ALL THE WAY INTO TOWN IS ENOUGH TO GIVE ME A MONSTER HEADACHE!
HI YOU GUYS! READY TO GO?
WE DON'T DO THAT!
WANNA BET?!
OH! HI KIM!
I AM! C'MON, KIM, LET'S GET AWAY FROM OL' SOURPUSS!
SUITS ME! NO OFFENCE, LIL.
WHAT'S HER PROBLEM?

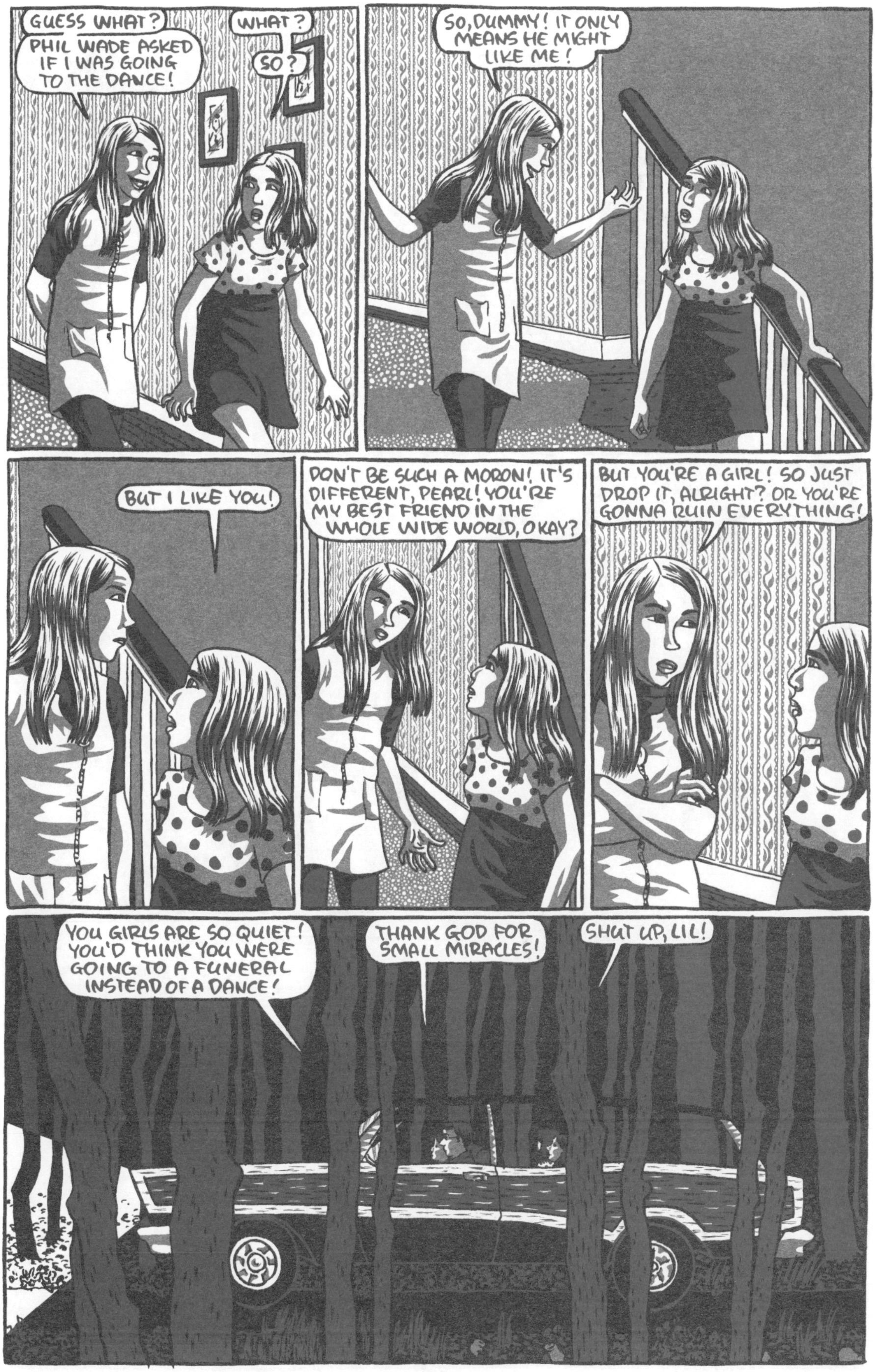
GUESS WHAT?
PHIL WADE ASKED IF I WAS GOING TO THE DANCE!
WHAT?
SO?
SO, DUMMY! IT ONLY MEANS HE MIGHT LIKE ME!
BUT I LIKE YOU!
DON'T BE SUCH A MORON! IT'S DIFFERENT, PEARL! YOU'RE MY BEST FRIEND IN THE WHOLE WIDE WORLD, OKAY?
BUT YOU'RE A GIRL! SO JUST DROP IT, ALRIGHT? OR YOU'RE GONNA RUIN EVERYTHING!
YOU GIRLS ARE SO QUIET! YOU'D THINK YOU WERE GOING TO A FUNERAL INSTEAD OF A DANCE!
THANK GOD FOR SMALL MIRACLES!
SHUT UP, LIL!

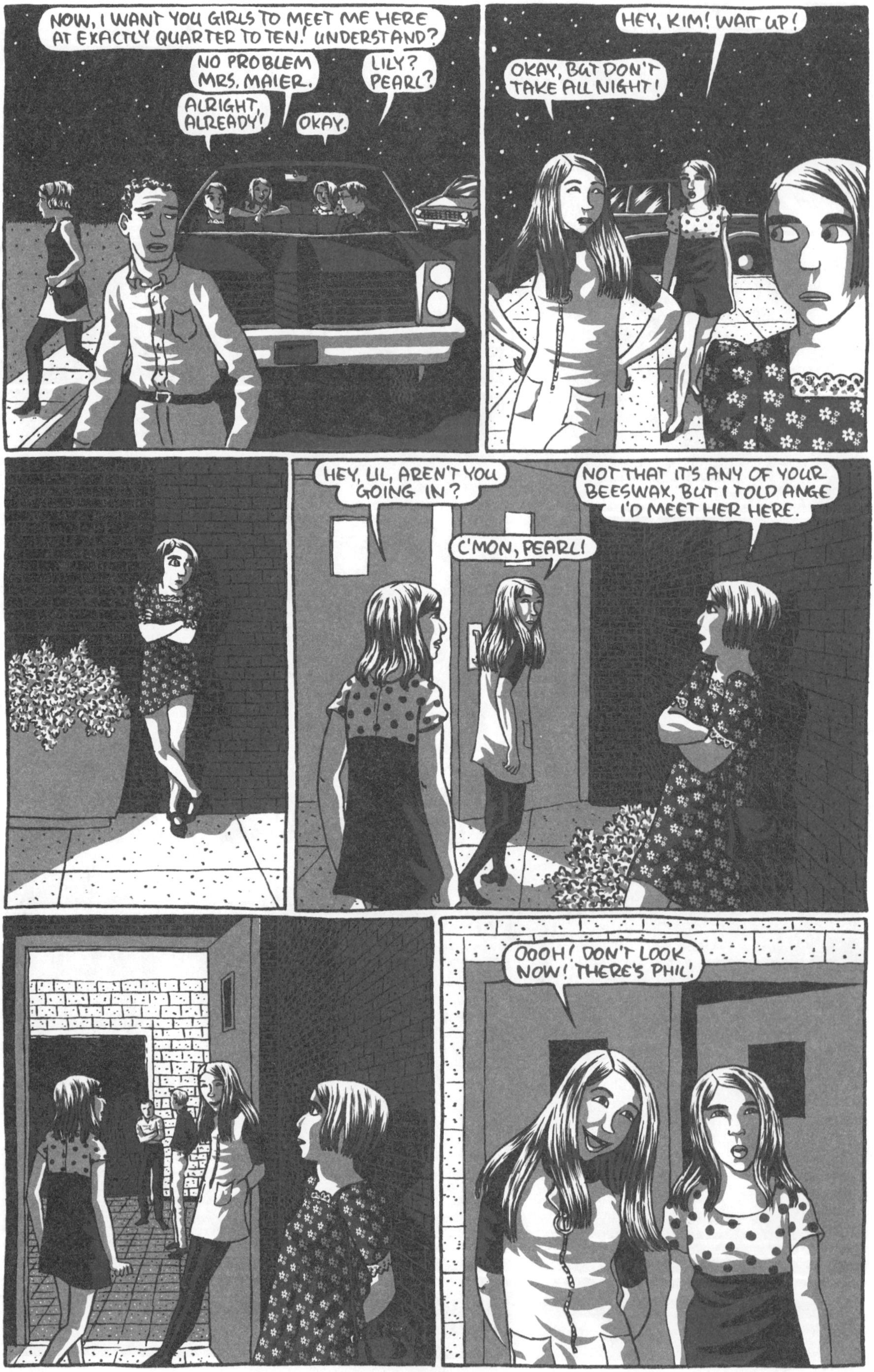
NOW, I WANT YOU GIRLS TO MEET ME HERE AT EXACTLY QUARTER TO TEN! UNDERSTAND?
NO PROBLEM MRS. MAIER.
LILY? PEARL?
ALRIGHT, ALREADY!
OKAY.
HEY, KIM! WAIT UP!
OKAY, BUT DON'T TAKE ALL NIGHT!
HEY, LIL, AREN'T YOU GOING IN?
C'MON, PEARL!
NOT THAT IT'S ANY OF YOUR BEESWAX, BUT I TOLD ANGE I'D MEET HER HERE.
OOOH! DON'T LOOK NOW! THERE'S PHIL!

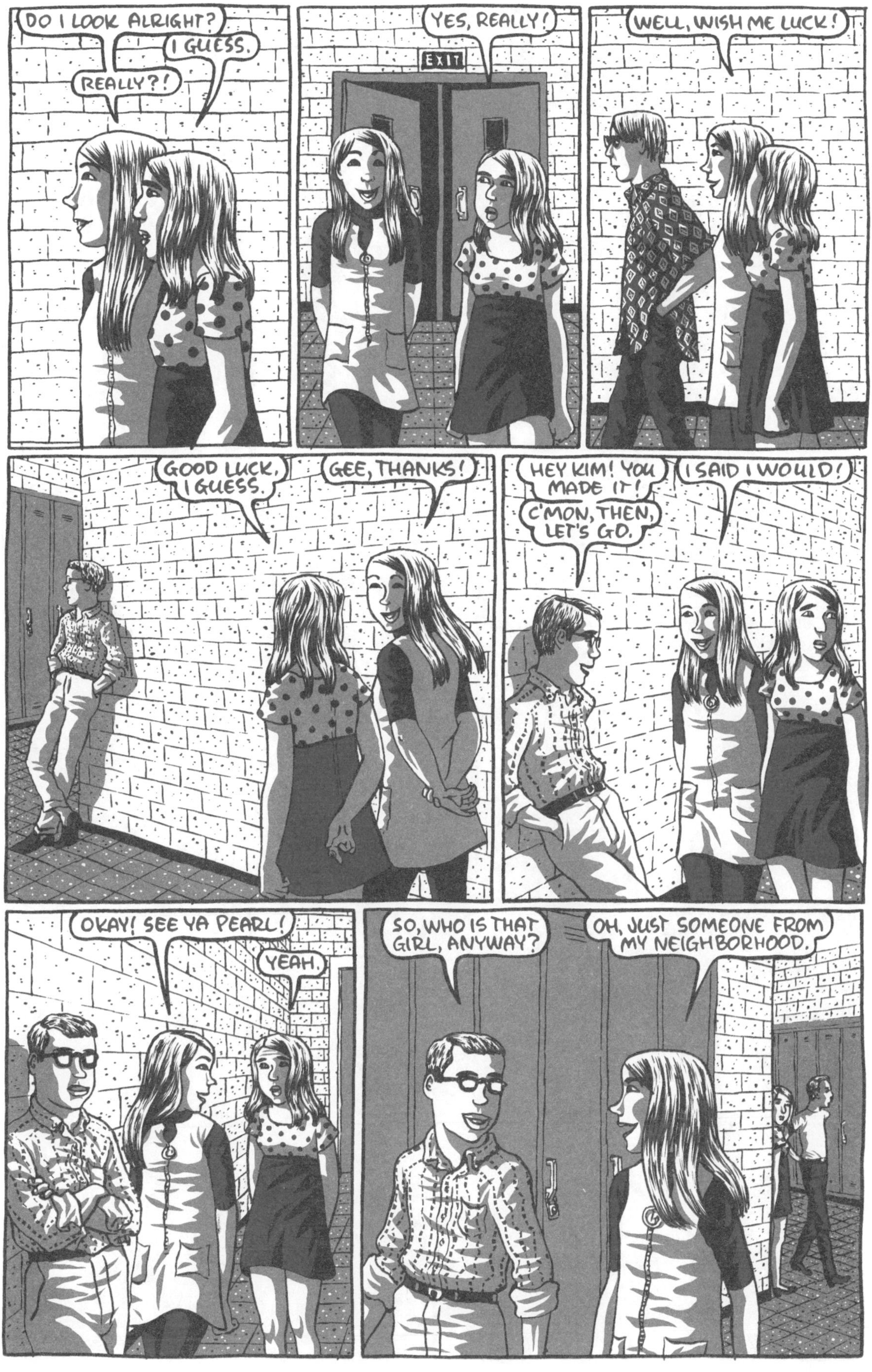
DO I LOOK ALRIGHT?
I GUESS.
REALLY?!
YES, REALLY!
EXIT
WELL, WISH ME LUCK!
GOOD LUCK, I GUESS.
GEE, THANKS!
HEY KIM! YOU MADE IT!
I SAID I WOULD!
C'MON, THEN, LET'S GO.
OKAY! SEE YA PEARL!
YEAH.
SO, WHO IS THAT GIRL, ANYWAY?
OH, JUST SOMEONE FROM MY NEIGHBORHOOD.

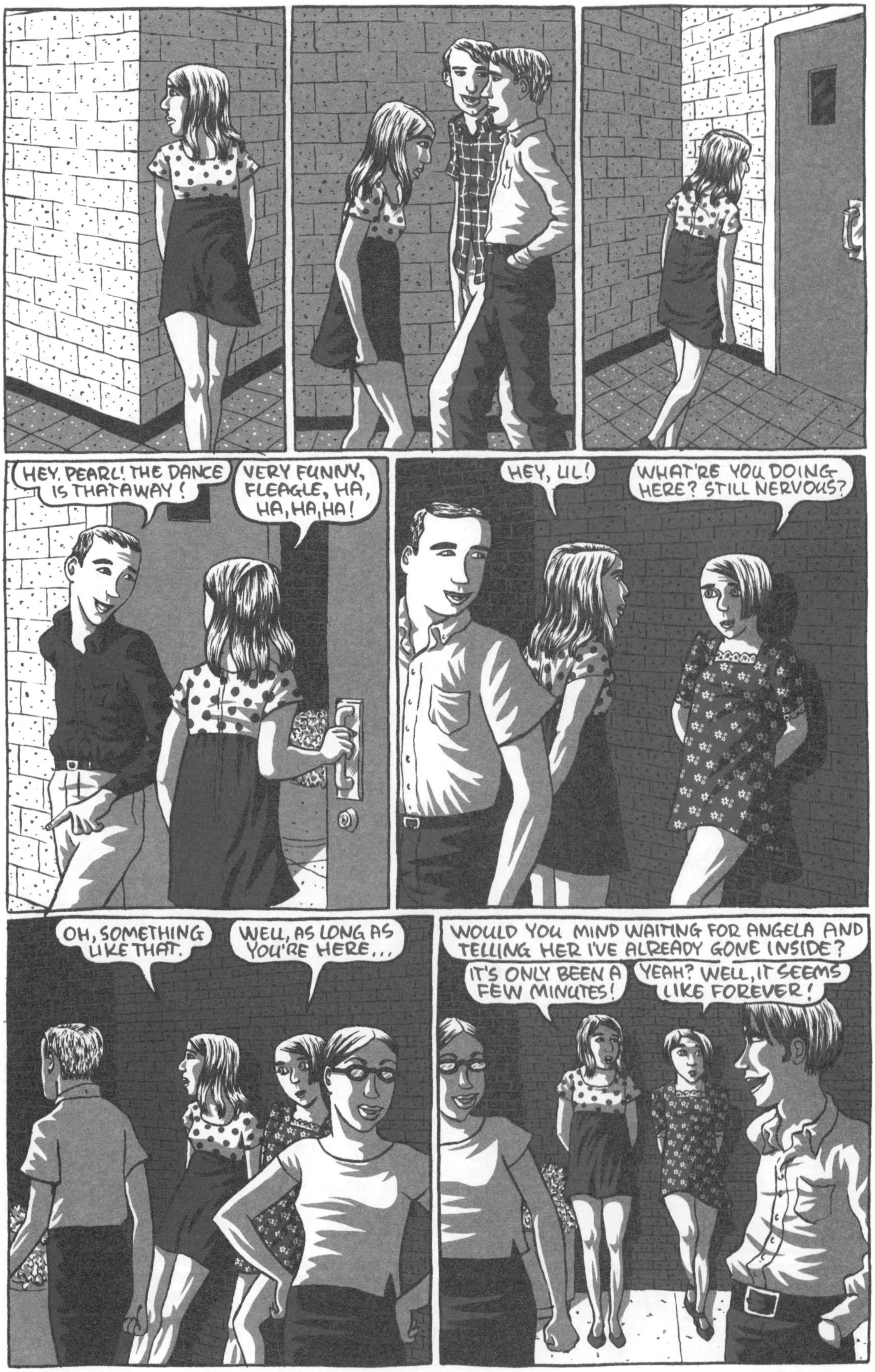
HEY, PEARL! THE DANCE IS THATAWAY!
VERY FUNNY, FLEAGLE, HA, HA, HA, HA!
HEY, LIL!
WHAT'RE YOU DOING HERE? STILL NERVOUS?
OH, SOMETHING LIKE THAT.
WELL, AS LONG AS YOU'RE HERE...
WOULD YOU MIND WAITING FOR ANGELA AND TELLING HER I'VE ALREADY GONE INSIDE?
IT'S ONLY BEEN A FEW MINUTES!
YEAH? WELL, IT SEEMS LIKE FOREVER!

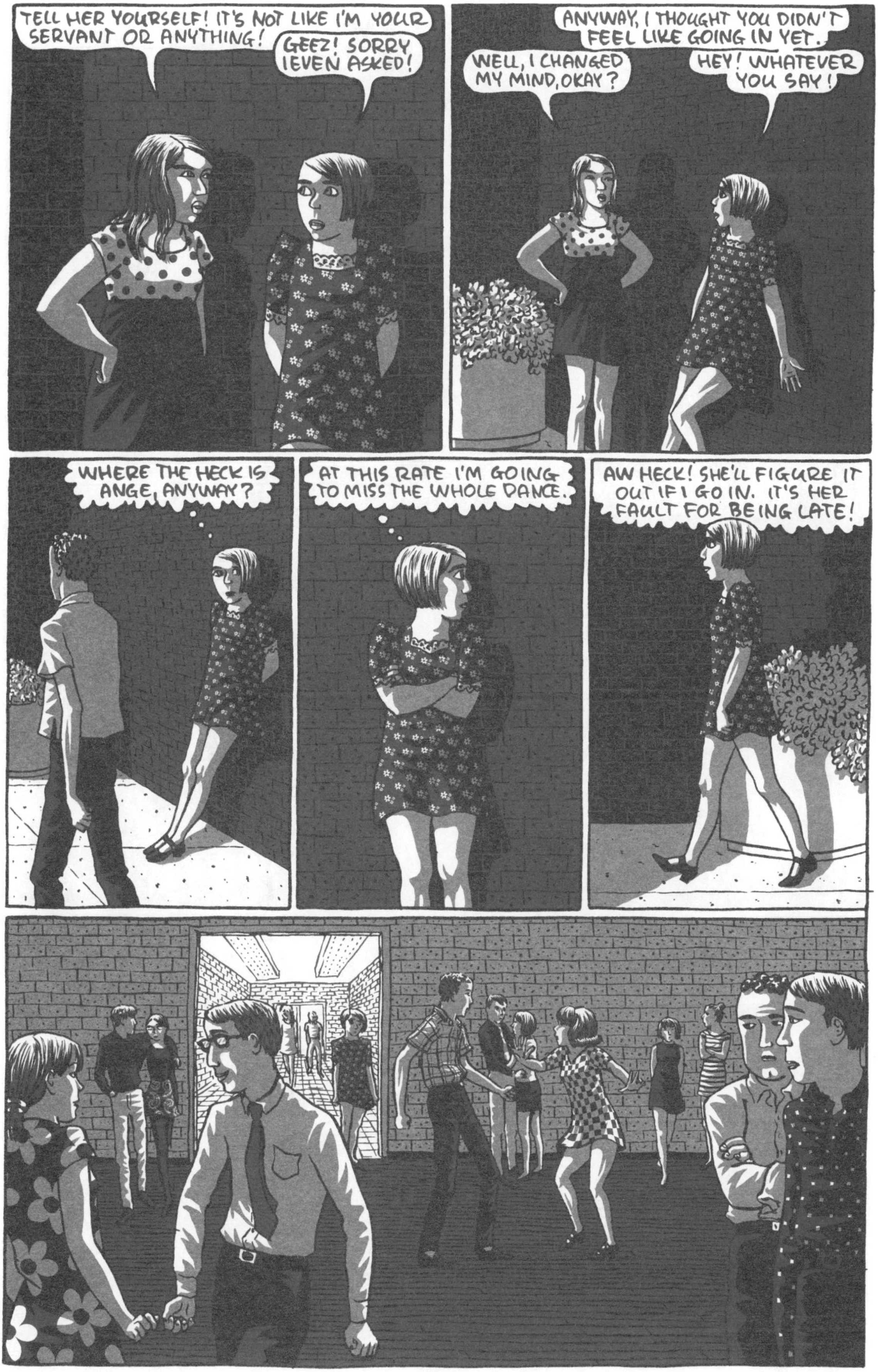
TELL HER YOURSELF! IT'S NOT LIKE I'M YOUR SERVANT OR ANYTHING!
GEEZ! SORRY I EVEN ASKED!
ANYWAY, I THOUGHT YOU DIDN'T FEEL LIKE GOING IN YET.
WELL, I CHANGED MY MIND, OKAY?
HEY! WHATEVER YOU SAY!
WHERE THE HECK IS ANGE, ANYWAY?
AT THIS RATE I'M GOING TO MISS THE WHOLE DANCE.
AW HECK! SHE'LL FIGURE IT OUT IF I GO IN. IT'S HER FAULT FOR BEING LATE!

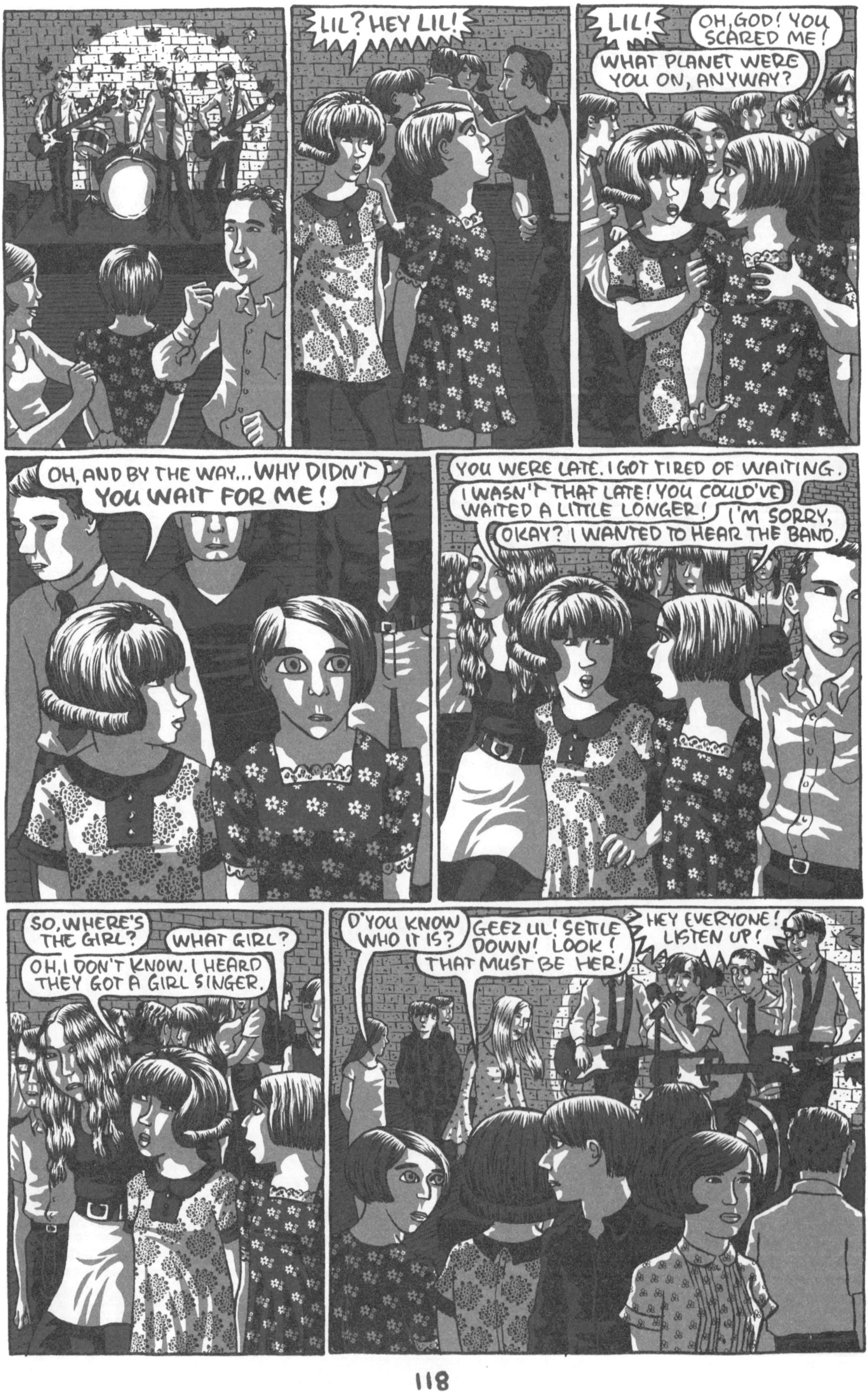
LIL? HEY LIL!
LIL!
OH, GOD! YOU SCARED ME!
WHAT PLANET WERE YOU ON, ANYWAY?
OH, AND BY THE WAY... WHY DIDN'T YOU WAIT FOR ME!
YOU WERE LATE. I GOT TIRED OF WAITING.
I WASN'T THAT LATE! YOU COULD'VE WAITED A LITTLE LONGER!
I'M SORRY, OKAY? I WANTED TO HEAR THE BAND.
SO, WHERE'S THE GIRL?
WHAT GIRL?
OH, I DON'T KNOW. I HEARD THEY GOT A GIRL SINGER.
D'YOU KNOW WHO IT IS?
GEEZ LIL! SETTLE DOWN! LOOK! THAT MUST BE HER!
HEY EVERYONE! LISTEN UP!

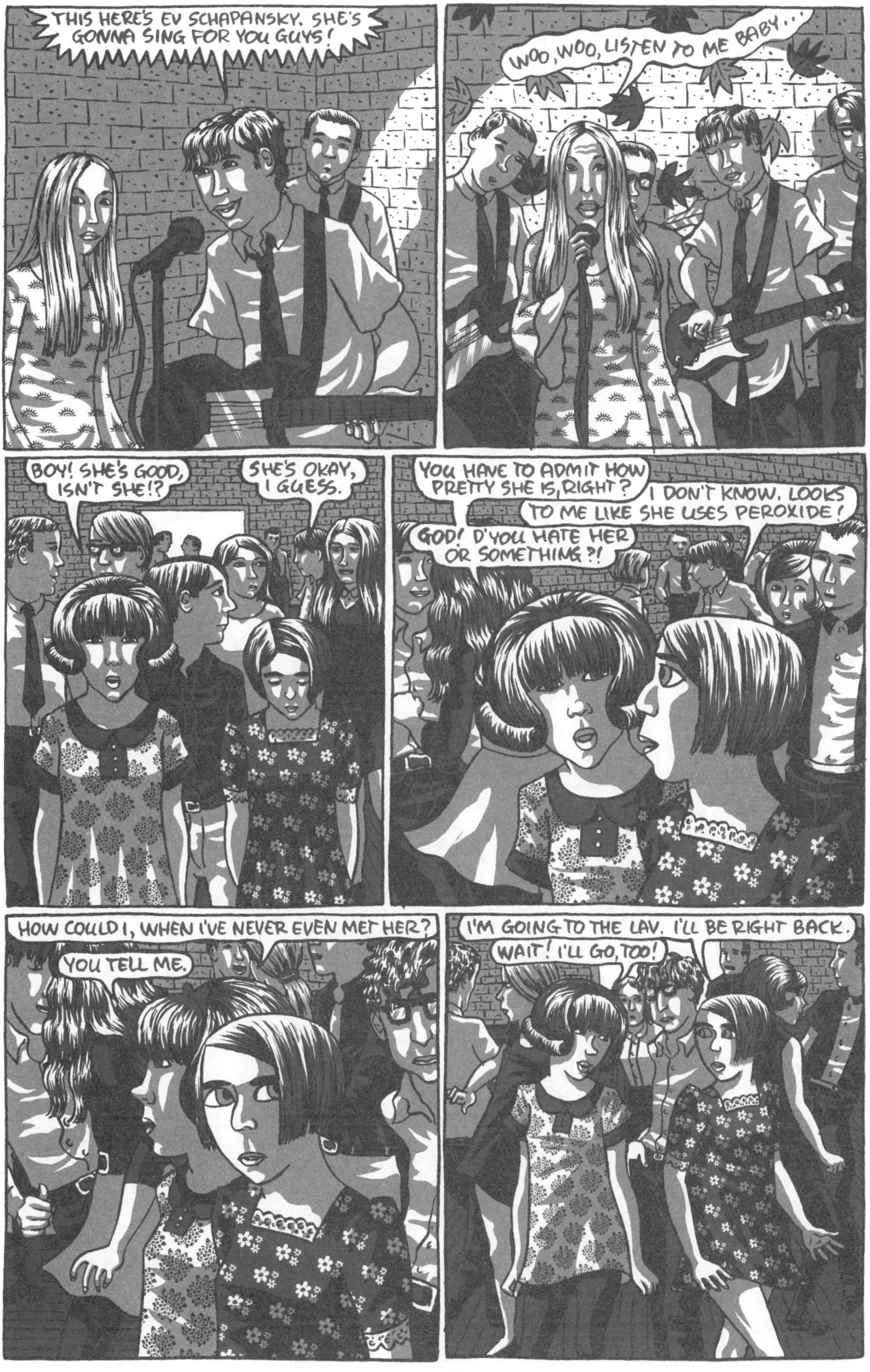
THIS HERE'S EV SCHAPANSKY. SHE'S GONNA SING FOR YOU GUYS!
WOO, WOO, LISTEN TO ME BABY...
BOY! SHE'S GOOD, ISN'T SHE!?
SHE'S OKAY, I GUESS.
YOU HAVE TO ADMIT HOW PRETTY SHE IS, RIGHT?
I DON'T KNOW. LOOKS TO ME LIKE SHE USES PEROXIDE!
GOD! D'YOU HATE HER OR SOMETHING?!
HOW COULD I, WHEN I'VE NEVER EVEN MET HER?
YOU TELL ME.
I'M GOING TO THE LAV. I'LL BE RIGHT BACK.
WAIT! I'LL GO, TOO!

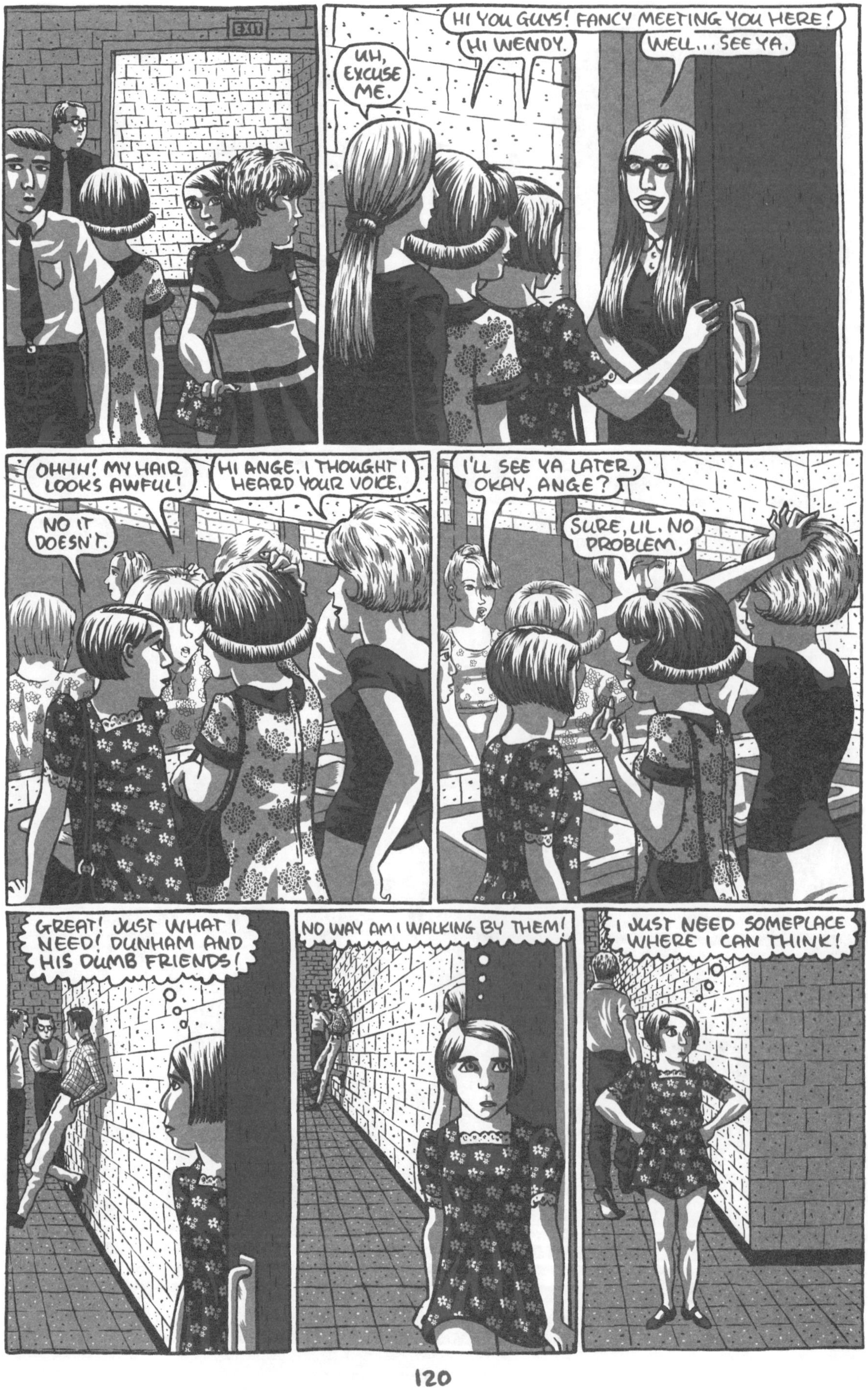
EXIT
UH, EXCUSE ME.
HI YOU GUYS! FANCY MEETING YOU HERE!
HI WENDY.
WELL... SEE YA.
OHHH! MY HAIR LOOKS AWFUL!
NO IT DOESN'T.
HI ANGE. I THOUGHT I HEARD YOUR VOICE.
I'LL SEE YA LATER, OKAY, ANGE?
SURE, LIL. NO PROBLEM.
GREAT! JUST WHAT I NEED! DUNHAM AND HIS DUMB FRIENDS!
NO WAY AM I WALKING BY THEM!
I JUST NEED SOMEPLACE WHERE I CAN THINK!

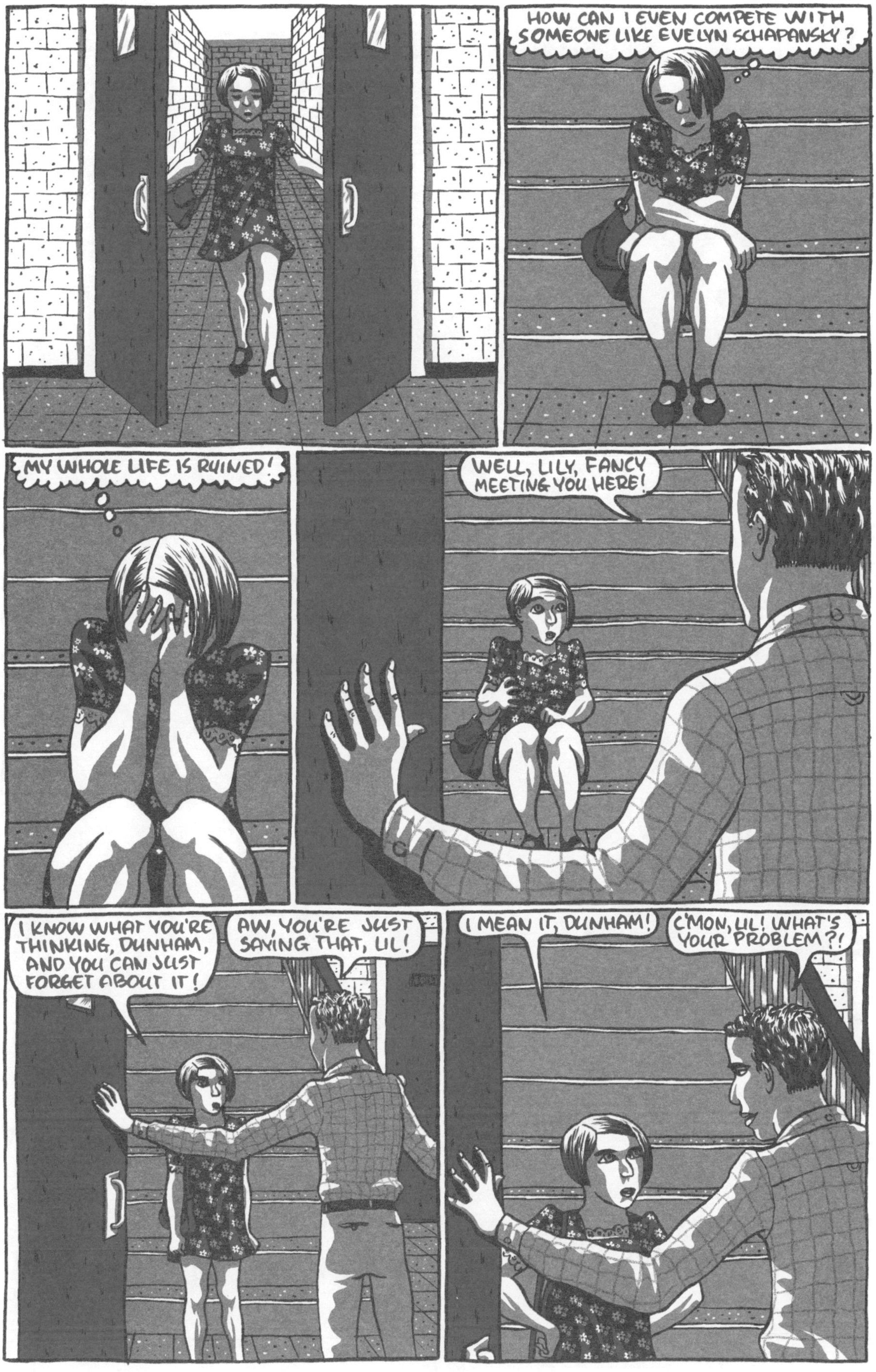
HOW CAN I EVEN COMPETE WITH SOMEONE LIKE EVELYN SCHAPANSKY?
MY WHOLE LIFE IS RUINED!
WELL, LILY, FANCY MEETING YOU HERE!
I KNOW WHAT YOU'RE THINKING, DUNHAM, AND YOU CAN JUST FORGET ABOUT IT!
AW, YOU'RE JUST SAYING THAT, LIL!
I MEAN IT, DUNHAM!
C'MON, LIL! WHAT'S YOUR PROBLEM?!

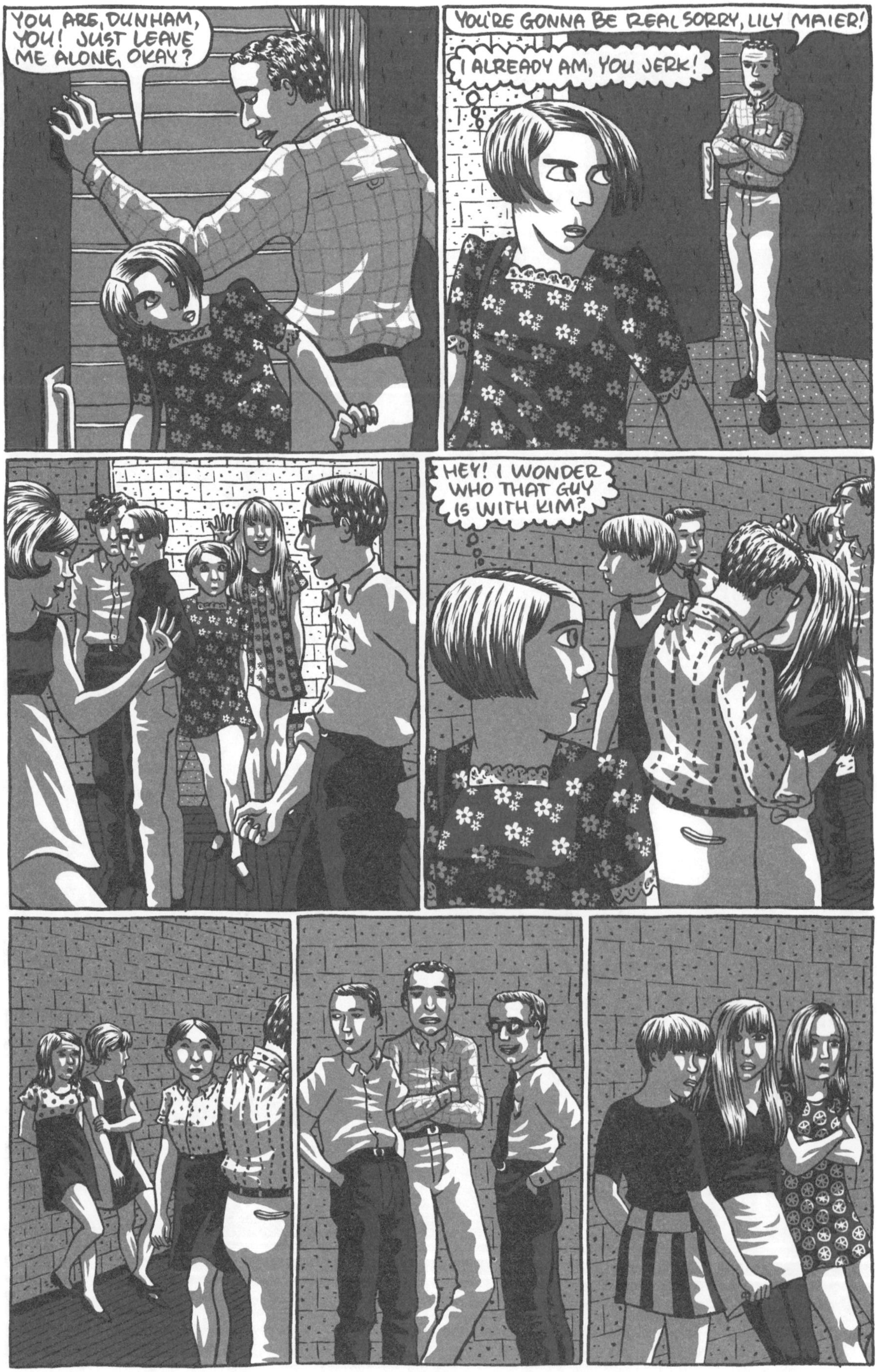
YOU ARE, DUNHAM, YOU! JUST LEAVE ME ALONE, OKAY?
YOU'RE GONNA BE REAL SORRY, LILY MAIER!
I ALREADY AM, YOU JERK!
HEY! I WONDER WHO THAT GUY IS WITH KIM?

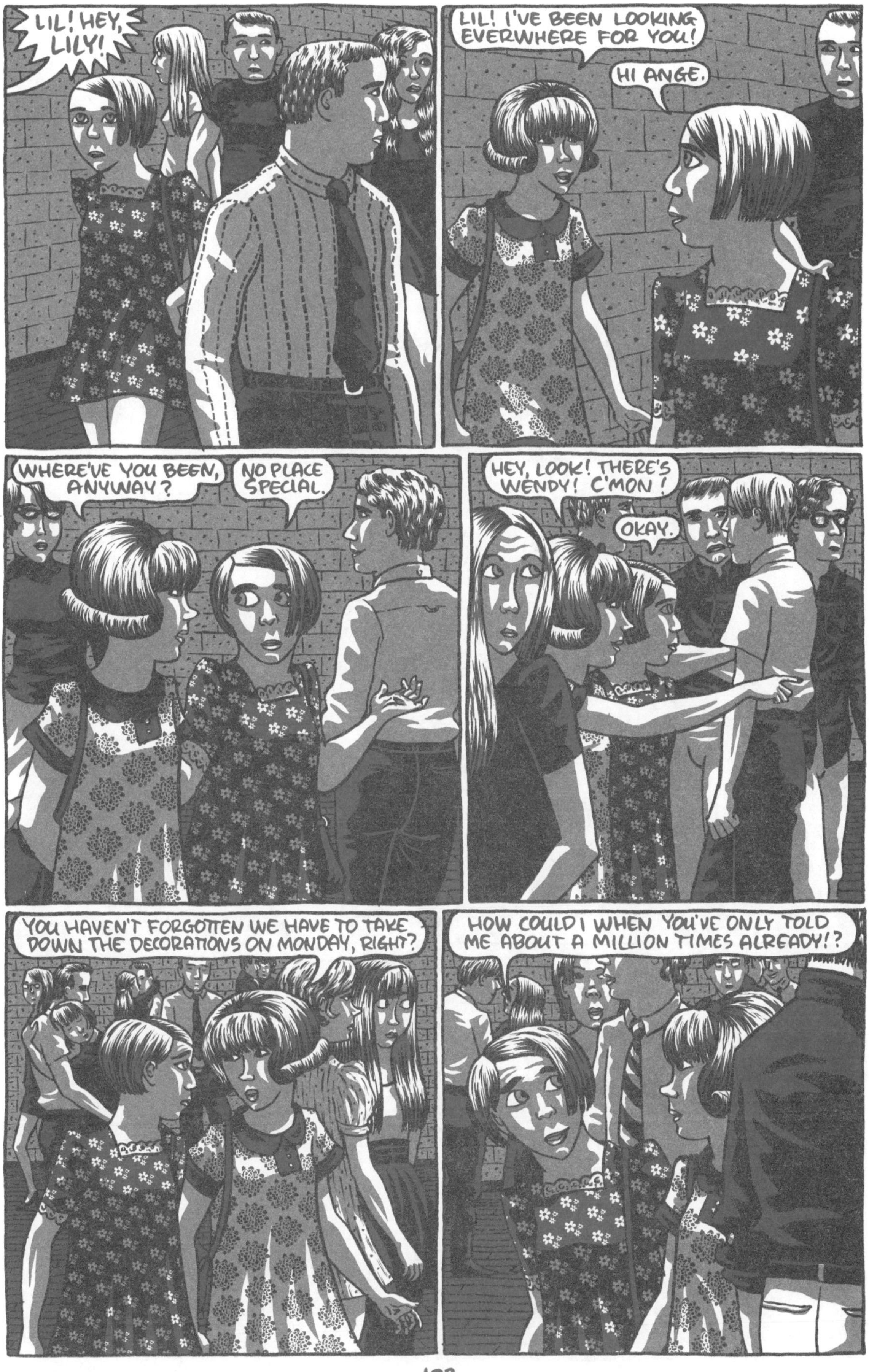
LIL! HEY, LILY!
LIL! I'VE BEEN LOOKING EVERWHERE FOR YOU!
HI ANGE.
WHERE'VE YOU BEEN, ANYWAY?
NO PLACE SPECIAL.
HEY, LOOK! THERE'S WENDY! C'MON!
OKAY.
YOU HAVEN'T FORGOTTEN WE HAVE TO TAKE DOWN THE DECORATIONS ON MONDAY, RIGHT?
HOW COULD I WHEN YOU'VE ONLY TOLD ME ABOUT A MILLION TIMES ALREADY!?

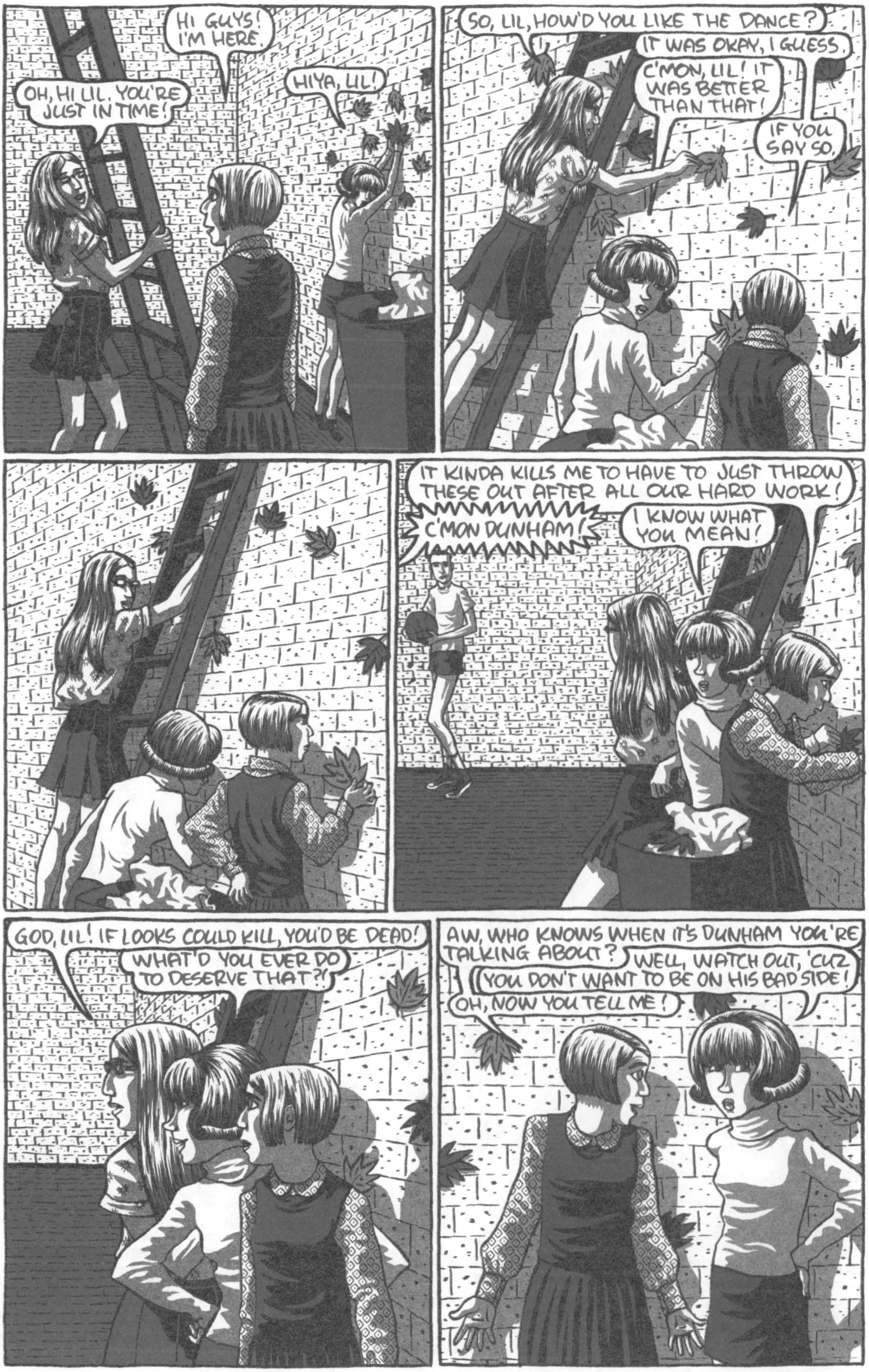
HI GUYS! I'M HERE.
OH, HI LIL. YOU'RE JUST IN TIME!
HIYA, LIL!
SO, LIL, HOW'D YOU LIKE THE DANCE?
IT WAS OKAY, I GUESS.
C'MON, LIL! IT WAS BETTER THAN THAT!
IF YOU SAY SO.
IT KINDA KILLS ME TO HAVE TO JUST THROW THESE OUT AFTER ALL OUR HARD WORK!
C'MON DUNHAM!
I KNOW WHAT YOU MEAN!
GOD, LIL! IF LOOKS COULD KILL, YOU'D BE DEAD!
WHAT'D YOU EVER DO TO DESERVE THAT?!
AW, WHO KNOWS WHEN IT'S DUNHAM YOU'RE TALKING ABOUT?
WELL, WATCH OUT, 'CUZ YOU DON'T WANT TO BE ON HIS BAD SIDE!
OH, NOW YOU TELL ME!

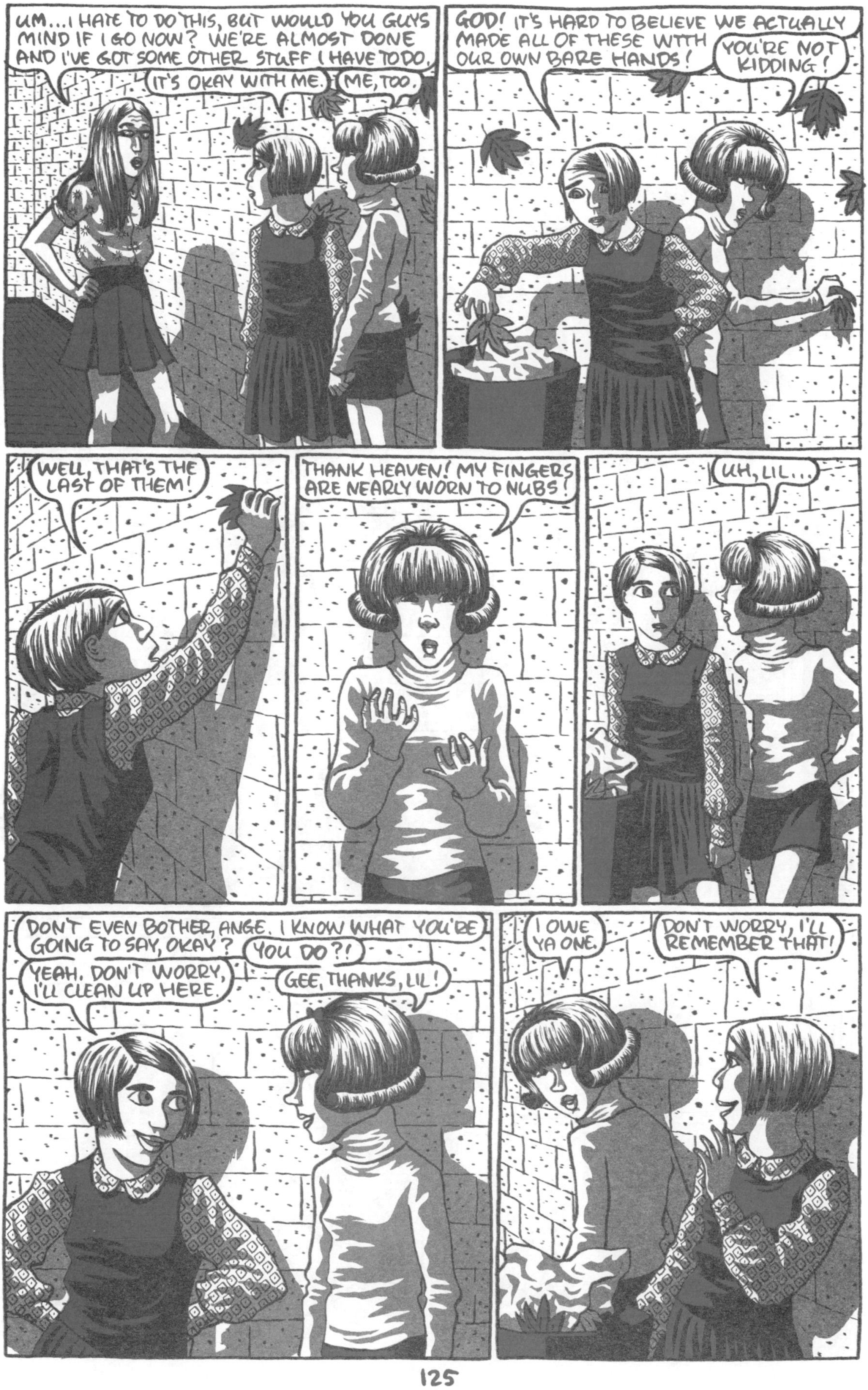
UM... I HATE TO DO THIS, BUT WOULD YOU GUYS MIND IF I GO NOW? WE'RE ALMOST DONE AND I'VE GOT SOME OTHER STUFF I HAVE TO DO.
IT'S OKAY WITH ME.
ME, TOO.
GOD! IT'S HARD TO BELIEVE WE ACTUALLY MADE ALL OF THESE WITH OUR OWN BARE HANDS!
YOU'RE NOT KIDDING!
WELL, THAT'S THE LAST OF THEM!
THANK HEAVEN! MY FINGERS ARE NEARLY WORN TO NUBS!
UH, LIL...
DON'T EVEN BOTHER, ANGE. I KNOW WHAT YOU'RE GOING TO SAY, OKAY?
YOU DO?!
YEAH. DON'T WORRY, I'LL CLEAN UP HERE.
GEE, THANKS, LIL!
I OWE YA ONE.
DON'T WORRY, I'LL REMEMBER THAT!

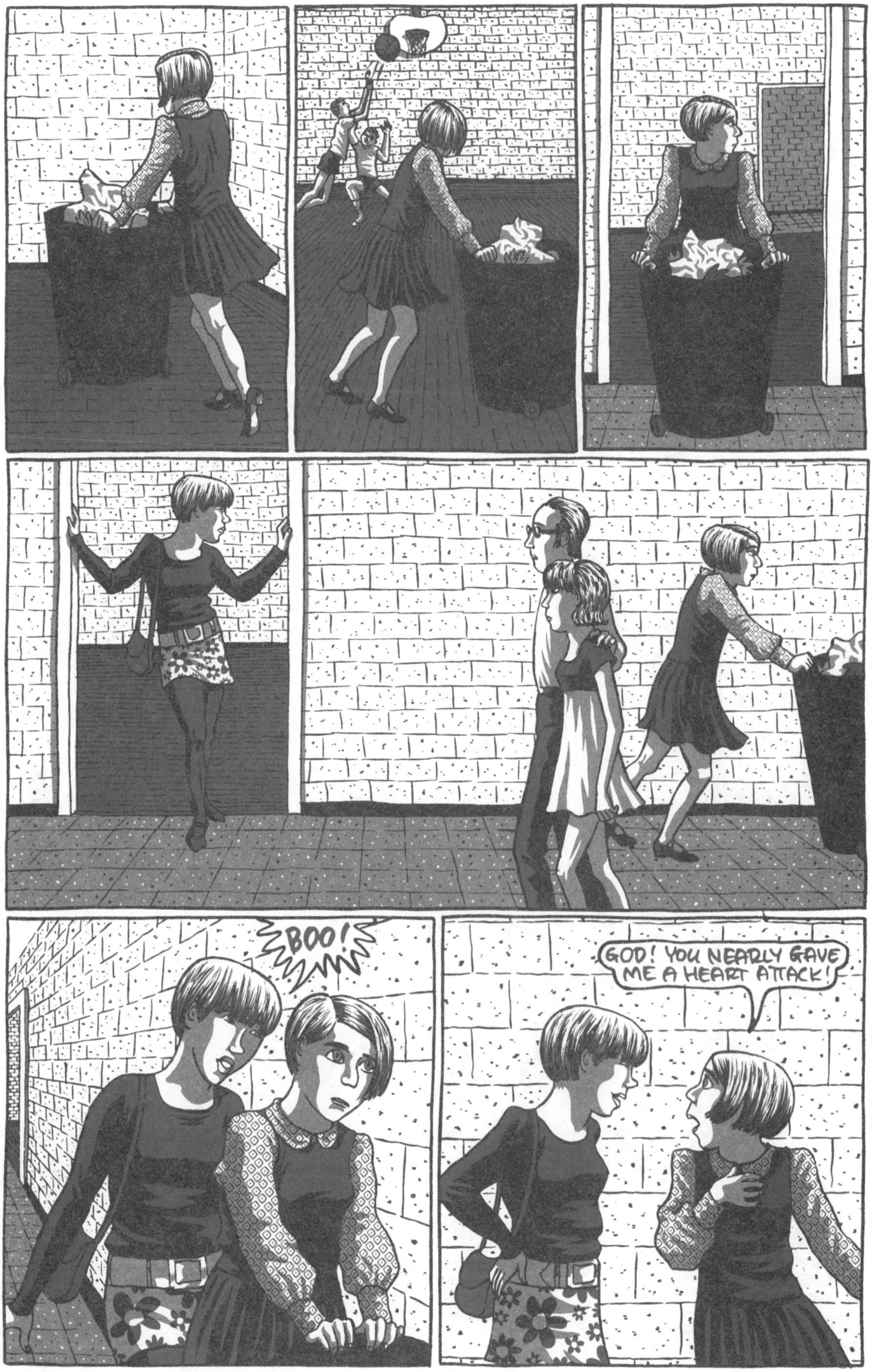
BOO!
GOD! YOU NEARLY GAVE ME A HEART ATTACK!

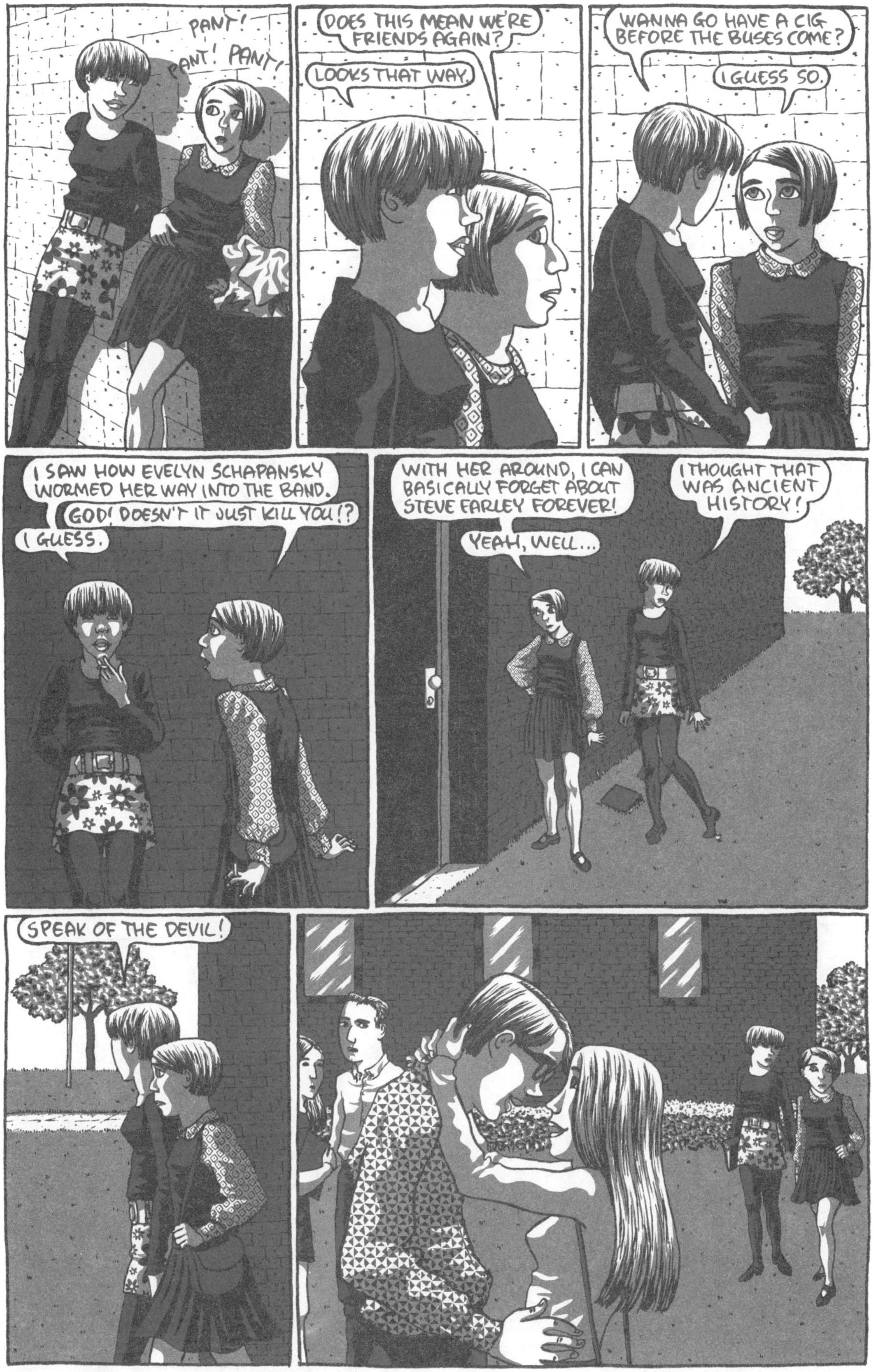
PANT!
PANT! PANT!
DOES THIS MEAN WE'RE FRIENDS AGAIN?
LOOKS THAT WAY.
WANNA GO HAVE A CIG BEFORE THE BUSES COME?
I GUESS SO.
I SAW HOW EVELYN SCHAPANSKY WORMED HER WAY INTO THE BAND.
GOD! DOESN'T IT JUST KILL YOU!?
I GUESS.
WITH HER AROUND, I CAN BASICALLY FORGET ABOUT STEVE FARLEY FOREVER!
YEAH, WELL...
I THOUGHT THAT WAS ANCIENT HISTORY!
SPEAK OF THE DEVIL!

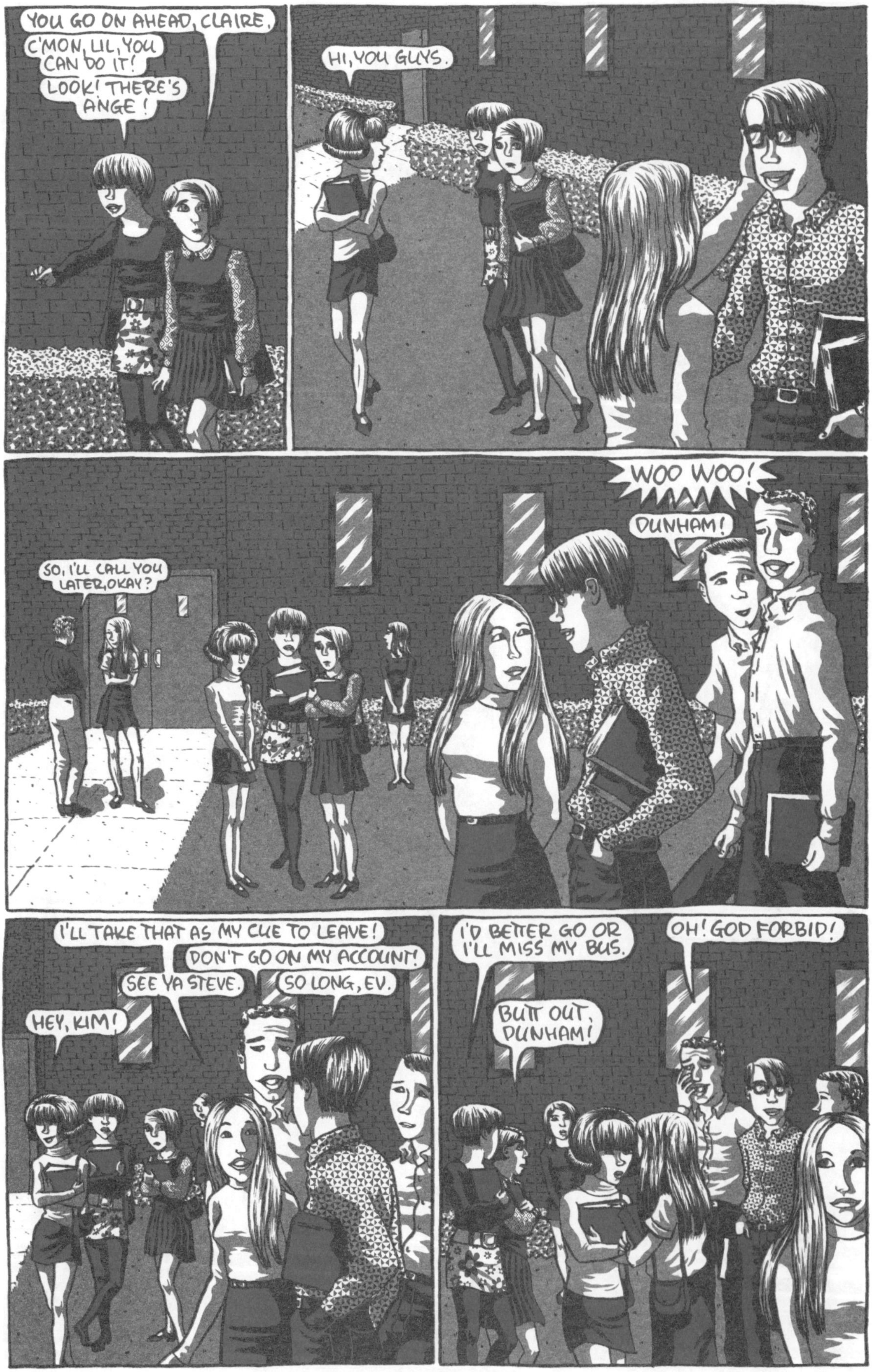
YOU GO ON AHEAD, CLAIRE.
C'MON, LIL, YOU CAN DO IT!
LOOK! THERE'S ANGE!
HI, YOU GUYS.
SO, I'LL CALL YOU LATER, OKAY?
WOO WOO!
DUNHAM!
I'LL TAKE THAT AS MY CUE TO LEAVE!
DON'T GO ON MY ACCOUNT!
SEE YA STEVE.
SO LONG, EV.
HEY, KIM!
I'D BETTER GO OR I'LL MISS MY BUS.
OH! GOD FORBID!
BUTT OUT, DUNHAM!

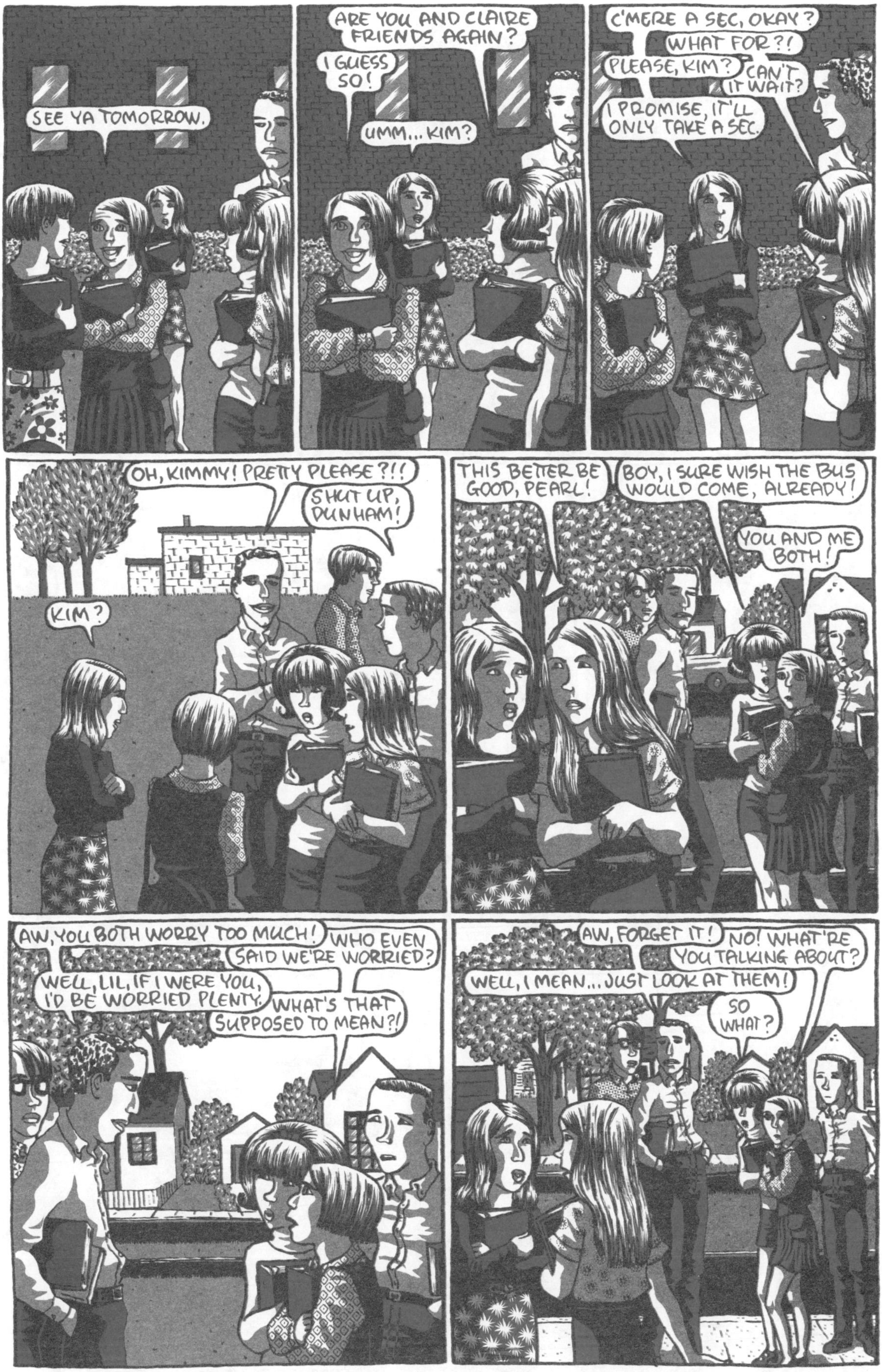
SEE YA TOMORROW.
ARE YOU AND CLAIRE FRIENDS AGAIN?
I GUESS SO!
UMM... KIM?
C'MERE A SEC, OKAY?
WHAT FOR?!
PLEASE, KIM?
CAN'T IT WAIT?
I PROMISE, IT'LL ONLY TAKE A SEC.
OH, KIMMY! PRETTY PLEASE?!!
SHUT UP, DUNHAM!
KIM?
THIS BETTER BE GOOD, PEARL!
BOY, I SURE WISH THE BUS WOULD COME, ALREADY!
YOU AND ME BOTH!
AW, YOU BOTH WORRY TOO MUCH!
WHO EVEN SAID WE'RE WORRIED?
WELL, LIL, IF I WERE YOU, I'D BE WORRIED PLENTY.
WHAT'S THAT SUPPOSED TO MEAN?!
AW, FORGET IT!
NO! WHAT'RE YOU TALKING ABOUT?
WELL, I MEAN... JUST LOOK AT THEM!
SO WHAT?

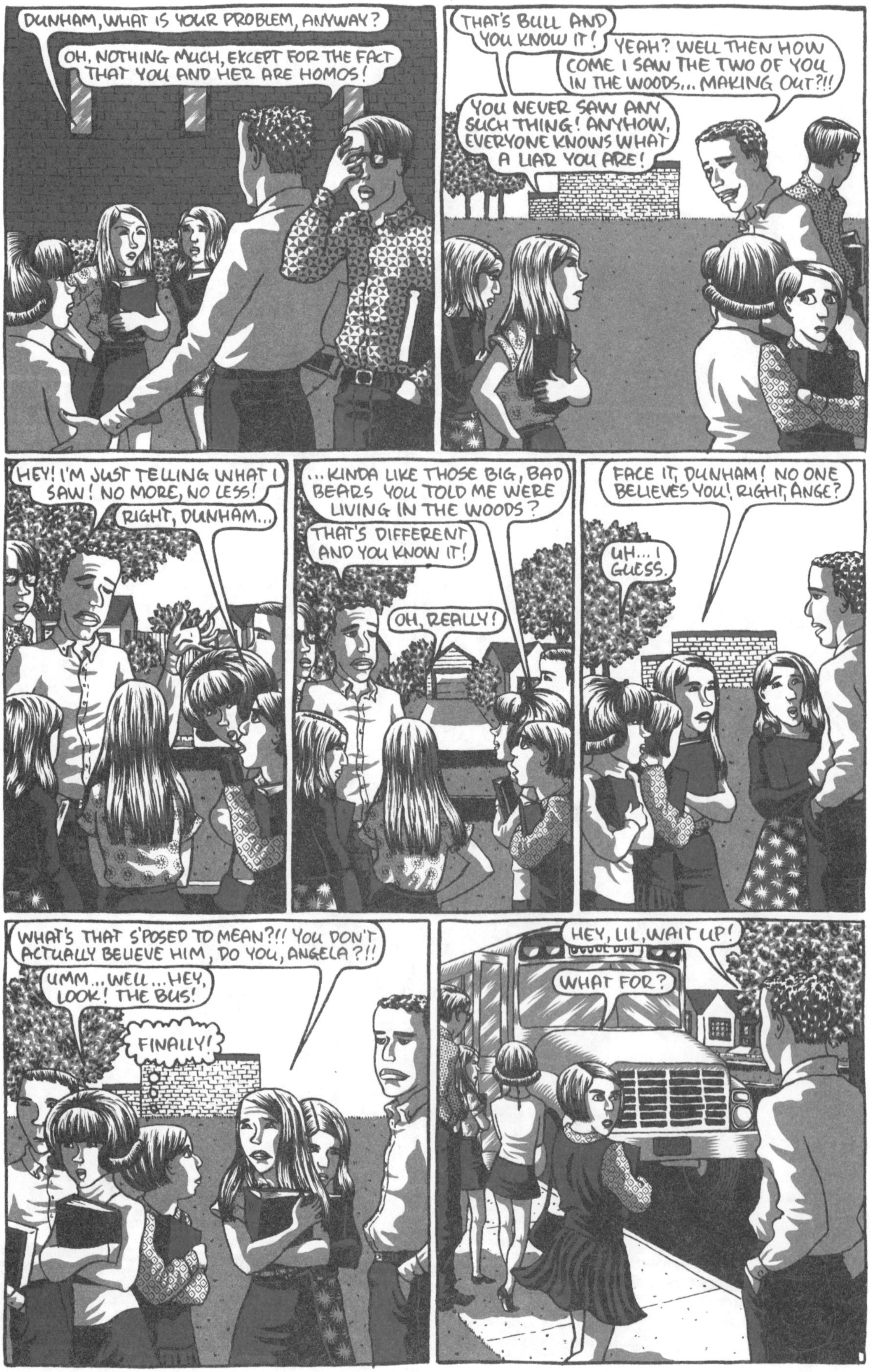
DUNHAM, WHAT IS YOUR PROBLEM, ANYWAY?
OH, NOTHING MUCH, EXCEPT FOR THE FACT THAT YOU AND HER ARE HOMOS!
THAT'S BULL AND YOU KNOW IT!
YEAH? WELL THEN HOW COME I SAW THE TWO OF YOU IN THE WOODS... MAKING OUT?!!
YOU NEVER SAW ANY SUCH THING! ANYHOW, EVERYONE KNOWS WHAT A LIAR YOU ARE!
HEY! I'M JUST TELLING WHAT I SAW! NO MORE, NO LESS!
RIGHT, DUNHAM...
...KINDA LIKE THOSE BIG, BAD BEARS YOU TOLD ME WERE LIVING IN THE WOODS?
THAT'S DIFFERENT AND YOU KNOW IT!
OH, REALLY!
FACE IT, DUNHAM! NO ONE BELIEVES YOU! RIGHT, ANGE?
UH... I GUESS.
WHAT'S THAT S'POSED TO MEAN?!! YOU DON'T ACTUALLY BELIEVE HIM, DO YOU, ANGELA?!!
UMM... WELL... HEY, LOOK! THE BUS!
FINALLY!
HEY, LIL, WAIT UP!
WHAT FOR?

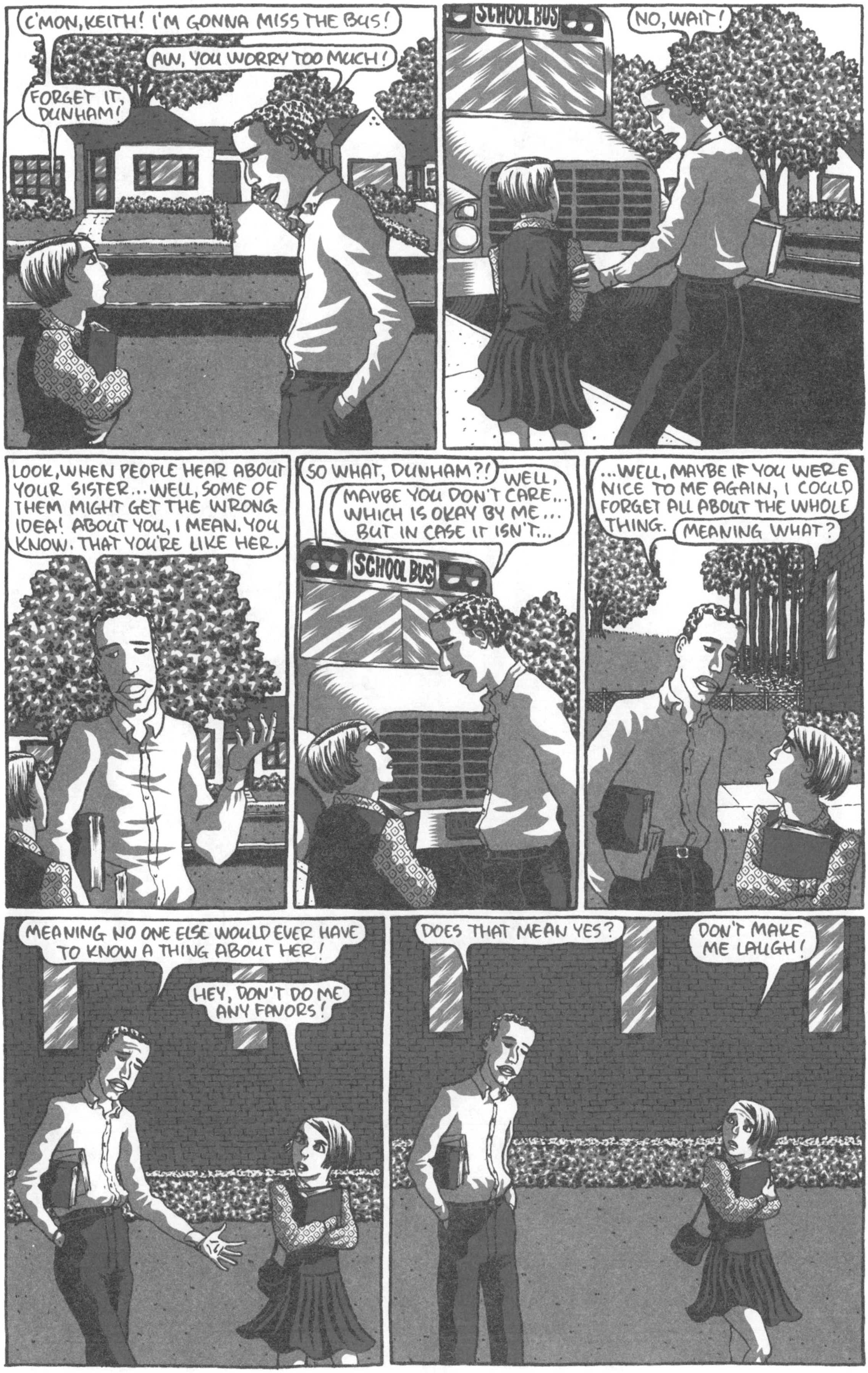
C'MON, KEITH! I'M GONNA MISS THE BUS!
AW, YOU WORRY TOO MUCH!
FORGET IT, DUNHAM!
NO, WAIT!
SCHOOL BUS
LOOK, WHEN PEOPLE HEAR ABOUT YOUR SISTER... WELL, SOME OF THEM MIGHT GET THE WRONG IDEA! ABOUT YOU, I MEAN. YOU KNOW. THAT YOU'RE LIKE HER.
SO WHAT, DUNHAM?!
WELL, MAYBE YOU DON'T CARE... WHICH IS OKAY BY ME... BUT IN CASE IT ISN'T...
...WELL, MAYBE IF YOU WERE NICE TO ME AGAIN, I COULD FORGET ALL ABOUT THE WHOLE THING.
MEANING WHAT?
MEANING NO ONE ELSE WOULD EVER HAVE TO KNOW A THING ABOUT HER!
HEY, DON'T DO ME ANY FAVORS!
DOES THAT MEAN YES?
DON'T MAKE ME LAUGH!

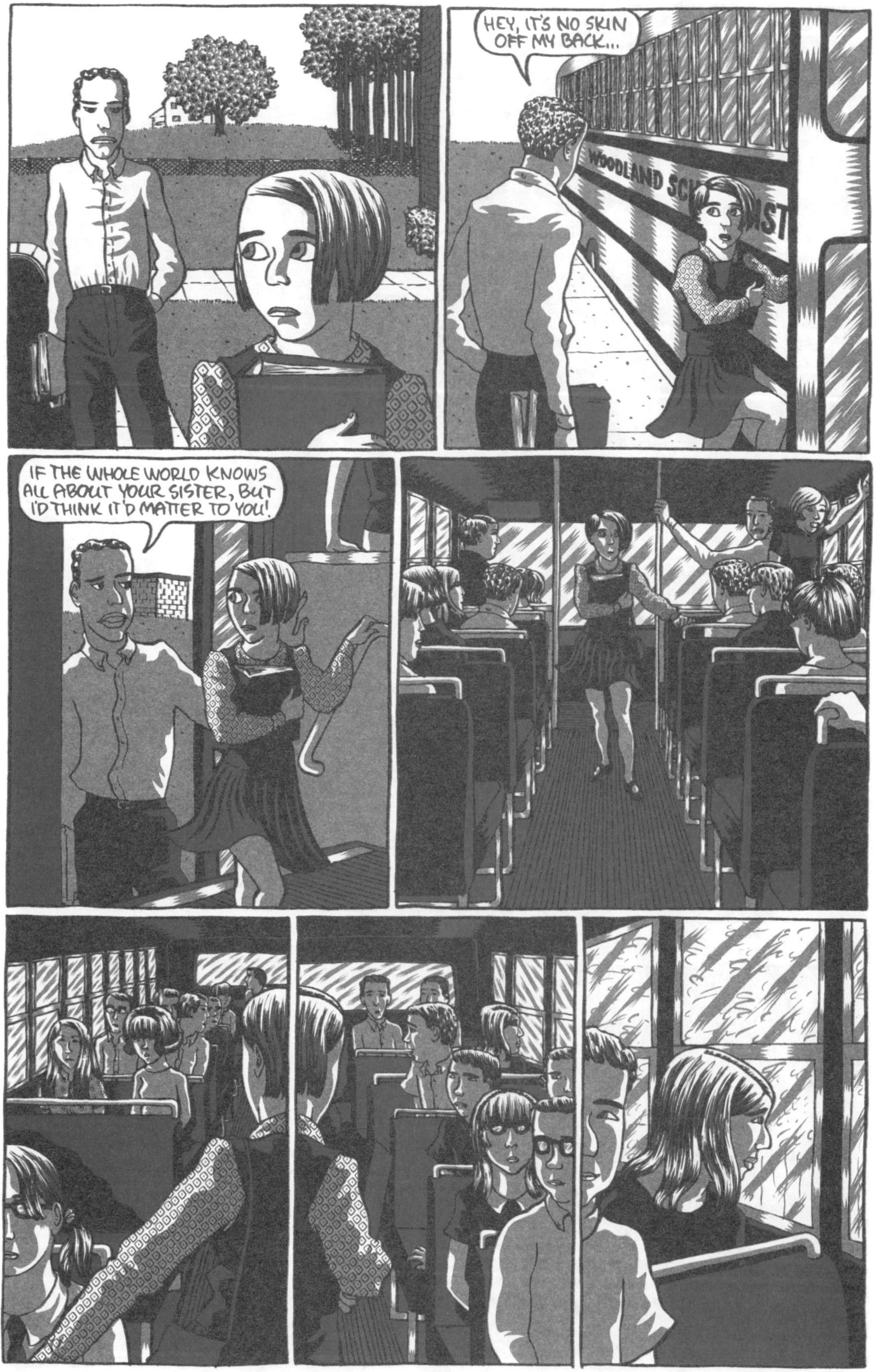
HEY, IT'S NO SKIN OFF MY BACK...
WOODLAND SCH
IF THE WHOLE WORLD KNOWS ALL ABOUT YOUR SISTER, BUT I'D THINK IT'D MATTER TO YOU!

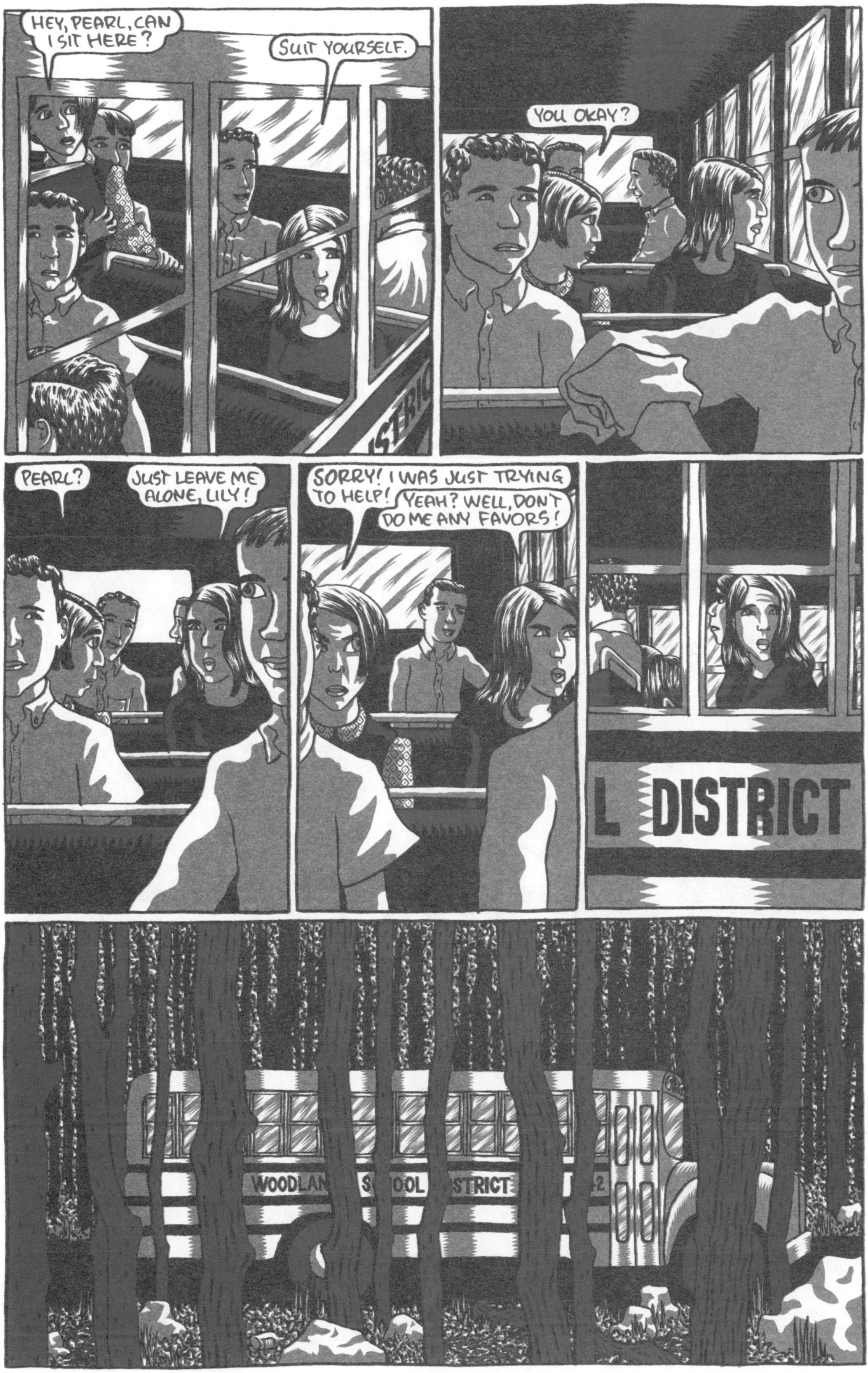
HEY, PEARL, CAN I SIT HERE?
SUIT YOURSELF.
YOU OKAY?
PEARL?
JUST LEAVE ME ALONE, LILY!
SORRY! I WAS JUST TRYING TO HELP!
YEAH? WELL, DON'T DO ME ANY FAVORS!
L DISTRICT
WOODLAN SCHOOL ISTRICT

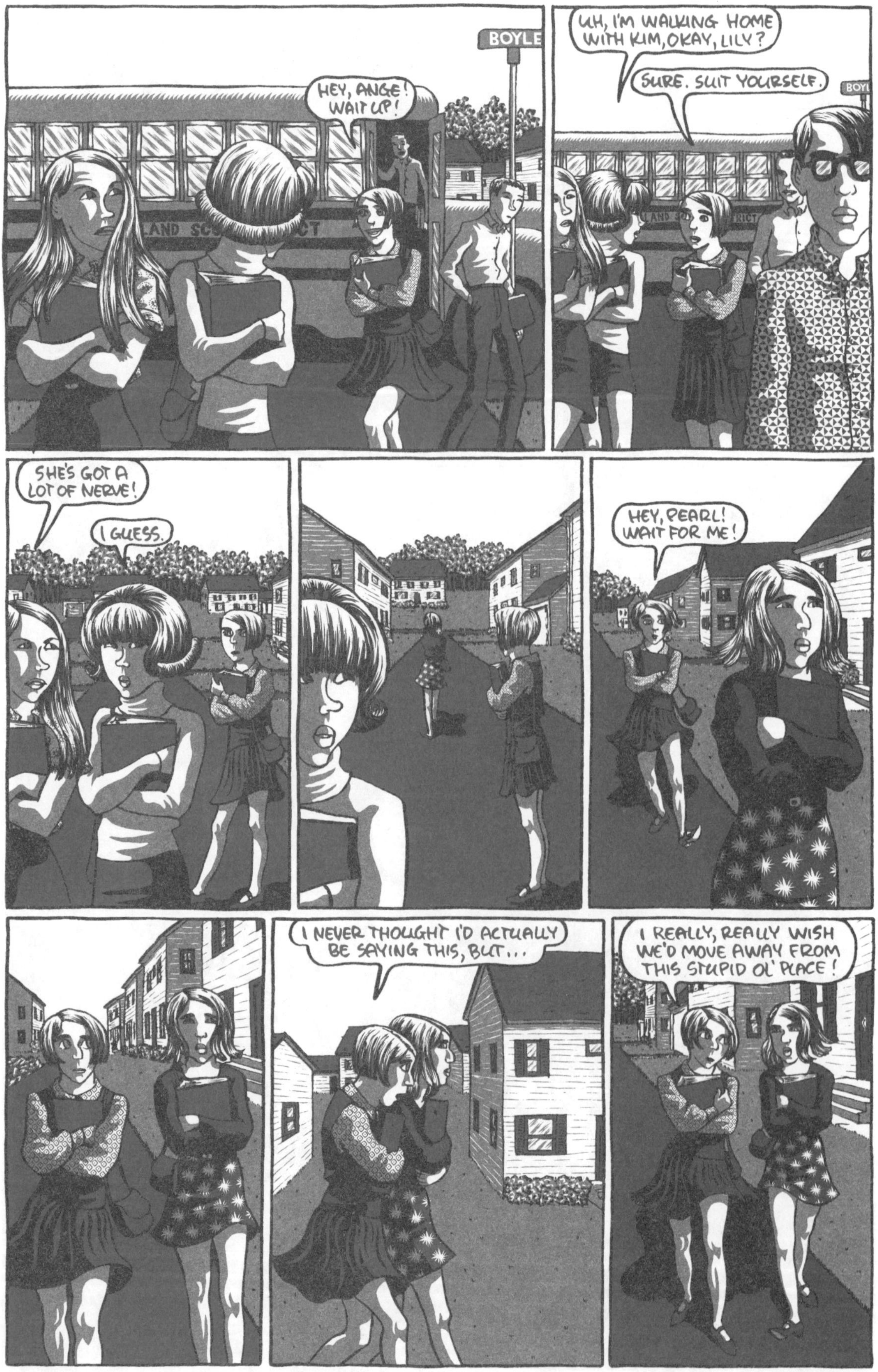
BOYLE
HEY, ANGE! WAIT UP!
LAND SC CT
UH, I'M WALKING HOME WITH KIM, OKAY, LILY?
SURE. SUIT YOURSELF.
BOYL
SHE'S GOT A LOT OF NERVE!
I GUESS.
HEY, PEARL! WAIT FOR ME!
I NEVER THOUGHT I'D ACTUALLY BE SAYING THIS, BUT...
I REALLY, REALLY WISH WE'D MOVE AWAY FROM THIS STUPID OL' PLACE!

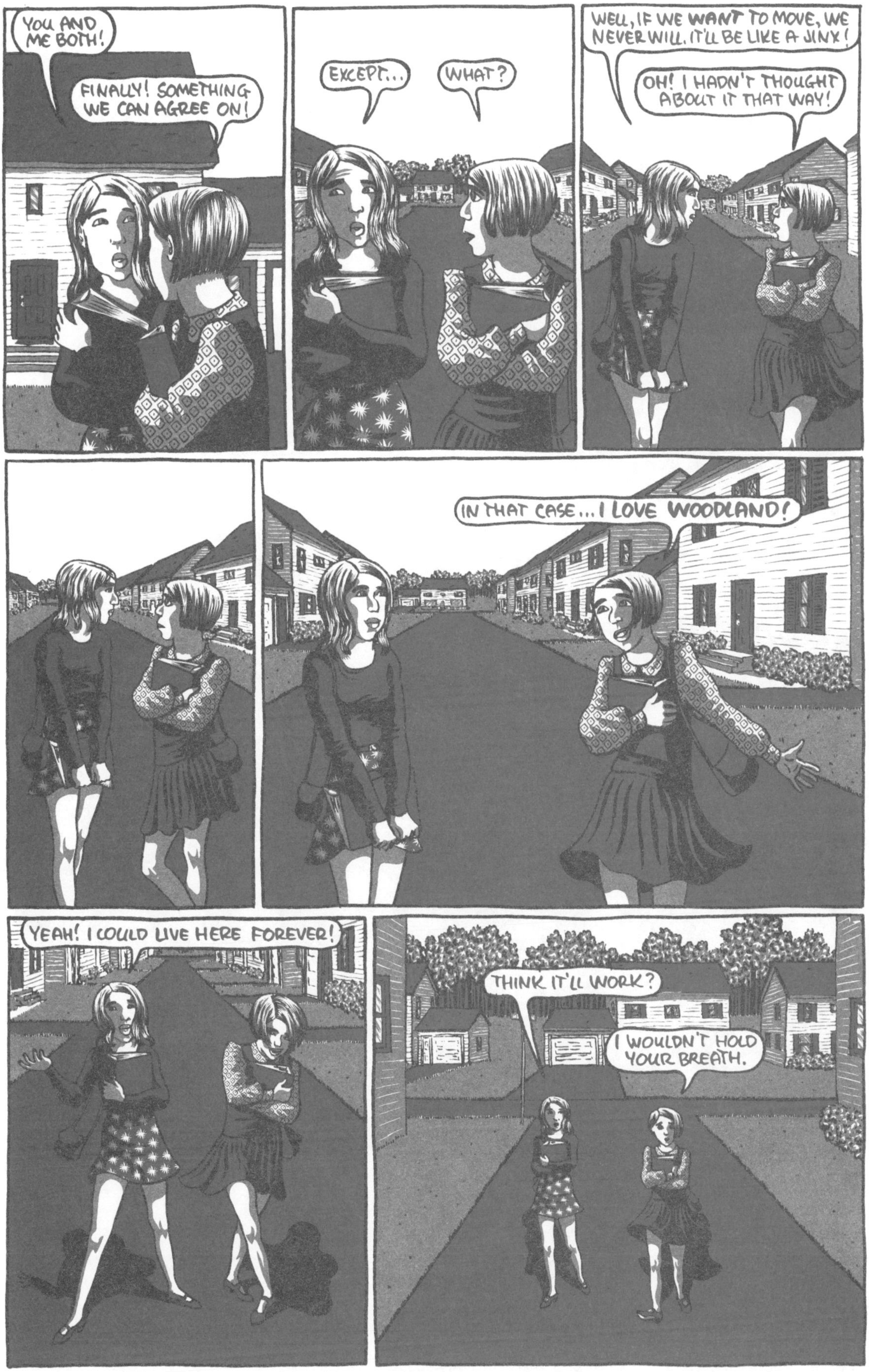
YOU AND ME BOTH!
FINALLY! SOMETHING WE CAN AGREE ON!
EXCEPT...
WHAT?
WELL, IF WE WANT TO MOVE, WE NEVER WILL. IT'LL BE LIKE A JINX!
OH! I HADN'T THOUGHT ABOUT IT THAT WAY!
IN THAT CASE... I LOVE WOODLAND!
YEAH! I COULD LIVE HERE FOREVER!
THINK IT'LL WORK?
I WOULDN'T HOLD YOUR BREATH.

Debbie Drechsler has been drawing pictures since she could first hold onto a crayon. For several years she's been an illustrator for clients such as *Redbook, Fast Company, Cicada, U.S. News & World Report, Hotwired, Business Week, Child, Parenting, Texas Monthly, Natural Health, Condé Nast Traveler, Bantam Books, Algonquin Press, The Los Angeles Times* and *Avon Books*.

Her first comics appeared in *Drawn & Quarterly, NY Press* and *The Stranger* in the early 1990's. In 1996 she began the series *Nowhere*, which eventually became this book.

She lives in Santa Rosa, California, about 50 miles north of San Francisco, with two cats and a guy.

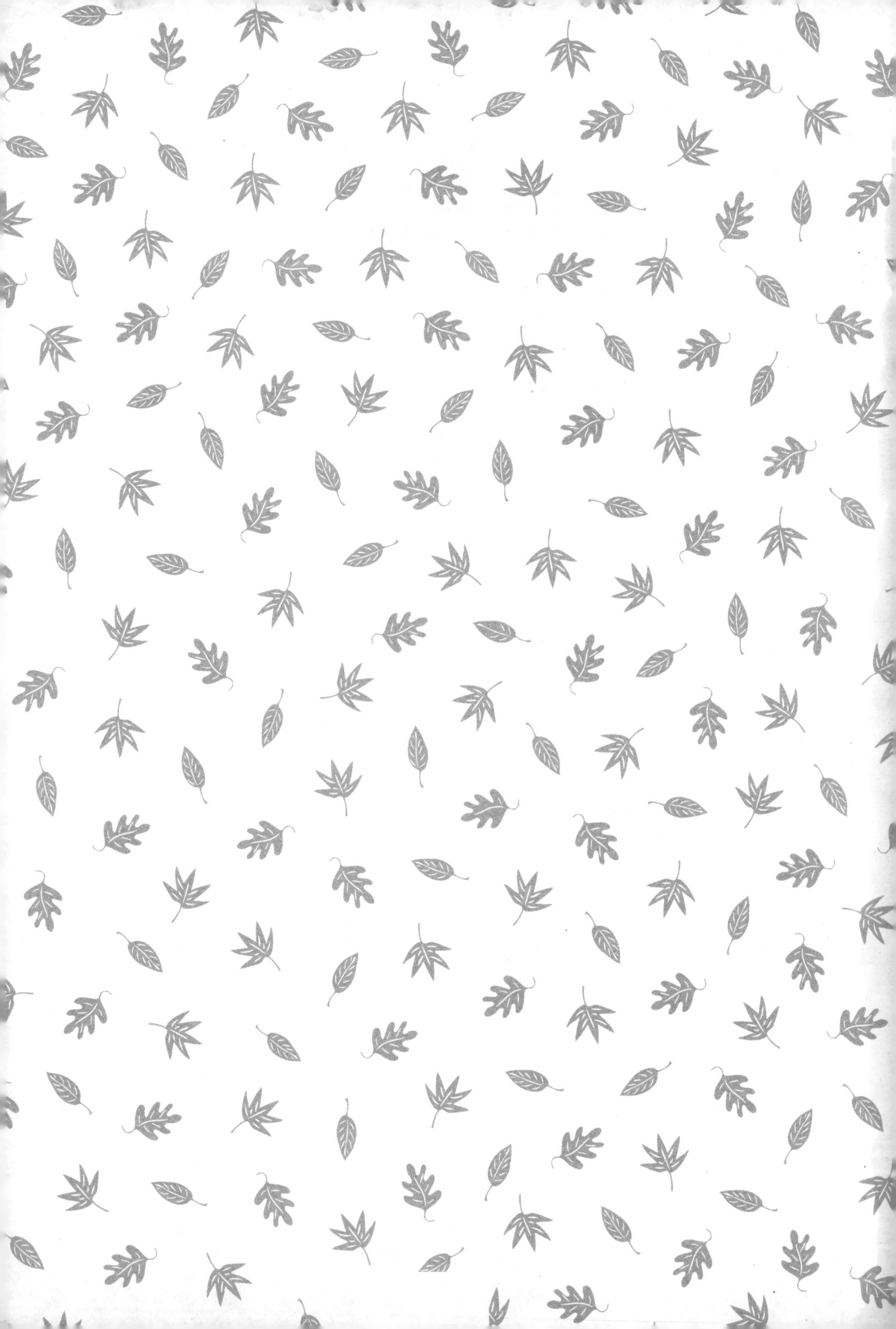